VIOLENT LOVE

VIOLENT LOVE

Jerry Oster

BANTAM BOOKS

New York · Toronto · London · Sydney · Auckland

The characters, events, and institutions depicted in this book are wholly fictional or are used fictitiously. Any apparent resemblance to any person alive or dead, to any actual events, and to any actual institutions, is entirely coincidental.

VIOLENT LOVE

A Bantam Book / May 1991

Grateful acknowledgment is made for permission to reprint the following: "VIOLENT LOVE" by Willie James Dixon copyright 1950. Renewed 1978 EMI MUSIC PUBLISHING LTD. All rights Controlled and Administered by SCREEN GEMS-EMI MUSIC INC. All Rights Reserved. International Copyright Secured. Used by permission. Caption on page 57 from a drawing by Cline © 1988 *The New Yorker* Magazine, Inc. Captions on page 256 from a four-panel drawing by A. McCarthy © 1989 *The New Yorker* Magazine, Inc.

Library of Congress Cataloging-in-Publication Data

Oster, Jerry.
    Violent love / Jerry Oster.
        p.   cm.
    ISBN 0-553-07127-0
    I. Title.
    PS3565.S813V36   1991
    813'.54—dc20   90-43589
                                                         CIP

Published simultaneously in the United States and Canada

Bantam Books are published by Bantam Books, a division of Bantam Doubleday Dell Publishing Group, Inc. Its trademark, consisting of the words "Bantam Books" and the portrayal of a rooster, is Registered in U.S. Patent and Trademark Office and in other countries. Marca Registrada. Bantam Books, 666 Fifth Avenue, New York, New York 10103.

PRINTED IN THE UNITED STATES OF AMERICA

BVG 0 9 8 7 6 5 4 3 2 1

For Susan Rice

I had help, in many forms. Grateful thanks to Diane Cleaver, Lauren Field, Trisha Lester, Kate Miciak, Lily Stein Oster.

—J. O.

VIOLENT
LOVE

1

"READY ALL."

The Harlem River, stretched smooth by the conflict of tide and current. Three thin racing shells hovered like water striders.

"Ready."

It was only just spring and here and there along the banks were winter's leftovers, patches of dirty old snow; but the oarsmen had warmed to their task and had their sweatshirts off and stowed down along the gunwales. The varsity, as was their privilege, wore betting shirts— T-shirts won from rivals in regattas past: Harvard crimson, Yale blue, Penn and MIT and Cornell. The junior and third varsities wore rags.

"Row!"

The shells groaned. A seagull, startled by the flash of oars, flapped up and up. The coxswains pounded cadence with the wooden handles of the rudder ropes, calling the changes. The tri-var cox was a woman, and her soprano rang from bank to bank, Manhattan on the starboard side, Randalls Island to port. They were far from home, the boathouse at Spuyten Duyvil; it was spring break and twice-a-day practices and the coach was kicking ass.

Twelve-foot oars of ash, blades painted light blue and white, bit into the water. Eight slender oarsmen, as long and smooth as oars themselves, extended their legs, driving against the stretchers—metal stirrups in which their feet were held by laced leather straps, sliding toward the bow on wheeled seats mounted on metal rails. Halfway through the slide, they cocked their backs and strained to pull the oar handles into their guts. Finally, leaning back past the vertical, the oarsmen could pull no

1

farther; flicking their wrists sharply downward, they freed the blades from the river's grasp. Where the blades had been buried were baby maelstroms.

Their wrists still cocked so that the blades were parallel to the water, the oarsmen slid sternward on their seats, compressing until their knees threatened their chins, guiding the oar handles out over the gunwales, rolling their wrists forward, squaring the blades for the next catch.

Swinging, they call it. Swinging together. A moment that doesn't come every day (doesn't come ever to some crews) of harmony, unity, symmetry. Every catch is crisp, every stroke long and full, every release precise, every recovery unhurried, so that the sternward movement of the seats on their slides does not contradict the forward movement of the shell. Swinging together, there is no checking at the catch, no shooting the slides, no bucking the oars, no washing out. A shell is precisely set up: all heads are in a line, all hands reach out over the gunwales without the bodies' weight following, which would tip the shell, which has no keel. Swinging together, striking together, the eight become one and the one, one with the shell. Sitting so close to the water, the sensation is of terrific speed; there arises the possibility of flight.

Nearly to the tip of Randalls now, nearly to Hell Gate, where the Harlem meets the East, all three shells were swinging. First one led, then another, then the other, then the first, surging ahead by half a deck, maybe, never more. A coach's dream, three boats vying to be the var, and the coach, in the following launch, leaned out over the windshield and bellowed deliriously through his bullhorn.

Then he sputtered, and smote the air melodramatically, and slammed the bullhorn down on the launch's console, for the varsity bowman had caught a crab, had buried his oar too deep and been unable to release it, getting punched in the chest with the oar handle. The shell was dead in the water.

"Shit. Shit, shit, shit." The coach called after the other shells to finish up with power tens, then motioned to the student manager to bring the launch around to the var, for a little lecture. He was surprised to see that the other oarsmen had swiveled around and were pointing fingers of contempt at the clumsy bowman. He hoped he wasn't crafting a team of future whistleblowers.

No, they were pointing at something in the water. So maybe the bowman hadn't crabbed out and it wouldn't be the first time something had heaved up out of the Harlem and grabbed an oar: mattresses, packing crates, telephone poles, stoves and refrigerators, toilet bowls, chairs, sofas, beds, bicycles, motorcycles, cars and trucks—a city river's jetsam.

Something white.

Something smooth and white.

A department-store mannequin. Or one of those dressmaker's dummies, just the torso. (The coach had never told anyone this, but when he was a kid he used to slip into the sewing room on the second floor of his grandmother's house and, well, experiment on a dummy that stood in the corner by the window. Nothing weird— just, you know, cop a little feel.)

Oh, christ, now what?

The bow and two were hanging over the gunwales, vomiting into the river. Pansies. Work them hard and they toss their lunch.

. . . Oh, Jesus, no.

It's not a mannequin, it's a . . .

3

Oh, Jesus, it's a woman.

He couldn't help it. He was going to be sick himself, but he couldn't help it if he noticed that it was a woman.

With breasts, with pubic hair.

But with no hands. No feet. No head.

2 SITTING SIDESADDLE ON THE VERY front of a metal folding chair, Val Fox poised her hands on an imaginary furled parasol. She was a little plump to be sitting that way safely, but in her mind's eye, she was thin as smoke.

" 'I do hope we won't have any unseasonably cold spells.' " Tenny Cullen read Val's cue without enthusiasm. Val was Tenny's best friend, but all Val wanted to do anymore was rehearse; she never wanted to do anything else; she was becoming a rehearsal nerd. " 'It brings on so much influenza and the whole of our family is susceptible to it.' "

Val lifted her chin prettily. " 'My aunt died of influenza. So they said. But it's my belief they done the old woman in.' " Nowhere as thin, okay, but she sure *sounded* like Audrey Hepburn. "Tenny," Val said when Tenny didn't prompt her. "Freddy's mother says, 'Done her in?' "

Tenny slumped. "If you know this, Val, what do you need *me* for?"

"For the sense, geekette—sorry, you're not a geekette; you're helping—for the sense of what it's going to be like onstage. For the *tim*ing."

"Couldn't we go get pizza? Couldn't we do this later?"

"Tenny. You promised."

Without a hint of inquisitiveness, Tenny read: " 'Done her in?' "

Liltingly: " 'Yes, Lord love you. Why should she die of influenza when she come through diphtheria right enough the year before? Fairly blue with it she was. They all thought she was dead. But my father, he kept ladling gin down her throat. Then she come to so sudden, she *bit* the bowl off the spoon. Now, what call would a woman with that strength in her have to die of influenza, and what become of her new straw hat that should have come to me? Somebody *pinched* it, and what I say is, them as pinched it, done her in.' " Val stamped a foot. "*Tenny.*"

"Uh, 'Done her in? Done her in, did you say? Whatever does it mean?' "

"I'll do Professor Higgins," Val said. " 'That's the new small talk. To do somebody in means to kill them.' Now, you do Freddy's mother."

" 'But surely you don't believe your aunt was killed.' "

Val drew herself up. " 'Do I not? Them she lived with . . .' "

As the pause grew longer, Tenny smirked, then read from her script: " 'Them she lived with would have killed her . . .' "

Val slid all the way back in the chair and faced front and sat like the chubby, gnarly fourteen-year-old she had been born and would die, the toes of her L.A. Gears hooked over the crosspiece, her hands under her thighs.

Falsetto, Tenny repeated: " 'Do I not? Them she lived with would have killed her . . .' Val? . . . *Val.*"

Val watched Tony Justice coming down the aisle toward the stage. Seeing her stepfather's face in the window of the door at the rear of the auditorium, she had been reminded of the vignettes in the margins of the dictionary her father, her real father, Stephen Fox, had given her for her tenth birthday—the last of her birthdays of his life. It was not her first dictionary but her first grown-up dictionary; it had entries for *fuck* and *cunt* and *prick*. Val's favorite vignette was one of Marilyn Monroe that illustrated the entry for *décolletage*, her least favor-

6

ite a close-up of the mouth of a lamprey eel. She would never be as thin as Audrey Hepburn (or a lamprey eel), but she had a shot at having boobs like Marilyn Monroe's. In some future edition of the dictionary, a vignette of Val Fox might illustrate *décolletage*. In some future edition of the dictionary, would a vignette of Tony Justice illustrate *The Last Great Newsman*, as *Newsweek* or one of those magazines had called him a couple of months ago, in an issue with his picture on the cover? The *cover*, like he was Madonna or something.

Tenny tried one more time, getting pretty close to Val's imitation of the real thing: " 'Do I not? Them she lived with—' "

"Tenny?" Tony Justice said.

Tenny startled and nearly dropped her script. "Oh, uh, hi, Mister Justice."

"Hi, Tenny."

"I didn't hear you come in."

"Would you please excuse us, Tenny? I need to talk to Val privately."

"Yeah. Sure. You know, okay."

"Thanks, Tenny. I appreciate it."

"Uh, Val, I'll be in the, you know, in the study hall when you need me, okay?"

Val nodded.

Free at last, Tenny clattered down the stage stairs and ran up the aisle and out the door.

Tony Justice, the Last Great Newsman (and don't forget best-selling author—fiction and nonfiction—talk-show regular, three-hour marathoner, gourmet cook, jazz piano player, husband, stepfather. What couldn't he do? He couldn't, so far as Val knew, fly a plane or remove a brain tumor), put one hand on the edge of the stage and vaulted lightly up. He held his hands out, inviting her to stand. When she didn't, he smiled shyly, the smile of a man who can bear momentary immovability because he knows (on top of everything else, he was better-looking than Kevin Costner, and had a dandy's taste in clothes) that over the long haul he's irresistible. "Hey, come on, a hug, hunh?"

Val got up and let him hug her. Her hands didn't touch him, nor did she exert any pressure with her arms. Still, he gave her an extra squeeze before standing back from her. "Val...."

Them she lived with ... "What?"

"I'm sorry, Val."

"For what?"

A tiny sty of impatience flared in a corner of one eye and then was gone. "You know why I'm here, Val."

Them she lived with would have killed her for a hat pin ... "Yes."

His lower lip quivered and in his eye now there was a tear.

He was going to make *her* say it, the bastard. Val jerked her hands free. "They found Momma."

"I'm sorry, Val."

"Dead."

Tony Justice nodded.

Them she lived with would have killed her for a hat pin, let alone a hat.

3 LATER THAT NIGHT, A LITTLE SOUTH OF Canal Street and thirty stories up, in a club you've never heard of because it has no name. Its members, even when they know each other, call each other only Frère, which is French for brother and also means fellow-member, brother-in-arms.

Leather chairs, burgundy carpets, gilt-framed faintly Impressionistic paintings, brandy, cigars, a stock ticker, men in pin-striped suits, snowy-white shirts, muted silk ties, burnished shoes whose heels never ever show signs of wear—you know the sort of place it is.

Glints of light flashed like fireflies as understated jewelry sparkled in the gloom—cufflinks, a wedding band, a tie pin, a wristwatch, a chain and fob, a hand-cuff, the brass zipper of a leather mask, the chain-mail codpiece of a pair of leather chaps, a cock ring worn by a naked man sitting in the lap of a man his father's age.

Three chamber musicians sawed sotto voce in a corner. A laugh burbled up here, an exclamation there; someone called a greeting—"Frère! Frère!"—until the frère in question looked his way. But mostly there was the murmur of intimate conversation, the sweet nothings of couples absorbed in each other.

A man came into the room, a tall trim man with a brush mustache, bringing to fifty or a hundred or a hundred and fifty the number of tall trim men with brush mustaches on the premises. Seeing without looking hard that he for whom he was searching wasn't in the room, the tall trim man crossed it, nodding hello over here, flicking a finger in salute over there, and went through a heavy leather door held open for him by a page done up like Mozart.

He was in a sanctum now, a square amphitheater with wide padded tiers. He stood back against the wall while his eyes adjusted to the near-dark—and so that his arrival would not upset the room's psychic trim.

There was no music in this room, and no conversation, though a score of men, some paired, some single, some lying, some sitting, were arrayed on the tiers. Their cynosure was a hospital gurney in the center of the arena.

Chest-down on the white silk sheet that covered the gurney's mattress, neck arched, chin high, hands gripping the mattress's sides, arms tensed, hips cocked, legs spread wide, was a small, muscled black man with short, oiled dreadlocks. He wore nothing but a copper bracelet on his left wrist and a braided anklet on his right leg.

Alongside the gurney, left arm braced against the mattress, legs flexed, the muscles of his thick neck and vast back knotted with tension, a tall man, six-five or more, with pale pale skin and platinum-blond hair, groped deeper inside the small black man. His right arm was already buried in the black man's anus to above the elbow.

The tall trim man with the brush mustache breathed in and out through his nose, in sympathy with the effort and with the pain, then stepped down one of the four flights of narrow stairs at each corner of the amphitheater until he reached the second tier above the arena.

The tall trim man moved down the aisle, past a couple, all entwined, who were slowly jerking each other off, and sat next to another tall trim man, clean-shaven, who sat all alone, sipping something on the rocks from a tumbler, smoking a long cigar, watching the watched, but also watching the watchers.

"You rowed in college, didn't you?" said the tall trim man with the brush mustache.

10

The other man cocked his head. "Sorry."

"On the crew."

"Ah. Yes. I didn't understand you at first. I thought you were asking if I'd done something risqué."

The tall trim man with the brush mustache smiled. "I wouldn't have to *ask* that."

The other man smiled back. "Yes, I rowed. I rowed for four years as an undergrad and two more on a club crew when I was in B-school. Why?"

"Because then you'll appreciate this even more. Karen Justice—"

Just then, the black man screamed, and the tall trim man with the brush mustache bent closer to convey his message.

4 "I'M GOING TO BE SICK."
"Think about something else. Anything else."
"*Base*ball?"
"Anything."

Ann Jones took a big breath, held it, expelled it. "*All* I can think is: in that coffin is what's left of Karen."

Joe Cullen put an arm through the crook of Ann's and squeezed, which probably wasn't the right thing to do, for it called attention to arms. "Count celebrities."

By the time Karen Halley Fox Justice (what was left of her, Ann was surely not alone in thinking) had been lowered in that coffin into a family plot in Sag Harbor measured out by her whaling ancestors, Ann and Cullen had each counted a bunch. Tony Justice was the Last Great Newsman, after all, and Karen, well . . . "the Cher of Manhattan luxury real estate," *City* magazine had once called Karen, an allusion to both her famous beauty (she had been a ubiquitous fashion model before tiring of the catwalk and the strobe lights) and to her unembarrassed self-promotion.

The upper crusts of the worlds of commerce, government, charity, culture, and publishing were represented. Emissaries from Seventh and Madison avenues had made the long trek out to the East End, and so had those from the Great White Way and Tin Pan Alley. (Karen's first husband, the late Stephen Fox—himself, eerily, a murder victim—had been a producer of Broadway musicals, and the indefatigable Tony Justice had written a couple of books on popular music and its musicians.)

Just friends included a diplomat, an opera singer, a rock star, a Grand Prix race driver, a world-class tennis

12

player, a reclusive novelist, a stand-up comic. Haute-couture mannequins in black black black skittered here and there like grieving flamingos. The afternoon was chilly, for winter had sneaked back in to pay *its* last respects, but the swarming reporters and photographers were so busy logging the famous that perspiration flew from them as from the coats of rollicking wet dogs.

Ann and Cullen counted too the many, many enemies of the widower, and noted the irony that such was the clout of Tony Justice that even those who had had the lids lifted by him off some simmering irregularity in their businesses or their bailiwicks were obliged to publicly mourn Justice's dead wife. "Lots of these people *hate* Tony. Any of them enough, do you think, to kill Karen?"

Ann Jones was a reporter, Joe Cullen a cop: speculation about who killed whom was second nature to them. Though a reporter—she had written that very *City* profile—Ann was there as a civilian: she and Karen had liked each other enough at their first meeting over Ann's tape recorder to have had lunch together two or three times a year since. Cullen, though a cop, was along for moral support: he was Ann's boyfriend (a word neither used if they could help it, for it called attention more to their differences—he was forty-eight, divorced, with teenage kids; she was thirty-four, never married, wanted a baby—than to their affinities).

A man who looked like a mogul, not a cleric, stepped up to a microphone and began the eulogy.

"Who he?" Ann said.

Cullen shrugged.

"He looks like Ray Brand. You read that he died?"

"I heard it on the radio."

"AIDS."

Cullen nodded.

"Rock Hudson, Ray Brand. All the movie stars I had crushes on when I was a kid are turning out to be gay. Can you imagine what that's going to do to me emotionally?"

Whatever the eulogist was saying, the wind was expurgating before it got to the rear of the crowd. "Can't we get closer?" Ann said. "We're like a team of playwrights in the back of the orchestra on opening night. Oscar and Hammerstein."

"I like to watch the way people react," Cullen said. "My training."

"You didn't catch this job."

No, but as a cop Cullen couldn't not be curious about any unnatural death. That the deceased had been seen last getting in a taxi after working late one night in her Madison Avenue office, a vital woman with a briefcase in one hand, a squash racquet in the other, and had been seen next six months later floating in a foul river, a virtual torso roped to a sandbag (which had burst, freeing the body to bob to the surface), made him wonder along with Ann not only whodunit but in what rage.

After a while Ann said, "What if that's not Karen in the coffin?"

"The X ray, the identifying marks." Cullen meant the X ray reproduced on the front page of every newspaper in town, showing a mended break in the corpse's right shinbone, a break that matched an X ray from an orthopedist's files of the right shinbone Karen Justice had once upon a time broken skiing; and he meant the scar from a cesarean section, the three moles on the left shoulder blade, the polytheliac nipple on the left breast—marks you didn't have to be a forensics expert to know meant the corpse was Karen Justice, Karen Justice was the corpse.

"Headless torsos," Ann went on anyway. "I came across one on the very first page of a mystery novel once and I said, 'I don't need this shit.' I probably don't want to know this, but exactly how do you do it? And with what?"

"Shhh."

"I'm not writing about this." It was well known in her circles and in his that Ann and Cullen were a couple, and there was therefore no mystery about where she got inside cop info that turned up in her pieces, which was why he often wouldn't talk shop with her.

"Whatever."

Ann looked up at him from under the brim of her black gaucho hat. " 'Whatever' is the refuge of scoundrels. On *Dallas*, this guy says to J. R., 'You don't want any killing, do you, Mister Ewing?' and J. R. says, 'Whatever.' "

Cullen picked at the bark of a tree and wondered what kind of tree it was. Ann probably knew: she'd grown up in a suburb and gone to a college with a campus. He was a city kid for whom a sidewalk, a street, the ground, grass—all were *the floor*, for whom a tree was a tree.

Ann again: "Did you—you, the cops, I mean—ever find the taxi driver who picked Karen up?"

This had been all over the papers too. "A photograph was circulated in all the garages. Plenty of drivers remembered picking her up at one time or another, but none that night."

"If trim like Karen Justice got in my cab, I'd sure as hell remember."

"Plenty did. But none that night."

A woman in black Chanel and a power hairdo, hennaed and wild, turned on them. Ducking from her glare

15

caused Cullen to look right at Diana Romano, who was looking at him. Mourning became her, slim and olive-skinned with dark, dark hair cut like Elvis's, a pompadour and ducktail (it was all the rage and Diana Romano had started it, according to Ann, whose job required her to keep tabs on things like that). And she wore glen-plaid pumps. "Bruno Magli," Ann had said when Cullen pointed them out, the way she would say *sycamore*, or whatever, were he to point out this tree.

Cullen felt . . . captured by Diana Romano's eyes. She was a photographer, after all, *the* photographer of the moment—Herb Ritts, Annie Leibovitz, Bruce Weber, eat your hearts out—winner just the other day of a prestigious prize for her photographs accompanying articles in the *Bulletin* on Vietnamese street gangs in Chinatown, photographs, the citation said, that "do not merely illustrate, but illuminate, the text"—that text by Tony Justice, by whose side she now stood, a friend in need, a colleague in distress.

To free himself, maybe—he hardly knew her—Cullen nodded once, a nod that said—what?—*courage?* And Diana Romano nodded back: a perfect communion.

One just as perfect, maybe even more so, took place when Tony Justice straightened after laying a rose on the coffin that held all that was left of his wife. He'd been stony till now, but now he stared around him as if he didn't know where he was, didn't know who these people were; he looked as if he might flee. Diana Romano saw the look and was at his side in a flash; she took his head in her hands and nodded as if to say that it was time to weep, and she kept his forehead to her chest until the racking sobs stopped. Even those present who had squirmed at reading in the *Bulletin* detailed descriptions of their transgressions ferreted out by Tony Justice, who had seen on the *Bulletin*'s front pages photographs of their guilt-eroded faces made by Diana Romano, were moved.

VAL FOX was moved too, moved to wonder: Would they? Will they? How can they? How, so soon after Momma's death, can they be touching each other like that? Look at her hand on his arm, on the small of his back, on his shoulder. Look.

Okay, so it wasn't really *soon* after Momma's death because Momma was dead the whole six months she was missing—that's what Tony said the Medical Examiner said, whoever *he* was and how could he *know* something like that? And if he *did* know, how come he didn't know *who* killed her? And *why*? Tony said the Medical Examiner couldn't even say for sure that Momma *was* killed, like maybe she died of natural causes, like people died of a heart attack or something (influenza!) all the time, right, and then someone came along and chopped off their heads and hands and feet and tied them to sandbags and threw them in the river, right? *Them she lived with would have killed her for a hat pin, let alone a hat—* didn't the Medical Examiner, didn't the whole wide world, see that? Why was Val the only one who saw it? The same reason, probably, that she was the only one who saw that Tony Justice and Diana Romano were going to get married as soon as they could.

Well, okay, not the *only* person. Tenny Cullen saw it too. Tenny (whose father was a policeman, which probably meant she had genes that made her good at seeing things) had seen something else too. She had seen that it might look wack if Tony got married again so soon after they found Val's momma's body, but Val shouldn't for-

17

get that it was only a couple of months after Val's *father* was killed that Val's momma got married again, and Val hadn't thought that was wack, she'd thought it was bitching. (Val's father, Stephen Fox, was killed by an actor who was ticked off that he didn't get a part in a play, talk about killing someone for a hat pin.) Val had thought it was bitching, Tenny reminded her, because she was glad that her momma was getting her act together. Okay, so maybe it *was* a little wack that the guy her momma married, Tony Justice, was a reporter who met Val's momma because he was writing stories about Stephen Fox's murder. And it *was* a little wack that when the actor, Noel Cutler, finally gave up and turned himself in, he didn't give up and turn himself in to the police, he gave up and turned himself in to Tony Justice. Still, hadn't it been bitching that Val's momma got her act together so soon?

Hadn't it?

Val said it had.

And won't it be bitching that your stepfather, which is what Tony Justice now is, right, gets his act together so soon?

Won't it?

Val supposed it would.

5 CULLEN READ GRAVESTONES WHILE ANN went to find a bathroom before driving back to New York. Tony Justice came toward him, stepping across the flagstones as if out on floes of ice. A short trim man followed after Justice, taking much bigger steps.

"We've never really met. You're Ann Jones's friend. I'm Tony Justice. Thanks for coming."

"Joe Cullen. I'm sorry for your loss." In the line of duty, Cullen had been around a movie star or two, and Justice took up space in the same way they had, made you back away a little. He was average height, average weight, yet he seemed tall and broad-shouldered; he was average handsome, yet it was an effort to take your eyes off him. He had exquisite hair that dared the wind to muss it, and wore a beautiful cashmere coat. Notwithstanding Justice's loss, Cullen felt some envy.

"This is Og Slate." Justice included the small man with a big gesture. "Og, Joe Cullen—Sergeant Cullen, isn't it?—of the New York Police Department."

"Cullen, Cullen," Slate said. "*Cu*llen. You're Neil Zimmerman's partner." Slate was very thirties—round horn-rimmed glasses, slicked-down hair, polka-dot bowtie. He could have been forty years old or sixty. "Neil's mother and my wife, Michelle"—he pointed with his chin at the woman in the black Chanel who had turned on Cullen and Ann for chattering—"rampage around town together, robbing the rich for various good causes."

Ah, *the* Slates. Cullen said something banal about that kind of robbing's being preferable to the kind he was used to, blah, blah, blah, but he could have been

19

reciting the Periodic Table or the lyrics to "Splish Splash," for Ogden Slate wasn't listening; only pith sharpened stiletto-thin could penetrate his self-absorption. A couple of other thoroughbreds whinnied at him and that was all it took to entice him away; he cantered off to chat with them without even an insincere *Nize ta meetcha.*

"I'm glad Ann could get out here," Justice said. "There're newspaper and magazine brass here, but not a lot of reporters. Off-duty reporters, I mean. Reporters aren't like cops; they don't rally round their peers.... So: Do you think I killed Karen, Joe? Does Ann?"

Cullen was wearing just a suit coat, the collar turned up, and he pulled the lapels closer in front to keep out the chilly wind and to keep in a vapidity like *Er, uh, inappropriate to discuss a, uh, pending investigation.* It was a good question, a fair question, a question that had probably occurred to everyone who had wondered about what was left of Karen Justice in that coffin. "My daughter, Tenny, goes to school with Val."

Justice looked puzzled, then made the connection. "Ah. Cullen. Sure."

"Tenny and her mother—she lives with her mother—asked me to tell you Val's welcome to spend a night or a weekend or even longer with them anytime you can use a break."

Justice swallowed. "That's very generous. Thank them for me. And it's generous of you not to give some bullshit answer to what I just said in anger. Things are always what they look like—that's what I tell cub reporters and journalism students. People don't just disappear, so if a woman *does* disappear and it looks like her husband killed her, then that's what happened. I've believed that nine out of ten times it's ever happened and

I'll continue to believe it when it happens in the future. But I expected the benefit of a doubt from people— people I've been hard on as well as from my friends. I can see in their eyes, though, that they think I killed her. They all think I killed her. Killed her and cut her to pieces. What kind of animal—"

"Mister Justice, I don't—"

"Tony," Justice said, and put a hand on Cullen's arm to stress how much he wanted to be called Tony.

Call *him* Miss Manners, but Cullen thought people were spendthrift with first names. He didn't like it when his dentist's secretary or a bank teller or the doorman in his ex-wife's building called him by his first name; he hated the Knicks' radio announcer, who sounded as though he was doing the play-by-play of a schoolyard game: "Trent, over to Rodney, inside to Patrick." (Neil Zimmerman, his partner, born with a season ticket in his mouth, got Knick broadcasts as a standard feature on his Saab Turbo, whose vanity plate, honest to God, was NIXFAN.) Cullen mistrusted people who when he had called them by their surnames told him to call them by their given names; he couldn't think of one who hadn't been trying, in trying to get him to get familiar, to apply some grease, some juice, some—one of Zimmerman's favorite words—spin. "Things are what they look like and then you look a little closer, a little more calmly, and they look like something else. You look long enough and something you could almost call the truth emerges— that's what I tell rookie cops and criminology students."

Justice ducked his head into the lapel of his cashmere coat. When he looked back up there were tears that might or might not have been wind tears in his eye. "Thanks. Thanks, that helps." And then he was gone, swept away by a trio of ululating fashion models.

21

*   *   *

ANN CAME back, walking arm-in-arm-in-arm with her boss, Mark Talbert, the publisher of *City* magazine, and his wife, Linda, a Broadway press agent. This was just like being in the big city.

"Mark was one of the last people to talk to Karen," Ann said. "He called her just before she left work the night she disappeared. They were both going to be in Boston the next day and were going to meet for a drink. Stephen Fox was a client of Linda's."

"A married couple murdered four years apart," Linda said. "The odds have got to be against it."

Mark Talbert didn't give Cullen a chance to respond. "Dismemberment, Joe—that's not usual, is it?" He looked right past Cullen's ear as he said it, checking out one of the mannequins, probably.

"Usual?" Cullen said.

"Doesn't it take—I don't know—special skill?"

"I think it takes a sharp tool and a strong stomach."

"And a lot of hate," Ann said.

"That too."

Linda Talbert gripped her husband's arm and gave him a look that assured him she could never hate him that much. He tried to give her one in return but it kept sliding into a look that was full of curiosity as to just *how* you'd go about it.

Ann took Cullen's arm. These were touchy people. "I told Mark my Ray Brand idea. He likes it."

"What Ray Brand idea?"

"A piece on a generation of women traumatized by loving men who secretly loved men."

Cullen didn't ask Talbert why *City* magazine always had pieces about one person's traumas written as if they were a generation's. "Sounds provocative."

"Mark and Linda have a house in Water Mill," Ann said. "They've invited us out some weekend."

"You've got to come, Joe." Talbert got his other arm around Ann and looked as though he'd put a third arm around Cullen, if only he had one. "You'll love it. You can take the sailboard out; you'll pick it up in no time. Tennis, walks on the beach, biking—you won't be bored for a second. Take the Jitney—you can read or sleep or neck"—there his eyes went again, thinking about necking—"and drive our spare car while you're out there. It's an old Healy with right-hand drive, but you'll love it."

Cullen just nodded. When the Talberts had gone off, Ann said, "What's the matter with you?"

"I guess I don't like being told that I'm going to love something or pick something up or won't be bored."

"You *guess*?"

"I don't like it. Where's the bathroom?"

Cullen followed Ann's directions into the church and down the stairs to the basement and made a left (did she say left?) and opened the second door (the second door?) on the right.

It was a storeroom: music stands, folding chairs stacked on racks, a volleyball net swaddling its stanchions, an old phonograph and a box of forty-fives, a bass drum (*Noyac F.D.*), a legless Ping-Pong table propped on its side against a wall, a pew burnt around the edges (from a sermon's brimstone?), a blackboard on wheels with the message *Paraliturgy will meet in the rectory* erased but still legible, copies (is there a basement or attic anywhere where there are not?) of *National Geographic*.

And Diana Romano, perched on an upturned steamer trunk, her black mourning dress up over her olive thighs, black French-maid French-whore garter-

23

less stockings, glen-plaid pumps (Bruno Magli), her right hand clutching Tony Justice's exquisite hair, her left hand jammed in her sucking mouth so she wouldn't cry out, as Tony, trousers down to his knees, elbows pinning his cashmere coat back out of the way, moved in and out of her, in and out.

To his envy of Justice's hair, of his coat, Cullen added envy of having a woman not averse to seizing the day.

As quiet as a mouse, as quiet as a Peeping Tom, Cullen shut the door behind him, but not before he had exchanged another of his perfect looks with Diana Romano.

"Find it?" Ann said when Cullen got back outside.

"Yup."

6 "NICE WEDDING," PHIL HRINIAK SAID.
Cullen said, "Umm."

The East End again, Shelter Island this time, spring about to turn to summer, the air crazy with dandelion rays.

"Some house." A native of a city with few surprises left up its sleeve, Commissioner of a Police Department whose internal politics were nearly Lebanese, Hriniak acted sometimes as though he'd just gotten off the local from Podunk.

Yet Cullen agreed. "Some house." As big as a barn, as white as snow, a cupola at one end, a widow's walk at the other, it sat in the middle of five football fields' worth of lawn on a bluff that looked west out over Peconic Bay, littered with sails. Complete with an outdoor dance floor, made of some smooth substance for the ultimate gliding experience, set in the shade of extravagant trees (their names unknown, of course, to Cullen), it was a typical working stiff's summer bungalow. Or was Cullen, whose idea of a summer vacation was two P.M. Saturday to eleven A.M. Saturday in a three-bedroom house shared with three other couples and eight or ten kids five blocks from the beach in Ship Bottom, New Jersey, the one who was out of step?

"Belonged to Justice's last wife and her first husband, I understand. His name was Fox. It's confusing." Hriniak turned to watch Tony Justice, in a morning suit, and Diana Romano, in a long white dress ("Azzedine Alaïa," Ann had said), waltzing expertly at the hub of encircling guests. "Not to this crowd, I guess. They look like they can tell the players without a scorecard. Didn't know this was your scene."

A long white dress, white stockings, white lace garters, Cullen saw as Diana Romano was passed on to a
new partner, and spun giddily. "Ann went to the funeral.
A lot of reporters didn't. The wedding invitation cleans
the slate."

"You at the funeral too?"

"Yup."

Hriniak shook out his pocket handkerchief and
mopped the back of his neck. "I was at a law-
enforcement convention in Dallas. People who know
about such things tell me it was a serious breach of local
protocol not to fly up for the afternoon. A reporter who's
one of the first on the scene every time the cops fuck up,
well, the PC ought to be at his wife's funeral, is how they
see it. I'm not only lucky to've been invited here today,
I'm lucky I didn't lose my table at Elaine's. Does Elaine's
have tables? It was right at the same time Ray Brand
died. Maybe that could be my excuse. Ray Brand—I still
can't believe it. I try to be broad-minded about that kind
of stuff, but Ray Brand? I don't know. Ray Brand was my
hero. He was like . . . I don't know—"

"Rock Hudson?"

"Exactly. Rock Hudson. . . . I can't think of that
many married couples in the news business, can you?
Must be the hours. Or maybe it's the egos."

"Ask Neil," Cullen said. Neil Zimmerman collected
marriages: Cullen's partner knew what actor was married to what actress in the same TV series (not the one
who played his wife, the one who played his *partner's*
wife); what baseball player was married to what former
belly dancer; what arbitrageur to what interior decora-
tor; what U.S. attorney to what radio consumer adviser;
what novelist to what novelist. He knew the husbands of
soap-opera sluts, bathing-suit models, talk-show host-
esses and country singers, the wives of couturiers, come-

dians, computer whiz kids, and congressmen. Why he knew, Cullen didn't know. Zimmerman wasn't searching for a pattern from which to fashion a marriage of his own; he had miles to go before he had slept with every baby boomerette on the Upper East Side. Ann thought— Ann *knew*—that Zimmerman's matrimonial expertness was the flip side of Cullen's ignorance (Cullen was certain that his father was married to his mother and that he had been married to his ex-wife, and that was about it): namely, that there is more than one way to keep one's distance.

And speaking of Ann, she was just stepping out on the dance floor on the arm of Ogden Slate, of all people, who had acted as though he'd never met Cullen before when Zimmerman introduced them earlier today, then, when reminded, had embraced him like a prodigal relative. "What does Ann think about this?" Hriniak said.

Cullen watched a purple-sailed catamaran (a Hobie, Zimmerman had called one like it, for he, like Ann, knew the names of things, especially the playthings of the rich) tear-ass across the bay, shattering the sun-dazzled surface, going faster than anything should that doesn't have an engine. "She thinks: Who are any of us to say it's too soon?"

Hriniak nodded. "Cal Calhoun, Jimmy Fontino, and I came out of the Academy together. It's always three guys who're tight, you ever notice that? Not two, not four. The musketeer thing, maybe. Not that everybody's tight with somebody; sometimes there're loners—like you. . . ."

Cullen didn't cross over into the space Hriniak left for him to defend his solitariness; he preferred to save his energy for jousts on the subject with Ann, whose guerrilla war to make him tighter with her was entering its third year.

"... Point is, within three years we were all married, after another four, both their wives were dead, two years after that they'd both remarried. I thought it was too soon, Beryl said who the fuck was *I*—those were her words and you know she doesn't talk like that unless she means it—who the fuck was *I* to say that? So I know what Ann means, I guess."

"Where's your car, Phil?" Cullen said.

"Over there somewhere." Hriniak waved beyond the house, where still more lawn swept down toward an Italianate garden, a tennis court, a boathouse, a dock, a beach, all around deep protective woods.

"You have a driver?"

Hriniak shrugged and smiled and shrugged again; he'd been Police Commissioner for two years and First Dep for four years before that, but he was still embarrassed about the perks. "He's the big guy eating the left side of the buffet."

"I'll go tell him you and I're going for a drive."

THEY DROVE for ten miles, but the bends of the shoreline were such that they ended up about two hundred yards from where they had been, on a spit of beach just across a small bay from the big old white house. They took their suit coats off and sat on a driftwood log. Down the strand, some kids with sticks flicked a dead jellyfish at each other.

"Zimmerman and I caught a job back around Christmas," Cullen said. "A lieutenant in Brooklyn Anti-Crime named Thomas Muldoon, known as Blond Tommy so as not to confuse him with redheaded Tommy Muldoon, Brooklyn Emergency Services. We got a tip from a bailiff in State Supreme Court who saw Blond

Tommy more than once in a bar on Tenth Avenue with some guys up on a hijacking rap."

Hriniak tipped his chin up and squinted into the sun. "Remember that summer just after I turned captain, I filled in as CO of the Six?"

Cullen knew that Hriniak would venture into the forest of uncertainty only if he could blaze his trail with reminiscences, the better to find his way back out. So he waited.

"The Bomb Squad works out of the Six," Hriniak said. "They were shorthanded—they had guys out with mono, hepatitis. Redheaded Tommy was good with explosives, he was temped over there for a couple of months. I knew him to say hello to. You started out in the Six, didn't you? I kind of forgot that."

Hriniak had caught up, and was waiting for him now, so Cullen said, "The DA suspects the guys are Westies."

Cullen paused, but Hriniak didn't have any Westie stories—or none that he felt like telling. "Blond Tommy retired in March, just in time not to have to answer some questions we had for him. Neil was for staying on him, Maslosky and I thought we should give him the benefit of a doubt as a retirement present. The guys were not nice guys, but we couldn't tie them to the Westies or Blond Tommy to anything they were doing that wasn't kosher."

Hriniak looked thoughtful. "Sometimes a guy doesn't have a good sense of who he is, what's his place in the scheme of things, he spends so much time around bad guys, he starts thinking they're his friends, it doesn't mean *he's* a bad guy, just confused."

Cullen nodded. "Blond Tommy works for a due diligence outfit around Princeton. He lives down the shore, as they say in Jersey: Little Silver."

"I always like the sound of that," Hriniak said. "Little Silver. There's a place out on the island I like the sound of: Brightwater. Turns out it's just a wide spot in the road, not a place you'd want to live."

They were coming up on their reason for being there, the reason they'd left a perfectly nice party with lots of comfortable lawn furniture and shade trees to sit on a bumpy log on the sand in the sun. They took their time. "When I was a kid," Cullen said, "I wanted my folks to move out of Elmhurst to Mount Vernon. I'd never been there, but it sounded nice, nicer than Elmhurst. I probably thought it'd be like George Washington's Mount Vernon, though I'd never been there either."

"You know, Beryl went to college in Washington—American U. She's always saying we should go down there for a week or a long weekend, go to museums, see the monuments, the Vietnam Memorial. We never seem to get around to it. Your boy's going there for the summer, isn't he? James? Didn't you tell me that?"

Cullen leaned forward to watch the kids with the jellyfish, remembering when James had been merely thoughtless and cruel, not cunning. "That was the plan—a music program run by the National Symphony. Now he's saying he'd rather stay home and go to heavy-metal concerts at the Meadowlands."

"Con*certs*? There's more than one?"

Cullen shrugged. "He's a Bon Jovi wanna-be."

"A what?"

"He wants to wear his hair long and go around bare-chested with a fringed vest and leather pants."

"Didn't they do that in the sixties?"

Cullen sat back and pushed them over the hump. "On our list of people to talk to about Blond Tommy, Neil and I had Charlie Peck from Manhattan Crime

Scene. Charlie used to be in Brooklyn Anti-Crime. He was on vacation at Christmastime and by the time he got back we'd let it slide. Neil ran into him last week and they got to talking. Which brings us," Cullen said, "to Diana Romano."

Hriniak sat up straighter to look at the shallows just beyond the scumline, as if the name were a stone—a boulder—Cullen had tossed in and that was still radiating circles.

"Diana Romano does all kinds of photography— spot news, features, books, record albums. She especially does stuff about . . ."—oh, what the hell—"the *demimonde*, things a little bit off center. The work that made her reputation was a book about uncles. It was called *Uncles*."

"Whose uncles? Her uncles?"

"Our uncles."

"*Our* uncles—yours and mine?"

"The De*part*ment's, Phil. Uncles are undercover cops."

"I know what uncles are," Hriniak said.

They were at the hard place—the place where people complained that they knew what you were telling them in order to postpone your telling them what they knew they didn't know and weren't sure they wanted to know.

"I know you know it, Phil. I'm just trying—"

"You know, I think you're too fast and loose with the Phils sometimes. I'm the PC, you're the detective. I don't think I should always be Phil, *Ser*geant."

The place where people you'd known all your adult life pulled rank in the hope that you might think twice about telling them what they knew they didn't know and weren't sure they wanted to know.

"So what about *Uncles*?" Hriniak finally said.

31

"*Uncles* was actually pictures of ex-uncles because active uncles wouldn't let their pictures be taken. Blond Tommy was an active uncle, he met Diana Romano while she was working on the book, they had an affair."

"Gossip."

"Peck wouldn't mention it if it were only gossip. Peck's one of the best."

Hriniak shrugged. "It happens. People have affairs. This is her first marriage, so she wasn't married, right? Was Blond Tommy?"

"Still is, technically."

"Come on, Joe, don't fuck with me. The fuck does 'technically' mean?"

They were on a first-name basis again, or he was. "Blond Tommy's wife, Rae, got in her car on June 5, 1986, to go to an A&P in Baldwin. She hasn't come back yet."

Hriniak was silent.

"Blond Tommy's alibi was solid. Diana Romano was in Mexico doing a book on bullfighting. Rae Muldoon had run off before, with a guy, to get back at Blond Tommy for spending a weekend in Montauk with a paralegal from the Queens DA's office. She may just have decided enough was enough. Blond Tommy and Diana Romano didn't last very much longer after that, according to Peck."

Hriniak picked up a razor-clam shell from between his feet, turned it over, tossed it away. "Have you talked to the Homicide D who caught Karen Justice's K?"

"No."

"Talk to him."

"There's a problem. My daughter and Justice's step-daughter are friends. They go to the same school."

"That wasn't a problem back around Christmas."

"Back around Christmas we hadn't talked to Peck.

32

Back around Christmas Karen Justice was a missing person, not a torso in the Harlem. Back around Christmas Tony Justice and Diana Romano were colleagues, not spouses." Back around Christmas Cullen hadn't seen Diana Romano, perched on an upturned steamer trunk, her black mourning dress up over her olive thighs, black French-maid French-whore garterless stockings, glen-plaid pumps, her right hand clutching Tony Justice's exquisite hair, her left hand jammed in her sucking mouth so she wouldn't cry out, as Tony, trousers down to his knees, elbows pinning his cashmere coat back out of the way, moved in and out of her, in and out.

Hriniak stood up, stretched, put his coat on. "You didn't catch this job, just talk to him. Name's Henderson, Harold Henderson. His buddies call him Rickey."

BACK AT the big old white house, Diana Romano was dancing with Zimmerman. A long white dress, white stockings, white lace garters, white lace panties—she got more energetic all the time. Cullen didn't want to know about it, so he walked back out on the lawn to look at the bay. At the top of the bluff was a topiary hedge in the shape of an S. Mark Talbert, who knew lots of facts too, especially about the life-styles of the rich and famous, had said when they arrived that the S was the initial of the builder of the house, a turn-of-the-century railroad tycoon.

"I always bought the railroads in Monopoly," Ann had said. "If you owned all four, the rent was something like two hundred dollars."

"You ought to play with Romano," Talbert had said. "Loves Monopoly. Has one of those computerized versions."

"She strike you as the Monopoly type?" Ann had said to Cullen. "Ro*mano*?"

Cullen had just smiled. Ann could do five minutes on men who called women by their last names and the women who loved them.

The hedge was higher than Cullen's head and the boy in him wanted to circumnavigate it. He was halfway round when he stopped, for around the next bend came voices, stealthy, intimate, articulating emotions, not facts. He didn't want to know about this either, and veered off toward the edge of the bluff.

A big, big sailboat, a yawl or a ketch, heeled way over as it skimmed under the headland. Cullen could hear the hiss of the bow and the snap of the rigging and the skitter of the dinghy being towed after it.

Cullen heard a cheer and turned to see that Diana Romano had Hriniak by the hands and was pulling him after her into the center of the ring of dancers. Infected by tarantism, the New York City Police Commissioner danced with a woman with white lace underwear who had prevailed on two boyfriends to get rid of their wives. Allegedly. Possibly. Maybe.

Cullen turned back to see a white-suited, suntanned, bleached-blond, teenage boy come out from behind the hedge. He couldn't say for an absolute certainty, he would be speculating, concluding, that Mark Talbert, who had somehow materialized in the space between the hedge and the dance floor, had preceded the boy out from behind the hedge.

All this was giving Cullen a headache. He turned away again and there was Ann. "Hi, sailor. Want to dance?"

7 VAL FOX DIDN'T WANT TO DANCE. SHE
wanted to do just what she was doing, huddling
inside the igloo of despair she could build up
around her at a moment's notice lately and had
erected this time in her room on the second floor of the
big old white house, the house that somehow now belonged to Tony Justice and Diana Romano, who were
now, somehow, Val's parents or stepparents or guard-
ians but in any case were in charge of her life.

And who wouldn't leave her alone. Right now, there
was Diana Romano, calling at Val's door like a . . . a . . .
Val couldn't think of the word—a word she had learned
in Miss Banta's mythology class, one of those women
Ulysses tied his men to the masts for, so they wouldn't
freak when the women sang.

A siren.

"Val?"

Tie me up, Ulysses. Plug my ears up with wax.

"Val, it's Diana."

*Tighter, Ulysses. Tighter, dude. I can snap my fingers, I
can tap my toes. If she starts singing, I'll start dancing,
snapping, tapping.*

"We need to talk, Val. Just us. Just you and me.
Hiding's going to solve nothing."

Tighter, Ulysses.

"Val?"

Tighter!

"Val, I can never take your mother's place. I would
never even promise to try. It would be arrogant of me to
say I could."

*I can hear her, Ulysses. What happened to the ear
plugs?*

"Val, I'm going to open the door, okay? I have a key."

Shit, Ulysses, no wonder it took you ten years to get home. You give people keys.

"Hi, Val."

She touches me, Ulysses, it's all over.

"I'm just going to sit here on the bed, okay? Ah, that feels good. I didn't realize I was so tired."

She touches me . . .

"Your head's hot, Val. Do you feel all right? Let me loosen your collar. I'll rub your neck."

Thanks for the help, Ulysses. I really appreciate it.

"Your neck's like iron."

"Ow."

"Sorry. There—how's that?"

"Better."

"Feels good?"

". . . Yes."

"So what do you think of all this, Val? Do you think it's too sordid for words?"

"I don't know. No."

"What do your friends think?"

"I don't know. You know."

"You've talked this over with them, haven't you—the marriage?"

"Mostly with, you know, Tenny."

"Her real name's Stephanie, isn't it?"

"When her brother was little, he couldn't say Stephanie."

"What's her brother's name?"

"James."

"Not Joseph Junior?"

"Who? Oh—her dad."

"He's here today, her dad."

"I saw him. He said hi."

36

"Tony says he's a friend of Ann Jones, who writes for *City*."

"I guess so. I don't know. He and Tenny's mom are, you know, divorced."

Diana stopped working on Val's neck, but let her hands lie lightly on her shoulders. "I have a sister. Her name's Roberta. When I was little I couldn't say Roberta, so I called her Rivvy."

"Really?"

"No, Rivvy."

Val couldn't help it, she laughed.

Diana laughed and squeezed Val's shoulders gently.

"I didn't know you had a sister," Val said.

"Umm. She's dead, actually."

"Oh, no."

"It's been a long time."

"You said 'have.' You said, 'I *have* a sister.'"

"I probably did."

"Is that because you think of her the way she was, when she was alive?"

"Yes. I always think of her as alive."

"That's how I think of Momma."

"It's how you *should* think of her."

"How did your sister die?" *Did someone kill her? Would them she lived with have killed her for a hat pin, let alone a hat?*

"In a car crash. With a boy. It was their first date, their first and last date. They went to a party and he got drunk and smashed into a car stopped for a light. Rivvy and the three people in the other car were killed. The boy broke a leg and got a few scratches, the son-of-a-bitch."

"Where did this happen?"

"California. Ojai, near San Diego."

"I've never heard of Oh-high."

"It's spelled o-j-a-i. Like jai-alai."

37

Val put her hand up to her shoulder, put it over
Diana's hand. "I'm sorry, Diana, about your sister."

Diana shifted on the bed, taking her hands from
Val's shoulders but slipping one arm around her waist.
"Tell me about that photograph—the one on the
dresser." In it, a man and a woman stood with their
arms around each other at the railing of a sailboat;
behind them on the shore was this very big old white
house.

"It's Momma and Daddy, right after they got married."

"That would've been when—seventy-five?"

"I was born in seventy-six, so yes, seventy-five."

"Nineteen seventy-six. You were a Bicentennial
baby."

"That's what Daddy used to say."

"I didn't know they'd had the house so long."

"They didn't. It wasn't theirs when that picture was
taken. That's what's so funny about it. It wasn't their
boat, either; it belonged to some friends of theirs who
have a house in Greenport and keep the boat in a marina
here on Shelter Island. Coecles Harbor."

"Cuckles?"

"It's spelled c-o-e-c-l-e-s."

"Coecles Harbor."

"Momma and Daddy were sailing with their friends
one time and saw this house from the water and fell in
love with it. For the fun of it, and, you know, as a kind of
wish that maybe it would someday be their house, they
took that picture and hung it on the wall of Daddy's
office. Then one day, a man came to see Daddy about
investing in a play. He walked up to the picture and said,
'That's my house. What's it doing in your office?' His
name was Mister Wister, which always made me laugh
whenever anybody said it. Momma and Daddy had an-

other blowup of the picture made and gave it to Mister Wister and said he should hang it in his house and tell people it was his boat."

Diana laughed and squeezed Val tightly.

"The play was a big hit and Momma and Daddy and Mister Wister became good friends. Then Mister Wister died and left Momma and Daddy the house."

"So they got their wish."

"They got their wish."

"From Mister Wister."

Val laughed. "From Mister Wister."

Diana stretched up to kiss the top of Val's head. "It's nice to hear you laugh. . . . I should get back to the party. Will you come and join us?"

Them she lived with . . .

"Please."

Would *them she lived with . . . ?*

"Please, Val."

". . . Okay."

They both laughed and Val crawled up out of the igloo and they hugged and held each other for a long time without moving, barely breathing.

8 THE SILK SHEET THAT COVERED THE
hospital gurney in the center of the amphitheater was burgundy this time, and chest-down
on it this time was a tall, lank boy with blond
hair that hung down between his winglike shoulder
blades. Slowly slowly slowly sliding a foot-long plastic
phallus into the boy's anus was a dwarf who stood on a
step-stool to get a better angle.

There was music this time, Don Henley, "A New
York Minute," for it was a Saturday afternoon and the
audience was younger. On a television monitor that
hadn't been on the last time, the Cubs soundlessly
played the Reds in the network game of the week. On a
padded tier close to the arena, three couples fucked side-
by-side: hoping to come in unison, the sodomizers kept
each other advised of their relative progress, chirping
like jockeys at their mounts. Only one of the sodomized
was really into it, encouraging his partner to speed up;
one chewed gum indifferently, the other's face was blank
with pain.

The half-dozen others in the room were solitary. One
masturbated with a hockey glove, another with a sheet
of fine sandpaper; one napped, one watched the ball-
game with an apparent rooting interest (for the Cubs),
one picked his nose. The tall trim clean-shaven man
sipped something on the rocks from a tumbler, smoked a
long cigar, watched the watched and watched the
watchers.

The tall trim man with the brush mustache came
through the heavy leather door and went directly to the
clean-shaven man, not even glancing at the *exhibition*.
He sat on the tier behind him and leaned down close to

his ear. "Justice knows names. He got hold of some kind of list. Who the hell made a list? There are no lists. The point is there be no lists."

The tall trim clean-shaven man put his tumbler down next to him and held up an admonitory finger. "Take it easy."

The tall trim man with the brush mustache snorted. "Take it easy? How the hell am I supposed to take it easy?"

"I'll take care of it, that's all. I'll take care of it."

"I don't know."

"*I* know. Don't worry. I'll take care of it."

The sodomizers came all at once just then, cheering themselves and getting cheered by others around them. Even the indifferent gum-chewer and the man in pain flashed smiles of accomplishment at each other. The lank boy and the dwarf, distracted from their performance, paused and squinted into the spotlights to try to make out what had upstaged them.

The tall trim clean-shaven man raised his tumbler at the sextet in salute. He took a sip, then put the tumbler down and patted the cheek of the tall trim man with the brush mustache. "Hey, come on. I *said* I'll take care of it."

9 "RICKEY HENDERSON. WELL, WELL."

"Tony. Justice." Harold Henderson paused a beat between given and surnames, like a public-address announcer reading the starting lineups, waiting for the echo to bounce back off the center-field fence.

"This isn't the last place I'd expect to run into you, Rick," Tony Justice said. "The last place is a pizza parlor in Howard Beach."

Henderson laughed. "I scoped you lamping here, homes, I thought, 'This is the *very* last place I'd expect to scope the Tone man.'"

This place was the mezzanine of the Port Authority Bus Terminal, south wing, outside the men's room where slim black and brown and yellow boys in tight bright clothes vogued for, while pretending indifference to, furtive white men shopping for fast sex. Chickens and chicken hawks, in the argot, but really more like tropical birds and rats. Bus exhaust fumes seeped in from the bus levels above and below to season the smell of pizza and boiled hot dogs and cigars and cigarettes and industrial-strength disinfectant and incense burned by a vendor in a caftan, on his table of wares this sign:

I ♡ Allah

"I'm just waiting to phone home." Justice tipped his head toward the bank of pay phones where Latinos, West Indians, Asian Indians, Koreans, dialed long distance direct, using purloined calling-card numbers bought from opportunists who stood by on the lookout for cops and new customers, twitching and hopping like little kids with full bladders.

"You're not writing about that scam, are you, Tone? Shit. That's down there with monte and the money-in-a-hanky hustle. That's wack. Not for an artiste like yourself, a man with a nose for def Watergate-like, Contragate-like scandal, government-toppling shit, career-enders. I hope not. No sir." With a flourish, like a magician, Henderson took off his hat, a red baseball cap with the insignia of the University of Nevada-Las Vegas. He twirled the hat back on and flipped a thumb at a store behind him that sold sports fan accessories. "A most recent acquisition."

"Nice," Justice said. "But you went to Fordham, Rick. Remember?"

"Had it to do over, though, I'd go to UNLV, major in roulette and chemin-de-fer." *Shoomain doo fur*, Henderson enjoyed pronouncing it. "So, uh, why *are* you lamping here, Tone? You want some B-boy to put a liplock on your love sausage, you got to wear fresher threads. It's dissing them to dress like that."

Justice plucked at the basic gray sweatshirt he wore along with Levi's and Asics. "Like a five-O in clothes?"

Henderson, in a blue sweatshirt, Levi's, Adidas, laughed. He leaned down for a closer look at the Walkman on Justice's hip. " 'Stead of a piece, you're strapped with sound. Who you listening to, bro—Tiffany? Debbie Gibson?" Henderson laughed again.

Justice took the earplug phones from around his neck and handed them to Henderson. "Check it out. Willie Dixon."

Henderson put the plugs in his ears and listened, dipping his shoulders, swinging his hips.

I wanna kiss every night, to squeeze and hold you tight.
I wanna make violent love to you.
I don't wanna be frantic, I don't wanna cramp your style.

But you're driving me into a panic, you almost drive me
    wild.
I wanna make whoopee-do, and have a little fun with
    you.
I wanna make violent love to you.

Henderson took the earphones out and handed them
back. "Down, homeboy. Out there. 'Violet Love.' 'I
wanna make violet love to you.' "

Justice smiled tensely. "Don't front me, Rick. The
name of the song is 'Violent Love.' "

"Is it?" Henderson said. And they looked, really
looked, into each other's eyes for the first time.

THE FIRST time *this* time. *The* first time, Henderson had
explained the rules: "I'm the deejay, you're the suspect.
Any time a woman gets killed, her old man's got a lap
head start on the rest of the field of possible perps, even
after I tell the press that he's not under suspicion, that
he's cooperating fully with the investigation.

"And here's what else's going to go down, homeboy.
I'll be doing the investi*gating*, you'll be getting investi-
gated. We'll be like Elmer Fudd and Bugs Bunny, Sylves-
ter and Tweetie, Holmes and Moriarty, Batman and the
Joker, Bond—James Bond—and the dude with the fluffy
white pussy—adversaries but also, like, intimates. Word
up, brother, I mean, check us out, like a bitch and a
homey on our first date. You dressed your best, I dressed
mine. We're both hoping to come off as well-groomed,
well-mannered, well-spoken, as modest about our ac-
complishments, up-front about our shortcomings.
Pretty soon, I'll know what you think's funny, you'll
know what I think. I like Richie Pryor, but I do *not* like

44

Eddie Murphy. Eddie Murphy is *not* an authentic black individual.

"I like white women country singers—hey, call me Uncle Tom. You wrote a novel, I already know this, about a black blues singer people say is kind of like Ida Cox. Least I know who Ida Cox is, I can't be all bad, but, hey, maybe we *did* get mixed up in our cribs, you're the soul brother, I'm the honkie. You run marathons—I read that too—I like to play round ball and ride an exercise bike. I can't *stand* riding the son-of-a-bitch, if you want to know the truth of it, but I can study for the sergeant's exam while I'm pedaling, so we're talking efficiency, like—expeditiousity.

"My favorite junk food's a Whopper, hold the mayo. Yours too? You fronting me? Holy shit. You went to Cornell, I know. I went to Fordham. See? Five minutes— *two* minutes—already we know all *kinds* of shit about each other. Don't ever think, homey—this is the point I'm making—that if and when the time comes, I'll feel, like, filial, and won't bust the shit out of you so fast I'll be out dragging you in cuffs down the stairs before the doorbell's even finished ringing."

In the spirit of their intimacy, they would have conversations like this, light on the hip-hop, the shtick:

"I told you, Rickey, didn't I, that it was on our honeymoon that Karen broke her leg skiing?" Justice might say.

And Henderson might answer: "That must've been a bummer, Tone."

"So I know there exist X rays of Karen's broken tibia that would match X rays of the broken tibia of the woman in the river. I also know about the moles on her shoulder, the scar from the cesarean, the extra nipple."

Rickey would wish he could ask about that extra

nipple: Was it, you know, sensitive? "So why would you go through the fuss and bother of chopping Karen's head and hands and feet off, knowing that if we ever found the body we'd be able to ID her anyway, without dental records or fingerprints, using the X rays, the identifying marks? That what you're saying, Tone?"

"Exactly."

"Why *would* you do that, Tone?"

"To make you think I didn't kill her?"

"That's possible."

"Anything's possible."

"Well, not *any*thing, Tone. *Any*one didn't kill Karen. Only one person killed her."

"You're speaking figuratively, aren't you, Rick? Two people could've killed her—or three or three dozen—but they were a *unit*."

"Exactly, Tone."

"And you're keeping an open mind about who that is, right, Rick?"

"Wide open."

IN THE spirit of their intimacy, Justice dropped the pretense that this meeting was by happenstance. "As I told you on the phone, I got a tip. Not even a tip, a call, an anonymous call. Yesterday afternoon, at the paper. I usually answer my own phone in the late afternoon. That could be significant. Someone who knows I do, who knows he wouldn't have to go through the switchboard. A man, a white man, probably, no pronounced accent, maybe Midwestern—a little flat in his A's. Age, anywhere from twenty-five to fifty-five. No preliminaries, no attempt, really, to be sure it was me. He said, 'Look for a brother.' I said, 'Hello, hello, who's this, who're you

calling?'—all the stuff you say when you've heard perfectly well what someone said but you want them to say
it again. He did say it again—'Look for a brother'—then
he hung up.

"Does it mean anything to me? Yes, it does. I haven't
said anything to you, because it's very speculative, but
more and more I've been inclined toward a theory—a
self-serving theory, I admit—that Karen was killed to
keep me from writing something. Yes, Rick, I can see in
your eyes you think that would be extreme. It *would* be
extreme. Even the mob doesn't kill reporters; they can
take the heat. That's the point: it's not the mob, it's a new
kind of bad guy who can't take the heat. Drug posses,
they can't take the heat. The Brothers, they can't take the
heat."

"*The* Brothers," Henderson said. "So it's not *a*
brother, like *a* homeboy, it's one of *The* Brothers, capital
T, capital B."

"I've been working for a while," Justice said, "on a
story about a resurgence of promiscuity among gay men.
A lot of leather bars are back in business, a couple of
bathhouses disguised as health clubs or tanning parlors
have opened up. West Street, the Loop, the Stroll, this
place—things're starting to look the way they did in the
late seventies. Some important people are into the scene.
The names would surprise you. Some of them are as
well-known for whom they're married to as for anything
else. I don't know whether they've been in the closet all
along or whether they're branching out."

"Ray Brand," Henderson said. "My hero."

"Ray Brand was a little different: show business
makes strange bedfellows. These are businessmen. I
have a respected historian of sexual behavior saying on
the record that a world that elevates to heroic stature

junk-bond traders and unfriendly takeover specialists can be expected to produce a good number of aggressive deviants with a taste for experimentation.

"There's supposed to be a club, a private club, I've heard only bits and pieces, I don't know where it is, I don't know how big it is, I don't know for an absolute certainty *that* it is. Or I didn't, until I got the call. They call themselves Frères, The Brothers."

"So it's like a frat," Henderson said. "You had me scared, homey. I thought you were talking black-magic voodoo mumbo-jumbo. But you're talking a bunch of yuppie brokers sipping martinis and playing with one another's johnsons."

"I'd think it was silly too, Rick, if Karen weren't dead and in pieces. These are extremely wealthy people who can't afford exposure."

"They got that big nut to keep up."

Justice agreed. "They got that big nut to keep up. I'm looking for a way into the group, the club, whatever it is. A weak link. I got a tip—a separate tip, a different kind of tip—that a couple of nights a week a very well-known businessman-benefactor-social animal can be found here indulging a taste for Chinese food." Justice paused just then as an Oriental transsexual in Lycra bicycle tights and a *Don't Believe the Hype* tank top sashayed by. He and Henderson both had to fight off grins.

"I don't know if this man's a Frère, I don't know if he knows anything about Frères. He's a story in his own right; he's not only prominent—on Wall Street, anyway—but he's also—and this is what gives it an irony that's pretty irresistible—he's also married to a woman who's widely admired for her vigorous efforts to raise money to fight AIDS. Is that a def-enough scandal, Rick?"

48

Henderson salaamed defensively. "Hey, Tone, you don't have to house me, homes. I'm a big fan. Word up."

Justice smiled. "You're full of shit, Rickey. Word up."

Henderson pressed his hands to his chest. "Tone. Knee. Don't dis me, bro. It hurts my heart."

They stood like that for a while, looking at nothing, saying nothing. Then Justice said, "What?"

"Say what?"

"There's something you want to tell me, Rick. There's something you want to ask me. Don't say there's not. I know you too well."

Henderson took his cap off again and molded the brim, still too new and too flat, needing some curve to give it character. "Things keep coming up, Tony. You know how it is. Questions, ideas, theories."

"Such as?"

"Such as back when your wife, your *first* wife, I mean, back when she—"

Justice pointed a finger like a dagger to cut Henderson off. "Don't. You dig? Yes, I got married very soon after Karen was found, but *not* very soon after she disappeared. Don't try to make something of it by tripping over it."

Henderson put the cap back on and pulled it low. "This hasn't been in the papers, and I don't want to see it in your paper, but some models who did a bathing-suit spread last spring in a well-known national magazine have been getting hate mail from an anonymous fundamentalist nut. Back when Karen was modeling, did she ever get any threats about anything she did that was, you know, provocative?"

"I didn't know Karen when she was modeling," Justice said, "except as a face in a magazine. She talked a few times about crazies who bothered her—and bothered just about all the other models—with phone calls, telegrams, love letters, flowers, candy, perfume. You should talk to the people she used to work with."

"How about enemies she might've made in the real-estate business?" Henderson said. "I don't mean competitors. I mean clients who might've gotten ticked off that she couldn't get them an apartment. New Yorkers're intense when it comes to real estate."

Justice took a look at Henderson and read in his eyes *white New Yorkers.* "Karen always had stories about less-than-satisfied clients: people who couldn't make their closing, people who hesitated and lost a penthouse, land-lords who wanted the diva and got the soubrette. Less-than-satisfied enough to murder? Well, Karen never forgot that her first husband was killed by a disgruntled actor."

Henderson watched two hamsters with fade hair-cuts and prison biceps pimp-roll by. "Can you explain to me, Tone, the logic of a system that puts weight rooms in the joint so the motherfuckers doing points won't get bored, they'll just get stronger? Most cops're pumping Budweiser, not iron. When the fighting in the streets comes—and it'll come—we're going to get our butts whipped." He took a squashed pack of Trident Original Flavor from the hip pocket of his jeans, stripped away the silver wrapper and offered Justice a stick. Justice shook his head. Henderson took the stick out and un-wrapped it and put it in his mouth and got it going. He rolled the paper up between thumb and forefinger and shot it from over his head at a trashcan five feet away. It went in. "Yesssss."

Justice laughed. "You never walk by a mirror, do you, Rickey, without checking your attitude?"

Henderson looked at his watch, suddenly a man with places to go. "I got to catch my bus."

"Pardon the expression, Rickey, but you're a jive motherfucker. You didn't come here to catch a bus."

"You keep a secret, homey?"

A secret? Sure. They were *this* close. "You're on your way to Peapack for a moonlight gallop with Jackie Onassis."

Henderson laughed. "For about a year now, I've had myself a little *pied-à-terre*"—*peed uhtare*—"up on Boulevard East. My main trim lives right close by. Don't tell the PC or nobody, will you. It's against the regs and all. Look. Nice seeing you, Tone. Small world, homey, ain't it?"

"That's a good hat, Rickey. Take care now."

Henderson swung around, then back. "Oh, yeah— one other thing, Tone."

Justice's face got hard. Finally—the spiel about threats to bathing-suit models had been smoke—the point.

"You know Rae Muldoon?" Henderson said.

Justice said, "No."

"Diana knows her. Maybe Diana mentioned her."

"Diana has lots of friends she hasn't mentioned."

"Rae wasn't a friend."

"Diana has lots of enemies she hasn't mentioned."

Henderson looked at his watch again. "Got to run. Catch you later, homes."

"I hope not, Rick, because now *I'll* tell *you* a secret: I'm sick of you."

"I'm like your worst nightmare, hunh, babe? Hey, I can understand that."

"No. You're like diarrhea."

Rickey Henderson was truly shocked. Tony Justice could be coarse, he could be vulgar, he could be obscene, but he was never cruel; in the nearly a year they had known each other Rickey had seen Justice make many people mad—it came with the territory, with his having for a pulpit a newspaper with more readers than any other afternoon paper in the country—but there was no one whom Justice had offended. The basic gray sweat-shirt, the Levi's, the Asics, were a disguise, mufti for a prince of a homeboy who understood better than any politician Rickey knew, any appointed honcho, any de-partment brass or union brass, any DA or judge or high-priced defense attorney, any movie star or goddamned overpaid *ball*player, that was for goddamn sure, the *ex-tent* of his noblesse oblige (a concept Rickey understood perfectly, though he deprecated his understanding by pronouncing it *noh-bless oh-blee-zhay*).

Heavy stuff, but Rickey was snowed, seduced, smit-ten, and had been from the moment he'd met Tony Justice, notwithstanding his I'm-the-deejay-you're-the-suspect speech. Which didn't mean he couldn't imagine such a prince of a homeboy butchering his wife (*I wanna make violet love to you*). Rickey could imagine such a prince of a homeboy butchering his wife because along with his *noh-bless oh-blee-zhay* Tony Justice had another trait that Fordham and the street had along the way taught Rickey to recognize: full-blown arrogance. They coexisted, the *noh-bless oh-blee-zhay* and the arrogance, and they would have to, wouldn't they? You would have to think you were better than anybody else—than every-body else—in order to also feel that it was your respon-sibility to be nice to them, wouldn't you?

(Not incidentally, Rickey could also imagine what Tony Justice had butchered his wife with, for Justice was a serious cook who in the kitchen of his Central Park West apartment had some serious knives, including one electric motherfucker that an old high school friend of Rickey's who was now a wholesale butcher in the meat district told Rickey that if it was the model he thought it was, it could turn a cow into cow parts in just a couple of minutes, let alone a former fashion model, still skinny after all these years.)

Rickey pressed his chest again. "He don't mean it, heart. He's just running his mouth."

Justice cupped a hand around his ear. "I think I hear your bus, Rickey."

"Later, homey."

"Later."

10 ANN HAD AN ORGASM JUST AS CUL-len's beeper went off. She clutched at him and hit at him gently but unmistakably to encourage him to keep on after one for himself, but he soon stopped.

"You all right?" Ann said.

"Yeah. Just tired." And it was too crowded in the room, with Diana Romano perched right there on the upturned steamer trunk, her black mourning dress up over her olive thighs, black French-maid French-whore garterless stockings, glen-plaid pumps (Bruno Magli), her right hand clutching Tony Justice's exquisite hair, her left hand jammed in her sucking mouth so she wouldn't cry out; with Tony right there, trousers down to his knees, elbows pinning his cashmere coat back out of the way, moving in and out of her, in and out.

"Did you ever think you might have a better sex life if you weren't umbilically connected to your office?" Ann said. "If you were a stockboy at Lamston's?"

"I'd get calls to come in on a Saturday. An unexpected shipment of Kean paintings."

Ann shifted under him so she could see his face. "That reminds me. I had lunch with Perry at the Museum of Modern Art. He told me something amazing. That Rodin statue of Balzac in the garden?"

Cullen stretched to reach the alarm clock on the side table: a minute to midnight, not an hour for getting good news.

"Balzac's wearing an opera cape. Perry says it's what he wore when he was writing—the way I wear my *Ten Fe* sweatshirt. The cape was cast separately from the rest of the statue; under it is a complete nude figure of Balzac—"

"Masturbating," Cullen said.

Ann punched the mattress. "How the *hell* did you know that?"

"There's a Rodin room at the Brooklyn Museum with a whole corner devoted to that statue. Photographs, plaster casts, models."

"When were you at the Brooklyn Museum?"

"The Courbet."

"The Courbet was years ago."

Cullen had slipped out of Ann, so he lifted off her and sat up. "Balzac was a satyr. It was Rodin's little joke." He found the phone down under the bed and punched out the Command Center's number.

"Satyr. What an old-fashioned word. I've never known a satyr. Have you ever known a nympho-maniac?"

"Operator Two-Three."

"This is Sergeant Cullen, IAU."

"Wait one, Sergeant."

"Have you?"

Tony Justice still moving in and out of her, in and out, Diana Romano looked into Cullen's eyes, curious to hear his answer. To evade her, and out of respect, he supposed it was, for Ann, he got up and began to dress.

Ann flounced on her stomach. "My favorite moment—your jumping out of bed."

A bed that could be at one moment the softest place in the world, the next cold barbed steel. The way plain old Ann Jones could turn into Anna Magnani. "Perry wears a beeper," Cullen said.

Ann stared. *"What?"*

"He may be a carpenter, but he's still on call. You romanticize his work: Perry, the happy craftsman."

"Sergeant, I'm going to patch you through to Captain Maslosky at home. Wait one, please."

"Thank you, operator."

"Are you *jealous* of Perry?" Ann was on her side now, head propped on a bent arm, an odalisque who wanted an answer. Actually, there were two plain old Ann Joneses: affixed by a magnet to the refrigerator door of one of them was a greeting card, in the style of an adventure-comic-book cover, depicting a business-suited woman in full stride:

Watch out, everyone!! Here comes
URBAN JUNGLE GIRL
The adventures of an overworked
female in such a hurry she
barely has time to finish
reading this comic book.
Jungle girl needs no approval from the likes of you.
Looking out for No. 1
She rises with the dawn!
She shoves her way to work!
She swims with the sharks!
She collapses at home in front of the TV!!!

Arrows pointed out the Urban Jungle Girl's "Grim Look," "Mace," "Briefcase," "Stylish Running Shoes," "Businesslike Yet Sexy" suit, "Only 10 Lbs To Go On Diet" figure. In the lower right-hand corner was a nervous-looking man: "Also starring Flinchley the gulping boyfriend."

But: Pushpinned to the bulletin board above the desk of the *other* Ann was a photograph taken at the wedding of a college classmate. On the left was the just-married (*finally* married) bride; on the far right, a clutch of women her age, bridesmaids, friends, relations, backing nearly out of the frame in their collective effort to be as far as possible from the bouquet the bride had just tossed; in the center, giggling, shrieking, in the proper spirit of the moment, little girls from twenty months to thirteen years, reaching up vainly as the bouquet passed over their unnubile heads; and, rising out of the group on the right, seeming to have eight or ten hands, one of them on the shoulder of one bridesmaid, one pulling the hair of another, one ripping an ear off a third, an elbow in the mouth of a fourth, leaping higher than Michael Jordan, than Akeem, than Spud, than Dominique or Alonzo, gathering the bouquet in with two or three sure hands, Ann Jones.

The card and the photograph had survived many winnowings of the stuff (Annana, Cullen called it) on the bulletin board and the refrigerator door. The recipe for chili for one thousand from a newspaper article about feeding forest firefighters ("1. Bring 250 gallons of water to a boil") was gone; gone was a clipping saying the average American woman is five three and a half, one hundred forty-three pounds, 36-29-39; gone were the descriptions of episodes of "thirtysomething" ("Hope searches the basement for radon contamination." "Gary has his tenure review." "Ellyn learns her building is going co-op."), saved from the TV pages for Ann to re-read "when I think *I've* got it tough"; gone the quotation from Estée Lauder: "I try to walk in in a hat. It makes you look like someone"; gone the Cline cartoon, two white men strolling: *"So much to learn about rap music, so little time"*; gone the photograph of Darryl Strawberry kissing Keith Hernandez. But the Urban Jungle Girl marched on, the Vaulting Bridesmaid still leapt.

"You are jealous."

Once, when *Rolling Stone* had listed two albums by Richard and Linda Thompson among the one hundred best albums of the last twenty years and Cullen had had to confess that he'd never heard of Richard and Linda Thompson, Ann had said, "I know them from Perry, the great eclectic." Cullen had been sure that, as far as rock and roll was concerned, *he* was the great eclectic. He *was* jealous of Perry for that. "No." Gulp.

"You are. And maybe you're right to be."

Maybe there weren't two Anns; maybe the two Anns were one. It was confusing sometimes. It was confusing always. "Oh?"

"You still there, Sergeant? The captain's line's still busy. I'm asking the telco operator to interrupt."

"Yes, operator. I'm here. Thank you."

"Well?" For some reason, Ann was grinning.

"Well what?"

"Aren't you going to get upset? Aren't you going to ask if I'm sleeping with him?"

"You're not sleeping with him." Flinchley Cullen tried to keep his voice from cracking. "The point of all this is so you can say, self-righteously, that you're *not* sleeping with him and since you're such a faithful lover, why am I not more appreciative and why don't we get married?"

That stare again. "You're losing me, officer."

Was he? She was a lot to lose. They had so much in common: both liked anchovies, and both could stand to listen to just about any radio station as long as it wasn't Soft Rock or National Public Radio and didn't have too high a Pink Floyd ratio; both knew what ever became of Madonna Louise Veronica Ciccone, Prince Roger Nelson, Steveland Judkins Hardaway, Cherilyn Sarkisian; both had crushes on Kris Kristofferson and Michelle Pfeiffer. Their favorite book was *The Year of Decision: 1846*, their favorite movie *I Know Where I'm Going*, their favorite name Peabo Bryson. Both knew that to hear over a pay phone on a city street you had to cover the mouthpiece, not your ear; both laughed at just the thought of John Candy, both preferred Betty Grable to Ginger Rogers; both knew what a thrum was, an allograph, a crang, that at sea level the horizon is three miles away, that if you dig a hole straight down under New York City you'll come out not in China but in the Indian Ocean off Australia. Both went through *Vanity Fair* before reading it and tore out the scented perfume ads; both remembered Earth Shoes and Marjoe. Neither used acronyms when they could say the whole thing (the Museum of Modern Art), neither could comprehend New Yorkers who rooted for the Red Sox; neither had read *The Fountainhead* or *War and Peace*, listened to *The Prairie Home Companion*, thrown the *I Ching*, made love in a water bed. Both now knew about the satyrical Balzac.

Was he losing her or was he maybe throwing her away, clearing the decks, winnowing *his* refrigerator, to make room for black French-maid French-whore garterless stockings, glen-plaid Bruno Magli pumps? "*Are* you sleeping with him?"

"With Perry?"

"Damn you, Ann."

"No, I'm not."

"But you'd like to."

"I'd like, not to put too fine a point on it, to live with a man. With you. But if you can't hack it"—Flinchley—"then with a man who can."

Gulp. "A stockboy at Lamston's?"

Grim look. "If necessary."

"Look, Ann. This isn't—"

"*Cullen?*"

Richie Maslosky wasn't the ball-breakingest commander Cullen had worked under, but he had his own style. He ran the Internal Affairs Unit from behind a totaled government-issue metal desk set squarely in front of his wide-open office door; he always knew who was in, who was out, who, though in, was fucking off. He liked to phone detectives he saw leave their desks to go to the bathroom, the coffee machine, the smoking lounge, leaving no message, just word that he'd called. If you'd been out on the street a long time, he'd pass you in the hall as though you'd never left; if you hadn't gone out in a while, he'd give you a big greeting, ask where you'd been, how things were going. Cullen had never been so glad to hear his voice. "Yes, Captain?"

"I just got off the horn with the PC, Cullen. He tells me he told you to brief a Homicide D named Rickey Henderson on a job you caught a while back." Maslosky was never on the phone, always the horn; he never went to the bathroom, always the crapper (where he took not a crap, but a dump). Sex was the dirty deed, unless it was the nasty, lunch was chow, women were skirts, blacks spades, Hispanics beaners, Orientals slopes, homosexuals limpwrists, fruits, butt jockeys. Cullen, right now, loved him deeply. "Yes, Captain. That's right. Zimmerman and I talked to Henderson a couple of days ago."

Ann was lying back with her arm over her eyes. *Drained from grappling with the spineless Flinchley, the Urban Jungle Girl recoups her strength.*

"Well, we got a little problem is the thing."

Cullen waited. At seven minutes after midnight, there were no little problems.

"Henderson's been K'd."

11 "K'D BY A PRO OR A VERY COMPETENT amateur. One bullet behind the left ear with a small-caliber handgun, a twenty-two or twenty-five. Yesterday evening sometime, at the Port of Authority. Sundays're light on the suburban level; buses run every half-hour, maybe. The shooter rolled Rickey under a disabled bus; some mechanics jacked it up to work on it and found him. His watch, his wallet, his off-duty piece were taken, but that doesn't make it a robbery. Midtown West and the Port of Authority Squad caught the job, but Hriniak wants us in on it. We report to Maslosky."

Cullen and Zimmerman were in a coffee shop on Hudson Street where it was hard to get served if you weren't smoking at least two cigarettes. A waitress finally brought their coffee and Zimmerman smiled his best smile at her. She had a shaven and tattooed head and an iron-cross earring, a chain-mail skirt over torn fishnet stockings, a black sleeveless T-shirt with *Die Yuppie Scum* in letters like dripping blood on the back; although Zimmerman wore a navy double-breasted blazer with six hundred buttons and a pink-and-blue knit tie, although Zimmerman was *Mister* Yuppie Scum, she smiled back. Sinéad O'Connor meets Ralph Lauren.

Why didn't any of Zimmerman's women (he'd gone out with *all* kinds—a lawyer, a doctor, a *tree* doctor, a body-builder, a fund-raiser, a former nun, a massage therapist, a book editor, a chorus line of actress/dancer waitresses) want to live with him? Why did they want only what he wanted—someone to scratch a transitory itch?

"Rickey's nominal address was in Bayside," Cullen

61

said, "a place he shared with another cop, Bobby Trumbo, a uniform in the One-twelve. Trumbo told Midtown West that most of the time Rickey lived in West New York, Guttenberg, Cliffside Park, Trumbo didn't know what it was called—Jersey opposite midtown. He didn't live *with* a woman, apparently, but near one. I didn't know this until Legal Affairs explained it to me, but the reason it's not kosher to live in Jersey—or Connecticut—is the gun license isn't reciprocal."

Cullen took a sip of coffee, which tasted like boiled leftovers from last week. He stirred it to bring the temperature down. "Crime Scene figures Rickey was K'd on a stairway at the south end of the suburban level and dragged to the disabled bus. They found heel marks. It's not a stairway that's used to get to outgoing buses; it's for incoming passengers."

"Meaning?"

"Meaning maybe he wasn't just there to catch a bus, maybe he was meeting someone somewhere out of the way."

Zimmerman moved around some sugar packets, like an augur, until they told him this: "The kind of stairway you're talking about is one out in the open around the perimeter of the bus driveway, right? The stairways to the gates are enclosed, so as not to asphyxiate the passengers—or do it slowly. Maybe Rickey was late for his bus, so rather than go to the gate, he took any stairway, the nearest stairway, knowing he could flag the bus down if it had already pulled out. Sundays're light; if he missed his bus he'd have a long wait."

Cullen shrugged, but it was a good thought—especially from someone who'd grown up on Riverside Drive and who when he said public transportation

62

meant taxis. "He wasn't so late he didn't have time to buy a baseball cap, University of Nevada-Las Vegas, at a sporting-goods store on the mezzanine."

Zimmerman nodded. "I know the place." And clearly didn't think much of it. Fluent in Russell, Reebok, Everlast, Hind, he knew his sporting-goods stores. As for Nevada-Las Vegas, well ... Zimmerman had gone to Yale-New Haven. He wasn't snobbish about it, exactly; it just accounted for so many differences.

"And he wasn't so late," Cullen said, "that he didn't have time to hang around outside the store for a while, wearing the hat, talking to someone, a guy. The clerk who sold Rickey the hat noticed them."

"Good description?"

"A white guy. Shirt, pants, shoes, hair."

Zimmerman smiled. Anyone who thought all God's chillun had wings had only to try to get one chile to describe a chile of a different color.

"Thin," Cullen said. "The clerk kind of remembered the guy was thin. Not two hundred fifty pounds. And not that old—not a hundred and ten. They talked for about ten minutes."

"One of Rickey's snitches?"

"Could be."

"A hamster he made and was telling to get scarce."

"Could be."

"An ounceman."

Cullen didn't answer right away. *Things are always what they look like,* Tony Justice had said outside the church in Sag Harbor. *That's what I tell cub reporters and journalism students.* And Cullen had countered: *Things are what they look like and then you look a little closer, a little more calmly, and they look like something else. You look long enough and something you could almost call the*

63

truth emerges—that's what I tell rookie cops and criminology students. Whatever the fuck had he meant?

What this looked like, cub reporters, rookie cops, students of journalism and criminology, ladies and gentlemen, honored guests, was that Rickey Henderson, cop, had been K'd by a small-time drug dealer in the course of a small-time drug transaction. The closer they looked, and the longer, the likelier it was that it would still look that way, like what it looked like. Unless he'd been K'd in the course of taking a small-time bribe. "An ounceman, a bagman. But if Rickey was wack, this was the first and last time he'd done anything suspicious."

Now Zimmerman waited. Then he said, "Are you going to say it or am I?"

Cullen pulled rank. "You say it."

"Maybe the thin young guy was a chicken."

Cullen studied his palm. On his way to meet Zimmerman, he had stopped at a newsstand in the Village to get the afternoon papers. The vendor, a handsome Indian, had been flirting with a redhead in black jeans and a black satin *Chess: the musical* jacket, trying to get her to let him read her palm. Cullen had volunteered his hand, to assure the redhead that it was okay—and to send into the ether a reminder to the Urban Jungle Girl that Flinchley had lots of opportunities to meet attractive women.

The vendor had turned Cullen's wrist gently to see his palm better. "You are a rich man, my friend," the vendor had said, and Cullen had had to laugh. "Then you *will* be," the vendor had insisted. "You will never be wanting for money." The redhead—her bad luck—had gone off without hearing the prophecy, absorbed in a copy of *Backstage*. Was it written on her palm that she had come *this* close to a man who could have liberated her from cattle calls and casting couches? And could you

64

really tell about people from their palms, from their being thin and young?

"I know we met him only once," Cullen said, "but did Rickey strike you as gay?"

Zimmerman shook his head. "Nope."

Cullen tried his coffee. Now it was cold and old, and stank of cigarette smoke. "*And* he'd be the first person we ever read wrong." He held up the *Post* he'd bought and showed Zimmerman the headline:

TORSO COP SLAIN

IN BUS STATION

" 'Torso Cop'?"

"It took me a while to figure it out too," Cullen said. "You catch a dismemberment, you're the torso cop."

"What does the *Bulletin* say?"

Cullen held it up:

DETECTIVE SHOT

AT PA TERMINAL

"The *Bulletin* mentions, doesn't it, Rickey's connection to its own star reporter?" Zimmerman said.

"It takes some reading, but you could put it together." Cullen put some change on the table and slid to the edge of his seat.

Zimmerman didn't move.

Cullen said, "What?"

Zimmerman said, "Well . . ."

"Say it, Neil."

"Well, is there a connection?"

"Talk to me."

"It's nuts."

"That'd be a first too."

65

Zimmerman pushed a packet of sugar front and center, so they could pretend they were talking about playthings, not flesh and blood. "Di Romano had a thing with Blond Tommy Muldoon. Rae Muldoon went off the scope. Are we working on the premise that Di and/or Blond Tommy killed Rae?"

"It's—what do they call it in diplomacy?—a talking point." Cullen could see that Zimmerman, who had studied foreign affairs at Yale-New Haven and believed that the NYPD's gain was the State Department's loss, liked the sound of that.

Zimmerman pushed another packet up alongside the first. "Karen Justice went off the scope. She was hardly out of the water before Tony Justice married Di Romano. Were they having a thing before they got married, and if they were, is it another talking point that Di and/or Tony K'd Karen?"

Tony Justice still moving in and out of her, in and out, Diana Romano took her left hand out of her sucking mouth and put her forefinger to her lips. But Cullen wasn't looking, Cullen was way ahead of her. "They were partners. Partners *are* married."

Zimmerman nodded. It wasn't something they ever joked about, for it was true.

Without looking, Cullen knew that Diana Romano was smiling. "The ME's never going to be sure when Karen Justice died, except that it was most likely close to the time she disappeared—last September seventeen, the Bon Jovi wanna-be's birthday."

"Who? Oh—James."

"Tony was home that night, with his stepdaughter. Diana Romano was at the movies. Movies're a nice alibi because you can see them anytime to find out what they're about and say you saw them at the time you need an alibi for."

"It wasn't the movies, it was a screening," Zimmerman noted. "At Cinema I. She was checked off on the guest list."

Cullen waved at the distinction, though he knew it meant a great deal, maybe everything, to Zimmerman, who never passed on an opportunity to get invited to a screening. "She could still have walked out."

Zimmerman moved up a third packet of sugar. "The point is: Suppose our talking points *aren't* talking points; suppose Di and/or Blond Tommy *did* K Rae Muldoon and suppose Di and/or Tony *did* K Karen Justice. And suppose Di knew that Rickey Henderson had made the connection. Did she and/or Tony K Rickey? It's nuts; it doesn't throw us off the trail, it puts more of us *on* the trail."

"I don't see a trail, Neil," Cullen said. "I see a dance floor polished so you can see your face in it, and a great-looking couple ready to just break your heart, they're so smooth and graceful. Fred and Ginger. Gene and Cyd. And standing at the edge of the floor I see us, needing to venture out there to find out more than we know, which is virtually nothing, but afraid to smudge the floor with our shoes that have diesel oil all over them from tromping around the Port of Authority. Mutt and Jeff."

"Poetic this morning," Zimmerman said.

"Yeah, well." Flinchley the gulping poet.

"Who're Mutt and Jeff?"

Christ. How old *was* he? Was he older than water? And how young was Zimmerman? Younger than springtime? "Let's take a ride to Jersey, to see where Rickey lived and how."

12

HIGH UP IN A HIGH-RISE, SHAG RUGS on the parquet floor, Naugahyde and chrome and glass furniture, framed posters of Patrick Ewing, Jesse Jackson, and the Judds. From the skimpy so-called terrace, leaning farther out than Cullen liked to, there was a view of a little bit of Manhattan's Upper West Side, Riverside Church, and Grant's Tomb. (Being older than water, Cullen remembered Groucho Marx's radio show and the booby-prize question: Who is buried in Grant's Tomb?) The imposing cameras, one still, one film (FTN and Arri, Zimmerman greeted them familiarly), mounted on imposing tripods and aimed out a bedroom window at another high-rise next door, testified to Rickey Henderson's preference for sights closer by.

There was no one home in the apartment under Rickey's scrutiny, but a detective from the Port Authority Squad who was going over the apartment told them he had glimpsed the tenant earlier that day. "Outstanding equipment," the detective said, patting the Arri's zoom lens but meaning the tenant's equipment as well. "It's like you're *in* the apartment. It's unfuckingbelievable."

So were the five-drawer filing cabinets, three of them, brimming with eight-by-ten photographs of Rickey's neighbor, the Port Authority Squad detective told them, and of dozens, scores, hundreds of other women, in apartments, on rooftops, on the street, at the beach, in the park. Black, white, brown, yellow, they had in common youth, shapeliness, and ignorance that they were being photographed.

Not unfuckingbelievable, but "weird," the Port

68

Authority Squad detective said, were the tapes from the answering machine on Rickey Henderson's desk (a Panasonic, Zimmerman noted). "He had two incoming tapes. One was in the machine. It had two messages, one from someone named Tiny, no positive ID, about a date to 'shoot some hoops,' one from someone named Roz, no positive ID, but he had a sister named Rosalind. The other was in the desk drawer. It looks like it was a backup tape. My wife does something like that: any messages come in for me or the kids, she doesn't feel like writing them down, she doesn't have time, whatever, she takes the tape out of the machine, puts another tape in. The messages for us don't get recorded over, we can play them when we get home."

The Port Authority Squad detective paused, wanting some reaction to his having figured that out. Cullen could never get excited about answering machines or answering-machine tapes, and just shrugged. "And?"

"Listen." The Port Authority Squad detective put the backup tape in the machine and played it:

"There are different kinds of voyeuristic relationships, Alan. The purest kind, arguably, is one in which the subject has no idea that she's being watched. But there's another kind, no less pure if it can develop to its fullest, in which the subject is not only aware of being watched, but approves of being watched, cooperates in it, plays an active role in it—but, and this is the important point, Alan, never communicates that awareness to the voyeur. She knows he's there, she knows he knows she knows, she pretends she doesn't know, she pretends he doesn't know she knows. Such a relationship, Alan, is extremely, powerfully, erotic. . . ."

The Port Authority Squad detective stopped the tape. "That's it. There's another short message after it, from a doctor's office, confirming an appointment."

"Could you play it again, please?" Cullen said.

The Port Authority Squad detective rewound the tape and played it again: A man's voice, youthful, bright, enthusiastic; accent, urban.

"Once more, please," Zimmerman said.

Once more.

"It's Rickey," Zimmerman said. "Not as uptown as usual, but Rickey. Rickey on his own answering machine."

"I told you it was weird," the Port Authority Squad detective said.

"Who's Alan?" Cullen said.

"Beats me," the Port Authority Squad detective said.

Cullen bent over the Panasonic. "Can you tape a call on this machine—your own call, I mean—as you're making it?"

Zimmerman bent over the Panasonic and said you could.

"So could this be Rickey recording his own call? Because it had to do with a job he'd caught, say?" Cullen himself answered the question that raised. "Then why didn't he tape the whole conversation?"

"It sounds kind of like ... well, like an interview," Zimmerman said. "Could you play it again, please. My name's Neil Zimmerman, by the way."

"Johnny Diehl."

"Joe Cullen."

Though they had already shaken hands, they shook again. Diehl played the tape.

"*There are different kinds of voyeuristic relationships, Alan. The purest kind, arguably, is one in which the subject has no idea that she's being watched. But there's another kind, no less pure if it can develop to its fullest, in which the*

70

subject is not only aware of being watched, but approves of being watched, cooperates in it, plays an active role in it—but, and this is the important point, Alan, never communicates that awareness to the voyeur. She knows he's there, she knows he knows she knows, she pretends she doesn't know, she pretends he doesn't know she knows. Such a relationship, Alan, is extremely, powerfully, erotic. . . ."

His ear to the Panasonic, Zimmerman said, "That time, I heard a hang-up."

"John, one more time, please," Cullen said.

"Play it again, John?" Diehl said, and laughed.

"Please," Cullen said.

Diehl played it again.

"I heard it too," Diehl said. "The hang-up."

"I did too," Cullen said. "A hang-up like you'd get if this were an *in*coming message."

"Right," Diehl said. "So . . ." But he couldn't come to a conclusion.

Zimmerman tried: "So it's a recording of an *in*coming call. Henderson called his machine from another phone, and left this message." He laughed. "Don't ask me why."

Diehl laughed. "Don't ask me either."

Cullen said, "Maybe . . ."

Diehl said, "Maybe there's a tap on this phone, someone taped Rickey making a call, then called *him* and played it back, to show him what he had on him." He laughed. "Don't ask me why."

Zimmerman said, "Excuse me for changing the subject, but why the hell"—from a bulletin board over the desk, he unpinned a clipping from the *Times*—"was he saving an article about Michelle Slate?"

"Who?" Diehl said.

71

"A friend of my mother's. They do charity things together."

"They rampage around town, robbing the rich," Cullen said.

"They do what?" Diehl said.

"I met Ogden Slate at Karen Justice's funeral, Neil. That was his description of his wife's and your mother's activities."

"I remember this article," Zimmerman said. "Here—Mother's mentioned in it. Mrs. Mordecai Zimmerman. My father's been dead for fifteen years, but that's who she still is and who she'll always be—Mrs. Mordecai Zimmerman."

Zimmerman put his fingertips to the other stuff on the bulletin board—a Mets schedule; a printed list of 976 phone numbers; a postcard from Ocean Grove, New Jersey; a Tower Records ad, with a circle drawn around a new K. T. Oslin album; some phone numbers; an ad for a Precor rowing machine; some reminders—"call Paulie," "toothbrush," "Letterman Tues."

"Why?" he said again. "Why does he have this? 'An Unlikely Warrior in the Fight Against AIDS.' "

And Cullen wondered again could you really tell about people from their palms, from their being thin and young? "Who said 'interview'? Back to this tape, guys. One of you said something about an interview. Who?"

"I did," Zimmerman said.

Cullen snapped his fingers. "That's it. This is an interview. An interview with Rickey. By a newspaper reporter."

Diehl snapped his fingers. "Or a radio show."

Zimmerman snapped his. "A talk show. Alan *Colmes.*"

"Or that other guy," Diehl said. "Alan Lang."

"Henderson was on the radio," Cullen said, "talking about being a Peeping Tom—"

"And someone heard him," Zimmerman said.

Diehl patted the filing cabinet. "One of these femmes, maybe, wanted to—what?—get back at him?"

Cullen said, "Henderson was on the radio, talking about being a Peeping Tom, someone heard him, someone who knew him. They called him, they put the phone next to the radio so Rickey'd hear his own voice on his machine."

Diehl laughed. "Why, though? Why do that?"

"I think you just said it. To get back at him, to get *at* him. John, call Colmes, call Lang, call any other radio Alans you can think of, and find out if anyone—"

Snap. "I got it," Zimmerman said. "Sorry, Joe, but I got it." *Snap, snap.* "Colmes or Lang or some radio Alan did a show on Peeping Toms. Rickey was on the show. He didn't use his real name, he used a pseudonym. Someone who knows Rickey heard the show and recognized his voice. They called this number, they put the receiver next to the radio, they played Rickey a little bit of his own voice."

Cullen nodded. "Good. Very good."

Diehl spread his hands wide. "I'm going to say it again, guys: why do that?"

Zimmerman said, "Maybe . . ."

Tony Justice still moving in and out of her, in and out, Diana Romano took her left hand out of her sucking mouth long enough to whisper the answer to Cullen. He talked right over her, he didn't need to hear her. "To let him know he was blown," Cullen said. "Not to let him know by whom, just that. A Peeping Tom unmasked by an eavesdropper. It's kind of elegant."

"It's beautiful," Zimmerman said.

Cullen didn't look at Diana Romano, but he knew

she was smiling again. He put his hand on Diehl's shoulder. Total strangers just a few short minutes ago, now partners in detection. "Call Colmes and Lang, John, and any other radio guys named Alan. If Rickey kept a diary around, check it for the name of the doctor whose office called on this tape. That could give you the approximate date of the radio show."

"I like it," Diehl said.

They shook hands all around.

"Where're you guys going?" Diehl said.

"Next door to see if we can find out about the woman at the other end of these." Cullen patted the camera lenses. The FTN's and the Arri's.

"Her name's Dee Blue," Diehl said.

Cullen and Zimmerman raised their eyebrows at each other.

"Dee Blue?" Zimmerman said.

"A stage name, probably. She's a dancer or something."

"A singer," Zimmerman said.

"You've heard of her?"

"Joe and I had a talk with Rickey Henderson last week—to do with a job he'd caught. Dee Blue's name came up. She's got a gig coming up at the Ballroom. She was Rickey's girlfriend."

Diehl had now heard everything. "He *spied* on his girlfriend?"

13

ANN CLAMPED THE PHONE BETWEEN shoulder and ear and wondered: If she ever had a child would it be born with its head tipped to one side, a victim of its mother's acquired characteristic? "Ann Jones."

"Hello, beauty. I like a woman who answers her own phone."

Ann hung up. She didn't like men who said *I like a woman who* . . . And as for the *beauty*, well . . .

When the phone rang again she let it ring five times so the receptionist would pick up. After a bit, the intercom buzzed.

"Thanks, Trace. Who is it?"

"Noel Cutler."

At a friend's summer place in Fair Harbor once, Ann had played a parlor game: With what historical scoundrel would you most like to have dinner? The villain would be brought back to life if necessary, and if necessary shackles and armed guards would be provided. Hitler, Caligula, Jack the Ripper, Charles Starkweather, Billy the Kid, Charles Manson, Ted Bundy—the choices had been uninspired, although interestingly (it was a girls-only weekend outing), many were sex maniacs and only one was a woman: Bonnie Parker, whom the selector—selec*trix*—miscalled Bonnie Barrow. Ann had picked Lee Harvey Oswald ("Now, once and for all, Lee, *about* the grassy knoll . . ."), but she realized right this minute that Noel Cutler would have been worth the price of the swordfish. "No. Really? Put him through. . . . Hello?"

"Not very friendly, beauty."

"I have a thing about telephone etiquette, Noel. I

do answer my own phone, and *you* begin by saying who *you* are."

"*Meet me at the carousel in Central Park, beauty. Four o'clock.*"

"I'm on deadline," Ann said, "so I won't be there, so don't hold your breath," but the phone had already gone dead, and she had turned in a piece for next week that morning, and even if she hadn't she knew she would have dropped everything and gone to meet him.

Mark Talbert put his head in Ann's door as she was getting her stuff together to leave. "Sliding out early?"

"Meeting someone."

"A source?"

"Not exactly. Someone I wrote about once."

"What you write is the property of the magazine. You really should tell me what's up."

"Mark, honestly."

Talbert backed off. "Linda and I've been going over our date books: You and Joe have got to come out to Water Mill. We won't take no for an answer. You'll love the place. You can sailboard, play tennis, take walks on the beach, ride bikes—you won't be bored for a second. Take the Jitney out—you can read or sleep. Or neck. Or join the fifty-five-mile-an-hour club—the highway version of the mile-high club. You *are* a member of the mile-high club?"

This was brand-new. Talbert tried to see down her blouses and up her skirts as much as any man, and there were times when he stood closer than he ought in the elevator, but he had never come on to her so overtly and annoyingly. She gave him a look that she hoped communicated that she had no interest in joining any club whose initiation involved copulating in toilets aboard common carriers, and that she didn't want to hear that anyone she knew was a member either, especially the boss. "I'll talk to Joe, but I'm not sure it'll be possible. His hours are so irregular, it's hard to do anything except on the spur of the moment."

Talbert flipped a hand carelessly. "That's the kind of people *we* are, Annie. Just call from the station, from the Jitney stop. Just show up on the doorstep. Just walk right in. Door's never locked. You can drive our spare car while you're out there. An old Healy with right-hand drive, but you'll love it."

"I'll talk to Joe," Ann said. "Now please excuse me."

Talbert held up a finger. "One more thing. How would you feel about writing the text for some pictures Romano's making?"

"Diana Romano?" Ann said.

He looked bewildered, as if he were suddenly in the world where the Regency, the Four Seasons, Le Cirque, had ceased to exist, where the names he dropped, instead of ringing true, clinked on the floor, wavered, wobbled, toppled over. "*Yes*, Diana Romano."

"I didn't know she was doing a job for us, Mark, that's all. What on?"

Talbert waved his hand. "Whatever she wants."

Ann laughed.

"What?" Talbert looked like a magician offering looks up his sleeve, turning out his pockets to show they were empty of guile.

"I've worked here eight years, Mark, and if anyone's earned the right to write whatever she or he wants, it's me. I. I would resent it, I will resent it, I do resent it, if you give carte blanche to a freelance photographer and then ask me to write her *cap*tions. Also: Ro*mano*'s husband's ex dead wife was a friend of mine. It would be . . . awkward."

Ann hefted her bag and went out the door.

*　*　*

ANN GOT to the carousel ten minutes early. Noel Cutler made her wait till ten after, then came out from behind a wide oak tree near one of the softball diamonds, where he had been the whole time. Dressed all in black when last she'd seen him, being led from a courtroom with his hands cuffed in front of him, he was dressed all in black now; in between, black had become fashionable.

"Hello, beauty." Same nervous alto, but warped, as if being played back too slowly, which was why she hadn't recognized him right away on the phone: Tony Perkins on 'ludes.

"Stop calling me beauty, Noel. You sound like a psychopath in a slasher movie."

Noel Cutler laughed soundlessly, pressing his hands against his stomach as if he were a jolly fat man, instead of thin as a stick. "But you *are* a beauty. You haven't aged a bit. It's really not fair."

That from a man with Meissen skin and a perfect mouth. "When did you get out, Noel?"

He ran his hand over his cropped hair, brushed forward like a Roman emperor's. He did it again and again, as if determining whether he really *was* out. "A month tomorrow. Don't be offended that I didn't look you up first thing, beauty. I was starved for cock that wasn't protruding from someone with an attitude."

Aren't we all? Ann thought. "So that's how it goes: you kill someone and in no time at all you're back on the street. No wonder victims' families always feel they didn't get a full measure of revenge."

"Four years, nine months, beauty. Two-thirds of eight and a third, another third off for good behavior."

Hardly *no time at all*, Ann knew he meant. She tried to remember four years, nine months ago, and could

78

barely. She could remember the architect she'd been thinking about marrying (unaware that *he* was thinking about moving to Australia—and would); she could remember exercising anorectically, getting ready for her second marathon and considering triathlons; she could remember screening all the calls on her home answering machine, picking up one in six or eight, and hoping she'd get other people's machines when she called them and that they wouldn't pick up for her. She could remember too much Bruce Springsteen on the radio and too much Michael J. Fox on the tube *and* at the movies. (Mojo Nixon was right: Michael J. Fox had *no* Elvis in him.) She liked herself better now, but she'd be that woman again in a New York minute rather than spend the interval in a cage. "And how was it, the joint?"

"I survived. *Comme tu vois.*"

What she saw was someone once funny and fragile become obdurate and frightening. "And now you want to tell your story? Or is it *sell* your story?"

"It's a hell of a story, beauty."

They had walked away from the carousel and its maddening recorded calliope music (and away from children, Ann kept thinking; keep this man away from children) along a path leading toward the West Drive. Noel Cutler stopped suddenly and sat on a bench.

Ann sat, not beside him exactly, but on the same bench to be sure, and watched a Broadway Show League softball team taking batting practice. She was reminded of a time, a geological era more than four years, nine months ago, when she had hung out a lot in another part of the park, near the Metropolitan Museum, watching people and dogs but mostly dogs on a rise of land known as Dog Hill. Just as there had been all kinds of dogs, there were all kinds of softball players—players who were whippets and players who were bulldogs and players

79

who were Newfoundlands and players who were Chihuahuas. Setters, collies, Scotties, mixed, mutts, just plain generic dogs.

"Did you used to play?"

"Always picked last, beauty. Always shunted out to right field, out of harm's way. Always batted ninth."

Ann hadn't looked at Noel Cutler before she asked the question, but looking now, she saw that he had become less stony, that he was studying the activities through eyes that had a moist lens of nostalgia over them. "Bullshit," Ann said. "You were a star, weren't you?"

He worked his mouth until he had swallowed the awkward memory. "I'm counting on *you* to make me a star, beauty. Best-seller, Carson *and* Letterman, Oprah *and* Donahue, movie-of-the-week, a long-running series, lifetime syndication. Spinoffs, T-shirts, sequels, beaucoup bucks, beauty. Noel Cutler dolls with suction cups to stick on your car window." The phantom laugh again.

Ann could see the pileups that would result, could smell the smoking rubber and the spilled gas and the devastation. "I don't do murderers. An interview is a seduction, and I don't sleep with killers."

"Your boyfriend's a cop, beauty."

That went through her like electricity. This creep *knew* things about her. She would never shower again, she would have to sleep with a light on—*all* the lights. She would become one of those trigger-happy paranoid wackos with a .357 magnum under her pillow, a Doberman on a choke collar drooling on the stoop, an electrified fence frosted with razor tape running around the perimeter. Laager: she would get to say laager. She would get to spraypaint ZOG on the sides of buildings. She would wear a Coors cap and drive a Blazer with halogen lights and those big motherfucking tires and a gunrack with a double-barreled 12-gauge and a .22 long. She would join the Klan and have a boyfriend named Slick or Bubba who wouldn't take crap like this from some faggot actor, he'd rip his faggot-actor heart out. "Listen—"

"No, beauty, *you* listen. Listen good. Tony Justice killed Stephen Fox."

Ann's dismay came out in a burst of laughter. "That's absurd. *You* killed Stephen Fox, you confessed, you knew every detail, you did four years, nine months for it. What're you saying—that it was all some goddamn Method *ex*ercise?"

Cutler leaned away from her to take her all in. He smiled. "I like you, beauty. I always have—even before I got to know you personally. I *loved* the piece you did on Marty."

Who? Oh—Scorsese. "Listen, you starfucking phony"—Cutler laughed a real-life tickled-pink laugh, giving her another jolt—"I stopped thinking a long time ago that I was anything special just because antisocial assholes found it easy to tell me their life stories. I stopped doing murderers and rapists and child abusers. I stopped doing anybody, in fact, who doesn't have an investment in making the world a better place. Call me Mary Poppins, but don't call me a mindless sensationalizer. So peddle your story somewhere else. I'm simply not interested." She got up and started across the outfield, on a beeline for the way out of the park at Seventh Avenue. Her goddamn high heels (Christian Lacroix) sank into the turf and she staggered like a drunk.

Noel Cutler caught up to her and took her arm chivalrously. He guided her along an archipelago of hardpacked dirt where the outfields of two facing diamonds melded together and where the going was easier. Like an animal, his ears perked up, his eyes got wide at the thump of a bat on a ball and shouts of "Heads up. Heads up."

Looking up and here and there, he found the white ball against the white sky. He let go of Ann and started running—drifting, really, a gait that said that a whole lot more speed than what you were seeing was being reined in. He had his back to the plate; his head was tipped all the way back and his eyes were all the way back in his head. The ball was coming down and down, hard and heavy, and from her angle Ann could see that he wasn't going to get to it before it hit the ground.

Then Cutler accelerated just enough and put both hands straight out in front of him and gathered the ball in so gently, so carefully, that it was as if the ball were a cherub that had tumbled from a cloud while napping and he a passing hero who would now swoop up into the sky and put the little fellow back in his bed without missing a wink.

Instead of swooping, Cutler stopped. He juggled the ball in one hand, twisting it to read the label or trademark or whatever it was called, a thing men did for reasons Ann had long ago given up hope of ever understanding. He turned toward the plate—applause and shouts and facsimiles of great roaring crowds had followed his catch—and smiling a little, he threw the ball back in to the shortstop. The throw was low to the ground and popped in the shortstop's glove.

Cutler walked back to where Ann stood, his eye on the game, his hands held cupped up in front of him as if some dew of ball essence had rubbed off and he didn't want to spill it. He took Ann's arm again and escorted her to another path and sat her on another bench and took her back five years, two months. After a catch like that, how could she not go with him?

14

BACK TO THIS:

"Turn the fucking music down, asshole."

"It's the Boss, *ass*hole."

"Then turn the fucking Boss down."

"You're hopeless, Noel. Hopeless."

"Anyway, Sinatra's the Boss. Since when is Springsteen the Boss?"

"Sinatra's Chairman of the Board, asshole. Did you just get off the boat or what, Noel?"

"Suck my dick, Andrew."

"I don't do lips, you pansy."

"Faggot."

"Nelly queen."

"Takes one to know one."

"God, Noel. What a *cut*ting retort."

"Fuck you, you fucking shithead asshole scumbag."

And on and on, day and night, night and day, week in and week out, month after month. Andrew Steiger and Noel Cutler, roommates when one or the other didn't have a lover, lovers when they were roommates unless someone more interesting caught one or the other's eye, aspiring actors, fellow waiters, friends, rivals, intimates, adversaries (Springsteen and Tina Turner versus Sinatra and Peggy Lee, health food versus junk food, books versus television, among many other antagonisms)—all rolled into one.

Andy had hit New York first, out of St. Louis, and the apartment on way West Forty-ninth Street was his. He got hired at a theater-district restaurant first too, and was the first to enroll in acting and voice and dance classes. But the early bird must still *catch* the worm and that takes talent and Andy had little. Noël, on the other hand, forever late, forever forgetful, a shiftless congenital liar and petty thief from Orlando, Florida, was a natural and an original. On a stage, Noël took people's breath away, knocked their socks off—if he didn't oversleep, or forget the audition or the interview altogether, or if he didn't just say fuck it, and go to a movie to get laid or get high—or best of all, all three: a couple of lines, a couple of tokes, a ninja double bill in a theater off Times Square, on Forty-deuce, the Stroll, some lips or hips in the balcony before the show, during the show, between shows, after the show. Death was in those balconies, in the bathrooms, in the alleys, in the truck trailers parked down by the river, on the decrepit piers, and everybody knew it, but fuck it, hey, I mean, you only live once, right?

Right?

THEN:

"You fucking *what*, Andy?"

"You heard me."

"I didn't hear you, Andy. Your fucking face is stuck in the fucking pillow. I can't hear you when your fucking face is stuck in the fucking pillow, can I?"

"It's so like you, Noel, to try and hurt me by making me say it again and again."

"I can't heeeeear you, Andrew."

So Andy Steiger sat up and spat it in Noel Cutler's face. "I. Have. AIDS."

"Fucking great. Fucking terrific. Outfuckingstanding. Were you going to tell me? Were you? Were you fucking planning on fucking telling me?"

"I just told you, Noel. I just found out and I just told you."

" 'Found out'? The fuck do you mean 'found out'?"

"Just what I said. I *found* out."

"You got tested, you mean."

"*Yes*, I got tested. Did you think I read it in the *Advocate*?"

"You got tested, which they don't do overnight, it takes a couple of days or a week or whatever the fuck, but you didn't *tell* me you were fucking getting fucking tested."

"I didn't tell you I was *getting* tested. I'm telling you now that I've *been* tested."

"Why not? Why didn't you fucking tell me you were fucking getting fucking tested?"

"Because the test might've been negative, Noel. You would've worried about nothing."

"*Noth*ing? You think having fucking AIDS is fucking *noth*ing?"

"Noel, I'm the one with AIDS, not you. Of course I don't think it's nothing."

"How do you *know* I don't have AIDS? If you have it, I sure as fucking hell could have it. We *have* fucked each other, Andrew, though not fucking lately, what with you spending so much time fucking fucking Roy. Does fucking Roy have AIDS?"

"He's being tested. You should be tested too."

"Oh, right. I'm going to fucking take the fucking test so some spic lab technician can have the pleasure of telling me I have AIDS? '*Pobrecito marico. Tienes SIDA.*' Not fucking likely. Not fucking likely. . . . Who'd you get it from, Miss Promiscuous?"

"What're you trying to do, Noel?"

"I'm not *try*ing to do anything, Andrew. I'm *ask*ing

85

you who you got fucking AIDS fucking from, that's what I'm fucking doing. Who, Miss P?"

"It could've been anybody."

"Not *me*, it couldn't."

"It could've been, Noel."

"No, it *couldn't*! It couldn't've been *me*. I don't fucking have fucking AIDS."

"You don't know that, Noel. You *can't* know that without taking the test."

"I don't need a fucking test to tell me I don't have those fucking blotches on me, those fucking sores."

"I didn't have them either, Noel, a couple of weeks ago."

"Look at my skin. Like a baby's."

"Noel."

"Don't touch me, you fucking leper asshole scumbag AIDSdick! You've got fucking AIDSdick and you didn't even fucking *tell* me?"

"How could I tell you, Noel, when I—"

"AIDSdick!"

"Are you going to keep on saying that, Noel?"

"AIDSdick!"

"Go ahead. Keep on saying it. Get it out of your system."

"AIDSdick! AIDSdick, AIDSdick, AIDSdick, AIDSdick, AIDSdick!"

". . . Are you finished now, Noel?"

"AIDSfuckingdick!"

"Anytime you want to talk, Noel, just stop saying AIDSdick."

"AIDSanus. AIDSfucking crotch rot asshole dickhead scumbag toejam cumstain dingleberry fistfuck rim ream rectumhead."

"Jesus Christ, Noel. . . . Noel? *Noel*. Don't cry, Noel, please don't cry. I hate it when you cry."

86

". . . I'm sorry, Andy. I'm sorry I said those things."

"I'm sorry too, Noel. Everybody's sorry."

"I really am, Andy. I'm really sorry."

"It's okay, Noel. This is heavy shit."

"I can't breathe, Andy. I can't breathe."

"Just take it easy, Noel. Take it easy."

"I need some air, Andy. I've got to get some air."

"I can't go out, Noel. Not right now. Not looking like this. Maybe later, when people're asleep."

"The roof, then. Let's go up on the roof."

"Okay. The roof."

"Can you make it okay, Andy? Do you want me to carry you?"

"I'll be okay, Noel. I'll just take it slow."

"Let me carry you, Andy."

"I'll be okay. I'll just take it slow."

"Please let me carry you, Andy. *Please!* Please *God* let me carry you, Andy."

"Okay, Noel. Okay."

"Put your arms around my neck, Andy, okay?"

"Okay, Noel."

"Okay?"

"Okay."

"You all right?"

"Yeah."

"You sure?"

"I'm sure."

"Here we go."

"Here we go."

THEN, FOUR years, eleven months ago:

"Noel Cutler?"

"My mommy told me never talk to strangers."

"My name's Justice. I'm with the *Bulletin*."

"You're a newspaperman?"

"Something funny about that, Noel?"

"Matter of fact, yeah, there's something funny about it. What's funny about it is once upon a time I worked at a porno house on Forty-deuce. I was overnight manager. The creeps who put newspapers over their laps while they're jerking off—we used to call them newspapermen. So you're a *news*paperman, hey?"

"And you're a jack-of-all-trades, aren't you, Noel? Cashier, waiter, stock boy, bike messenger, overnight manager. Now you're a soda jerk. Oh, sure, hey, Häagen-Dazs. An upscale soda jerk, but inescapably a soda jerk. I haven't seen your name up on any marquees, though, Noel—not on Broadway, not off-Broadway, not off-off, not on a movie theater—not even a porno house. Have you ever actually *acted*, Noel? I don't mean in Miss Russell's third-grade class, I don't mean in *Cyrano* in high school, I mean in the real world."

Hey, he'd been a good Cyrano, a *great* Cyrano. "The fuck do you want, Jack? The fuck do you know so much about me?"

"You're a hell of a softball player, though. Everybody talks about what a—"

"Hey! Motherfucker! The fuck do you know so much *about* me?"

"You mean, since you're such an insignificant creep?"

"Fuck you, asshole."

"Andrew Steiger, Noel. Andrew Steiger's something else I know about you."

"... You ... you a friend of Andy's?"

"This could be your big break, Noel, this part I'm offering you."

"What part?"

Two teenage girls came in just then and ordered cones and Noel Cutler made them. Tony Justice watched interestedly, taking mental notes. The girls left and Justice repeated: "This could be your big break, Noel, this part I'm offering."

"I don't know what the fuck you're talking about, Jack."

"You see, Noel, the part you've written for yourself is a cheap, sleazy part that'll lead only to more cheap, sleazy parts." Here Justice held his left hand out, fingers together, thumb hyperextended, and read from an imaginary newspaper's front page: " 'FAGGOT KILLS LOVER OVER AIDS. Fatal Plunge Follows Rooftop Squabble.' "

"I . . . I . . . I don't know what you're talking about."

"It's scary, isn't it, Noel, to have a complete stranger know *that* about you?"

"I don't know what you're talking about."

"Sunday April twentieth, Noel, Andy Steiger broke the news he'd gotten the day before: HIV-positive, Kaposi's sarcoma, up shit's creek without a paddle and as far as you knew, dragging you along with him right over the big old Niagara of life. It was a warm night, summery, and the two of you went up on the roof of Andy's building. You lived there too, at the time, but it was Andy's building, Andy was the one the neighbors knew and liked; to them you were just one of a bunch of losers who hung around with Andy, no one could quite figure out what Andy saw in all you losers.

"The two of you went up on the roof. You carried Andy in your arms. The climb was too much for him. The argument—you'd been shouting, slamming furniture around—had worn him out. You carried Andy in your arms, you carried him straight to the parapet, before he even realized what you were doing you dropped him seven stories to the courtyard, you went downstairs and typed out a suicide note on a piece of paper that must already have been in Andy's typewriter because it has his prints on it, you forged his signature, you went to the window and pretended to discover Andy lying down below, you screamed and yelled and someone called the cops. When they came, you told them you'd just come home and found the apartment empty, found the note, looked out the window and saw the body.

"Andy didn't even scream on the way down. It was probably a relief to know he was going to die. You probably *did* do him a favor, Noel, but that doesn't mitigate the underlying cheap sleaziness of the whole affair. Not a bit.

"The part I've written for you, Noel, is a lot more elegant. It's classy, clas*sic*, even. It goes like this. . . ."

A mother with a baby in a blue Snugli came in and ordered a cone. While Noel Cutler made it, Tony Justice let the baby play with his index finger and chatted with the mother about a woman friend of his who was convinced that the brightness and alertness of her seven-year-old daughter was due in part to the girl's having spent her babyhood in a Snugli, where she was part of every social interaction, rather than—Justice's version of his friend's words—"in splendid isolation" in a stroller.

The woman left and Justice stepped to the door for a moment to watch them go. "Babies. I've never had one. I know I'm missing something."

"What you're missing, Jack, is a few screws. I ought to pick up this telephone and call the cops and tell them there's a fucking nut case in my store, come on over and get him out of here, that's what I ought to do."

Justice came back to the counter and spread his elbows on it, as if surveying the flavors. "As I was saying, Noel, the part I've written for you goes like this: Stephen Fox, the theatrical producer, is mounting a musical version of *The Lady Eve*. Do you know the Preston Sturges movie?"

"Why don't you just get the fuck out of here, Jack, and we'll forget we ever had this little conversation."

"Fox wants Madonna for the Barbara Stanwyck part and an unknown for the Henry Fonda part. There's an open call next Thursday. To give you an edge, Noel, I've gotten some pages of the script for you to read over. 'Sides,' I believe they're called. Don't be so indelicate as to bring them with you. I can't do anything about getting you called back, of course, but it's my hope that you will be, so work hard on your lines. Here's a videocassette of the movie, forwarded to the scene in question, so you can have some idea of the ingenuousness Fonda brought to the part. I think it's one of his best performances. You should, of course, watch the entire film at some point before the audition; all the other aspirants surely will, you'll stand out if you don't."

Justice had taken the pages and the cassette out of a leather portfolio tucked under one arm. He zipped up the portfolio and put it back under his arm, like a messenger who has delivered the important documents. One, he held back, gripping it between thumb and forefinger and gently fanning himself with it. "It's vital, Noel, that you look like someone who *deserves* the part; if you're just another petulant psychopath it won't play anywhere near as well—"

"Talk about psychopaths, Jack, you are one fucking—"

"Shut up and listen, Noel. I have *not* finished. . . . You *won't* get the part, of course, called back or not, because word is out that you're a fuckup and Stephen Fox will simply not work with fuckups. You *won't* get the part, and *when* you don't, you're going to get a gun and go to Stephen Fox's office and kill him—"

"Jesus, Jack. Hey, shit—"

"Noel. Shush. Please. I don't have all day"—here Justice handed over the final document—"This is a list of gun shops. A couple in the city, a couple on Long Island. Take your pick. Fill out all the forms, everything on the up-and-up. I recommend a thirty-eight or a forty-five or a three-fifty-seven magnum. Anything smaller and he might live long enough to identify you. We want there to be some suspense as to who you are; we don't want your likeness on every front page, on every TV news show, on every post-office bulletin board. The best place to shoot him is in the face. You'll have the opportunity; he won't be expecting it. I want everything back by this time next week—the sides, the cassette, the list. At that point I'll be in possession of a key to Fox's office and a sense of when he's most likely to be there alone. He's an early-morning person, which is desirable, because New York may be open all night, but things're wound down real slow early in the morning."

"Justice, listen, let me ask you something. Did somebody—"

"Let. Me. Finish. Then you can ask away. After you kill Fox, you'll go about your business as usual. A junkie, not a disgruntled actor, is the kind of suspect the cops'll be looking for." Again, Justice held out his left hand, and conjured a headline: " 'CRACK ADDICT SOUGHT IN BROADWAY SLAYING.'

"As will many of my . . . peers"—the caesura said Justice didn't really think he had peers—"I'll be writing about the police investigation. When I've gotten all the mileage I can expect—scores of cops fanning through the theater district, indignant impresarios, terrorized tourists, all that drivel—then you'll confess." Justice put a finger to his lips to cut off yet another interruption forming on Noel Cutler's. "Confess to *me*, I was about to say, Noel—either by letter or over the phone; I haven't decided. In either case, the text or the transcription of your confession will be printed in the paper, and subjected to the usual analyses by professional psychotherapists and criminologists to determine the state of mind of such a villain.

"Between the confession and your actual surrender, some more time will elapse. How much depends on how interested my readers are in your story. Days, weeks—I have no way of knowing. If I could forecast their enthusiasms, I'd be worth far more than my employers are currently—"

"What the *fuck* are you talking about, mother-fucker?" Noel Cutler could contain himself no longer. "Your *readers*. Your fucking scumbag dickhead *readers*?"

"You wanted to ask me something earlier, Noel. What was it?"

"*Readers?* Man, you are fucking whacked-out, Jack. You are—"

"What you wanted to ask me, Noel, was whether someone saw you. Isn't that it? You wanted to know if I know what I know about Andrew Steiger because someone saw you drop him off the roof, isn't that so?"

"—fucking whacked-out."

"Someone did see you, yes, that's right, Noel.

Someone, as luck would have it—my luck, not yours—who owed me a favor. A relative had a legal problem, I helped out, this was my repayment."

"Some fucking whacko, right? Or some fucking junkie wino dipshit crackhead whore passed out on the fucking rooftop, probably, right?"

"Actually not, Noel. Actually, a respectable, sober, straight, law-abiding citizen. Not that it matters, it really doesn't matter. *You* know you threw Andy off the roof and faked a suicide—that's all that matters. We're not talking about eyewitness testimony that'll stand up in court, Noel, because you're not going to court—not for killing Andy.

"Listen, I'm going to be off now, Noel, because I can see from your face that you're ready to overload. This is heavy stuff, I don't deny that, and you need some time to absorb it all. I'll be in touch. Oh, and, uh, don't kill *your*self, Noel, okay? Because that won't accomplish anything. I'm offering you a chance for real fame, Noel. Theatrical producers don't have much of a constituency, and a lot of people, maybe even most people, and not just actors and actresses and directors either, will think you have a lot of style for going to the extreme of killing one.

"Oh, yes, one more thing: If you should hear of anyone with AIDS, anyone who has it bad, anyone whose name in a headline would sell some papers, let me know, will you?"

"You scumbag. You bloodsucking fucking scumbag."

"*Ciao*, Noel. Talk to you soon."

15

"I HAD NO IDEA THE WACK MOTHER-fucker was copping peeks. *No* idea."

Cullen and Zimmerman had found Dee Blue at her mother's house in Fort Lee. George Washington Bridge traffic thwapped by outside, the air was blue with ozone. A larger-than-life replica of Diana Ross, huge hair, pop eyes, imperious, Dee Blue was taking up the hem of a borrowed matronly black dress to wear to Rickey Henderson's funeral. (Her own clothes, leather and Spandex, wouldn't do.)

"I had *no* idea the wack motherfucker was living in the next building for the first two months the mother-fucker was there. The washing machines in my building broke down, I took a load of laundry next door, there was Harold, folding his cute little bikini undershorts. The wack motherfucker."

"On the radio," Cullen said, "Rickey talked about a situation—sorry; we knew Harold as Rickey—about a situation in which a woman knows a voyeur's watching, but doesn't object. I take it that was hypothetical, that he wasn't talking about you."

For an answer, Dee Blue gave him the briefest of looks.

"The Alan Lang Show, June six. That is correct, isn't it, Ms. Blue?" Zimmerman said.

"My mother's birthday, the wack motherfucker. Now I'll get to be reminded of it every motherfucking year."

Cullen wondered if every motherfucking year, on his mother's birthday or any old time, he would remember Diana Romano, perched on an upturned steamer trunk, Tony Justice moving in and out of her, in and out. "I

95

know it's difficult, Ms. Blue, but could you please tell us everything—how you came to be listening, what you did when you recognized Harold's voice, what happened when you saw him next—"

"Saw him *next*? I never saw the wack motherfucker *peri*od. Oh, he called me plenty, tried to house me— 'Please, baby, please, baby, baby, baby, oh, baby, please. Let's get together, baby. Lemme 'splain, baby.' I told the wack motherfucker I'd love to get together so I could cut off his johnson, but other than that I never wanted to lay *eyes* on the motherfucker."

"How did you happen to be listening to the show, Ms. Blue?" Zimmerman said.

Dee Blue thrust a needle into the dress rather than into him. "It's a free country."

"Which is why there're a hundred or so radio stations to choose from. Are you a regular Alan Lang listener? A lot of women don't like him."

"He don't bother me none. I like the way he stirs people up."

"What we're wondering, Ms. Blue," Cullen said, "is, did someone tell you Harold was going to be on the radio, or was it just a coincidence that you were listening? Radio's awfully transitory: it's like one of your performances; you have to be there, or it's gone."

Dee Blue stitched fiercely for a while. "Harold has a friend who . . . who's been trying to romeo me. Nothing's gone down, but he let me know he was available if things didn't work out with Harold. He works nights, wakes up around three, turns on Alan Lang while he's shaving. He heard this homeboy calling himself Dex talking about spying on sisters with cameras and binoculars and shit. Dexter was Harold's middle name. He knew it was Harold, this friend; a deaf dumb blind fool would've known it was Harold. He thought I'd want to know, this friend, he called me and recommended I tune in."

"Harold was one of several guests on the show, yes?" Zimmerman said.

"There were four or five others, I think. One was a woman who liked to be watched, the others were men who liked to do the watching. I didn't listen hard; it ain't my trip."

"And while Harold was talking, you called his home phone, knowing the machine would be on, and held the receiver next to the radio for a while, so he'd come home and hear the sound of his own voice and know he'd been found out, is that right?" Diana Romano took her left hand out of her sucking mouth long enough to reward Cullen with a pat on the shoulder. "Or was it Harold's friend who did that?"

Dee Blue tried not to smile. "*I* did it. I thought it was def."

Cullen agreed. "We've been admiring it since we guessed that's what'd happened. And you say Harold eventually called to ask your forgiveness, but you wouldn't see him?"

"You been listening? I told the wack motherfucker I'd see him long enough to cut off his johnson." Dee Blue said it deliberately—slice, slice, slice.

After a nervous swallow at the thought, Cullen said, "Detective Zimmerman and I spoke to Ric—to Harold— last week. We had some information for him concerning one of his cases. Neither of us had ever met him, though we knew him by reputation—"

"As a wack motherfucker?"

"—We chatted a little bit and he mentioned he had a girlfriend who was a professional singer—"

"Not anymore the motherfucker didn't."

"He touted your gig at the Ballroom. He was very proud of you."

Dee Blue spread her hands helplessly. "What're you going to do with a motherfucker like that? The motherfucker didn't have a conscience."

Zimmerman made a small move that meant he wanted to throw out a different kind of question. Cullen nodded at him to go ahead.

"Harold had a newspaper clipping on his bulletin board," Zimmerman said. "About a woman named Michelle Slate."

"The wack motherfucker."

"She's a wealthy woman, the wife of a Wall Street banker, who's active in different charities. Did Ric— Did Harold know her?"

"You're axing me?"

Zimmerman fought a smile. "Harold was working on the murder of a woman named Karen Justice. You knew that?"

Dee Blue nodded. "The K, he called it. The Karen Justice K. That what you call it, between yourselves?"

"Pretending people don't get murdered, they get K'd makes the job a little easier sometimes," Cullen said. "Did Harold say anything to you about that K? Did he tell you any theories he had?"

"Harold thought she got K'd on account of her husband knew something."

"Did he? Knew what?"

Dee Blue just shook her head.

"Someone K'd Karen Justice to keep Tony Justice from writing something he knew—that was Rickey's theory? Sorry—Harold's theory?"

Dee Blue shrugged. "Something like that."

In police work as in everything else, there comes a time when you have stayed too long, and this was it.

Cullen sat forward, ready to get up and get out. "Ms. Blue, we're not directly involved in investigating Harold's murder, and we're out of our jurisdiction anyway, but I feel I should warn you that your discovery of Harold's ... pastime"—Diana Romano stopped Tony Justice moving in and out of her, in and out, so she wouldn't miss any of this—"could be construed as a motive for murdering him. Add to that your admission that there's another man in the picture—"

"Nothing's gone down with Alonzo. I explained that to you already."

Cullen and Zimmerman looked at each other and back at Dee Blue.

"Alonzo?" Zimmerman said.

"Alonzo Paul?" Cullen said. "Midtown North Squad?"

Dee Blue pouted and stitched.

Cullen got up. "Get a lawyer, Ms. Blue. And don't leave town."

"ALONZO?" CULLEN put his head out the window of Zimmerman's Saab, parked down the block from Midtown North.

Alonzo Paul's left hand went up to his chest and his thumb flicked at his Levi's jacket, checking what there had better be no doubt about—that he was strapped. "Who may I say is calling?"

"Cullen. Internal Affairs."

Paul ran the backs of his fingers under his chin, getting reassurance from the smoothness of his beard. "I hearda you. Word is don't fuck witch you, the PC's your rabbi."

Sometimes months went by, sometimes only hours, without someone mentioning that away from the job

99

Cullen and Hriniak were friends. The friendship had been born when Cullen, then a college student, worked part-time as a clerk in a record store that Hriniak, then a patrolman, then and now a jazz buff, dropped in at often when walking his beat; at the outset, the friendship had gotten Cullen a good reference to put on his application for the Police Academy and gotten Hriniak a discount on records. Cullen didn't know what Hriniak would say the friendship meant to him lately; what it meant to Cullen lately was extra work and innuendo.

Cullen reached around and opened the back door. "This is Detective Zimmerman. Have a seat. We need about five minutes."

Alonzo Paul pushed the door closed just hard enough to make his point. "I gave at the office." But he didn't walk away. He leaned against a cobra-head lamppost, folded his arms across his chest, looked out from under his lowered lids at everything but them. For their part, they pretended to be tough guys too, guys whose job—whose métier—it was to sit inside a parked car on a rare lovely June afternoon, imaginary fedoras tipped back on their heads, imaginary cigarettes dangling from their lips, admiring the creases of their imaginary sharkskin suits, the shine on their imaginary two-tone shoes.

Alonzo Paul gave in first. "So this is your cover— two faggots in a foreign car?" He laughed, but his eyes were bright with apprehension. He'd done *something* he didn't want them to know about. But then, who hadn't?

"Where were you Sunday night?" Cullen said. "Between five and nine."

"Who wants to know?"

"Santa Claus. We're his helpers."

"Kinda early for Santa, ain't it?"

"You know how long it takes to make a list and check it twice?"

"I axed for a Reatta last Christmas. Didn't get it."

"A Reatta's a Buick," Zimmerman said, in case Cullen had no idea—*knowing* Cullen had no idea—what Alonzo Paul was talking about.

"Sunday, Alonzo," Cullen said. "From five till nine." He hadn't smoked in years and drank a beer at bedtime and he was already exhausted by the repartee, which only sounded right when it was smoky and boozy.

Alonzo Paul mimed recollecting. "Around the time Rickey got K'd, you mean?"

"Harold, Dee Blue calls him. Dex, he called himself at least once."

Alonzo Paul breathed deeply through his nose and breathed out slowly, savoring the oxygen as if it were suddenly in short supply. "Dee's stupid fresh. But nothing's going down between us."

"That's what she said. So you got your stories straight—big fucking deal."

Alonzo Paul heard that Cullen was out of patience. "Sunday five to nine I was at my mother's for dinner."

Cullen had to laugh. "That's so pathetic it's got to be true. You win, Alonzo—you win the Nobel Prize for best alibi."

"I'll settle for the Reatta."

"Don't take any trips, Alonzo, without letting us know. Cullen and Zimmerman, IAU."

Alonzo Paul took a step, then took it back. "You know one thing, don't you, Cullen?"

"What's that?"

"I wanted to K Rickey, I wouldn't do the K in the Port of Authority. Or then again," Alonzo Paul said, "knowing you know that, I might."

16 THEY DROVE DOWNTOWN BEHIND A Beamer with the vanity plate LLB MOM. Zimmerman just about drove through the rush-hour crowds on the sidewalk to see the driver and got enough of a glimpse to fall in love with her. Cullen knew Zimmerman would have DMV run the plate and would know by this time tomorrow whether she was a married Lawyer/Mom or a divorced or separated or unwed Lawyer/Mom. Lawyer/Mom peeled off in the Twenties (Chelsea Lawyer/Mom) and they kept on going back to the diner, back to where it all began.

Sinéad O'Connor was working a double and Zimmerman eased his pain at not having met Lawyer/Mom by chatting her up. "I have tickets for Mike and the Mechanics at Radio City a week from Thursday. You interested?"

Sinéad looked dubious. "Me?"

"Mike Rutherford. Used to be with Genesis."

Cullen stuck a napkin in his mouth to keep from laughing. Mike and the Mechanics was Zimmerman's idea of raunch; Jane's Addiction—maybe—was the closest Sinéad had ever been to the middle of the road.

Sinéad sponged the Formica vigorously. "You want to go with *me*?"

"Absolutely. Do you work Thursday?"

"Till six."

"I'll pick you up. We'll have something to eat first. Not here."

She laughed at the thought. "Not here is right."

"My name's Neil. Neil Zimmerman."

102

"Jan Spellman."

"Jan, it's nice to meet you. This is my partner, Joe Cullen."

She wiped her hand on her apron and held it out. She had a good grip. "Jan."

"Hi. What kind of partner?"

"We're cops," Zimmerman said without a flinch, as though she'd be as glad to hear that as if he had said *We're white supremacists.*

"*Really?*" She was impressed. You *never* knew what was going to impress someone. "Like, you know, 'Wise-guy'?"

"Vinnie's a fed," Zimmerman said. "We're local."

"You *know* Vinnie?"

"We know his rep."

This wasn't happening, was it? Sinéad O'Connor and Ralph Lauren weren't talking about a television character as if he were real, were they?

"The thing is," Sinéad said, "I have a class Thursday nights."

"What kind of class?"

Memory and Desire: The Poetry of Heavy-Metal Music.

"Life Drawing."

"Really?"

"Portraits, figures, botanical forms."

"No kidding?"

"Plus, I'd have to get a babysitter."

"No kidding? Boy or girl?"

Two-headed love child, probably.

"Boy. He's six."

"What's his name?"

Jell-O.

"Stiv"—Sinéad looked offended *and* defensive

when Cullen chuckled—"but I'm going to change it. His, you know, old man named him, but he's never coming back, the scumbag."

"Uh, Jan." Cullen tried not to sound older than water. "Neil and I have a couple of things to talk over. If you wouldn't mind, could we have five minutes? Then he's all yours."

She giggled. She was blushing. She went off with a flirty look over her shoulder.

Zimmerman watched her go. "Cute."

Cullen sighed the sigh of a man older than water who will never understand what makes people do the things they do, nor what will impress them.

Zimmerman read the sigh differently. "Don't groan like that. Just say it. Say you think I screw around too much."

"I wasn't groaning."

"You've got a good relationship, you know—with Ann."

He did?

"One like that isn't easy to find these days."

It wasn't?

"If I seem kind of desperate sometimes, well, I am."

He was? "Neil, I wasn't making a judgment. It's been a long day, I'd like to wrap it up."

Zimmerman nodded. "Yeah."

"I'm sorry if I—"

"It's okay. I said it's okay."

"... Okay. ... So: Rickey Henderson had an eccentric hobby and his girlfriend found out about it. Did she K him for it? I don't think Dee could, and if Alonzo did, as he said, he wouldn't do the K in the Port Authority. Or then again, as he said, he might. If Rickey's K has nothing to do with his hobby, then does it have to do with Karen Justice and/or Rae Muldoon? You said it sitting here seven or eight hours ago: if Diana Romano was worried that Rickey had made the Justice-Muldoon connection, K'ing Rickey doesn't throw us off the trail, it puts more of us *on* the trail."

"And sitting here seven or eight hours ago," Zimmerman said, "you said you don't see a trail, you see Fred and Ginger and Mutt and Jeff."

"Whoever they are."

"Whoever they are," Zimmerman said. "Am I making too much of the Michelle Slate clipping? Could it be it means nothing?"

"People don't put things that mean nothing on their refrigerators and bulletin boards"—the Urban Jungle Girl, the Vaulting Bridesmaid—"Maybe ..." Cullen lost it, so fleeting was it. He tried again, tried harder. "Maybe it wasn't Michelle Slate that made him save the clipping, maybe it was AIDS. Maybe he wanted to know about AIDS, maybe he was afraid of getting AIDS, maybe— Tony Justice. AIDS and Tony Justice. Dee Blue said Rickey thought Karen Justice was K'd because of something Tony Justice knew. Something about ... someone who had AIDS, and couldn't afford to have it be known. Maybe he told Rickey who it was. Or maybe he didn't, and Rickey had to guess, and thought Michelle Slate could help him make a better guess ... I don't know. I'm just rambling on, I don't know."

Cullen unscrewed the top of a salt shaker, then screwed it back on. Sinéad hadn't brought their coffee. Had they ordered coffee? He guessed maybe they hadn't. "Let's split up for a while. Check out Alonzo's alibi, check out the other women Rickey photographed. Would any of them want to K him, and could they if

105

they wanted to? Call Alan Lang. He's an opinionated guy, does *he* have an opinion?"

"And you?"

"I'm going to see Blond Tommy."

Zimmerman nodded and waited, but there was nothing more. "That's it?"

Cullen ducked his head so he wouldn't see behind the hand jammed in her sucking mouth the smile in Diana Romano's eyes. "And I guess Diana Romano."

"How're you going to handle her?"

Yes, how? Diana Romano's eyes asked.

"I can't come on too strong." *That's okay*, those eyes said. *I like it strong.* "We don't have a thing on her."

"Except that women turn up missing when she's around."

"Karen Justice isn't missing anymore. I don't know if that changes things or not."

"You mean, undoes the connection?"

"Well, yes."

Sinéad came back with coffee and pieces of apple pie that they hadn't ordered but she'd thought they looked like they needed. She sat down to make sure they ate every bite (PUNK MOM, her plate probably said) and Cullen took the opportunity to get away, lying and saying he had dinner plans. He stopped between the cash register and the door and almost went back to the booth and said *Look, Neil, there's something about Tony Justice and Diana Romano you should know: in the church, after Karen's funeral ...* But Sinéad and Zimmerman had their oh-so-different heads together and were laughing over something and someone was tugging at his sleeve.

When he turned, he saw that it was Diana Romano. She wasn't perched on an upturned steamer trunk anymore, she wasn't wearing a black mourning dress and black French-maid French-whore garterless stockings, glen-plaid pumps, Tony Justice wasn't moving in and out of her, in and out. She was alone and wearing a virginal white shift. Her feet were bare and she was stepping backward into a calm ocean, inviting him with just the energy of her fingertips to come swim with her.

17

"I DON'T LIKE IT. IT'S GETTING OUT of control. Too fucking many people know."

"Relax. You're halfway to an ulcer and you're not even forty."

"I don't think relaxed is what *you* are. I think you're oblivious. I think you don't give a shit."

Standing with his back against a railing running around Battery Park, watching secretaries, office boys, messengers, runners, middle-management drones eating their lunches in the sun, the tall trim clean-shaven man finished his hot dog and dabbed at his lips with a paper napkin. "Of course I give a shit. But there are things that can be influenced and things that can't, things that have to run their course."

"Don't lecture me. Okay?" The tall trim man with the brush mustache, facing out over the harbor but not taking in any of its sights, grasped the railing with both hands—he wasn't eating, and hadn't; his stomach was roiling—as if he might wrench it loose. "I argued from the start that we had to control the membership as carefully as if we were running a covert operation. Suddenly, we not only have members who haven't been properly vetted, we have pho*tog*raphers roaming around shoving strobe lights in people's faces."

The tall trim clean-shaven man took a leather cigar case from an inside pocket of his double-breasted suit coat. He removed a cigar and smelled its aroma, but didn't trim it or light it, just held it between his first two fingers, like a child playing at smoking. "There's *one* photographer working with available light—working very discreetly, quietly, unobtrusively. That kind of exaggeration is just tiresome. The energy required to refute it is twice that required for its creation. Let's change the subject, shall we?"

The tall trim man with the brush mustache struggled to, but failed. "Just tell me again—why? Why do we need these pictures?"

"We don't *need* them. They'll be entertaining."

"They'll be evidential."

The clean-shaven man laughed. "Lawyers. What a wonderful world it would be without lawyers."

The man with the mustache turned his back to the harbor. "I have just one question, then I'll shut up. How many more killings are there going to be?"

The clean-shaven man raised his eyebrows. "There have been only two."

"How many more?"

"As many as necessary."

"Necessary?"

"To ensure our survival."

"Is that what it's a matter of?"

"Isn't it? . . . *Isn't* it?"

"I suppose."

"You sup*pose*?"

The man with the mustache touched the corner of one eye with the tip of his little finger.

The clean-shaven man leaned over to look at him closely. "A tear?"

"Yes, a tear."

"On behalf of the victims?"

"On behalf of us. I thought . . ."

"You thought the whole world would flock after us, that we'd be pioneers."

"Well, yes."

"We are, in a way. And as such, we're occasionally beleaguered. We have to get the wagons in a circle, we have to send out war parties." The clean-shaven man looked at his watch. "I've got to get back to the office. I won't be around tonight. Some benefit. I'll be by tomorrow, though."

The man with the mustache shoved his hands in his pants pockets like a petulant boy. "With your wife?"

"My wife? Of course not. What a thing to say."

"I meant, are you going to the benefit with your wife?"

"Of course. Listen. Don't start. Okay?"

Singsong, the man with the mustache said, "Listen. Don't start. Okay?"

"Oh, christ. I haven't got time for this now."

"For me, you mean. You haven't got time for me."

"I'll see you tomorrow."

"A kiss. Can't I at least have a kiss?"

"Not here, for christ's sake."

"Please."

"Get fucked."

"Would you? Would you do it here in front of all these people?"

"Stop."

"I would. That's the difference, the real difference between us. You love to fuck with people watching, I love to fuck *you* with people watching."

"Not. So. Loud."

"I love you."

"I'll see you tomorrow."

"I love you."

"Christ."

"I *love* you."

18

IN THE MEADOWLANDS, A BRUSHFIRE smudged the sky. A west wind whipped the heat across the Turnpike. Driving through the fierce banner, the car shrieking, Cullen thought for the first time in a decade of Evel Knievel.

On the radio, Imus flirted with a listener who had called to wangle Mets tickets but really wanted a date. Imus liked her voice but was afraid she was a dog; she said she'd fax him her driver's-license picture. Imus played a Joe Pepitone bit Cullen had heard before and he switched to Dave Herman in time for the Morning Bruce Juice, appropriately, "Jersey Girl."

If Ann were there, she'd tell the story of her first trip to Los Angeles, how on the radio in the taxi from the airport was Bob Seger's "Hollywood Nights"; or she'd tell about the time she got ripped in the bathroom at the Market Diner and on the jukebox when she came out Brewer and Shipley sang "One Toke over the Line"; or the time she drove through a thunderstorm on the Taconic and just as the sky cleared the radio played the Beatles' "Here Comes the Sun"; or the time she broke up with a guy and went to the White Horse to feel sorry for herself and the bartender played a homemade tape with Dolly Parton's "Single Bars and Single Women." Ann could do five minutes on how often the right song was on the radio or the jukebox.

Dave Herman played the Stones' "Beast of Burden," then Guns N' Roses' "Patience," then "the number-one song in the land two years ago this week," Fine Young Cannibals' "She Drives Me Crazy."

If Ann were there, she would say she couldn't understand how come, if "She Drives Me Crazy" had been the number-one song in the land, Toni Childs's "Stop Your Fussin'" hadn't been a number-one song too. Ann thought "Stop Your Fussin'" was the best song that never got to be a hit since Suzanne Fellini's "Love on the Phone," that Toni Childs's failure to be hugely famous was the result of a conspiracy at least as insidious as Iran-Contra, since the plotters included her record company, which had released as a single "Don't Walk Away," the worst song on Toni's first album. Ann could do five minutes on Toni Childs.

Dave Herman played his anti-AIDS public-service spot, a couple of white guys sitting around rapping, urging men to "wrap the rascal." If Ann were there, she would say Dave Herman had gotten too commercial: he had a newscaster, a sportscaster, a weatherman, a traffic woman; he had contests, he played jingles. She had liked him better in the seventies when he'd done the show all by himself and the only regular features were the Morning Bruce Juice and Old, New, Borrowed, and Blue. If she were here, she'd recall how on nice days Dave had sometimes given his listeners permission to "call in well" and take the day off; she would tell the story of how she and other listeners had called the station to help Dave trick Vin Scelsa, the late-night man, into switching shifts with Dave, ostensibly so that Vin would concede that morning drive was harder than late-night but really to help Dave get away early on his vacation. And she'd recall how Vin, on K-Rock on Sunday nights now, Mister Opinion, flogging Anne Tyler novels and playing garage tapes by obscure Jersey bands, had introduced a cut the other day saying "Who would have thought at the time that we would one day feel nostalgic for the Clash?" And she'd wonder how Vin, who so clearly loved his wife and daughter, could write for *Penthouse*. Ann could do five minutes on Dave Herman and/or Vin Scelsa. She could do five minutes on longing for what when it had been present had been merely average. She could do five minutes on men who thought of their penises as rascals.

The Parkway now: Woodbridge, Perth Amboy. If Ann were there, she'd recall a *New Yorker* cartoon she'd had up on her refrigerator for a while: a couple in a car approaching a highway exit marked *Yo, the Amboys.*

Cullen switched back to Imus in time to hear him say the fax of the driver's license was too dark and he couldn't make out the woman's face. If Ann were there, she would do five minutes on Imus's agoraphobia, on Charles McCord's talent as a straight man, on Lisa Glassberg's inability to pronounce "cellular." She would do five minutes on how she missed Roz Frank, five minutes on fax machines.

Back to Dave. The smoke was a memory and the sky was almost too blue. Dave's weatherman said it was Ten Best Days of the Year number thirteen and Dave played Jimi Hendrix singing about kissing the sky.

If Ann were there, if Ann were there . . . They hadn't had a fight, exactly, they just hadn't spoken since the night Maslosky called with the news that Rickey Henderson had been K'd.

All right, all right—that was revisionist. The problem had begun before the phone call, the problem had begun before that night, the problem was older than water.

"I'M SORRY," Cullen had said after telling Ann the gist of Maslosky's call. "Sorry to bring murder into your house."

"Murder is your business," Ann had said.

"I'm sorry about *that.*"

"I knew what I was getting into. And anyway, that's not what's upsetting me. What's upsetting me is what we've been talking about. . . . You've forgotten already, haven't you?"

"No."

"What were we talking about?"

"Ann."

"That's how my father used to say 'Ann.' It meant I'd done something ineffably stupid or intensely irritating."

"I don't want to have this conversation: The Difference in Our Ages."

"The difference in our ages doesn't account for the difference in our outlooks. I want to get married, you don't."

"I've never said I didn't want to, I just said I didn't want to now."

Ann was sitting on the edge of the bed, still naked but all business: Urban Jungle Girl Says What She Needs *And* What She Wants. "You're happy the way things are. You've got your time with your kids, you've got your time to yourself, you've got your time with me. I'm not *al*together *un*happy with the way things are myself. I haven't figured out, for example, what responsibilities I want to have toward your kids: Do I want to legally be their stepmother, do I want it spelled out what my role would be if something happened to you *and* to Connie and to Doug? I don't know."

Who was Doug? Oh, right—Connie's new husband, Doug Aiello, no relation to Danny (though the Bon Jovi wanna-be kept asking Doug if he was sure, because Danny had been in that movie with Cher and more than the Bon Jovi wanna-be wanted to be Bon Jovi, he wanted to meet Cher). Doug wasn't new at all, he'd been married to Connie for nine years, three years longer than Cullen had been married to her. Doug *was* new, though, insofar as Cullen was worn. "I don't know either. That's something we'd have to talk about."

"The point, Joe, is this: your life's complicated, mine's not. I could do with a little complication, but not as much as you've got. If someone comes along—"

"Like Perry the happy craftsman?"

She gave him a *Watch it, Flinchley* look. "—someone who's not so complicated but could do with a little complication himself—"

"Kids, you mean."

"Kids, I mean."

"Marriage."

"Yes. If someone like that comes along, I'm going to be real interested in getting to know him a little better."

"I see."

"Joe, don't look so beaten down. You've got a fighting chance. If I said I was looking for a four-hundred-pound Samoan whose pastimes were the oboe and Texas lap dancing, then you wouldn't have a chance. But I'm not talking physical, I'm not talking mental, I'm not talking superficial. I'm looking for someone who'll take some risks along with me. I know you've already taken some risks—having kids is a risk—but you haven't taken them with me. I want to do a little emotional hang-gliding and I don't want to fly solo." She waved a hand, as if to say she didn't want that metaphor in the record. "I'm too tired to say just what I mean. Think about it, okay? This isn't an ultimatum, it's not a threat, but it's something more than just a vague notion. . . . You better go. Duty calls."

And go he had. He had kissed her first, and she had kissed him back, but she hadn't gotten up to do it and hadn't made room for him on the edge of the bed to sit and kiss her, so there had been no embrace, no thighs and hips and stomachs and chests brought into play. No real contact, just . . . well, just a vague notion.

PARKED DOWN the street from Blond Tommy Muldoon's house in Little Silver, a split-level with a high chain-link fence around it, a satellite dish on the lawn, and a big wide gas-guzzling Coupe de Ville in the driveway, Cullen was reminded of parking down the street at one time or another from the split-level fenced-in houses of mafiosi.

A mafioso or his sidemen, though, would have made a staked-out cop; Blond Tommy came out of the house and got in his car like a man with no secrets, with barely a look at what kind of day it was. He drove thoughtlessly too, skimming through stop signs as he made his way out of the back streets to the main drag. He turned without signaling into a McDonald's and hogged two parking places, one of them reserved for handicapped drivers.

When Blond Tommy had ordered and sat down, Cullen went inside, got a coffee, and sat with a booth between them. Tommy had gotten two sausage-and-egg biscuits and two coffees. He put three creams and four sugars in one of the coffees and ate both biscuits. He ate as if destroying evidence. He drank off the first coffee and put cream and sugar in the second. He read a local paper while he ate and it wasn't until he finished the sports section that he looked up and noticed Cullen. He just slumped and shook his head, like a man who has once again had his worst opinion of his fellow man confirmed.

"Shit, hoss." The moniker went with Blond Tommy's outfit, serious western—Resistol hat, Larry Mahan boots, something-or-other silver belt. Cullen had forgotten what little he'd known from the time when Zimmerman had gone briefly cowboy, shopping at Billy

Martin's and Whiskey Dust, eating at the Cowgirl Hall of Fame restaurant (*"Call* Girl Hall of Fame?" Ann had deliberately misheard him), until a woman Zimmerman had liked, a writer who had since moved to Los Angeles to work on *Murphy Brown,* had told a joke: "Why is a cowboy hat like a hemorrhoid? . . . Because sooner or later, every asshole gets one."

"I know, hoss," Blond Tommy said to Cullen. "You're on your way to Atlantic City, you stopped off for breakfast. Had no idea you'd run into me. Or don't you gamble? 'Course you don't, 'cause you're a pussy. You can drag a pussy to the edge of the envelope, but you got to beat him to death to teach him one fucking new thang."

Cullen had to smile at Blond Tommy's mixing of metaphors. He more than mixed them, he puréed them.

"Still kissing the PC's ass, hoss?" Blond Tommy said.

There *was* a pattern to the mentions that Cullen and Hriniak were friends: Those who did the mentioning were friends of neither his nor Hriniak's. It was that simple. "Everybody says hello, Tom."

Blond Tommy drank off his second coffee and crushed the container, as if it were Cullen. "Bullshit. They fuck you over, you stay fucked over, they don't fucking send their fucking regards. What's so fucking funny, Cullen?"

"What's so funny, Tommy, is how time plays tricks on you. You called it quits just in time not to have to answer some questions about drinking buddies of yours who were up on a hijacking rap. There were those in IAU who were for keeping on breaking your hump; there were others who thought you should have the benefit of a doubt as a retirement present. You did bust Carlos Pelaga, Tommy, no one's ever forgotten that, it

117

was a classic, you're a legend. So nobody cut you loose, Tommy, you jumped, and you were very lucky there wasn't a noose around your neck to bring you up short." Cullen sat back and got his breath. This was what happened when guys started shredding Styrofoam in your face: you talked back tough and purple.

Blond Tommy gripped the table of his booth so hard it yelped. "Yeah? So? Go ahead, hoss—break my hump. You didn't have a fucking thing on me then, you don't have a fucking thing on me now.... The fuck're you going?"

Cullen dropped his coffee cup in the trash and went out to the parking lot and got in the passenger's side of the Coupe de Ville. He turned on the radio: Country 103.5, Hank Williams, Jr., "All My Rowdy Friends Have Settled Down." If Ann were there ...

There was a pay phone just outside the door of the McDonald's and Blond Tommy made a call from it. He punched in a bunch of numbers, which meant he was paying with a credit card, but it could have been a local call or it could have been long distance. Whatever kind of call it was, it was a call Blond Tommy didn't want to kick Cullen out of his car and make from the portable cellular phone sitting right there on the front seat.

Acting like he was just getting comfortable, Cullen slid down in the seat and sprang the glove-compartment lock with his knee. He rummaged among the usual shit and found two videocassettes with handwritten labels: One label said *Girl Duos*, the other said *Girl Solos*. You didn't need to be Karnak the Magnificent to know that they weren't tapes of the Judds and Ann Murray, that the first had sets of two girls doing it to each other, the second, single girls doing it alone. Cullen put the cassettes back and shut the compartment with his knee.

Blond Tommy finished before the song did. He sauntered over to the car, looking every which way this time, wondering if Cullen had backup or had he gone rogue or what. He got in and turned off the radio just as Hank Junior finished and Lucinda Williams started singing "Passionate Kisses."

"I like that song," Cullen said. *Cullen* could do five minutes on Lucinda Williams, on her superiority to the inexplicably popular Nanci Griffith.

"Fuck the song," Blond Tommy said. "And fuck you, hoss."

Cullen smiled. "What'd your lawyer have to say?"

"He said you got a warrant or a subpoena, bring it by his office."

"Where's his office?"

"Miami Beach."

Cullen laughed. "Do you ever miss it, Tommy, police work? Or is due diligence the same thing? It probably is: you try to find things out, people try to keep you from finding them out; you talk out of the side of your mouth, they talk out of the sides of theirs. You have a calendar on your watch? A date thing, I mean?"

Blond Tommy cupped a protective hand over the face of his watch, suspicious. "Yeah. So?"

"So today's—what?—the tenth?"

Blond Tommy peeked. "So?"

"So it's just five weeks over five years since your wife disappeared. You probably heard Diana Romano got married. To Tony Justice. The newspaper guy?"

Cullen longed to see Blond Tommy's face, but he made himself keep looking straight ahead. Tommy's voice sounded pale, though. "The fuck're you fishing for, Cullen? The *fuck* are you fishing for?"

"I don't fish, Tom. I don't gamble, you were right, I don't fish, I don't do anything that requires a whole lot of luck or very much patience. Rickey Henderson was K'd.

119

I know you heard that too. He caught the Karen Justice job. Justice's first wife? She turned up near Hell Gate minus her head, hands, and feet. You read about that too. There's a very good chance Justice was having a thing with Diana Romano before his wife disappeared, just the way you were having a thing with Diana Romano before your wife—"

It was a measure of Blond Tommy's skill at such things that the forearm he slammed into Cullen's neck didn't kill him, just advertised how easy it would have been. Blond Tommy leaned across Cullen, smiling when Cullen flinched a little as he did. He opened the door and pushed it wide with his fingertips. "Mosey, hoss."

Cullen got out somehow, for he couldn't breathe, couldn't see clearly, didn't have a real good sense of which way out was, or up. He thought the Coupe de Ville came very close to his toes as Blond Tommy backed up, but he was reluctant to look down to make sure, lest he topple into the car.

He blinked and blinked and gasped and hawked and was able to focus on one thing before Blond Tommy lurched out into traffic: Blond Tommy's license plate said SOUTHPAW, which Cullen guessed meant Blond Tommy was a lefty, which made Cullen glad Tommy had hit him right-handed.

Two things: Blond Tommy drove out the In driveway.

19

"MISTER SLATE? *OGDEN?*"

"Hello, N-Neil."

"What're you, uh ...?" But Zimmerman couldn't say it, couldn't ask Ogden Slate what he was doing there. He couldn't ask because he knew the answer, there could be only one.

"How's your mother, Neil?" Slate hurdled lightly the discarded question. He was a world-class small-talker, an expert at prodding reluctant conversations along steep winding paths. The investment banker was outfitted for his trek in a white linen suit, blue shirt, blue bowtie with white polka dots, blue canvas deck shoes. His teeth, hair, fingernails, jewelry, all were gleaming. He would have stood out more—but not much more—in a tutu and tights.

"She's, uh, fine. Fine. She's fine."

"Knew that, actually. Had dinner with her yesterday, ha ha," Slate said, uncharacteristically overcome by the altitude, by the ridiculousness of it all.

"Ha ha," Zimmerman agreed.

"Ha ha."

"Ha ha. . . . How's Michelle?" And what do you think a newspaper article about her was doing on the bulletin board of a dead cop who was into voyeurism in his spare time?

"Tip-top. Ha ha."

"Ha ha."

And then, like the Mad Hatter (or was it the White Rabbit? Zimmerman's mother would remember; he would ask her the next time he went over for dinner—and would ask her what *she* thought a newspaper article about Michelle Slate was doing on the bulletin board of

121

a dead cop who was into voyeurism in his spare time),
Ogden Slate was gone, leaving Zimmerman all alone
with the burden of his enlightenment.

IT HAD been a day for finding things out:

Zimmerman had found out that between five and
nine on the Sunday night Rickey Henderson got K'd at
the Port Authority, Detective Alonzo Paul, Midtown
North Squad, had indeed been at dinner at his mother's
in farthest east Far Rockaway, practically in another
time zone.

"Who says he wasn't?" Alonzo's mother said
through the screen door.

Zimmerman, kept standing on the porch of the wea-
thered frame house, couldn't see her because of the way
the light fell. A confessional must be like this, he imagined. But which of them was giving absolution? "No one
says he wasn't here, ma'am. All we want to know is—"

"Who's 'we'?" Alonzo's mother pushed her face up
against the screen and tried to see into the corners of the
porch. "Who's there 'sides you?"

"All the P*olice* Department wants to know, ma'am,
is your son's whereabouts when certain other events
were transpiring."

Alonzo's mother said, "Hunh?" and Zimmerman
couldn't blame her. There was no course at the Police
Academy on Interrogating Suspects' Mothers, and even
a twenty-year man like Cullen could lose himself in the
maze of his own circumlocution while talking to one.
Best to just let her have it. "A cop was killed Sunday
night at the Port Authority bus station. Alonzo and the
victim were, uh, interested in the same woman."

Alonzo's mother unhooked the screen door and
pushed it open. "You want to come in, come in."

Zimmerman went in.

"You're in, sit."

He sat where she pointed.

"You're staying, have some ice tea."

Still a little bit his own man, Zimmerman said, "No thanks. I'd just like to confirm Alonzo's account of where he was that night."

"His alibi, you mean?"

"His alibi."

Alonzo's mother didn't pretend to think it over to make it seem more credible. "He got here around five, I guess, right around the seventh inning of the Mets versus the Hollyweird Dodgers, right when Jefferies kicked that double-play ball. Couldn't you, like, go to the videotape, confirm what time that was?"

Zimmerman smiled. "Yes, we could go to the video-tape."

"Jefferies is a candy-ass cry-baby." Alonzo's mother made her voice candy-ass cry-baby high. " 'I don't wanna play second base. Please don't make me play second base. A runner might could try and take me out. I might could hurt myself.' Shit. He should go around to Twenty-second and Seagirt, tell it to the junkies lamping there. They'd be real happy to go play second base for him for what he gets paid. They'd play with no mitt on. They'd play barefoot on a field of fire. Shit.

"I'd already cooked up some chicken in the cool of the morning," Alonzo's mother went on. "We ate in the living room and watched the game. We had chicken and cornbread and salad and ice tea. Alonzo had a beer, just one, he was driving, he knows when to say when. The Hollyweird Dodgers won five-three in eleven. I hate those sons-of-bitches almost more than I hate the Yankees. They ever play each other again the way they did back in seventy-seven, seventy-eight, I'll root for a neuron bomb to fall on the park.

"After the game we switched over to "Sixty Minutes," after that we watched "Murder, She Wrote." Alonzo kept his promise to me to for a change not run his mouth about how any resemblance between "Murder, She Wrote" and real-life police work is purely coincidental. On top of that, he was wrong about who done it, it wasn't the lawyer, like he thought, it was the ballet dancer.

"He washed the dishes, Alonzo, he went home ten, fifteen minutes after nine. He called me to tell me he was safe home. That was just after ten, 'cause I was watching the news, watching the videotape of candy-ass cry-baby Jefferies kicking that double-play ball again."

Like all good alibis, it was colorless, and loosed a million new questions. If not Alonzo . . . because of . . . then who . . . and why?

Alonzo's mother had a question too. "Who's the woman? Not that bald bitch?"

". . . Bald?"

"One of those, you know, skinned heads. She's a cop groupie, works in a diner downtown where lots of cops go."

"Not, uh, Jan Spellman?"

"See? You know her too."

"Alonzo's seeing Jan Spellman?"

Alonzo's mother tipped back laughing. " 'Seeing'? Sweetknees, I'm the boy's momma, I don't fool myself that all he's doing is 'seeing' her. The young lady likes po-leecemen, 'specially when the meat is dark."

AND ZIMMERMAN had found out that Alan Lang, the radio talk-show host, had had Rickey Henderson as a guest more than once, so frank was Rickey about his perversion, so like a fish did he take to the water of Shock Radio.

"Have a seat, Neil, take a load off your feet. The Rickster? Jesus, babe, I swear to God, man. I broke in this racket the year after Marconi, man, and I have seen only a few amateurs with the *cojones* of the Rickster to sit down at a fifty-thousand-watt clear-channel mike and tell listeners in ten states what a pervert he is and to what degree, bro. The Rickster loved it, man, he especially loved when listeners called to say how much he disgusted them, how they scrubbed their radios with Lysol, man, after listening to him, how the station should give away rubber gloves, babe, rubber *suits*, man, when the Rickster was going on the air. Most guests, Neil, no matter who it is, unless it is some pablum-puking bleeding heart, it is *me* the listeners wind up getting PO'd at, babe. With Dex, it was invariably him. Dexter was his *nom de* airwaves. The Dex."

They were in the studio where in an hour Lang would do his show: the only light was a gooseneck halogen lamp on the engineer's board; it was as cold as a meat locker; acoustical carpeting and paneling dulled every sound. All in black with black Serengeti Drivers, Lang was hard to make out. Could questions raised by events in the outside world be answered satisfactorily in this place of deprived senses? "Did any callers ever threaten him?" Zimmerman said. "Did he ever say anything about threats off the air? At home, in the mail, whatever?"

"Hey, Neil, threats, man? You are in call-in radio, bro, you do *not* get threats, you begin to worry, you begin to ask yourself certain fundamental questions, questions on the order of: *What the fuck am I doing wrong? Did I not say* some*thing that offended* some*body?* Holy shit, I hope

125

the PD does not hear about it. PD is inside radio for program director, babe; it does not mean what it means to you, Police Department.

"The Rickster grooved on the outrage, bro, he dug it, got off on it, got high. The Rickster was born to be broadcast. He would call my producer sometimes, Neil, if he had been on a show during a sweeps period, to see how the ratings had been. He was the perfect guest. I hope he gets his own show in heaven, babe, he will get a ten share, man. Easy."

"The threats did not concern him, then? They were not threats to be taken seriously?" Now Zimmerman was doing it—talking without contractions, like Nathan Detroit.

"Seriously, bro? I take all threats seriously, man. We all do. After the Berg thing, babe, the thing in Denver, all us talk-jocks do. Soon as I heard the Rickster bought it, bro, the first thought through my mind, *the first thought—af*ter thinking What a Terrible Tragedy, of course, *after* thinking The Poor Rickster's Family and Loved Ones—*the* first thought was Holy shit, I probably actually *know* who took out the poor son-of-a-bitch, I have probably actually *talked* to the guy who took him out, because the guy who took him out is probably actually one of my *lis*teners."

"Any thoughts on which one?"

"Hey, babe, it could be any one of them. *The* one who took out the Rickster it grieves me to say I do *not* know."

"Did the listeners know the guest who called himself Dexter was a cop? Did he ever mention his work on the air?"

Lang put a finger up, like, Now *there* is an interesting question. "One time. Not on the air, but after a show, we were sitting right here, the Rickster and me, shooting the shit, finishing up our coffee, kind of half-listening to Les

126

Glatter's show. Les was in Studio B, talking about Ray Brand. It was a week or so after he died, it was finally official that it was AIDS, people were still surprised that a macho hunk like Ray Brand was turning out to have been a little light in his loafers.

"I was saying something like I was surprised you could keep something like that a secret considering that if you were light in the loafers yourself and had been in the sack with Ray Brand, you would probably have to fight off an understandable inclination to brag about it, the way a straight cat would feel full of himself if he had been in the sack with—who?—Kim Basinger. Am I right, Neil? If you had been in the sack with Kim Basinger, would you not want to tell somebody about it, and not even necessarily somebody you knew all that well?"

Zimmerman was bored by Kim Basinger, his fantasy was for Laura San Giacomo and Mary Elizabeth Mastrantonio—small dark girls with big names. But he nodded.

"I said I wondered if maybe Ray Brand had had to pay out some hush money," Lang said. "The Rickster said he would not be surprised if it had been hush money in considerable quantities. Being a Ray Brand fan—hell, who was not?—the Rickster said he certainly hoped Ray Brand had not also had to have anybody killed. He said he was working on a case where it looked like someone might have gotten killed because somebody did not want it known he was gay. I was a little surprised to hear that. I guess you guys handle more than one case at a time, but I had read in the papers that the Rickster was working on the Karen Justice thing, Karen Justice who did an Amelia Earhart."

Zimmerman's mother had sometimes talked about hearing the news that Amelia Earhart's plane was missing; she ranked it in indelibility with Pearl Harbor and Roosevelt's death and Hiroshima and the Kennedys and Martin Luther King and the *Challenger*. Other than that she had disappeared, Zimmerman didn't know anything about Amelia Earhart. He would have to ask his mother about Amelia Earhart the next time he went over for dinner. He wondered if Alan Lang, who was somewhere in that unknowable space between Zimmerman's age and Zimmerman's mother's, knew about Amelia Earhart from *his* mother or from memory. "And that was it?"

"Someone came in, my producer or somebody, and we got off the subject. It was the PD, come to think of it and speaking of PD's. He wanted the Rickster to know what a terrific guest he was and me to know I was still the finest talk-show host in North America. I said Make that the world, Rick—the PD is also a Rick; all PD's are named Rick, unless they're named Scott—and since that is the case, how come you are getting away paying me only eight hundred grand a year?"

Zimmerman wasn't especially good with numbers, but he was able to calculate that he would have earned eight hundred grand around the time he had worked long enough to retire.

AND ZIMMERMAN had found out that of all the facts Rickey Henderson had assembled about the murder of Karen Justice, the one he liked the most, his favorite, the one he hummed in the shower, and sometimes just sat and stared at the idea of, was Karen Justice's squash racquet.

"Squash racquet?" Yale-New Haven '76, Zimmerman knew whom he expected to say squash racquet and whom he didn't. He no more expected Bobby Trumbo to say squash racquet than to sing "The Whiffenpoof Song."

Bobby Trumbo was Rickey Henderson's roommate at the apartment in Bayside where Henderson had nominally lived, and Zimmerman could understand why maybe Rickey had preferred living in New Jersey. Bobby Trumbo was a wrestlemaniac, and had turned the apartment into a Smithsonian of his fanaticism, a chapel of love: posters, autographed pictures, magazine covers, newspaper clippings, buttons, banners, shreds of capes and mantles, facsimiles of masks and helmets and war bonnets, replicas of championship belts with elephantine buckles—the walls dripped memorabilia.

In the place of honor was a photograph of Bobby himself. It had been made at an exhibition (Bobby called it a "bout") at Madison Square Garden (Bobby called it "the square garden"), the night a referee had disqualified the current local hero for what most of the crowd—including Bobby—had perceived to be a mere misdemeanor. Bobby, near ringside, had been struck above the left eye by a shoe fired from the cheap seats. Snapped at a first-aid station under the stands, he smiled for the camera and fingered his Band-Aid lovingly, a valediction in blood.

"It's a game like handball, you know what I'm saying?" Bobby swung his arm back and forth mechanically.

"I know what *squash* is, Bobby," Zimmerman said. "I don't understand what Karen Justice's racquet has to do with anything."

Bobby Trumbo explained, offering a warmed-over soup of policese and shorthand that had been concocted by his late roommate: "Karen Justice disappeared last seventeen September, you know what I'm saying? A night porter in her office building, Six-one and Mad, saw her get in a cab, headed, most likely, for her apartment at Eight-one and CPW, carrying a briefcase and a squash racquet. She played squash three or four times a week at the Vertical Club, Six-one between One and Two, either early, before work, or at lunchtime, you know what I'm saying? That day, a Monday, she didn't play, but she was set to go to Boston the next day on business and had a date to play with somebody at the Harvard Club, or maybe just at Harvard, the gym or something, you know what I'm saying? . . . You all right, Detective?"

Inculcated—inoculated, practically—while at Yale-New Haven, with antipathy to Harvard, Zimmerman was feeling a stirring in his gut that clearly showed on his face as well. "Yeah. Fine. Long day. Go on."

"She didn't play squash that day, she was supposed to play in Boston the next day, so she sent her secretary around to the Vertical Club to get her racquet out of her locker, she'd take it home with her that night. Karen never made it home, but the racquet did. Rickey always wondered how that could be."

"Rickey found Karen Justice's squash racquet in her apartment?" Zimmerman said.

"In her bedroom closet, you know what I'm saying?"

"Maybe she had two racquets."

"I don't know anything about squash." Bobby Trumbo added redundantly: "I'm a wrestling fan, you know what I'm saying? But from what I understand of what Rickey said, the racquet was an older kind of racquet—wood instead of fiberglass or whatever, made by hand. The manufacturer used to put a number on each one, a registration number, you know what I'm saying, so you could have another racquet made to the same specs—"

130

"Bancroft," Zimmerman said. "The racquet was a Bancroft."

Bobby Trumbo gave Zimmerman a nod of approval that few non-wrestlemaniacs had ever earned. "How'd you know that?"

Because he was Yale-New Haven '76, and knew a squash racquet from a handsaw, and especially one crafted of wood from one bent out of something synthetic. "So Rickey checked the registration number?"

"And there was only one made," Bobby Trumbo said. "The one in Karen Justice's bedroom closet."

"And did Rickey have a theory on how the racquet got there?"

Bobby Trumbo shrugged. "I don't see how he could *not* have a theory, you know what I'm saying? But he kept it to himself."

"What about Tony Justice? How did he explain the racquet's being there?"

"Rickey never asked Justice about it. The racquet was Rickey's trump card."

Zimmerman wondered when he had hoped to play it, or if he already had. "Did Rickey ever tell you about his picture collection?"

"What picture collection?"

"Did he ever tell you about his being on the radio?"

"*Rick*ey?"

"Did he ever mention a woman named Michelle Slate?"

"She somebody he went out with before Dee? Long as I've known Rickey, he was only with Dee."

"Did he ever talk about AIDS?"

"You mean about . . . having it?"

"Having it, being afraid of having it, knowing someone who had it?"

Trumbo shrugged. "Well, you know, Ray Brand was like Rickey's favorite actor. He was real shook-up by that. Rickey didn't screw around. I mean, he and Dee had their donnybrooks, just like anybody else, but if he ever got any on the side, he never said anything about it to me."

"Did he ever say Karen Justice's K had something to do with AIDS?"

Trumbo made a face at that. "You're bullshitting me, right? Didn't you and your partner have a meet with Rickey about a week before he got polished?"

"We did, yes."

"And you reminded him in case he forgot or maybe he never knew it in the first place that Tony Justice's new wife used to be tight with Blond Tommy Muldoon."

"That's right."

"And you reminded him in case he forgot or maybe he never knew it in the first place that just like Karen Justice went off the scope when Tony Justice was maybe getting tight with another femme, Blond Tommy Muldoon's wife went off the scope when Blond Tommy was tight with the same femme."

"That's right."

"So he went to the Port Authority to meet a guy who knew something about it."

" 'It'?"

"You know—the whole megillah."

"Why the Port Authority?"

"He didn't say."

"Did he say what guy?"

Trumbo shook his head. "At the time, it didn't seem like a major omission, you know what I'm saying? I may not've even noticed that he didn't tell me what guy. Someone's telling you something sometimes, you're not expecting them to get K'd, to be in a condition where they're unable to tell you everything they didn't tell you in the first place, you don't notice what they're *not* telling you, you know what I'm saying?"

"He did say *guy*—as opposed to woman."

"He said guy."

Zimmerman touched Bobby Trumbo's shoulder. "Thanks, Bobby. Sorry about your friend."

Bobby Trumbo nodded. "Yeah. Hey, listen, good luck. You know what I'm saying?"

AND ZIMMERMAN had found out from the clerk at the sports-accessories store on the mezzanine, Port Authority south wing, that the man Rickey Henderson had talked to after buying his University of Nevada-Las Vegas baseball cap hadn't looked at all like Blond Tommy Muldoon and had maybe looked something like Tony Justice or maybe he hadn't.

Zimmerman hadn't had time to put together a good ID package, and showed the clerk, Kareem Jordan, a Xerox copy of a year-old photograph of Blond Tommy from his last pistol permit. And he showed Kareem Jordan a photograph of Tony Justice clipped from a New York *Bulletin* house ad for Justice's column. The photograph of Blond Tommy was badly lit and contrasty; the photograph of Tony Justice was grainy. Neither photograph was as interesting to Kareem Jordan as the photographs in the copy of *Tawny* he was paging through down behind the register. But he took a second look at the photograph of Blond Tommy.

"This homeboy big?" Kareem Jordan said.

"Six-two, two-twenty, maybe more. The last time I saw him, about six months ago, his hair was a lot longer, almost to his shoulders."

"He was here," Kareem Jordan said.

133

"When?"

"That day."

"The day the officer was killed?"

"Uh-hunh." Kareem went back to his magazine.

"You're sure?"

"Word up."

"Before the shooting? After? When?"

"Before. Early. I start at noon, it was a little after noon."

"Here in the store or outside, on the mezzanine?"

Turning pages, Kareem said, "He bought something. I forget what. Paid with plastic. Copped a 'tude with me when I gave him the carbons, like he didn't want to get his fingers dirty."

"Whom do I see to get the credit-card receipts?"

"Manager. He'll be in in the morning."

"This other picture—any other thoughts?"

Kareem Jordan turned *Tawny* around for another angle on a photograph. "Like I said, thin lips, straight hair, no mojo working, you white folks tend to look kind of all alike to me."

"Thanks. Thanks a lot."

AND NOW, standing outside the sports store on the mezzanine, Port Authority south wing, bus exhaust fumes seeping in from the bus levels above and below to season the smell of pizza and boiled hot dogs and cigars and cigarettes and industrial-strength disinfectant and incense burned by a vendor in a caftan, on his table of wares a sign saying *I ♡ Allah*, listening to the babble of Latins, West Indians, Koreans dialing long distance direct, using purloined calling-card numbers, Zimmerman found out something that he could tell his mother the next time he went over for dinner, in exchange for her telling him whether it was the Mad Hatter or the White Rabbit and what, besides disappear, Amelia Earhart had done.

He could tell her that Ogden Slate, of the investment-banking firm of Tindale, Slate and Cooper, dweller of a neighboring Park Avenue penthouse and a neighboring East Hampton beach house, married to a woman who, along with Zimmerman's mother, raised money for innumerable good causes (not the least of them the fight against AIDS), in his spare time picked over the slim black and brown and yellow boys in tight bright clothes who vogued for, while pretending indifference to, furtive white men shopping for fast sex.

20

TENNY CULLEN STOPPED AT THE edge of the woods. "What about ticks?"

Val Fox kept on going. Just a few steps and she vanished. Her voice came back. "What about them?"

"My mom said look out for them, okay? She said Shelter Island's famous for ticks, they live in high grass like this." Tenny felt wack standing on the verge of Route 114, Shelter Island's only serious road, talking to the trees, so she went through the high grass so fast only a very fast tick could jump on her, and ran after Val, who had a destination in mind and was walking briskly.

It took a while, but Tenny caught up and struggled to keep up. Between breaths she said, "I just don't want to get sick . . . okay? My mom's cousin lives in Lyme . . . Connecticut."

"So?" Val said.

"So it's called Lyme Dis*ease*, okay? . . . The disease you get from the ticks. My mom's cousin has a friend . . . who got bitten. She has arthritis so bad . . . she can barely open and close . . . her hands."

Val sped on. "If you want to go back to the house, Tenny, then go. I'm going to the meadow."

"Well, do one thing . . . for me then."

"What?"

"Slow . . . down!"

Val stopped and waited for Tenny to catch up.

"Thanks."

"Sorry. I'm used to hiking alone."

"Oh, pardon me."

"Tenny, I didn't mean anything by it, okay? It's just a fact, okay? Let it go, okay?"

136

"Okay, okay?" Tenny concentrated on stepping on nothing, brushing against nothing that looked like a haven for ticks. She could hear the ticks shouting *Here comes another sucker* and hear tick trumpeters playing tantaras. "What does it mean anyway, Mashomack?"

"It's not *Mash*omack," Val said. "It's Ma*sho*mack."

"Well, what does it mean?"

"It's some Indian word."

"High Grass Where Ticks Live," Tenny said.

Val laughed and put her arm around Tenny's waist.

"It's good to hear you laugh," Tenny said. "You don't laugh much these days. I understand why, but you don't."

They walked on. The air was heavy with heat and humidity and the smell of sap and earth. Tenny felt drowsy, as if they'd walked a very long way, instead of just down the drive of the big old white house, and a little way along a paved road past an apple orchard, then out onto 114 and across it. Or did she already have Lyme Disease? "Well, who owns Ma*sho*mack?"

"Nobody. It's a nature preserve.... Listen."

They were walking single file now, along a path traveled only just enough before them to be called a path. There were hardly any birds singing and they could hear the whoosh of an occasional car on 114, a light plane overhead. Then they heard again a heavy, anomalistic clank.

"So like what was that, okay?" Tenny said, thinking about Jason, thinking about Freddy Kruger.

"The ferry gates," Val said, keeping on.

"The *ferry*? We're nowhere *near* the ferry."

"We're not that far. We've been heading south. And sound travels different out here." At a fork in the path, Val went left. Pointing right, she said, "If we took that path, we'd come to Smith Cove, to a beach where you could see the ferry. We can go there tomorrow. It's pretty. Or we can take the Sunfish and sail around."

Tenny stopped. She didn't know why, but she asked, "Well, are there *ghosts*?"

From up ahead, Val—Tenny *thought* it was Val—laughed.

"I mean it, Val. *Are* there ghosts?"

Val hooked the air. "Don't be silly, come on." It was her Katharine Hepburn voice and it was what Hepburn says in *Desk Set* when she and Tracy get caught in the rain and he's nervous about going to her apartment to dry off. *Don't be silly, come on*, Hepburn says. She makes him stay for dinner and says *How do you like your chicken fried?* How do you like your chicken fried? was what Val's mother had said to Val every time she got ready to make chicken, which she never fried, she slow-baked it after rubbing it with tarragon and stuffing it with a few tarragon leaves—a Shaker recipe.

Tenny hadn't budged, so Val went back and took her by the hand and led her along the path a little farther, then out from under the canopy to a meadow swarmed over by bees and dragonflies and gnats and the pollen of a thousand wildflowers. A million.

"Oh, wow," Tenny whispered.

"Radical, *non*?" Val said.

"No ghosts here." Tenny took a look back over her shoulder at the woods, all the darker now that they were out in the light. Perhaps there was another way back, across a field and alongside a broad, bright river. Did islands *have* rivers?

Val sat on a hard hummock and leaned back on her hands. "There's *something* special here, though. I used to come here with Momma. Fairies lived here, she thought."

138

Tenny looked around for fairy middens, but there were none. She looked back at Val and saw that she was weeping. Tenny squatted down next to her and put her arms around her. After a while, her legs ached, so she sat and held Val in her lap and tried not to think about the ticks lining up at the hem of her shorts, ready to charge up her thigh.

When Val could finally speak, she said, "I don't know if it's better to be with you, or worse. I don't cry when I'm by myself."

"Then it's better," Tenny said. "Being with me, I mean."

"But I *cry*."

"It's not good to hold it in."

"I don't know how to behave anymore. I don't know who I am or what I'm supposed to do. When my dad was killed and Momma started, you know, going out with Tony, well, I was her daughter and he was her boyfriend and that made sense, I knew who I was. And then they got married and I was still her daughter and he was my stepfather and that made sense too.

"Now, though, well, Momma made Tony my guardian—in her will; she doesn't have any brothers or sisters and her parents are dead—and so that's who Tony is—my guardian. And Diana's Tony's wife, and sort of my stepmother, I guess, except she's not really, because he's not really my step*father* anymore.

"And that's not the point anyway. The point is, who am *I*? I mean, I'm like an orphan who's not an orphan. I mean, I kind of sort of have a family. Some kids don't have any family at all, so I guess I'm like better off than they are. And I have friends and, you know, stuff I like to do, activities and all. But . . ."

Tenny waited. She could hear the head tick exhorting the other ticks to take no prisoners.

"Do you ever talk to your father about his, you know, girlfriends?" Val said.

"There's only one," Tenny said. "Ann. Ann Jones. Dad went out with her for like a year before he introduced her to me and my brother. I mean, it was like I guess he didn't want us to be where we had to, you know, think twice about saying stuff in front of Mom or anything. Anyway, I like her and my brother likes her. She was at your dad's wedding. I know he's not your dad, okay, but I don't know what else to call him. You call him Tony, but I can't call him Tony. My dad and Ann came out here to the wedding."

Val nodded. "I remember. We talked about you, Diana and I."

"Me?"

"She wanted to know if Stephanie was your real name. I told her it was."

"Oh, rad. Thanks. Great."

"She already *knew* it, okay? She said, 'Her name's Stephanie, isn't it?' What was I supposed to say—'I don't know'?"

"She *knew* my name?"

"I told her you were called Tenny because that's what your brother called you because he couldn't say Stephanie, okay? And *she* told me *she* has a sister *she* called Rivvy because when *she* was little *she* couldn't say Roberta."

"Hunh."

"Yeah, well, she was lying."

"Diana was lying?"

"*Yes!*"

"Don't yell at me, Val, okay?"

"I'm not yelling."

"You *are* yelling."

"*You're* yelling."

140

Tenny cocked her head and put up a hand. "Shhh."

"Well, you are," Val said.

"Val, shut up and listen. Someone's coming."

They listened. They heard the meadow, the bees, the dragonflies, the gnats, the birds, the trees and flowers and grasses and woods. They heard the sky. No light planes now, no cars, no ferries. No fairies.

"The ghosts're coming," Tenny said. She tried to hug Val but Val wriggled away on her belly, Indian-style, to where she could see the way they had come into the meadow.

Tenny lay as flat as she could on the floor of the meadow. She could feel the ticks racing all over her body, but it didn't matter. "No, no, no, no, no."

Val hissed at Tenny to be quiet and motioned her up alongside her.

Tenny crawled up next to Val, but was afraid to lift her head. There were ticks in her ears, in her nose, in her mouth. There were ticks crawling into her brain, into her vagina even. Still a virgin and she would have arthritis of the vagina. There would be stories about her in the *Enquirer*.

Val said, "Hunh."

Tenny said, "What?"

"Look."

"I can't look," Tenny said.

"Tenny, look, for God's sake, okay? There aren't any ghosts, okay?"

Tenny moved forward a little on her elbows, but still kept her head down.

"It's *her*. It *is* her? *Isn't* it her?"

"Who?"

"Look!"

Tenny looked, and saw not ghosts, but something strange. She saw Tony Justice, Val's guardian and maybe not her stepfather anymore, but *something* to her, something kind of sort of like family, saw him coming into the meadow with his hand on the arm of the woman Tenny and Val had been talking about just a little while ago, the woman Tenny's father had gone out with for like a year before Tenny and her brother met her, like maybe their father didn't want them to be where they had to, you know, think twice about saying anything in front of their mother or something. Ann Jones.

21

"ANN? I'LL BE DAMNED."

"Tony, hi."

It had been one of life's little coincidences, aboard the ferry *Shelter Island*, making the minuscule crossing of Shelter Island Sound from North Haven to Shelter Island. While the crewmen finished loading the cars, Ann Jones had climbed out of her red rented Lumina, Tony Justice out of his ancient blue Volvo wagon, parked one behind the other. They had leaned side by side over the starboard gunwale to look down into the foaming water; ghastly jellyfish wavered just below the surface. They had looked out into the glittering morning, then had finally seen each other—and, in each other's sunglasses, themselves.

Justice took his Vuarnets off and let them hang from a cord around his neck. "Visiting the island, or on your way to the North Fork?"

Ann would have liked to keep her Wayfarers on, the better to deceive him by, but in the spirit of his gesture she parked them up in her hair. "I'm having lunch at a friend's in Greenport. Orient, actually. I'm at Mark and Linda Talbert's in Water Mill for the weekend. And of course you're out here in your big old white house." She turned and pointed back down the sound. "That's it there in the trees, isn't it? Are you just getting out?"

"I came out yesterday," Justice said. "I had to go to the hardware store in Bridgehampton this morning. Why don't you stop by on your way back? Or come over for lunch tomorrow."

"I'd love to. I don't know if I'll have time. I hadn't planned on waiting half an hour to get on this ferry."

"You may wait even longer at the North Ferry. Con-

143

sider leaving your car on the Shelter Island side—there's parking at the North Ferry slip—and going across on foot. You can take a cab to Orient. It's worth it, if time's a factor; there'll be even more traffic this afternoon. Also: did you get to North Haven through Bridgehampton and Sag Harbor?"

"Speaking of traffic," Ann said.

Justice reached through his passenger window and got a map off the dash. He spread it on the Lumina's hood. "A shortcut going back. Take One-fourteen off the ferry to the first stop sign, a flashing red light. Left at the light would take you east, back the way you came, through Sag Harbor. Instead, go south about a mile— this is a beautiful beach, European-looking—to this intersection. There's a restaurant on the right, the Salty Dog. Go left and keep bearing right for about half a mile, past one, two, three forks, to this road. It's called Brick Kiln on the map, but Bricklin on the sign. You wind south through the woods another mile or so and when you come out you're on Scuttlehole. It's a wonderful spot, one of the highest points on Long Island, the terminal moraine of the last Ice Age glacier; you can see all the way to the ocean. West on Scuttlehole a couple of miles to the Montauk Highway, west again, and you're practically in Water Mill. You can keep the map."

Ann's neck hairs tingled with pleasure. This was classic summertalk, roads and place names, compass points and distances. (*Go a couple of blocks that way and make a left at the Papaya King*—that was as colorful as New Yorkers got to talk. Once in a lifetime you got to say *Great Jones Street* or *Little West Twelfth*.) And Justice looked the classic summerguy: a knit tennis shirt (not with anybody's silly logo on it, just *a shirt*), its original navy washed out of it until it was a nameless blue; white Lee painter's pants with rolled cuffs; navy espadrilles, new this season; a black-faced diving watch with yellow bezel and yellow rubber strap. Standing close to Ann as he'd traced the route with a fingertip (his little finger, Ann had remarked, less imperious than a forefinger, a finger for suggesting, not bullying), he had smelled good—not of any bottled scent but of sun and toolshed and hardware store and old car.

Ann stumbled as the ferry got under way and her breast bumped Justice's arm. He had put his shades back on to cut the glare off the map and she hadn't been able to tell if he had taken advantage of their closeness to look down her shirt. Why would he not have? It was a full-cut cotton shirt (only seven thousand dollars at Banana Republic) and they were, she had decided after a period of not liking them, nice breasts. And he was a man and wasn't that what men did—looked down your shirt, between your buttons, up your sleeve, as if your breasts were lodestones and their eyes little iron spheres? You could hear the noise on the street sometimes—boing, boing, boing.

The ferry trembled as it crawled across the current, and Ann had to grip the gunwale to keep her balance. She reminded herself, speaking of balance, that this man's curriculum vitae was dappled with dead bodies, what difference did it make how he smelled or where he looked? "How's Diana?" Ann said. Thanks be to small talk.

"Working, I'm afraid. A book—women in prison. She's just begun and already she's finding it extraordinarily draining."

Ann folded up the map and stuck it in the hip pocket of her shorts, boy-style. "I can imagine. I was in Sing-Sing once, years ago. I was writing about some filmmakers shooting a documentary of a concert by B. B. King and Joan Baez and the Voices of East Harlem. At the end of the day, they had to do what they called 'clear the count'—account for every inmate, either in his cell or on a job or with a visitor. It took two hours. We couldn't leave. I thought I'd die. I still get antsy when I see a prison scene in a movie, hear those doors clang shut."

Why was she telling him this? It wasn't a very good story, and never had been. She hadn't been taken hostage, hadn't even been hit on by any inmates, who each and every one of them had only wanted her to write about how he was innocent, about how he'd been set up or mistaken for someone else or lied about by his old lady's ex-old man or by his ex-old lady's current old man. She had been home and had showered and had a Stoly martini and some Zabar's takeout by nine o'clock. *Mary Poppins Goes to the Big House*, starring Ann Jones, fashions by L. L. Bean and Weiss & Mahoney, the peaceful little Army & Navy store.

She was telling him because she was nervous, that's why, and she was nervous because she was lying. There *was* a house in Water Mill, Mark and Linda Talbert's house, but the house in Greenport (*Orient, ackshewly*) was fictitious. Ann's plan, such as it was, had been to take the ferry to Shelter Island and drive up to the big old white house and bluster: *Tony, hi, no, don't worry, you didn't forget you invited me for the weekend, I'd never been on Shelter Island before your wedding, I liked it a lot, I'm staying with friends in Water Mill, I thought I'd drive over and look around, I didn't mean to drive right in, I thought this road went around the place, I'm really sorry to bust in on you, just point the way and I'll be gone.*

Justice would have laughed at her transparency, would have asked her in, and they would have spent an idle hour on the porch, telling journalism stories, looking out over Peconic Bay, sipping ice tea or maybe a gin

146

and tonic, what the hell, it's Saturday. And finally Ann would have said *Oh, and, uh, by the way, Tone, I've been meaning to ask you—is it true you blackmailed Noel Cutler into murdering Stephen Fox and surrendering to you so you could play the hero to Karen Fox and after a while marry her and have an apartment on Central Park West and this big old white house to play in? Hunh, hunh, is it, hunh?*

Instead, *he* had sneaked up on *her*. For half an hour at least, he had sat a couple of cars behind her in the ferry line (the car directly behind her had ended up to the left of her on the boat; that was the way they loaded—one here, one there, one here, one there, for balance), and she hadn't even noticed, so what kind of sleuth was she?

A QUESTION Ann had been asked at dinner the night before when she had explained to the Talberts that her acceptance of their open invitation to visit them in Water Mill had nothing to do with loving to sailboard or play tennis or take walks on the beach or ride bikes or drive the old Healy with right-hand drive, it had to do with a tale told by a sublimely unstable pervert.

"Here's the problem I have with all this," Mark Talbert had said. "The problem is, Noel Cutler *didn't* get famous. Oh, maybe for about two minutes, but that leaves him thirteen minutes shy of his allotment. No newspaper or magazine that I read or television station I watch cared enough a month or so ago that he was getting out of jail to even cover it. *We* didn't cover it; *you* didn't cover it. Did you even know he was due to be released? You didn't because Noel Cutler's history."

As vexatious to Ann as just about anything were people who parroted Andy Warhol's *In the future everyone will be world-famous for fifteen minutes* remark as if it

147

were profoundly true, which it emphatically wasn't. The way Ann saw it, some people would be known locally or maybe regionally for as long as they could be collectively stomached, then would vanish—like Sukhreet Gabel; others would be known internationally for reasons no one could articulate even at gunpoint yet would never go away—like Joan Collins; others would flash across the sky momentarily and leave on the eyes of some who chanced to glimpse them an indelible photogene—like Noel Cutler. She let it pass, though, and addressed Talbert's objection. "Cutler had kept his part of the bargain by killing Stephen Fox; he couldn't bring him back just because Justice didn't make him mythic."

Linda Talbert, one of a species of Broadway press agent for whom journalists indicated their respect by calling her *savvy*, had asked the more important—the more savvy—question. "What does Joe think of all this?"

"He doesn't know about it."

"You're not serious? You hear about a murder and you don't tell your boyfriend?"

"You mean, because he's a cop?"

"Yes, because he's a cop."

"So far, it's just a rumor. I'm not a rumormonger."

"When you hear it from the horse's mouth, is that a rumor?"

"When it's a psychotic horse."

"You didn't come all the way out here because you think Cutler's psychotic."

"This fish is delicious," Ann said.

"Ann," Mark Talbert said, "what have you told me several times Joe always says he wishes reporters wouldn't do?"

"What's in the marinade?"

"Play cop," Talbert said.

148

"Are things all right with you and Joe?" the savvy Linda said.

"Things are . . . transitional."

"Because he's been married and you haven't?"

"That's how he looks at it. Because I want to get married and he doesn't, is how I look at it."

"All of which is another reason you shouldn't be doing this alone," Linda said. "Tony Justice is dangerous."

"It'll be broad daylight," Ann said. "There're bound to be people around his house. Tony always has people around."

Linda sat back from the table and folded her hands in her lap, looking matronly, asking to be taken seriously. "I don't just mean dangerous because some people say he's a killer; I mean because of what he does to those people he always has around. When Tony Justice walks into a room, you can see the men checking their reputations the way they check their wallets when there might be a pickpocket around; you can see the women glancing at themselves in mirrors, wondering if they look good enough to be noticed by him. You can hear their nipples getting hard."

WAS THAT why, even though he had his shades on and she couldn't tell for sure, Ann didn't think Tony Justice had looked down her Banana Republic shirt? Because he knew without looking, from experience, that nice breasts or droopy, big or small, any kind of breasts at all, their nipples would be hard?

Which they were. From the cool breeze, Ann told herself.

Or did he not look because nipples are surface, and he was interested in her depth?

22

"WE'VE ALL WISHED OUR SPOUSES or our lovers dead at one time or another," Tony Justice said. "Sometimes, when there're problems, that seems the only solution, or the simplest. Don't deny that you've had thoughts like that."

A plot, an acre, a prairie of gravestones, testimony to the lovers Ann had wished dead, how could she?

"And we *were* having problems back then, Karen and I. Not serious problems—or maybe they were; I can't even remember now. It was mid-September of last year, we'd closed this place up and were back in the city, but it was still very hot and we were still in summer clothes and a summer mode. Val was back in school. It was time to knuckle down to work and study, to order those concert tickets, those Film Festival tickets, to at least visualize Thanksgiving and Christmas, but none of us felt like it. Not extraordinary problems, is what I'm trying to say. At the time, though, they were vexing, frustrating, productive of fantasies of accidental death. Not fantasies of murder, I'm not talking about fantasies of murder, I'm talking about passive daydreams: we *hear* someone's dead, we get the news, but we aren't the instruments of their dying or even witnesses to it. The accidents are arcane, exotic: *téléfériques* falling in the Alps, suspension bridges collapsing in the Andes, avalanches in Nepal, tidal waves in Sri Lanka, flash floods in the Badlands, cattle stampedes in Montana. Locusts.

"When Karen was late that night, that's how my fantasies were running: the dirigible in which she was crossing the Atlantic had been hit by lightning. Her yacht had been sunk by a submarine volcanic eruption

150

off Tahiti. She's dead—good. We won't have to thrash *that* over anymore, whatever *that* was. She was in New York, of course, just a mile or so away, so of course then came the worry, the— Did you see it, the meteorite?"

Shooting star, Ann could only call it. Meteorites were tedious chunks of rock in the lobbies of planetariums; you slumped against them while an earnest teacher failed to convince you that the dusty plastic balls in pathetic orbit around the ceiling were the heavens in miniature. Shooting stars were silvery elves, quick and clever, like fish in deep black pools.

Stretched out in a pair of Adirondack chairs at the edge of the bluff looking out over Peconic Bay and up into a sky whose stars were dim through a scrim of sea mist, she and Tony Justice had seen several shooting stars already, in different regions, traveling in different directions on different missions. "That one was more middle-aged," Ann said. "More matronly. Matronly, not patronly: I'm still working on why, but they seem to have gender."

Tony Justice reached across the distance between the chairs. He didn't touch Ann's arm or hand or the arm of her chair, but he made contact. "You must come back in August to see the Perseids. They can be a bust or they can be extraordinary, depending on I don't really know what, but it's worth the risk."

The risk that there wouldn't be Perseids to see, Ann wondered, or the risk of becoming a habitué? And where, by the way, were all the people? *It'll be broad daylight,* Ann could hear herself saying. *There're bound to be people around his house. Tony always has people around.* So here she was, sitting in the dark with him, sitting all alone.

Justice had his head back against the back of the chair now and his hands loose in his lap. Ann remembered Linda Talbert, sitting back from the table and folding her hands in her lap, looking matronly (like the shooting star), asking to be taken seriously, saying seriously that because he had the power to tarnish reputations, the power to harden nipples, Tony Justice was dangerous.

He certainly was attractive. He was beautiful. Ann supposed that she had always been aware of that, and had suppressed it, or had had it suppressed for her by her professionalism—and by her vague rule, many times excepted, not to seek pleasure from guys in her business. Thus when her and Justice's paths crossed—at crime scenes and disaster sites, mostly, or at ritual equivocations by public servants—her nose was for news. The meat puppets, male and female, from local TV news elbowed one another to be the center of attention at such confluences, but Ann honestly wasn't sure which of them was which. ("Hi, Ernie." *Oh, shit*, was *that Ernie, or was it David?* "Hi, Kaitie." *Connie?*) Justice, though, had a way of holding back that enabled him to see everything, and *that* she'd noticed.

Justice picked up what he had let fall: "Anyway, as I said, next came the worry, the anxiety, the suspicion. I suspected Karen of stopping for a drink with a friend, of noticing a man at the bar who would notice her, would notice that she noticed, thinking: *Why not? Tony's being an asshole lately, so why the hell not?* Maybe I projected what I would've done. It *is* what I would've done when I was younger, long before I knew Karen."

When he was younger, he would have looked like something out of *Elle*, something illegal. Had she known him when he was younger? Of course she had, but she couldn't remember him well. Or maybe she remembered him perfectly, remembered that he'd been too good-looking. Those had been the days when Ann—younger herself, of course—decided that looks weren't everything and had made a point, almost, of going out with guys who looked like Meat Loaf, big burly hairy guys she didn't need professional help to tell her she was attracted to because of imperfections in her relationship with her father. Or something. (Once she had even almost gone out with Meat Loaf himself, but as much as she would have liked to have him on her life list, she hadn't wanted to be on his, and she knew that, after going out with him a couple of times, which is all it would have amounted to, she wouldn't have been able to listen to "Paradise by the Dashboard Light" anymore, one of her all-time Top Ten, and that wouldn't have been worth it. So she settled for going out with varieties of Hamburger Helper.) Something out of *Elle* wouldn't have turned her head in those days.

Justice went on: "I had to lie to Val. Ten o'clock came, her bedtime, and I lied and said Karen had called while Val was taking a shower: She was hung up at the office and wouldn't be home till after midnight. Karen didn't have that many late nights, but enough that Val didn't suspect anything. Sometimes when Karen did work late—this was the chance I took—Val would call her at the office to say good night. For whatever reason—maybe I hinted that Karen was very busy and wouldn't appreciate a call—Val didn't try to reach her. . . .

"At twelve-ten, I made the first of sixteen calls. I know this because the cops checked the phone records—*my* alibi. Sixteen calls to friends. For the first few, I pretended I was just calling to say hi, and talking just long enough to determine that Karen wasn't there and that the friends didn't know she wasn't with me. That took longer than I really wanted to take, though, with the small talk, the talk about the weather—had I seen this new movie, was I going to that new play?—and by that time it was late enough that I was waking people up.

"The only thing I could do at that point was be straight and say Karen hadn't come home; I didn't know where she was; did they? The cops thought sixteen calls was extravagant, suspicious even; they thought I should've called *them* right away, that if I had they could've done *some*thing, though none of them has ever said exactly what. Their saying that also overlooked that it's Police Department practice—you probably know this—to wait until someone's been unaccounted for for twenty-four hours before declaring them officially missing. People have changes of heart.

"A good number of my friends and colleagues, once they'd put it all together, from the vantage point of their armchairs and with telescopic hindsight, thought I should have called the cops sooner too. What no one understands who hasn't been through it, though, is that taking the right course, the rational course, the course most likely to unravel the mystery, is something you hesitate to do because doing it requires that you admit the true nature of the problem confronting you. A doctor merely confirms that there's something eating away inside you; it's you, the patient, who make the initial diagnosis—and for a long time, for as long as possible, you ignore the symptoms. The police don't tell you your spouse is missing; you tell yourself—and for a long time, for as long as possible, you pretend she's just out for a walk. Am I making sense? The wine's doing its dirty work, assisted by the aftereffects of the sun and the wind and the water."

The wine—and the sun and the wind and the water—were working on Ann too. The little white lie that had burbled up out of her on the ferryboat about the friend in Greenport had forced her to the ridiculous inconvenience of driving the length of Shelter Island, parking in the North Ferry parking lot, taking the North

154

Ferry to Greenport, and hanging out there for the length of time she calculated it would have taken to go by taxi to Orient, have lunch, and take a taxi back.

There was a movie theater in Greenport, thank God, but, god damn it, it didn't open till evening, so Ann shopped and ate and walked and sat on benches and wished she hadn't left her Susanna Moore novel on the night table in the guest bedroom of the Talberts' house in Water Mill. Yes, there was a bookstore in Greenport, and she could have bought another book or another copy of the Susanna Moore, but she didn't like starting a book when another remained unfinished, and she didn't spend money on things she already had (except quarts of milk; she was always buying quarts of milk, then discovering she already had one or more in her refrigerator).

And the book was a Susanna Moore, which meant it was very special, meant that the copy she'd bought was already a keepsake. Ann moved in to Susanna Moore novels, shouted *Aloha!* from the truck as it bounced up the dirt lane, braced to throw her arms around Mamie and Claire Clarke and Lily Shields as they tumbled toward her off the veranda. For the too few days it took to read a Susanna Moore novel, Ann spoke pidgin, and chanted Hawaiian sex chants; she drank *mai tais* and sucked on mangoes and ate macadamia nuts; uncustomarily brave, she rode the water flumes and swam with the baby hammerhead sharks. Whatever the season, she felt hot and moist, she felt thin cotton against her skin, she felt her breasts budding all over again as the girls' breasts budded. She knew that Mamie's and Claire's and Lily's world would have changed, she knew she would never find it, so she didn't go looking for it beyond the pages of Susanna Moore's books. Hawai'i, Susanna Moore spelled it, the diacritic a warning to those who thought money for a plane ticket and the fortitude for a long flight over water were all that were needed to understand the place.

So after walking and eating and shopping some more, Ann had taken the ferry back to Shelter Island and had called Tony Justice to say lunch had been over a little sooner than she'd anticipated—her friend was elderly and needed her afternoon nap—and maybe she *would* take him up on his offer to stop by on the way back to the South Fork. Justice had said he was just on his way out to do a little sailing, and gave her directions to the marina at Coecles Harbor.

Ann had sailed Sunfish on lakes back in Michigan, and knew a beat from a reach and the luff from the leech, but Justice's Soling was out of her league, so all she did was play the bimbo on the prow, her back arched and neck attenuated. She hummed Jimi Hendrix, wished she could kiss the sky.

They didn't go far, just took a turn out to Gardiners Island and back, then sat with their bare feet dangling over the marina dock and drank Rolling Rock longnecks.

"It's been on the tip of my tongue a dozen times," Justice said, "and I keep forgetting to tell you: Val's houseguest this weekend is Joe's daughter. Or maybe you already knew that."

Joe Cullen? How interesting that this was the first time his name had come up today. When, on the ferry, Ann had asked, "How's Diana?" Justice hadn't asked back about her inamorato—though he might have if she hadn't gone blathering on about Sing-Sing. Nor, since the conversation with the Talberts at dinner the night before, had she had any thoughts of Joe Cullen on her own; she had left him back in the guest bedroom in Water Mill with her Susanna Moore novel, her tennis racquet, and her swim fins.

"No," Ann said. "I know Tenny, sure, but not her social schedule." That came out without a quaver, but Ann was sure she was pale under the tan she was accumulating. She wasn't doing anything she wouldn't tell her mother, which had always been her rule of thumb on propriety, but that didn't mean that this was really where she should be and with whom.

One more thing: back in the guest bedroom of the Talberts' house in Water Mill with her Susanna Moore novel, her tennis racquet, her swim fins, was her diaphragm. She traveled with it by second nature, and she hadn't put it in her daypack when she'd set out that morning, but still . . .

"I'm not sure we'll actually get a glimpse of them," Justice said. "They're getting a ride to Easthampton with the mother of a Shelter Island friend of Val's. They're going to see a movie and then sleep over at another girlfriend's father's house in Sag Harbor. They'll be back here around noon tomorrow."

"That's too bad," Ann said. "It would've been nice to see Tenny."

"I know you and Joe see each other, but are you, do you, is it—" Justice laughed. "Help me, Ann."

"Neither of us sees anybody else. That's our version of being committed to each other."

After a while Justice said, "What?"

"What what?"

"I thought you were going to say something else."

She had been considering telling him about the fantasy induced by Noel Cutler's knowing she had a boyfriend who was a cop—the fantasy of guns and dogs and electrified fences, telling him that it was of some interest to her that it wasn't the real-life cop boyfriend who she had fantasized would rip Noel Cutler's faggot-actor heart out, it was a fictive boyfriend named Slick or

157

Bubba—meaning maybe that when it came to taking affirmative action her cop boyfriend didn't come to mind. She had been considering telling him, but she didn't know how to tell him without naming Noel Cutler, whom if she was going to name she wasn't ready to name yet. "I guess I was going to try to clarify the relationship, but I don't know what else to say about it. It's a relationship in transition, but I'm not sure from what or to what."

They watched a gaff-rigged sloop jibe into its mooring. "Nicely done," Tony Justice said. Then he said, "I'd like company for dinner. Would you be my guest?"

Ann inexplicably remembered the retort that had been popular in her adolescence: *Be my guest.* Someone would say *Eat shit, you douche bag,* and you'd say *Be my guest.* That hadn't been his tone, of course; he had made a genuine invitation—and there was no doubt in her mind that it hadn't been inspired by her telling him she was involved in a relationship that lacked clarity. No, she was hearing someone else saying *be my guest* in that bratty, catty way. Anyone else.

Tony Justice invited me to dinner.

The Tony Justice whose wife was found floating near Hell Gate, no head, no hands, no feet?

Yes.

Annie, be my guest.

"Sure," Ann had said. "Sure I would."

They had gotten back in their respective cars and driven back to the big old white house. They stopped on the way at a fish market for mussels and sea bass and at a roadside stand for corn and tomatoes. The stand was unattended: you weighed the produce yourself and made your own change from bills and coins in a cigar box.

"So that's how far we are from New York," Ann said.

158

"So far that trust prevails?"

"Yes."

"Yes."

"That is far."

They stopped again at a dirt road marked by a sign:

MASHOMACK PRESERVE

The Nature Conservancy

"What's *Mash*omack?" Ann said.

"Ma*sho*mack," Justice said. "Follow me." And he led her down the road and along forest paths less and less traveled to a meadow filled with wildflowers.

"It's beautiful."

"You look like you're walking on thin ice."

"My friends in Water Mill said something about ticks."

Justice shrugged.

"You don't believe in ticks?"

"I believe that if there's a tick with your name on it it'll get you whether you're careful or not. Or a snake or a mosquito or a tractor-trailer truck."

Or, Ann wondered, a .38 or a .45 or a .357 mag, anything smaller and Stephen Fox might have lived to identify Noel Cutler?

23 ANOTHER SHOOTING STAR, THEN another. Then nothing for so long that Ann had to remind herself to breathe. "I think it's fairly brave," she said, "when your wife's been not only murdered but dismembered, to say you had fantasies about her dying."

Tony Justice sat forward in his Adirondack chair and waved a mosquito away from his bare ankles. "Rickey Henderson and I talked about it a number of times. At first, I thought having such thoughts meant I must be guilty. I imagined the thoughts as like a spotlight picking me out of the dark, freezing me against a wall. An image from some Jimmy Cagney movie. Rickey shared some of his fantasies in the area of difficult relationships; he helped me understand that they were normal. Did you know Rickey?"

Ann shook her head. "Who do the cops think killed him?"

"I thought you might know. I thought Joe might've said something."

"Joe and I . . . We've been busy the past couple of weeks, we haven't talked . . . shop."

"New York killed Rickey," Justice said. "It'll kill all of us. None of us has a chance, we're outnumbered. Look at all its motivations—poverty, disease, decay, indifference, hatred, filth, intolerance, greed. Look at its pool of potential hitmen—junkies, psychopaths, lunatics, the merely strung-out, the merely fed-up. Think of all the imaginary homicides you commit every day: the subway conductor who shuts the door in your face, the passengers who won't let you off the train, the counterman in the deli who sloshes just enough coffee on your corn muffin that everything's a mess by the time you get to your office—*and* you ordered black coffee, not light, *and* it was a bran muffin you wanted *and* you wanted the butter on the side. And that's just the first hour of the day, and it goes on and on and on. Imagine—if you were just a touch more volatile, and carried a gun—how easy it would be to kill some or all of those people.

"Rickey could've been killed by a crack addict for his watch and his wallet. He could've been killed by some ex-con he helped put away or at the orders of a con who's still doing points. He could've been killed by a kid who wanted to prove to his posse that he's a man. He could've been killed by a snitch who wasn't happy with what Rickey'd given him as payment for information—drugs, money, a marker, a thank-you. I remember that piece you did about how terrified the narcs were because the scutter they'd been seizing and giving to snitches was so heavily cut; the cops were thinking about making their own scutter. That was a nice piece.

"Rickey could've been killed by someone he was tailing. He could've been killed by someone who'd never killed anybody before, and wondered what it felt like. He could've been killed by someone who hadn't killed anybody yet that day. He could've been killed by someone with an overriding, undifferentiated hatred for cops—or for blacks—or for black cops. With such a range of styles and colors to choose from, is it any wonder that it's difficult to make a choice? Rickey was a wonderful guy. I'm shattered by his death."

Okay, here Ann had to ask herself, ask him, ask generally: if your basic fundamental execution-style cop-killing had shattered Justice, what had been the effect on him of the butchering of his wife? "Was it scary . . ." But she couldn't finish the thought. And why not? Because she didn't want to offend him? Because she presumed him innocent? She didn't presume him innocent; she presumed, as she did with just about every suspected murderer, that he was guilty, and might be found innocent because juries—if it ever got to a jury—sometimes did crazy things.

Justice finished her thought for her, unhesitatingly. "Was it scary when I found out the cop who suspected me of murder had been murdered? Sure.... But I didn't kill him, Ann. I didn't kill Karen either."

You see? Ann said to her mother, who was still wondering after all these hours if this was really where her daughter should be spending her time, and with whom. *He says he* didn't *kill her.*

"I feel terribly distanced from everything," Justice said. "I feel as though I'm watching a movie, or reading a book—except that I have none of the empathy a viewer or a reader develops for a character, and none of the contempt either. I watch myself come out here for the weekend, say, my wife butchered and the cop who thinks *I* butchered her executed, and I don't know whether to think I'm callous, to think I'm cold and calculating, to think I'm . . . I'm—"

"Maybe you just need a break." Ann shushed her mother with a karate cut of her hand.

"If you steal, steal a million, if you fuck around, fuck a queen," Justice said. "A Russian proverb I came across in *The Russia House.* I went off le Carré, so I'm just getting around to reading it. Do you like him?"

"I used to think he was the best. I'm off him too." Ann gave her mother a look that said she wasn't being a toady, she *was* off le Carré, who had turned contemptuous of his readers.

"If you steal, steal a million, if you fuck around, fuck a queen. If you kill—what?" Justice said. "Kill a president? Slay a dragon? Kill your wife? What is it? What would it be?"

"Kill your fears," Ann said, and ignored her mother rolling her eyes.

Justice turned his head toward her somewhat sharply, as if surprised at what she'd said, as if seeing her differently—as in a corny movie. It was too dark for her to know. "What're you working on these days, Ann?"

A piece about how you had Stephen Fox killed so you could marry his widow. "Oh, uh, I just finished something on some unpublicized racial incidents in the Bronx. Bedford Park."

Justice looked back up at the stars. "Do you ever wonder about the people you write about, about what they feel when they realize, even before you publish, usually, that it's not a puff piece you're writing, it's a hatchet job? I'm working on a piece right now about a return, a resurgence, a whatever-you-want-to-call-it, of gay promiscuity. Leather bars, bathhouses, cruising— they're back. Christopher Street, the Stroll, the Loop, West Street—things look like the late seventies. The difference is, there're some new players—some wealthy, powerful people, a lot of them former straights—and some new wrinkles—private clubs, hustlers who make house and office calls. Fist-fuckers, passive and active, are in big demand.

"One professional observer of sexual mores sees risky, illicit, unbridled sex as predictable behavior among bankers and brokers and businessmen, say, given their immoral appetite for acquisition. From junk bonds to bondage, he says, isn't a long leap. A leveraged buyout is plainly and simply a gang rape.

"One of the men I've been hearing stories about interests me particularly because his wife is an impor-

163

tant figure in the fight against AIDS. She's out on the front lines raising money and he's in the back alleys risking his life. I don't think he has a clue what I'm doing. He thinks I'm interested in a whole other aspect of his life—his business, his avocations. I feel—this is the point of all this—I feel contempt for him. I imagine Rickey Henderson felt contempt for me. And now some other cop will, some other cop does."

"But as you said, you didn't kill Karen." Ann heard the hopefulness in her voice and ignored her mother tugging at her sleeve.

Justice looked at her again. "No. I didn't." Again, she couldn't read the look in the dark.

Justice stood and stretched, then bent down for his wineglass and the empty bottle. He tossed the dregs in the glass into the high grass at the edge of the bluff, and slipped the glass through the loop, for hammers or whatnot, on the hip of his painter's pants.

Ann laughed. "Is that what that's for?" She could feel her mother's backhanded slap against her arm, and had to agree that she sounded like a tipsy freshman. When he took out his penis, would she say *And what's that for?*

Justice tucked the bottle under an arm and held out both hands to Ann. "Let's go inside. It's getting chilly."

Ann took one of his hands, but got up on her own. "I really have to go. It's late. The ferries stop at midnight, don't they?"

"Later, on Saturday. But you can't drive, Ann. You've had half of two and a half bottles of wine."

And had he or anyone—like her mother—asked her, she could not have calculated what half of two and a half was. "I'm fine."

Justice still had her hand. "Ann, it's no trouble. Really. You can be up and out in the morning as early or as late as you want. I'll be gone about quarter to eight to play tennis."

Ann got her hand back; her balance wasn't going to be retrievable for a while. "I'm fine." *I'm fine* was never the answer to a question. To the question *Do you want some more chocolate cake?* the answer was *No*, not *I'm fine*, yet *I'm fine* was often the answer people gave. It enabled them to change their minds: *Well . . . maybe a little piece.*

Do you want to spend the night?

I'm fine. . . . Well . . .

"Let me call a cab, then," Justice said. "One out of Sag Harbor, to meet the South Ferry. I'll drive you to the ferry, you'll go across on foot."

She patted his shoulder like a movie drunk in a parody of reassurance. "I'm fine, Tony. Really." She got her hand back and concentrated on crossing the lawn without stumbling. But she didn't stumble. *Look, Ma. No stumbles.* She went up onto the back porch and into the bathroom off the kitchen. She splashed cold water on her face and dried it; she didn't look at her face in the mirror.

Tony Justice was waiting on the porch with her daypack and her car keys. "I really shouldn't let you do this."

She patted his shoulder again. "I'll take your short-cut. There won't be any traffic."

"No, but the roads're twisty."

"Twisty's better. Twisty'll make me concentrate."

"Ann, please."

Suddenly, she *had* to get out of there, before the werewolf in him, if there was one, if that's what it was, clambered up out of his soul. "Thanks for dinner, thanks for the afternoon. Say hi to the girls. See you in New York." She stood on tiptoe to kiss the air next to his left cheek and got away before he could kiss her back, before he could sink his fangs into her neck.

The Lumina was on the grass alongside the house and Ann had to back it a ways between trees to get to the driveway. She made it, though she had the sensation that the trees were moving. Or the car. But not her.

She shifted out of reverse into drive and put her foot on the accelerator.

Then she stood nearly straight up to drive down the brake.

There in the middle of the driveway was Tony Justice, walking toward her, a gun in his hand, ready to kill her.

No, not a gun.

Just an audiocassette.

An audiocassette that he handed through the window. "Play it loud," Tony Justice said.

"I will. Thanks."

"Drive carefully."

"I will."

Justice stood aside and Ann drove down the drive and along the road she now knew was called Osprey and onto the road called Midway and along Midway to 114 and down 114 to the ferry. A car coming off the ferry didn't kill its brights and Ann panicked as her front seat was filled to overflowing with bright hot light. She thought she would drown in it.

The light receded and she breathed normally again. She pulled up to the stop sign at the head of the ferry line and shut off the engine and put her head back against the rest and shut her eyes.

A werewolf tapped on the window and she sat up straight and screamed.

"Jesus, lady. Holy shit." It was one of the ferrymen;

he was between her and the light of a spotlight on the ferry-company office and she couldn't see his features, just that he was short and broad.

Ann rolled the window down a crack. "Sorry. You startled me. I'm just waiting on line."

He was already rolling away from her with a nautical gait, and said over his shoulder, "Lady, you *are* the line. There *ain't* nobody else. You are *it*."

Ann looked in the rearview mirror and saw that that was so, that there were no cars lined up behind the Lumina. The other ferrymen waited at the gangplank, hands on impatient hips. They must have waved at her, signaled, yelled, and finally the short broad one had had to come out and get her, all alone at the stop sign. "Sorry," she called after the short broad one, too softly to be heard.

Ann would have liked to get out of the car on the trip across to North Haven, for the fresh air, but she feared the ferrymen's mockery. She put Justice's cassette in the tape deck. It was a homemade tape labeled *Blues Misc.* She didn't like blues. She could do five minutes on how all blues singers were actually one singer—Little Blind Howlin' Muddy Mississippi Jefferson Johnson McGee singing about slapping women around, shooting them, cheating on them, drinking. Like the first song:

> I wanna kiss every night, to squeeze and hold you tight.
> I wanna make violent love to you.
> I don't wanna be frantic, I don't wanna cramp your style.
> But you're driving me into a panic, you almost drive me
>   wild.
> I wanna make whoopee-do, and have a little fun with
>   you.
> I wanna make violent love to you.

167

Ann shut off the tape and shut her eyes. When she opened them, she thought the ferry was sinking; water poured down the windows all around.

Rainwater.

The ferrymen had put slickers on and stood with their arms folded on their chests as the ferry nudged into the slip. They let down the gangplank and opened the gates and folded their arms again as Ann started the Lumina, waiting to see what she would do for her next trick. All she did was drive off.

The slip was at the foot of a long hill. Water coursed down the road. The Lumina went up it like a salmon upstream, its tail wriggling mightily. Sheets of rain whipped in the headlights, like auroras. Tony Justice had said that she would come to a flashing red light, but there was no flashing red light; it had been washed away. The road had been washed away. She was lost. She was no longer driving, she was floating, floating out of control. She was drowning.

She came to the flashing red light. She wanted to get out and hug it.

She went through the intersection and along the beach road that reminded Tony Justice of Europe. It reminded Ann of Atlantis.

The puny little car—Lumina, for christ's sake; what kind of name was Lumina for a car?—shuddered in the wind. The wipers couldn't clear the windshield of the pounds and pounds of water.

Ann's hands on the steering wheel were steel clamps, her eyes popped out of her head, she gasped for air.

A sign that said something about *permit parking*, a shed, reflectors marking a turn off the road: Ann put it together—a parking area between the road and the beach. She crept into it and pulled around to the lee of

168

the shed and shut off the engine and turned out the lights. It was as dark as the darkest night of her childhood—darker, for she had been told repeatedly then that there was nothing to be afraid of and knew now that there was even more to be afraid of than she had been afraid of back then.

She fumbled for her daypack and found it and got her sweater out of it and struggled into it. She found the map of Shelter Island Justice had given her and shook it open and used it to cover her legs. She was wet and cold and couldn't have slept had she not also been drunk.

ANN WOKE to a clear windy cool morning and to another werewolf's face at the window.

She didn't scream this time. She was an old hand.

No werewolf. Just a cop. His car said Southampton Town Police but in his mind's eye he was in California— jackboots, jodhpurs, Sam Browne belt, gauntlets, aviator shades, the whole nine fascist law-enforcement yards. Pig, he was a pig. That was the only word for it— pig.

Ann sat up and cranked the window. "Good morning." The map slipped off her lap onto the floorboards and she covered herself with her hands reflexively. She registered that she was fully clothed, and tossed her hands, like a ditz.

The pig took it all in. "See your license and rental contract, miss?" *Miss*—get it? *Miss. Who would marry you, miss?*

Ann wondered: Could she be accused of drunk driving if she hadn't *been* driving, but had probably *driven* in order to get to where she was? They'd have to prove that she'd driven there, wouldn't they? She could say she'd driven there sober, and done all her drinking there in the

parking lot. She wished she had a couple of bottles rolling around down on the floorboards, for evidence.

Or did she?

"Uh, miss?"

"Yes. Right. Here. I took a nap, that's all." Ann got
her license out of her wallet and the rental contract out
of the glove compartment and handed them over.
Should she tell the pig her boyfriend was a cop? Should
she ask him if she could go behind a bush and pee? She
was dying to pee. What effect would peeing have on the
quantity of alcohol in her blood? Was there still alcohol
in her blood, or by now had it done whatever it did—
evaporated, metabolized, metamorphosed?

The pig took her license and rental contract to his
car and got on the radio to his dispatcher. He had the
door of his white-top open and a foot up on the running
board, California style, and when he wasn't talking on
the radio mike he held it backhanded against his hip in
one gauntleted hand, à la mode California.

Two women with short gray hair and gray sweat-
suits rode past on beat-up old bicycles. They'd been jabbering, but they stopped jabbering to stare, their necks
swiveling as far as possible, then snapping back just
before they snapped off. Jabber, jabber, jabber, they
started up again. The old biddies. The dikes. The old
biddy dikes.

A young couple jogged by. She wore white Nikes and
navy Hind tights and a yellow Russell tank top and a
white Campagnolo bicycle cap. She looked great. He
wore gray New Balance and black Adidas shorts and a
gray Russell tank top and a white Nike baseball cap. He
looked great. They had just had great sex, or were about
to, and had had it the night before too, and the afternoon
before that. They each made a hundred thousand a year
and they ate every meal out. Every meal. The assholes.

"Miss." He was back, the pig, her license and contract in his hand. He gave them back and touched the brim of his cap and walked back to his car. His radio squawked at him and he put a foot up on the running board and talked into the mike and listened and got in and drove off, peeling just a little rubber, California-esque.

Ann leaned her forehead on the steering wheel and wept.

24 "IS THERE SOMETHING I CAN HELP you with?" The black woman all in black chuckled, almost, and Cullen knew why: she wasn't saying she *would* help him, she was just genuinely honestly curiously dying to know what it was that *he* thought *she* could help him with—he with the tan poplin suit, the blue button-down shirt, the navy knit tie, the Weejuns, the barbershop haircut, she with the 109 off-the-shoulder minidress, the Capezio tights, the Tootsi Plohound shoes, the Soviet military watch, the Grace Jones fade.

And, Cullen not only looked as though he'd just gotten off the Greyhound from 1962, he needed a haircut; his barbershop trim (extra light, no clippers, thin out the back) was a month old and grown to a length that curled when the weather was this humid, making him look not like a moppet but deranged. His son, the Bon Jovi wanna-be, had the same hair, and despised his father for it, his father was sure, for in the Bon Jovi wanna-be's world, as in the world of the black woman all in black, hair was destiny.

"I'd like to see Diana Romano," Cullen said.

Another chuckle, a bigger one, a laugh, really. "And, is she . . . expecting you?"

"Tell her . . . Joe Cullen." The black woman had paused for the comic effect, Cullen to wonder whether he should tell her he was a cop, then, since clearly that wouldn't impress her, whether he should tell her he would never be wanting for money.

She thought maybe he was amnesiac. "*Are* you Joe Cullen? And anyway, even if you are"—she surveyed a big appointment calendar spread out in front of her on a

172

big shiny black table, an African queen looking over her ebony kingdom, her neck an arc, her chin and nose haughty, surveying supplicants, or candidates for sacrifice—"Cullencullencullen, you don't have an ap-*point*ment."

"Joe?" Diana Romano said.

Just like that, just one word, and the African queen was deposed and living in exile, sharing a two-bedroom apartment in the high East Nineties with two steward-esses and the daughter of a former Persian diplomat, washing out her tights nightly in Woolite in the bath-room sink, working as a secretary for a corrugated box company. Her hauteur melted into not humility exactly, but . . . r-e-s-p-e-c-t. "I beg your pardon, Mister Cullen."

"It's okay. I didn't mean to sound arrogant. I *don't* have an appointment."

"You weren't at all arrogant. I should've—"

With a mannish whoop, Diana Romano stepped be-tween them. "Here now. You're going to kill each other with kindness, you two. Joe, this is my assistant, Sum-mer Bainbridge. Summer, Sergeant Joe Cullen of the New York City Police Department."

If Ann were there, she could do five minutes on peo-ple with exactly the right names. "Summer."

"Sergeant."

Diana Romano laughed again. "Honestly." Then she backed toward the door through which she had mate-rialized, her hand out invitingly. That was how he had seen her last, through the cigarette smoke at the Hudson Street diner, stepping backward into a calm ocean, im-ploring him with just the energy in her fingertips to come swim with her.

Clearly, now, she wanted him to follow.

So he did.

Diana Romano's studio was in a loft building in the

West Twenties between Fifth and Sixth, across the street from a plush billiard parlor and an indoor miniature golf course. Cullen had once shot a frame or a set or whatever it was called of eight ball at the billiard parlor with Neil Zimmerman, who never let go by a bandwagon designed with the young urban professional in mind without hopping on at least the running board and taking a spin at least around the block; he had once played a round of miniature golf at the indoor course with Ann and Tenny and the Bon Jovi wanna-be. (Ann's hands-down winning scorecard, seventeen twos and on the thirteenth hole a ten, had been up on her refrigerator for a time, along with the Urban Jungle Girl.)

Around the corner from Diana Romano's loft was a rifle and pistol range (Ann called it the stamen and pistil range) where Cullen sometimes practiced when he was up for a marksmanship review. (The range had lately started advertising in the sports pages—*Like to shoot? Why commute?*—and had gotten popular with young urban paranoids, men in vests or suspenders, women with babies in Gerry packs, toddlers in Apricas; in the evenings there were waits for galleries as long as there were in health clubs for lanes in the swimming pools or turns at the Nautilus machines.) Around another corner and to the west, between Seventh and Eighth, was a dance studio where Tenny, then a Gelsey Kirkland wanna-be, had taken classes. Still farther west was an S&M club where Cullen and Zimmerman had last winter tailed a Narcotics Division detective captain who'd been acting like he was on the pad. (He wasn't, as it turned out, he was simply a paying customer who liked to take a turn on the wheel a couple of nights a week, dressed in a rubber hood with no eyeholes and a zipper mouth, a chain-mail jock, a chiffon skirt.)

So: Not Cullen's neighborhood or his stamping

ground, but a neck of the woods he'd been in more than just a couple of times—not enough for him to wonder now how come he had never run into Diana Romano, but enough to wonder what would have happened if he had.

The studio was postmodernist, postliterate hyperchic: white bare walls, black angled furniture, mantis lights, pterodactyl mobiles, highway fatality sculptures. The supporting cast, coming and going as if choreographed by a director of background action, carrying dripping ribbons of developed film, dripping enlargements, mounted finished photographs, squinting through loupes at contact sheets hot off the printer, juggling camera bodies, tripods, light stands, long long lenses, were David Byrne epigones, Dianne Brill/Tama Downtownowitz epigones, SoHoEuroTrash, East Village RetroNeo. From behind the backs of their hands, they dropped the names of celebrities, nightlifers, club kids, they dropped the names of clubs, names of doormen, sites of outlaw parties; if their clothes weren't black, they were blacker; if they saw Cullen at all through their Incognito shades, they looked right through him.

The music was a surprise, though: instead of the Talking Cowboy Replacements, instead of Depeche Dü or Lou Cherry or Neneh Reed, it was funky blues.

"You like?" Diana Romano said, seeing Cullen shorten his stride to listen.

"Muddy Waters?"

She looked impressed. "Very close. Willie Dixon. Muddy Waters covered a lot of Willie Dixon."

Cullen listened:

I wanna make whoop-ee-do, and have a little fun with you . . .
I wanna make violent love to you.

175

They were at the door to her office now, and Diana Romano opened it and gestured Cullen in. The decor was as different from the rest of the studio—a beat-up rolltop desk, a sprung wooden swivel chair with a leaky uncased feather pillow softening the seat, a black rotary phone, a cozy couch covered in worn chintz, a mock Oriental rug pocked with the small square craters of many previous furniture arrangements, an old streamlined floor lamp out of a forties movie set on a cruise ship, a sensible shoe of a coffee table artlessly arrayed with the books and magazines you'd expect (*Details*, *Rolling Stone*, *Vanity Fair*, the *Voice*, *Ms*, *Aperture*, *ARTnews*, the new John Irving, the new Trey Ellis, the new Mary Gaitskill, the new Bret Rudnick McInerney, the new Tama Downtownowitz) and with some you wouldn't (*Natural History*, *Popular Mechanics*, *Hit Parader's Heavy Metal Heroes*, *Utne Reader*, *Rodeo News*, Rider Haggard's *She*, le Carré's *The Naive and Sentimental Lover*, a biography of Edna St. Vincent Millay)—as Diana Romano was different from her staff: she wore a plain white logoless, sloganless, tabula rasa of a T-shirt, sleeves rolled up fifties-juvenile-delinquent-style, tucked into old washed-over-and-over Levi's; on her left wrist was a man-sized Cartier tank watch, on her left ring finger a blue-and-gold cloisonné ring, in her left ear a small gold loop, in her right a turquoise stud; her feet were bare, she had a dirty Band-Aid on her left little toe, her soles were black with grime, her heels were dry and cracked.

In his vision of her at the smoky Hudson Street diner, when he had stopped between the cash register and the door and had almost gone back to the booth and said *Look, Neil, there's something about Tony Justice and Diana Romano you should know,* but Zimmerman and Sinéad O'Connor had had their oh-so-different heads together and had been laughing over something,

Diana Romano had been barefoot too, wearing a white shift, stepping backward into a calm ocean. Cullen hadn't been able to see her heels; he doubted, frankly, that he would have noticed her heels, for the close-fitting shift had commanded all his attention. He could live, though, with the dry, cracked, blackened heels, he could suffer gladly the dry, cracked, blackened heels.

"You're very busy, for a summer Saturday," Cullen said.

Diana Romano had this gesture. She had made it a couple of times already—while standing alongside Summer Bainbridge's desk, after sitting in the sprung swivel chair behind her desk and directing Cullen to sit on the cozy chintz couch. She had made it while Cullen watched at her wedding and at— No, not at Karen Justice's funeral; he didn't remember seeing her make the gesture at Karen Justice's funeral.

The gesture was this: she lifted her left arm, always her left arm, up alongside her head, and with her left hand, palm downward, fingers pointed toward her forehead, grasped her Elvis pompadour and dragged her fingers backward through it.

Each time Diana Romano made the gesture, it had a different connotation. This time, it was boyish, impatient: she wanted to be asking the questions; she knew what she was doing there on a summer Saturday, she wanted to know what he was doing there.

"I'm beginning a book. Women in prison. I have to clear the decks: two album covers, a bunch of author portraits, a *GQ* spread on the Mets. Ballplayers—what children. And why're they all named Kevin and Keith and Greg? Whatever happened to Jim and Bob and Al— ballplayer names? And Joe. What do you want, Joe?"

Had they ever been formally introduced, or did they just *know* each other—because she sometimes worked

177

on the street and sometimes so did he and they saw each other sometimes across crime-scene cordons? Or because they both knew Ann—she being a professional peer of Ann's, he being Ann's boyfriend?

Diana Romano formed Cullen's christian name naturally, but Cullen didn't believe he had ever used just hers; she was always, even when he was talking to himself, Diana Romano. (He hadn't realized before, but he realized now, that he got annoyed when Zimmerman called her Di. Di Romano. It put her in the same category as Rickey Henderson's girlfriend, Dee Blue: small-time chanteuse.) And yet he knew secret things about her— knew about her black French-maid French-whore garterless stockings, her white stockings, white lace garters, white lace panties—and now about her dry, cracked, blackened heels.

"I'm looking for Tony," Cullen said. "Your housekeeper said he was on Shelter Island but she wouldn't give me the number and it's not listed. She said I'd find you here. I was in the neighborhood"—shooting pool and playing miniature golf and taking target practice and learning modern dance and getting whipped—"so rather than call, I thought I'd just come up." Up five flights of stairs, the elevator being down on a Saturday, and through a buzzer system controlled by the Janus-eyed Summer.

Diana Romano spun a paper clip on her desk around the axis of a fingernail. He wasn't a fingernail man, and hadn't noticed before how long hers were, and how well-cared-for, unpolished, unless with clear polish. "You know your daughter's on Shelter Island with Val, don't you? Or maybe you don't."

That made his heart race, as much as if Tenny or her mother had caught him here with Diana Romano. Or Ann. What was it Ann had said—that she could do with a little complication, but not as much as he had? *He* could do with not as much complication as he had too. "Uh, no. No, I didn't. Her mother and I, we don't clear the kids' every social activity with each other." Though they probably ought to, oughtn't they, if the kids were going to socialize with the children of murder suspects?

Diana Romano moved the stone cup her paper clips were kept in, as if this were a chess game, which it was, wasn't it? "If you had told the housekeeper your daughter was our houseguest, she would have given you the Shelter Island number. In case you're wondering."

Cullen smiled goofily. He hadn't wanted the Shelter Island number, he had wanted to come here. Didn't she know that? How could she not know that?

"What happened to your neck?" Diana Romano said.

Ah, yes—his neck. Summer and the epigones, blinded by their Incognito shades, hadn't noticed the blue bruise on Cullen's windpipe. Or maybe they had and had thought it a SoHoEuroTrash East Village Retro-Neo sort of thing to have, like a Jonathan Shaw tattoo. If it had been winter, Cullen might have worn a turtleneck and covered up his neck and wouldn't have had to talk about it; but it wasn't winter, and he had bared his bruise and now there was nothing to do but talk about it, and maybe that was why he was there. "Blond Tommy Muldoon. He didn't hit me, exactly, he just wanted to get my attention."

That gesture again. This time it was as if Diana Romano were exposing a wound of her own, a burn too ghastly to look at too long. When she figured Cullen had had enough, she let go of her hair and let her hand fall lightly into her lap. "And did he?"

Cullen sat forward. Somewhere in the Book—you know the Book, the Book you're supposed to do things

179

by—there was—or ought to be—a rule: never interrogate anyone when you're sitting on a cozy couch and they're in a chair behind a desk. You're too low down; your questions skip off them like flat stones off slippery water. "Diana— May I call you Diana? You call me Joe, but I always think of you as, well, as Diana Romano. Never just Diana, always Diana Romano. I don't like it when my partner calls you Di—"

She twitched fractionally, like a cornered animal running out of patience. "No one calls me Di."

Way way out on thin ice without any skates, Cullen slipped and slid. "Not to your face. I don't mean to your face. I don't think you even know him. Neil Zimmerman? He doesn't call you Di to your face. He—"

"He calls me Di when you're sitting around the station house wondering who killed Karen Justice and is she the same well-known photographer who killed Rae Muldoon? I thought you were in Internal Affairs, Cullen. Oh, right. Blond Tommy plus Rickey Henderson equals Internal Affairs. One of my lab assistants doubles as my bodyguard. He's in the darkroom. I should have him throw your ass right out this window."

Cullen—just Cullen now, Summer would certainly be happy to know, and probably not surprised—worked on a way to offer his as-objective-as-humanly-possible view that one's bodyguard ought to be where one's body was. Before he could, Diana Romano said, "Does Ann know you're here?"

Now that she mentioned it, he had called Ann that morning, so he could tell himself that he had tried to tell her where he was going. It wasn't his responsibility that she hadn't been home, it wasn't his responsibility that she played racquetball or tennis, depending on the season, every Saturday morning, and hadn't been home. Maybe she was at a friend's, maybe she was away for the weekend—they didn't clear every social activity with each other, it wasn't his responsibility. "I'm here professionally. I don't talk shop with Ann about pending cases." Well, well. Mister Integrity.

Diana Romano had a paper clip between her thumbs and forefingers now, and was pulling it apart, working sympathetic magic on him. "Ann and I talked shop once. We were at Federal Court on something. We talked about the Heisenberg Principle. Has she ever talked to you about the Heisenberg Principle?"

Cullen tried to see past her low regard for him to determine if he was being put on and to what degree. "The Heisenberg Principle?"

"Another name for it is—"

"Uncertainty," Cullen said. Listen to them: schmoozing physics.

That gesture again. This time it was as if she were holding herself back from attacking him—for interrupting her *and* for pretending he hadn't known what she was talking about. "That's right. Uncertainty. If you measure it, you change it."

If you measure it, you change it. Cullen had many times listened to Ann do her five minutes on Uncertainty. *The Moon. Think about the Moon: the day, the hour, the instant men landed on it, it was a different place; every observation the astronauts made, every characterization, every reading they took, was fundamentally false because all of a sudden there they were, mucking up the moonscape. It's the same with any and every news story anyone ever covered. Try this sometime: hire a reporter and a photographer to hang around your house for a day—hell, for a morning— and see if you can behave naturally, see if what you let them see of you even remotely resembles the true you.*

Ann could also do five minutes, either following out of the five minutes on Uncertainty or as a separate shtick, on the perverse little relationship that developed between a reporter and the people he or she reported about: *I pretend to love them when I'm hanging out with them, following them around, drinking coffee, drinking booze—usually their booze, almost* always *their booze, swatting flies, swapping lies. And maybe I really do love them: In the process of seducing them, maybe I seduce myself. But when I sit down at the computer, when I play back those tapes, it becomes crystal-clear to me what low-life sordid sorry sons-of-bitches they really are. My river-deep, mountain-high love for them never gets in the way of the number I do on them.*

Cullen said: "And you want to know: do I actually think I can find out the truth about anything when my looking into it changes it?"

"Especially," Diana Romano said, "when you're in love with me."

25

"UH, ANN?"

"Hi, Mark."

Mark Talbert stayed on the threshold of Ann's office, gripping the doorposts as if some poltergeist were trying to drag him in. Finally he said, "Can I come in?"

"Sure."

In, Talbert turned this way and that. "Uh . . ."

Ann wondered if he were going to propose that they have an affair, or only ask her to understand his giving someone else a choice assignment. She couldn't imagine anything else making him so edgy. "Would you like to sit, Mark?"

Talbert sat not in the chair right on the other side of Ann's desk, where he and everyone else usually sat, but in the one by the window, where no one ever sat. To do so, he had to remove from the chair a stack of books and magazines and put them on the floor, for there was no more room for books and magazines on the windowsill full of them. For just a moment, books and magazines in his arms up to his chin, his eyes going every which way in search of a resting place for them, Talbert looked as though he would cry.

Finally seated, Talbert hunched his shoulders and clasped his hands together, thrusting them straight down toward the floor so that his elbows touched the insides of his knees. He looked like something out of Dickens, someone named Sneep or Grool.

Leona Helmsley, Ann thought. He's been doing a Leona Helmsley, writing checks for the swimming pool at the house in Water Mill, for the Oriental rugs for the apartment on St. Luke's Place, and calling them busi-

183

ness expenses. He's about to be found out, he was going to confess to her, then jump out her window, which looked out the back of the building. If he jumped out his window, on the front of the building, a large piece of which he owned, he would land on Park Avenue, depressing real-estate values.

Instead of confessing, Talbert said, "So how was your weekend?"

Ann looked at him sideways. "My *week*end?"

He shrugged as much as his posture would allow. "Yeah. You know . . ."

"Didn't I stay with *you* this weekend?"

He recoiled from the innuendo. "*Me?*"

Ann sighed. "You and Linda, Mark."

Talbert nodded weakly.

"I had a swell time. I told you yesterday."

He perked up some. " 'Swell.' Swell's a good word. People don't use it much these days. They say . . . What *do* they say?"

"Rad. Chill. Dope, fresh, hard, hyped, down. Def. Do you want a piece on this, Mark? Street lingo. . . . Mark?"

He started. "What?"

With a clenched jaw she said, "Mark."

He took a big breath and blurted: "There's a cop here, Ann, a Suffolk County detective."

The mind works fast, but very imperfectly. From that little squeeze of inspiration, Ann painted an entire canvas, her in an off-the-shoulder tunic, Aphrodite-style, grappling with the California-dreaming jackbooted, jodhpured, Sam-Browned, gauntleted, aviator-shaded Southampton Town pig over an empty Tanqueray bottle he alleged he found on the floorboards of her red rented Lumina. (Her swiftly turning mind even had time to wonder why, if she conjured expensive duds, expensive gin, didn't she upgrade the car?) In the background, the two jabbering gray-haired biddy dikes in gray sweat-suits and the two-hundred-thousand-a-year-every-meal-out asshole couple cheered the pig on. "Oh?"

"A homicide detective."

Far too many movies, far too much television, far too many mass-market paperbacks—Ann was sure she had studied hard against the day when someone would say to her *There's a detective here to see you. . . . A homicide detective.* When that day came, she was sure, she would come back with a crack so wise, so hard-boiled, so *noir*, that Raymond Chandler would lurch up in his grave and slap his forehead that he hadn't thought of it, that Bogart's ghost would have to laugh that weird little heh-heh laugh, that Bette Davis and Betty Bacall would roll their shoulders and toss their hair and mutter *Bitch.* And now she knew that what in fact would happen was that her mind would go altogether blank, that she would nearly faint, that she would stammer "Wh-wha-wha . . . ?"

"Tony Justice died Saturday night."

"Tony Justice?"

"He was murdered."

"That's impossible. I was with him Saturday night."

Talbert's head was nearly down to his knees by now. He craned his neck so he would still see her over the top of her desk. "I'm not sure you should say that, Ann Romano . . ."

Ann snapped up what he'd let hang. "*Romano*? Ro-*mano* what?"

"She was in the city. You were with him."

"I *was* with him. Are you crazy, Mark? I was *with* Tony Justice on Saturday night."

Talbert's head sank. "That's why he wants to talk to you."

185

*   *   *

"Dowdy," the detective said, standing when Ann came into Talbert's office, but not offering his hand.

Ann guessed that that was his name—though his mud-brown suit was certainly unprepossessing. "Ann Jones."

Dowdy sat back down behind Talbert's desk. "That your real name?" Without waiting for an answer, he started scribbling in a tiny pocket notebook that Ann thought more suited to jaywalkings than homicides.

"You think someone would make up the name Ann Jones?"

Scribbling, scribbling, scribbling, like Dickens (speaking of Dickens) on deadline, Dowdy said, "That's just it. It's, you know, commonplace. It's not ordinary." Scribble, scribble, scribble.

Weren't those opposites? And what did it matter? "How come there hasn't been anything about Tony Justice on the wires, on the radio?"

Scribble, scribble.

"What're you writing?"

Scribble, scribble.

"You'll ask the questions, right?"

Dowdy glanced up, but didn't stop scribbling. "That's right."

Ann crossed her legs, folded her arms, looked out the window at St. Bart's, in whose chapel, she had never told anyone, she thought it would be nice to be married. "And I'll answer them when my lawyer gets here." Good going, Ann. Much better, very Bette, very Betty. If only she *had* a lawyer. She had a dentist, a gynecologist, a chiropractor, an accountant, a twice-a-month cleaning man who also washed her sheets and towels, but no lawyer.

Scribble, scribble. "You *were* with the victim Saturday night, you're not denying that, are you?"

The victim. How many Saturday nights had she been with someone and felt *she* was the victim? Should she deny it? Should she say anything at all? She had seen too many movies, watched too much television, read too many mass-market paperbacks not to know he was trying to trip her up. The dowdy pig. "Aren't you supposed to tell me what you know?" Was he? Where had she gotten that? One of those movies or TV shows or books— written by someone who had never been through anything like this himself. Or *her*self. Written by some *writer*, some *shut*-in, some *house*wife.

Scribble, scribble. "I know that the last time the victim was seen alive *you* were seen with him." Scribble, scribble. "Got a pretty good witness."

Yeah? Who? Mother Theresa? "Oh?"

"Someone who knows you pretty well." Scribble, scribble.

Mel Gibson or Paul Newman? "Who?"

Scribble, scribble. "Your boyfriend's kid. Stephanie Cullen. Tenny, they call her."

"ANN? How are you?"

"Joe, aren't you coming over?"

"I just got off the phone with Maslosky. He thinks I better not. He's sorry. I'm sorry."

"I can't do this alone, Joe. I can't do this alone."

"Remember Mabel Parker? She was an assistant DA in Leah Levitt's office. She's in private practice now, specializing in women's rights. She's handled a couple of self-defense homicides. I think you should call her."

"Joe, listen carefully, okay? I didn't kill anybody. In self-defense or cold blood or any other way."

187

"... I think you should call Mabel."

"Are you home? Can't you come over just for a minute?"

"I'm at Connie's. Tenny's shaky. She and Val found the body."

"*I'm* shaky."

"Ann, this is a tough one. I've got to go with flesh and blood."

"*I'm* flesh and blood."

"Call Mabel, Ann. Call Trisha, call Roz, call Susan, call Brooke."

Those were the names of her closest friends, but they might as well have been the names of aliens: Zerg and Trflz and Rachitt and Klint. "Did Romano and Tony Justice kill Karen?"

"Ann, try and understand that I can't be talking to you about related cases."

"They were fucking each other while Karen was still missing, weren't they?"

Diana Romano, in a loose black linen boatneck shirt, loose black linen pants, her feet bare, a fresh but already dirty Band-Aid on her left little toe, her soles black with grime, her heels dry and cracked, looked up at Cullen from a table in the corner of a damp and ratty basement somewhere off the Bowery where she had known there was an outlaw party. With a fingertip, she dabbed up from the tabletop the cocaine that had escaped being snorted up through a silver pipette. With that fingertip, she scrubbed her gums. She lifted her left arm up alongside her head and with her left hand, palm downward, fingers pointing toward her forehead, grasped her Elvis pompadour and dragged her fingers backward through it to the middle of her skull. This time it was as if she were offering her head to an executioner, to save him

188

the trouble of lopping it off. She smiled, though, and let her hand fall, when Cullen gave the right answer.

"We don't know that."

"I know it," Ann said. "I'm sure of it. Remember Noel Cutler?"

". . . Yes."

"Noel's out of the joint. He did his points for killing Stephen Fox. Karen's first husband? Val's father?"

"I know who he is, Ann."

She ignored his impatience. She was all alone and would take as long as she wanted. She didn't need anyone—not him, not Mabel not Trisha not Roz not Susan not Brooke not Zerg not Trflz not Rachitt not Klint. "Noel called me. I met him in the park, by the merry-go-round, like a Hitchcock movie. He told me he killed Fox as a blackmail payment to Tony Justice. Noel had killed his roommate—Andrew Steiger; look up his obit, I bet it's in the clips—because he had AIDS. He threw him off the roof. Someone saw him—"

"Ann?"

"—and told Tony Justice. Justice blackmailed Noel into killing Fox, then surrendering to Justice, so Justice could marry Karen Fox. Marry her for her money and her ten-room apartment and her summer house. And then what happened is Tony started fucking around with Romano, and they killed Karen, so *they* could have the money and the apartment and the summer house. And then, *then*, this is what happened, I'm *sure* it's what—"

"Ann, Noel Cutler's dead."

"—*then* Romano killed Tony, so *she* could have the . . . the . . ." Ann put the phone down on her desk, and took a step away from it. "No, not dead." She stepped back to the desk and picked up the phone and said again, "No, not dead."

"Stabbed. In a gay bar. I don't know the details. I heard a headline on the car radio."

"The *car*. That's *it*. I didn't stay at Tony's house, I spent the night in my rented *car*. In a beach parking lot in Noyac. Do you know where Noyac is? A cop woke me up, a Southampton town cop, he ran a check on my license. That's my alibi. Joe, I've got an alibi."

"They know you were asleep in your car at the beach at seven in the morning, Ann. They don't know when you got there, is the problem."

"The *ferry*. That's *it*. I talked to the ferrymen. They yelled at me for taking too long to drive on. They'll remember."

"They don't remember, Ann."

"How can they *not*? How can they *not* remember?"

"They take across hundreds of cars. Thousands."

"It was a Lumina. A *red* Lumina."

"So far, they haven't—"

"And we're not talking about a whole day's worth of cars. It was after midnight when I went across. We're talking about—"

"Ann, you've said too much to me already. Call Mabel Parker. I just spoke to her. She's at her office. Write down this number."

"I *have* her number. I have numbers you wish *you* had. I have numbers the dowdy Suffolk *hom*icide detective'll *never* have."

"I'll call you tomorrow—if Mabel says it's okay."

"What do you think of my theory? You didn't say anything."

"I'll call you tomorrow."

"No, really—what do you think? Tony had Fox killed; he and Romano killed Karen; Romano killed him. What do you think? Does Romano have an alibi? I bet she doesn't. Tony thought she was in the city working on a book—women in prison. Hah!—but *was* she? I don't think she was. I had dinner with Tony, I left, he was all alone. The kids went to a movie and slept over somewhere in Sag Harbor. Tenny told you that, right? It would've been easy as pie for Romano to drive out, kill Tony, drive back. That's who they should ask the ferrymen about. Did any ferrymen see Romano? And what about the North Ferry? She could've come that way, along the North Fork. Tony said some of his neighbors swear by that route, that it's faster even though it looks longer on the map.

"We talked about maps a lot—maps, roads, place names, compass points, distances. Summertalk. Osprey, Midway, Long Beach Road, Brick Kiln, Scuttlehole. Aren't they lovely? 'Go a couple of blocks that way and make a left at the Papaya King, the Manny Hanny'— that's about as colorful as New Yorkers get to talk. Once in a lifetime, you get to say 'Great Jones Street' or 'Little West Twelfth.' So what do you think? What do you think of my theory?"

". . . Diana Romano has an alibi, Ann," Cullen said.

"Yeah, what is it? I'd love to hear it. Don't tell me— she was at the Tunnel with Mick and Jerry."

". . . No."

"What, then? What? What? . . . *What?*"

"She was with me."

26 MORE ACCURATELY, CULLEN HAD been with her. With her as a consort is with a queen, always a deferential step behind, eclipsed.

First Diana Romano had found an out-of-the-way place to put Cullen while she shot one of the projects she was busy this summer Saturday clearing from her decks so that she could do her book on women in prison: an album cover for a SoHoEuroTrash East Village Retro-Neo band fronted by a man who looked like Annie Lennox and a woman who looked like young Bob Dylan. The lowest-of-the-low assistants who shlepped the lights around and loaded film and bracketed exposures and pulled focus and kept the bottles of Naya water coming sensed that even they were higher in the scheme of things than he with the suit, the tie, the Weejuns, the haircut.

Then Diana Romano had parked Cullen all by himself in her office while she worked for two hours in the darkroom, setting apprentices to developing the film just shot, to making contact sheets, to printing roughs of the best of the shoot. Cullen had already read the editions of *Rolling Stone* and *Vanity Fair* and the *Voice* that she had out on her sensible shoe of a coffee table, but he flipped through *Details* and *Ms* and *Aperture* and *ARTnews* and *Natural History* and *Popular Mechanics* and *Hit Parader's Heavy Metal Heroes* and *Utne Reader* and *Rodeo News*.

He let the new John Irving stay just where it was and read a few pages each from the new Trey Ellis, the new Mary Gaitskill, the new Bret Rudnick McInerney, the new Tama Downtownowitz. He recalled having loved

Rider Haggard's *She* when he was a boy and having liked le Carré's *The Naive and Sentimental Lover* when he was a younger man, but skimming the first chapters of both of them now he couldn't recall why. He would have guessed that Edna St. Vincent Millay had died in 1850, not 1950, and he didn't recognize a single poem from the index of titles, but he thought the biography looked interesting, if for nothing else than for its happened-upon revelation that Millay's wedding had been front-page news in the New York papers. A poet nowadays would have to kill someone (someone other than himself) to get that kind of ink.

Cullen got out from his wallet his list of books to read when he had the time, when he retired, in his next life, and added the Millay biography to it. For the fun of it, for the time it killed, he read over the list and tried to remember why he had thought he'd be interested in *Horse-Trading and Ecstasy, The Way to the Western Sea, Jack Gance, The Road from Cooram, The Eudaemonic Pie, Mary and Richard, The Bourgeois Experience, My Place, Equator.*

Next, Diana Romano had taken Cullen home with her. Not to the apartment on Central Park West where she and Tony Justice lived, but to her bachelor's loft on West Broadway that she had held on to against those nights, as she put it in the taxi on the way downtown, "when even a ten-room apartment's too small for the two of you—it's a couple of locked doors and a couple of miles you want between you and him." Taken him home and dumped him by the industrial-strength elevator along with her shoulder bag and a couple of cameras while she went off into the maze of ceilingless walls that partitioned the loft—to bathe and make a few dozen phone calls and have a session with an Icelandic-looking masseuse who was there when they got there, who

looked as though she might be there all the time, who—
Of *course*: she was a *per*sonal masseuse and this was the
wonderful world of personal masseuses, personal aero-
bics instructors, tennis pros, weight-lifting instructors,
physical therapists, nutritionists. Cullen glimpsed the
masseuse through the door to a room where Diana Romano lay prone on a high, narrow table, a towel around
her hips, a cordless phone in her hand.

"Ronnie?" she was saying. "Romano. . . . Christ, no.
Working. . . . Album cover. . . . Some band. . . . He's on
the island." She shifted on her side and raised up on an
elbow; her areolas were so deep red they were nearly
black. ". . . Yes. All alone."

The masseuse closed the door just then, but not before Cullen and Diana Romano, as they had on the rim of
Karen Justice's grave, as they had in the basement storeroom of the Sag Harbor church, exchanged another of
their perfect looks.

Cullen wasn't snooping exactly, he was just sidling
around in the maze to see what he could see. He had done
a day's, a weekend's, a week's worth of reading by now,
especially of things he didn't want to read, and had
ignored the bookshelves and that magazine rack that
Diana Romano had swept a hand at before going off to
indulge herself. He had scanned the shelves and racks of
records and tapes, but he couldn't focus, he couldn't get
a sense of her taste.

Except that the preponderance of her collection was
blues. The Muddy Waters chitchat had been smoke, Cullen was a blues illiterate. He felt about blues the way the
two white men in the Cline cartoon on Ann's refrigerator
felt about rap music, the way he felt about Europe: there
was so much of it and so little time that it was easier to
pretend it wasn't there than to stumble along its rustic
lanes, lose oneself in its historic alleys, brave its vaunted

high-speed roads, all the while stuttering its many tongues. Cullen wasn't proud of the feeling, he conceded its childishness, he understood that he was the only loser. Sometimes he blamed the feeling on Phil Schaap, a WKCR deejay who could tell you what color socks Benny Goodman wore at his Carnegie Hall concert and where he'd bought them. Phil Schaap knew more about jazz and blues and swing than it was healthy to know about anything.

Cullen picked up the sleeve for the record on the turntable: *Robert Johnson: King of the Delta Blues Singers*. The notes said Johnson was from the same neck of the woods as Muddy Waters (speaking of Muddy Waters), Son House, Charlie Patton, Bukka White, and John Lee Hooker. See? Cullen had heard of Hooker as well as Waters (the way he'd heard of, oh, Zaragoza and Wuppertal), but White and Patton and House were Rennes to him, they were Livorno and Pécs.

The Bon Jovi wanna-be had said something once about blues songs' being constructed of flatted thirds and sevenths, but that was Greek to Cullen, who could carry a tune in the shower but dropped it like a wet sliver of soap once he turned the water off and threw open the curtain. Cullen fingered the controls of the turntable, wondering what thirds and sevenths were when they weren't flatted and just how you flatted them, but in the end he didn't play the record. This wasn't the time or the place to be throwing a few shovelfuls of dirt into the Grand Canyon (to switch geographical metaphors) that was his ignorance about the blues. This was a time for . . . a place for . . .

"Dinner?" Diana Romano said. She was at a different door but somehow still a door to the room where she had gotten the massage. She had the towel up in front of her. She looked relaxed.

*   *   *

CULLEN HAD wanted to go home to change. (He hadn't mentioned that home was Queens. Kew Gardens. Diana Romano was someone who went to Queens because Queens was where the airports were, to catch a plane to Zaragoza and Wuppertal, to Rennes and Livorno and Pécs, to Oulu.) Diana Romano had said he looked fine, but if he really felt like a change of clothes, why not run down to Parachute or the Second Coming and pick out a little something? Suddenly, unexpectedly, remembering his Thoreau—*Beware of all enterprises that require new clothes*—Cullen decided to go as he was, in a suit, tie, Weejuns, haircut.

Cullen wasn't aware of another Thoreauvian observation—*The man who goes alone can start today; but he who travels with another must wait till that other is ready*—but he formulated his own version of it in the nearly ninety minutes between Diana Romano's query about eating and their no-turning-back departure.

In a loose black linen boatneck shirt, loose black linen pants, black silk slippers (Bruno Magli?), Diana Romano looked as though she had just thrown something on (something exceptional, to be sure, something rare), and she didn't explain what had taken her so long. (Maybe she was a Thoreauvian too, and agreed with her guru that *It is a great art to saunter.*)

Cullen played with Diana Romano's motorcycle while he waited. It was parked out by the elevator, a black Norton (he knew that by reading the insignia on the gas tank, not because he knew motorcycles) with not as much menace in it as many motorcycles but still not something he would like to have between his legs. Its fittings sparkled, but it had the lines of something old. Cullen pretended he was barreling down some French

196

country road, the poplars a blur, leather jacket and crash helmet, goggles, a dispatch case over his shoulder with orders to Patton from Ike himself.

Then he rifled Diana Romano's shoulder bag, dumped by the elevator with a couple of cameras, with Cullen. Well, not rifled exactly, but peeped into, to have a closer look at a contact sheet that was peeping back at him, a corner—more than a corner, a whole half practically—sticking out of the bag, just begging to be looked at. Cullen thought it might be from today's shoot of the SoHoEuroTrash East Village RetroNeo band and wanted to see whether the man who looked like Annie Lennox and the woman who looked like young Bob Dylan, both of whom were conducting love affairs with themselves, had had enough left over to have love affairs with the camera.

Cullen lately had found he couldn't read the phone book or the agate movie listings without a magnifying glass. Ann, who wore glasses for reading and had once gone out with an ophthalmologist, told him he had presbyopia—"Old eyes. As in Presbyterian, a church run by elders." But his eyes weren't so old that he couldn't tell that the contact sheet wasn't from today's shoot, it was from a shoot from hell.

Men alone, men together, men in groups, mostly naked, some in leather, some in lace, some in feathers, focused, all of them, like doctors in a surgery, like mechanics around a car, like hackers at a VDT, on the centers of their own or someone else's bodies, front and back. Because of his presbyopia, Cullen couldn't make out faces, and, thank God for presbyopia, couldn't tell just what it was the men were doing, only that they were doing it as far as they could, and with objects bigger and longer than he ever would have imagined.

He put the contact sheet back just the way he'd

found it and wandered around until he came across a television set. He watched a *Hunter* rerun, and was a step or two behind Hunter and McCall all the way through.

DINNER WAS chez the Ronnie (presumably) whom Diana Romano had called from the massage table. She spelled her name Ronee and wrote it large on the big abstract paintings—blobs of red and yellow and orange, gashes of black and blue—on the walls of her Wooster Street loft and in progress in the adjoining studio. Ronee was tall and skinny and had blond chopped hair. She and a bunch of her friends had stayed in town to go to an AIDS memorial service and she had invited them back to her place for seafood tabouleh and a vast salad. There were as many open mescal bottles around the studio as there were tubes of paint, and quite a few more around the living loft. Mescal was mother's milk to Ronee, who drank straight from the bottle closest at hand. Ashtrays she had almost none, and she merely let the ashes of her thin brown cigarillos fall of their own weight to the rough bare floors, not even bothering to flick them.

"I'm so glad Romano called," Ronee confided to Cullen in a voice hoarsened by alcohol and nicotine. "Imagine having to spend a summer Saturday night by herself in town. Christ. What do you do, Jeff?"

"It's Joe and he's one of New York's finest. *Aren't* you?" A trim little man in round horn-rimmed glasses intruded. He wore a yachting cap with scrambled eggs on the visor, a double-breasted navy blazer over a red-and-white *apache* shirt, white ducks, velvet slippers with no socks.

Cullen thought about saluting. "Mister Slate."

198

Og Slate whipped his cap off and did an extravagant *révérence*. "You *do* remember me. Oh, good. I'm touched. I'm e*lat*ed."

Ronee took a hit of mescal and, for effect, wiped her mouth on the sleeve of the oversized shirt, a replica of a Yankee uniform from another era, that she wore like a dress, belted with a paisley necktie. Number 5, Joltin' Joe. "Finest what, Og? As if I didn't know. Funny," she said to Cullen, "you don't look nelly."

Slate semaphored his hands. "No, no, *no*. He's a po*li*ceman." He hooked their arms and drew them into a conspiratorial circle. "And if you think *he's* cute, you should see his *part*ner."

Ronee leaned back from their huddle to see if she agreed that Cullen was indeed cute. She didn't seem to. "Straight or bent, you guys *all* have your brains in your dicks. You've got to get them out, you really do. You can't keep going on like this, you really can't, relating to people based exclusively on whether you want to screw them. It's the fucking nineties." Then just as quickly as she had lashed out at them, she forgave them, and held out the bottle to Cullen. When he shook his head, she took a long drink herself, setting the worm to bobbing. "So how do you two know each other?" Ronee said when she got her breath back.

"We met at Karen's *funer*al, which *you* were too hoity-toity to grace with your presence." The banker yanked them quickly backward before a sofa that had just been vacated could be reoccupied, and pulled them down on either side of him. It was a tight fit and they were practically on his knees, Charlie McCarthys to his Edgar Bergen. Cullen couldn't not wonder if he didn't have old eyes if he would have recognized Slate on the contact sheet of the shoot from hell. And he couldn't not notice that Ronee wore nothing under her baseball shirt. Where *had* Joe DiMaggio gone?

"Ronee and Karen broke in together, Joe," Slate said to Cullen. "The *stories* she could tell you."

Cullen had left his plate of tabouleh out of reach and the bottle of Corona he'd drunk half of had skipped over his empty stomach and gone straight to his head, brimful with the day's uncustomary events. "Broke, uh, *in?*"

"We were models," Ronee said. "Haute couture," she added in a Judy Holliday voice—*Oat coo-too-uh*. She put two fingers way down in the breast pocket of her baseball shirt and came up with a joint.

Slate got a Dunhill lighter out of his blazer and flicked it and flicked it and flicked it and finally got a flame out of it. "Glad it's not my fire you're trying to light," Ronee said.

"Silly girl," Slate said.

Ronee got the joint going and took a big hit and offered it to Cullen.

"I'm screaming," Slate said. "I'm peeing in my trousers."

"Take it, will you?" Ronee said. Then she figured it out and shrugged and took another hit and handed the joint to Slate. "Hey, fuck it. Bust me. I don't care."

"Why weren't you at Karen's funeral?" Cullen said.

Ronee puckered her face. "Funerals're for ghouls. Especially when the deceased"—she put the mescal bottle between her knees and made a gesture of slicing off her arms at the shoulders—"You know what I'm saying?"

Slate tapped Cullen's knee furiously, like a bratty child wanting attention. "What you really must be wondering, Joe, is how on *earth* Ronee and Romano can *possi*bly be *friends.*"

Ronee made a fist under Slate's face. "Hey, Og,

you're not saying Romano whacked Karen, are you? You're not saying that, *are* you?"

Whacked. Why was it interesting that she said *whacked*? "Who did kill her?" Cullen said. "In your opinion." *And in your own words.*

Ronee shrugged, got the joint back, took a hit, shrugged again. "Karen did some porn. Long time ago, before she got her break. I did too. Not fucking porn, jerk-off porn. We jerked off so the guys who bought the tapes would have something to jerk off to. Some guys don't like guys in their porn, you dig? Are you one of those guys? You look like one of those guys *and* you look like a guy who'd slap me around with one hand for doing porn and jerk off with the other 'cause it turned you on."

"Really, Ronee," Slate sniffled.

"It's not easy being taken seriously when you're a piece of ass," Ronee said. "Trust me on that. And once those guys get their hooks in you, they don't let go."

"Those guys, meaning the guys who make the movies?" Cullen said.

"Yes. Who'd you think I meant?"

Cullen shook his head. He was listening to himself telling Hriniak about this: *Diana Romano took me to this party, see, in SoHo, see, and then walked off and left me all by myself, see, and I got to talking with a woman, a painter, wearing a Yankee uniform with nothing underneath, drinking mescal out of the bottle and smoking a joint the size of the Goodyear blimp, and she said she thinks Karen Justice was killed by someone she crossed when she was younger, and made, you know, an X-rated movie.* Hriniak would ask if that was it and Cullen would say *Oh, and, uh, the uniform had Joe DiMaggio's number on it.* Hriniak idolized DiMaggio; he'd gotten an autograph as a teenager that he still carried in his wallet. Hriniak would ask if *that* was it, and Cullen would say *Well, the woman in*

*the shirt with DiMaggio's number on it didn't say 'killed,'
she said 'whacked.' Doesn't that seem odd to you, that she
would say—*

"Joe?"

Cullen startled. Joe Di*Maggio*? Here? The Yankee
Clipper?

"Joe, let's go."

Diana Romano, a hand extended, five or six people
watching her from the door, waiting for her, wondering
how he figured in, he with the suit, the tie, the Weejuns,
the haircut. "Uh, go?"

"To Maxwell's. Ronee, you're sure you won't come?
Og, you're sure?"

They were sure. The memorial service. Another
senseless untimely death. Weary, drained. *De trop.* Nice
to see you again, Joe. Say hello to the charming Neil.
Nice to meet you, Jeff.

27

BUT THEY DIDN'T JUST LEAVE, OF course. Diana Romano never just left. She had to make sure that everybody knew she was leaving, that they would be deprived of her for the rest of the night, maybe forever.

And while Cullen was waiting—the man who leaves alone can leave when he wants; but he who leaves with another must wait till that other is ready—he decided maybe it was time to get a little professional and call his partner and see what he was up to. He found a phone in the studio, the receiver encrusted with dried paint, and called Zimmerman's apartment. The machine answered and Cullen waited through the message to see if Zimmerman would pick up. He didn't, and Cullen hung up without leaving a message. He had forgotten what he was going to say, for he was distracted by the number on Ronee's phone. It was a number he knew, all sixes and nines, but that was impossible, wasn't it, because he hadn't met Ronee before. Had he?

Cullen went back into the living room and Ronee, behaving as though they'd not only met before, they'd really enjoyed it, came over to him and bumped him into a corner with her thighs. Was this it, finally, the gratuitous, disengaged, wild sex he had been searching for without requital since puberty—no underwear, no words spoken—and that he had always been led to believe would be his if he kept going "downtown," an entity that year after year crept farther and farther south, always just out of reach? Until now? "Jeff, what I was saying to you, about those guys? The porn guys? Don't say anything to Romano, okay?"

"Okay. . . . Why not?"

Ronee played with Cullen's tie—the only one in the room, the only one (this was "downtown") in the neighborhood. "Just because."

"Just because it's farfetched or just because it's right on the money?"

Ronee pouted. " 'Farfetched' means you don't believe me."

"I don't believe you, I don't not believe you, I'm along for the ride. And I'm curious. I'm curious that you and Og were tight with Karen Justice *and* are tight with Diana Romano. Have you known *her* a long time? Did she do any porn?"

"Ro*mano*?"

Cullen shrugged. "I'm sure it *is* hard, being a piece of ass. I'm sure I haven't a clue how hard."

"Joe?" Diana Romano put her hands on Cullen's shoulders and a whisper, a hint, of her breasts against his back and her thighs against his ass. Over his shoulder, a hint of her cheek against his neck, a hint of her breath teasing his ear, she said, "You can't have him, Ronee. I'm taking him."

Ronee shook his hand with ludicrous formality. "Nice meeting you, Jeff."

On the stairway down, bringing up the rear of the line of partygoers clattering on to the next exotic locale, Diana Romano put her hands on Cullen's shoulders again. "Having fun?"

"Sure."

Og Slate had come down ahead of them during their leave-taking and was pulling away in his car, a well-preserved old Benz. The vanity plate said something about STOX. . . . He honked the horn in farewell: it played the first few bars of "Appalachian Spring."

Someone who was going to drive them went to get his car. Cullen and Diana Romano stood around.

"Maxwell's in Hoboken?" Cullen said to say something. He'd already said what fun he was having; he couldn't keep on saying that.

"Maxwell's in Hoboken," Diana Romano said. "Six dollars to see twenty-two-dollar bands, the *New Yorker* described it."

That man is the richest whose pleasures are the cheapest: Henry David Thoreau.

IT WAS a six-dollar band and it played one hundred decibels, and this time Cullen was the one who left Diana Romano all by herself. He took a walk along Sinatra Drive to the river and counted the neon drops dripping from the neon coffee cup on the Maxwell House factory. After a while, he had to make himself see them as drops dripping; his mind wanted to make them into drops leaping upward back into the cup. A couple of years ago, when *Batman* opened and Batman merchandise was everywhere—batshit, she called it—Ann could do five minutes on the logo, contending that unless you made yourself see it as a bat it looked like a mouth with tonsils and a tongue. A fifty-million-dollar investment being flaunted by an ambiguous symbol.

But Ann wasn't there, was she? We weren't talking about Ann, were we?

In cars parked along the drive, on rocks down along the shoreline, in among the trees on the bluff below Castle Point and Stevens Institute, everywhere and all around the solitary Cullen, couples made out. It was a windless night, a windless morning, and their moans and sighs and shivers and shudders rose up all around in a goddamn symphony of lust.

Cullen didn't remember going back to Maxwell's. He didn't remember eventually leaving Maxwell's, or in

205

whose car. He didn't remember which tunnel they took back under the river. Or did they go over? What he remembered next was Diana Romano in her loose black linen boatneck shirt, loose black linen pants, her feet bare, a dirty Band-Aid on her left little toe, her soles black with grime, her heels dry and cracked, looking up at him from a table in the corner of a damp and ratty basement somewhere off the Bowery where she had known there was an outlaw party and where they had gone with the partygoers they'd started out with augmented by the partygoers they'd picked up at Maxwell's.

With a fingertip, Diana Romano dabbed up from the tabletop the cocaine that had escaped being snorted up through a silver pipette. With that fingertip, she scrubbed her gums. She lifted her left arm up alongside her head and with her left hand, palm downward, fingers pointing toward her forehead, grasped her Elvis pompadour and dragged her fingers backward through it to the middle of her skull. This time it was as if she were thrusting herself up against a wall and demanding answers to a few questions.

"Are you shocked?" Diana Romano said. "Or don't you shock? But you won't do some blow. You've never done any drugs. Not just because you're a cop, because you're straight. College, high school—you've always been straight."

"I used to shoplift," Cullen said. "Forty-fives, mostly, but once an album—Jerry Lee Lewis."

She didn't even smile. "But you've never done even grass."

"I'm older than you." Why was he debating her? "Half a generation. People didn't do drugs."

"You've never done even grass," she persisted.

"No," he admitted.

"So you are shocked. You're disgusted."

"No."

"Titillated? Curious?"

"Curious about you."

Diana Romano grasped her pompadour and dragged her fingers backward through it. This time it was as if the bad cop were taking over from the good cop. "How long you been on blow, Diana? How many toots a day? Ever try primo? Ever free-base? Ever do jumbo, love boat, ice? And what's the kick anyway, Diana? Where's the high? Is the going up worth the coming down? Ever try taking life straight up, Diana, or are you too scared, too weak, too fucking chickenshit?

"Where is the high?" Cullen said. Ann could do five minutes on the high's being that it was illegal, but the criminals Cullen had talked about such things with had to a man and to a woman gotten off on money.

Diana Romano craned her neck, looking a little defensive now, but going to tough it out. "It's expensive. I would no more do crack than I would shop at A and S. It's against the law; I drive faster than fifty-five whenever I can help it. It feels good; I try never to do anything that doesn't feel good. It's dangerous. I like danger: I like to ski, I like to climb rocks, I like to fuck where I might get caught. But you know that.

"Do you think about that day much, Joe? I do. Did you tell anybody? I didn't. Usually I would've told Tony. Usually that would've been why we did it where we did it—in the hope of getting caught. Getting caught makes it memorable—not just another fuck. Remembering it makes you talk about it. Talking about it turns you on all over again."

She was comfortable now. She had her elbow on the table and her fist under her chin. Her lips were wet, her teeth were wet. "Anything else, Joe? Anything else you want to know?"

Out on the floor of the outlaw club, their moans and sighs and shivers and shudders rising up all around in a goddamn symphony of lust, couples danced, couples ground their hips together, ground hips to asses, asses to hips. Men had their shirts off, women had their shirts off. One couple, he couldn't see well, he could barely see, it was so dark, he had been up so long, but he was pretty sure one couple, the girl, she had her legs wrapped around the guy's back, her black dress up over her white thighs, her white hands with red nails tugging the guy's black hair, the guy moving in and out of her, in and out.

"I want to know," Cullen said, "if you want to dance."

Diana Romano didn't say a word. She looked at him for a long time. She grasped her pompadour and dragged her fingers backward through it. This time it was as if she was grooming herself, trying to make herself look really fine, knowing that she *looked* really fine, but wanting to look *really* fine. Then she got up and put out a hand and stepped backward barefoot out onto the dance floor and implored him with just the energy of her fingertips to come dance with her.

And Cullen felt like a character in a Bret Rudnick McInerney novel, thinking of himself in the second person singular, thinking you're dancing with Diana Romano, thinking you don't have anyplace important to be, anything to do, you could go on dancing like this forever, you could go on dancing like this all night.

So you did.

28

"*ALL* NIGHT?" HRINIAK SAID.

"It was light when we left the place near the Bowery," Cullen said. "I didn't look at my watch."

Richie Maslosky looked at his watch now, having spent enough time, thank you, listening to one of his men telling the PC something he was hearing for the first time himself. "You bag her, Cullen?"

A question asked less crudely but no less pointedly by Cullen's ex-wife, Connie, by Urban Jungle Girl Ann Jones, even by his adolescent daughter ("Did you go to *bed* with her, Dad?"), whom he had hoped would never learn about such things, would grow up and grow old a happy, ignorant, innocent virgin. "She got a cab to her place, I got one to where I'd left my car, near her studio, and went home." (The Urban Jungle Girl, on hearing that answer, had said, "Ah well. I think it was Hemingway. I think he was talking about Gertrude Stein: He said it's hard to get anything out of a legendary woman.")

Chief of Department Powell Ruth: "She's got a bunch of places, Romano, it seems like. Which place?"

"Central Park West, I imagine. I heard her tell the cabdriver to go uptown."

Chief of Detectives Anthony Amato: "You live in Queens, isn't that correct, Sergeant? So when you say you got a cab to where your car was parked, then went home, you mean you went to Queens, don't you?"

Mild panic flickered on the faces of the other brass. The consensus Downtown was that Amato had lost it entirely: burn-out, Alzheimer's, degenerative slow-wittedness—speculation as to why was wide-ranging. His colleagues' fear gave way to hopeful looks that this would be Amato's only, *pro forma*, question, and not the first mile in a marathon interrogation on alternate ways to get to Queens from Manhattan, on ways to drive around in Queens once you got there, on the parking options that had confronted Cullen when he got to his neighborhood. "Yes, sir," Cullen said.

"Good." Amato sat back, entirely if inexplicably satisfied.

Hriniak again: "So. Bottom line. You're saying nothing went down between the two of you, you just danced with her, that's it, that's all."

Cullen looked at Zimmerman, who raised his eyebrows. Cullen had recently pledged to kill Zimmerman if he ever said *bottom line* again. "That's all."

"You weren't *int*imate with her, Sergeant? Not even a *little* bit?" That from Captain Elihu I. Novak of Homicide.

Being picked over by a roomful of brass, it turned out, wasn't as bad as Cullen's worst nightmare: in his worst nightmare, women past, women present, women only fantasized about demanded to know how the fuck he could live the way he did, then, when he tried to formulate an answer, interrupted to ask who the fuck was he trying to kid. The stage for their inquisition was always a slippery precipice over a turbulent void. This place was solid as a rock—a pleasant conference room off Hriniak's office, a glimpse of the river, the sky, freedom. Look! A bird! Okay, only a pigeon, but a bird, a heart-stirring bird, nonetheless.

"No sir," Cullen said.

Novak snorted. "You spent—what?—nineteen or twenty straight hours with her. I'd call that *int*imate. You might not've been *int*imate, but you sure as hell were *int*imate."

Among the many in-house jokes about Novak was

one that his middle initial stood for Italics. Novak's body language indicated a difference among his *intimates*, but Cullen couldn't figure out what it was. "What's your question, Captain?"

Novak sat forward. "The *question*, Sergeant, is what did she *tell* you?"

Cullen enjoyed the Novak jokes along with everyone else, but he was one of a few who held that Novak was smarter and meaner than just about anybody else Downtown, and therefore very desirable to get on the good side of—if he had one. "She neither confessed to any crime nor fingered any criminals, Captain," Cullen said.

Brevity is the soul of contempt as well as of wit, and Novak sniffed at Cullen's answer, in his eyes a warning to maybe be a little less succinct next time.

Hriniak still again, with slaps on the tabletop for punctuation: "Tony Justice, Karen Justice, Rickey Henderson, this Noel Cutler, a long time back Stephen Fox, and before that the Muldoon woman. Did I leave anybody out? What—besides their all being dead; I know we don't know for sure about the Muldoon woman, but let's just *say* she's dead—what is the fucking connection? Six people, six motherfucking people. Excuse my language, Detective Esperanza. I mean, are we talking a crime wave, are we talking a vendetta? What the *fuck* are we talking? Can anybody tell me? Yes, Detective?"

Detective Maria Esperanza, who had caught the job of liaison with Dowdy of Suffolk County Homicide: "First of all, Commissioner, respectfully, please don't apologize to me for using expletives. It's condescending and it's sexist. Second, your list should include Andrew Steiger, whom Ann Jones says Noel Cutler killed because he, Steiger, had AIDS."

Hriniak took a moment to marvel that she had so cleanly yet so subordinately told him off *and* had taken

211

such care with her pronouns, relative and personal. Then, to show he'd gotten all her messages, he said, "Seven motherfucking people."

No one said anything.

Finally Maslosky said, "Maybe we should take them one at a time, see what connects. I guess we should begin with the Muldoon woman."

So THEY took them one at a time, beginning with the Muldoon woman, even though that meant beginning with Cullen, whose questionable judgment was the reason they were there in the first place:

"June, nineteen eighty-six, Rae Muldoon, wife of Lieutenant Thomas Muldoon, Brooklyn Anti-Crime, got in her car to go to an A&P in Baldwin, Long Island, never came back. Muldoon at the time was having an affair with Diana Romano, who was doing a book of photographs on undercover cops. There was no evidence of foul play, and Rae Muldoon may just have been fed up with her husband's womanizing. Romano and Muldoon saw each other only a couple of months, Muldoon retired last March while under suspicion of associating with felons. He's doing corporate investigative work in New Jersey." Not bad: short and sweet.

Zimmerman put up a hand. "I think Stephen Fox would be next, sir. I can take that."

Hriniak nodded. "Take it, Detective."

"July nine, nineteen eighty-six, Stephen George Fox, a theatrical producer—"

"Excuse me, Commissioner," Maria Esperanza said. "And Detective. I don't want to seem obsessed with Andrew Steiger, but it would be appropriate to discuss his death *before* Fox's, occurring as it did in April, eighty-six, and serving as it may have as a catalyst for Fox's murder." She paused for permission, but she needn't have, for Hriniak and Zimmerman and all the rest were happy hostages to her big white teeth, her wide brown eyes, milk-chocolate skin, her tango-dancer slick black hair, the fascinating ways in which the pinstripes of her sober business suit veered away from the vertical in response to the curves of her body. Her obsessions were their obsessions.

"Please," Hriniak said, meaning *Please beat me, please make me pass bad checks.*

"You don't mind, Detective?" Maria Esperanza said.

"Not at all, Detective," Zimmerman said. *Cuff me, hang me by my thumbs.*

"According to Ann Jones," Maria Esperanza said, "Noel Cutler learned on twenty April, nineteen eighty-six, that his intermittent lover, Andrew Steiger, had tested positive for antibodies to human immunodeficiency virus. According to Ann Jones, Cutler threw Steiger off the roof of Steiger's apartment building in Clinton, then forged a note making it look as though Steiger committed suicide. There was a witness, according to Ann Jones, someone who owed Tony Justice a favor and told him about the incident. According to Ann Jones, Justice contacted Cutler and proposed that Cutler kill Stephen Fox as the price for keeping his secret about Steiger."

Everyone could have listened for several more hours, but Maria Esperanza stopped right there and smiled at Zimmerman, inviting him to run the next leg.

He took the baton from her, juggled it, got a grip on it, ran with it—but ever so reluctantly, looking back over his shoulder at her as he raced on, wanting only to go back—back to just what he had been wishing for, a small, dark girl with a big name. "Uh, Fox, Stephen Fox,

Stephen George Fox. July nine, nineteen eighty-six, Stephen George Fox, theatrical producer, was shot twice in the face with a Beretta Mod90 thirty-two-caliber double-action automatic. He was alone at the time in his office in the Brill Building, it was six A.M., approximately, he was often at his desk that early. There had been some crack-related muggings and holdups in the building, and the investigation focused on known addicts, especially those living in a welfare hotel just around the corner.

"About a week after the killing, Tony Justice wrote a piece in the *Bulletin* saying Noel Cutler had confessed to killing Fox. Cutler contacted Justice because he'd been writing pieces on how the theater community had been terrorized by the murder. Detective Esperanza, in her wish to be brief, didn't mention that Noel Cutler was an actor who auditioned for a part in a musical Fox was producing. Cutler telephoned Justice for four or five days running and Justice wrote pieces about their conversations. Cutler said he killed Fox because Fox overruled the director, who wanted Cutler for one of the male leads. The director denied it, but Cutler said he was lying. Whatever the motive, it was clear from the details Cutler told Justice that he'd been in the office when Fox was killed.

"Cutler finally surrendered to us, the police, at the merry-go-round in Central Park. He had the Beretta in his apartment, and a paperweight he'd taken from Fox's desk as proof that he'd been there. He pled to murder two, he was sentenced to eight and a third, he walked three weeks ago after doing four, nine. Friday night or Saturday morning— I'm not stepping on anybody's turf, am I, Commissioner, if I go ahead with Cutler?"

"Go ahead, Detective."

"Friday night or Saturday morning, Cutler was

stabbed in the neck in a fight or maybe a lovers' quarrel or maybe he was having fun at the Lash, an S&M bar on West Street. The place was crowded, there were plenty of witnesses. The Six Squad is looking for a male Hispanic, twenty-five to thirty-five, five-eight, one-thirty, straight black hair, mustache, white tank top, jeans and jean jacket, motorcycle boots, possibly riding a racing-type bike. His weapon—a switchblade."

Zimmerman looked first to Maria Esperanza, who was writing in her notebook, then to Hriniak, who said, "Who's next?" Maria Esperanza looked up and saw that Hriniak was looking right at her, depending on her, so she said, "Karen Justice."

"Powell, you were still at Homicide when Karen Justice went off the scope. Why don't you take it?"

Ruth, who had since become the highest-ranking uniformed officer on the force (Amato, the joke went, was the highest-ranking *un*informed officer), leaned forward as far as his medaled chest would allow, to see Zimmerman—and past Zimmerman, Maria Esperanza. "Detective Zimmerman neglected to mention that soon after Stephen Fox was killed, his widow, Karen, married Tony Justice, out of gratitude, presumably, in part anyway, for his help in bringing her husband's killer to, uh, justice."

Ruth smiled at his little wordplay and invited Maria Esperanza with his eyes to smile too. She ducked her head and wrote harder in her notebook. Zimmerman looked at Cullen and asked with *his* eyes for help, asked Cullen to say that Maria Esperanza had been just as guilty of neglect as Zimmerman, asked him to cite Zimmerman's generosity in attributing Maria Esperanza's failure to mention something to her wish to be brief. Cullen just smiled.

"Seventeen September last, a Monday, at approx-

215

imately twenty-thirty hours"—Ruth's delivery went with his uniform—"Karen Justice ingressed a taxicab at the northwest corner of Six-one and Madison, carrying a briefcase and a squash racquet. Her presumed destination was the apartment on Eight-one and CPW she occupied with Tony Justice. If that apartment *was* her destination, she didn't attain it, according to the testimony of the doorman on duty and other building staff. If she had another destination, we don't know what it was; fliers with her photograph were circulated at taxi garages in all five boroughs. They failed to produce any leads. Nor did our inquiries at airports, train and bus stations, and car-rental agencies. I believe at this point I should yield to Captain Novak."

Who had nearly crawled out onto the table in his impatience to get in on the action. "Thank you, Chief. As the Chief *said*, Karen Justice was missing and unaccounted for from last September seventeen until this March two-five, when the *torso* of a female Caucasian was found floating in the East River just north of *Hell* Gate. X rays revealed a *frac*ture of the right tibia identical to one suffered by Karen Justice in a *ski*ing accident some *years* ago. The torso *also* bore a scar from a cesarean section, had three prominent *moles* on the left shoulder blade and had an *ex*tra nipple on its *left*, uh, breast." Novak tried not to look condescendingly and sexistly at Maria Esperanza at that point, and failed miserably. She stared back at him and he looked away.

"Detective *Hen*derson," Novak said, "if I may continue on here, Commissioner, since Detective *Hen*derson was under my com*mand*, and was one of the detectives who caught the Karen *Justice* job, with *special* attention to verifying *Tony* Justice's alibi both at the time of his wife's im*med*iate disappearance *and* in the time thereafter during which he might have attempted to, uh, dis-

216

*mem*ber her body, Detective *Hen*derson, as I think is tragically fresh in *all* our minds, was whacked behind the *left* ear with a twenty-five-caliber *hand*gun in the *Port* Authority *bus* terminal. According to Detective *Diehl* of the *Port* Authority squad, *Hen*derson had an unauthorized apartment in New *Jer*sey which he utilized for the purposes of observing a *night*club entertainer who he had an *int*imate relationship with."

Novak's singsong was wearing him out along with everyone else and he paused to pour a glass of water from a carafe and drink it off.

While he did, Cullen thought: *Whacked.*

Then he thought about sitting on the sofa in Ronee's loft—what was Ronee's surname, anyway?—Og Slate in the middle, Cullen and Ronee practically on his knees, Charlie McCarthys to his Edgar Bergen, Ronee saying *Hey, Og, you're not saying Romano whacked Karen, are you? You're not saying that,* are *you?*, then Cullen asking her who did kill Karen, *In your opinion*, and Ronee saying *Karen did some porn. Long time ago, before she got her break. I did too. Not fucking porn, jerk-off porn. We jerked off so the guys who bought the tapes would have something to jerk off to. Some guys don't like guys in their porn, you dig?*

Then he thought about sitting in Blond Tommy Muldoon's car in the parking lot of the McDonald's in Little Silver, acting like he was just getting comfortable and sliding down in the seat and springing the glove-compartment lock with his knee; rummaging among the usual shit and finding a videocassette with the handwritten label *Girl Duos* and a videocassette with the handwritten label *Girl Solos*; not needing to be Karnak the Magnificent to know the first had sets of two girls doing it to each other, the second, single girls doing it alone.

Novak was just about to start up again, but Hriniak

looked at his watch and said, "I have to get over to the Hall. The Attorney General's in town, big to-do, war on drugs, all that. Detective Esperanza, if you could just brief us, uh, briefly, ha ha"—ha ha's all around the room—"on Tony Justice, we'll at least have covered all the victims, we'll be ready to move right along the next time we meet. Thank you, Captain Novak."

No one even noticed that Novak began gnawing in frustration on the edge of the conference table. All eyes were on Maria Esperanza.

"This is all according to Suffolk County Homicide," Maria Esperanza said. "There hasn't been time for independent verification. Tony Justice was seen around four o'clock Saturday afternoon, walking in a nature preserve on Shelter Island with Ann Jones, a reporter for *City* magazine. Justice's stepdaughter, Valerie Fox, and Stephanie Cullen, who is Sergeant Cullen's daughter and a friend of Valerie's, were in another part of the preserve and saw them from a distance. The girls then went to a friend's house and subsequently left Shelter Island to go to the movies and sleep over at yet another friend's. They got back to the island Sunday morning around ten o'clock. They were dropped off at the driveway, about a quarter-mile from the house, and took a while getting to the house because they spent some time trying to get a kite out of a tree. At ten-forty, the Southold Town Police, who log Shelter Island's nine-elevens, got a call that there'd been a K. According to the Suffolk ME, Justice was shot once in the back of the head with a medium-caliber handgun, a thirty-eight maybe. He died between ten P.M. Saturday and two A.M. Sunday.

"According to Ann Jones, she and Justice spent five or ten minutes in the preserve Saturday afternoon, then went to Justice's house, had drinks and dinner, and sat out on the lawn talking until about eleven-thirty. According to Ann Jones, she took the so-called South Ferry off the island, to North Haven, on the South Fork. She was headed for Water Mill, where she was a guest of Mark Talbert's, the publisher of *City*. According to Ann Jones, it started raining heavily as soon as she got on the ferry, she'd drunk quite a bit of wine, she didn't know the roads. She pulled off into a beach parking lot about a mile or two from the ferry, on Noyac Bay, and fell asleep. A Southampton Town Police officer woke her around seven and ran a check on her car. It was a rented Lumina, red. It was clean, obviously, but none of the South Ferry crewmen remembers taking it across, according to Suffolk Homicide, so there's been no independent verification of Ann Jones's version of the time."

Cullen wondered why no one applauded, since in the gap between her finishing and Hriniak's thanking her for her, uh, brief brief, ha ha, there sizzled and sparkled in the air the same electricity that fills a concert hall or an opera house or a theater when great music has just been made or a great performance given and a momentary respectful silence is the only adequate tribute. *Get a grip, guys*, Cullen wanted to scream.

"Thank you, Detective, for your, uh, briefing"—ha ha, ha ha—"Now I've really got to get a move on. Gentlemen, Detective, I appreciate the perspective. I do want to say though that I'm troubled that nobody used the word suspect, forget about perpetrator, in talking about any of these cases—except, I guess, the two K's this Cutler guy is apparently responsible for, and Cutler's K too, I guess, since Detective Zimmerman, I think, or was it Detective Esperanza, said the Six Squad is looking for a male Hispanic. Anyway, look. Ten A.M. Wednesday, same place, same faces. Anybody can't be here, send a well-informed stand-in. Anything develops on any of this between now and then, let Chief Amato know. Sergeant

Cullen, I'm not going to suspend you, but that doesn't mean I like what you did. I don't like what you did, don't do any more of it. Clear?"

"Yes, sir."

An unseemly rush to see who could get to the door to hold it for Maria Esperanza. Zimmerman, being Other Ranks, wisely held back.

"Coffee?" Zimmerman said.

"Hudson Street?" Cullen said.

". . . All right."

"We can go somewhere else."

"No. No, I should."

" 'Should'?"

"I'll explain."

29

"BEFORE YOU DO YOUR EXPLAINING, Neil, let me tell you something: after Karen Justice's funeral, in Sag Harbor, looking for a bathroom in the basement of the church, I took a wrong door and walked in on Tony Justice and Diana Romano. . . ." On the way to the diner, Zimmerman preoccupied with traffic (and with thoughts, Cullen imagined, of Maria Esperanza), Cullen had rehearsed ways to say it:

Gossipy, anecdotal: *There was this steamer trunk—you know the kind I mean? The kind people used to take on ocean voyages. It was standing up on end and she was sitting on it with her dress pulled up to her waist. She had on black garterless stockings, like a French maid or a French whore; she was wearing her shoes—glen-plaid low-heeled shoes, very distinctive, very unusual. She was grabbing his hair with her right hand, her left was jammed in her mouth so she wouldn't, you know, scream. He had his pants down around his knees, his elbows were pinning his overcoat back out of the way—a beautiful coat, cashmere. He was sort of rocking back and forth, rocking in, rocking out, rocking in, rocking out.*

Matter-of-fact: *She's sitting on a trunk, he's standing between her legs, they're having intercourse.*

Crudely euphemistic: *They were balling, they were doing the dirty deed, they were making the beast with two backs, they were getting it on.*

Quaint: *They were making love.*

Seated in a booth now, the cigarette smoke already drying out their noses, their throats, he decided on Middle English: ". . . They were fucking."

Zimmerman nodded, not as though he had known it

all along, but by way of saying he knew what such a taking of a wrong door could do to a guy, why he might not want to talk about it.

"And let me tell you that I went to see Blond Tommy," Cullen said. "He did this. . . ."

"Jesus." Zimmerman flinched from Cullen's bruise. "You should have someone look at that."

Cullen rebuttoned his collar and retightened his tie. "Neil, didn't Novak just say, just a while ago, that Rickey Henderson was whacked behind the left ear?"

"You said it too, sitting right here in this same booth last week, when you first told me about Rickey's K."

Last week? Didn't he mean last year? "That could mean a left-handed shooter."

"It could, if he was taken out from behind."

"Blond Tommy's left-handed. His vanity plate says SOUTHPAW. And I can see him pouring sugar in his coffee. I followed him to a McDonald's, he poured left-handed; he takes three creams and four sugars, he had two sausage-and-egg biscuits."

Zimmerman whistled. "His plate should say *CORONARY CANDIDATE*. Blond Tommy was in the Port Authority the day Rickey got K'd, just after noon. He bought a woman's Mets nightgown at the same store where Rickey got his UNLV hat. He gave the clerk a hard time, the clerk made a picture I showed him, remembered he'd paid with plastic, Visa. The manager pulled the credit-card flimsy: Thomas Michael Muldoon. I showed the clerk a picture of Tony Justice and he was maybe seventy-five percent sure Justice was the guy Rickey talked to after he bought the hat. I didn't see you at Rickey's funeral, or was Rickey one you didn't get around to?"

Cullen, sitting sidesaddle on his bench, had been worrying a napkin, and thought Zimmerman was ranting. He looked up and saw that Zimmerman wasn't talking to him about Rickey Henderson but to Sinéad O'Connor, who had seen them come in and had brought them coffee.

Sinéad seemed to understand Zimmerman perfectly, and stared down at the toes of her Doc Martens. "Does this mean no Mike and the Mechanics?"

"I think it's best," Zimmerman said.

Sinéad tromped off, chin up but trembling.

"A badge groupie," Zimmerman said. "Who would've thought? She was tight with Alonzo Paul, whose alibi, by the way, is solid. I talked to his mother."

"You've been busy," Cullen said.

"Also: Karen Justice's squash racquet, which everyone always mentions she was carrying when she got in the cab the night she went off the scope? It made it home to Central Park West."

Cullen shifted around and put both feet on the floor. "Now, *that's* interesting. Bobby Trumbo?"

Zimmerman nodded. "He called it Rickey's trump card. He didn't think he'd had a chance to play it.... Also: Alan Lang?"

"Is there anyplace you haven't been, Neil?"

"Something Rickey said once made Lang think Karen Justice's K had something to do with homosexuals. She knew someone who was gay, maybe Justice knew someone who was gay, she got killed because she knew or because he knew or because they both knew."

"Cutler," Cullen said. "I don't mean he's the some-one, I mean he's a gay connection, according to Ann."

"So, speaking of Ann, what's with you and Di Romano?" Zimmerman said.

Cullen swiveled sidesaddle again and went back to his napkin. It rang truer, at times—Di Romano. *"She's sitting on this steamer trunk, see—Di Romano—with her*

223

*dress hiked up, Justice has his pants down around his
knees, he's fucking her standing up, fucking Di Romano.*

"Joe?"

"I heard you."

"You're not addicted to her, are you, Joe? That
seems to be what happens."

"Addicted? No, I'm not addicted." He was a puppet
of his hormones, Ann had said, and would say again if
she were there. After hearing how he had spent his Saturday night and Sunday morning, she had done five
minutes on his marionette-hood, even coincidentally
echoing a line of Mescal Ronee's (or maybe it was a
current battle cry of The Sisterhood):

"It's all about trust, you know. That's all that matters. We go hunting for good looks and good sex and good
laughs, for someone who's read a book by someone other
than Joan or Jackie Collins; who's not afraid to go way
back among the Italian and Northern Renaissance stuff
at the Met, miles from the blockbuster exhibition and
the nearest gift shop; who has the self-esteem to stay
home four or five or six or seven nights a week. Outlaw
parties? Jesus Christ. What're you, Baryshnikov? Tama
Downtownowitz?"

(Yes, Ann had coined the name and Cullen had un-
scrupulously picked her pocket.)

"But the only thing that matters, the *only* thing, is
trust. I'm tired tired *tired* of dealing with men whose
brains are in their dicks. 'How was the movie?' 'Fantastic. The most gorgeous woman I have ever seen.' 'Right,
but how was the *mov*ie?' 'I just *told* you—fan*tas*tic.
You've got to see this woman.' I have conversations like
that every day at work. I hear them every day on the bus,
at the gym. 'How's your new secretary working out?'
'Great tits.' 'I hear your firm's got its first black woman
associate.' 'Yeah, and what a body.' To a woman, my

224

women friends say what's missing in their lives is intimacy. No shit, Lois Lane. How can you be intimate with
a penis, with something that *stands* up *eve*ry time it sees
something interesting? I'm tired of it, truly genuinely
bone-fucking-weary tired.

"See, what you do, you sleazebucket, is you pretend
to agree with things like what I just said. You say them
yourself sometimes: 'Neil's a terrific partner, a very,
very good cop'—she had made her voice newscaster
deep and self-important here—'but he's not a very
highly evolved human being. He's materialistic, he's
simplistic, he's sexist. He rationalizes his staring after
women on the street by saying he appreciates women's
bodies. He's a connois*seur* of women's bodies, is what he
means, the way he's a connoisseur of cutting-edge audio
equipment and stores that sell plain cotton T-shirts for
forty dollars. But he doesn't see that he's no different
from a construction goon or some garment-district rack
pusher going *"Mira, mira, chica."* ' You sound *great* when
you talk like that, Cullen, especially when you talk like
that in front of impressionable women. But it's really
just total fucking bullshit, because it's not *felt*, it's se*duc*-
tive; it's not your heart talking, it's your dick in collusion
with your conniving little mind. Your fucking tes-
tosterone pulls the strings and you dance."

"JOE? . . . JOE. . . . Joe!"

Cullen shook his head clear and looked at Zimmerman. "Did you say a Mets shirt?"

"A *what*?"

"You said Blond Tommy bought something at that
uniform store in the Port Authority."

"A Mets nightgown."

"A woman's nightgown."

225

"Yes."

Sinéad O'Connor stumped by with someone else's order and Cullen tipped his head toward her. "Do you mind if I ask her something?"

"I'd make sure she doesn't have a knife in her hand."

Cullen slid out of the booth and went to the back of the coffee shop, where Sinéad was dumping dirty dishes into the busboy's station. "Jan, you said you were a painter."

She didn't look at him. "So?"

"I'm blocked on the name of a painter. Contemporary. A woman. She does abstracts, big paintings. Her first name's Ronee—R-o-n-e-e. She signs her—"

"Ronee Baldwin." Sinéad aimed an elbow at Cullen's ribs as she pushed past him.

"Thanks." Cullen went to the pay phone and called information and got Ronee's number, all sixes and nines. He went back to the booth.

"What's going on?" Zimmerman said.

"I called the other day, Friday, and asked Cindy to get Jersey Bell to run the MUDS of a pay phone Blond Tommy used to make a call. I asked her to give you the number if she saw you first. Did she?"

Zimmerman got out his notebook and flipped through it. He found the page and turned it so Cullen could read it. Cullen read it, all sixes and nines, and turned it back and put his notebook down next to it, open to the page with the number he'd just gotten from information.

Zimmerman said, "Who's Ronee Baldwin?"

"She's a baseball fan, someone whose boyfriend might call a left-hander a southpaw. She says 'whacked' for killed, the way a cop's girlfriend might. She was once upon a time in some porn films. Blond Tommy had a

226

couple of porn cassettes in the glove compartment of his car."

"You know her, then?"

"We met at a party. She's a friend of"—*Di or Diana?*—"of Diana Romano's. Another friend was Karen Justice, before her first marriage, before her modeling career. Karen did some porn too, according to Ronee."

"Small world," Zimmerman said.

"Your friend Og Slate was at the party too," Cullen said. "He sent his regards. Did you know he's gay?"

"Not only that, he's a chicken hawk. I ran into him at the Port Authority, speaking of small worlds."

"Isn't his wife . . . ?"

Zimmerman nodded.

"Diana Romano," Cullen began, starting to tell Zimmerman about the contact sheet from the shoot from hell, "took some photographs—"

"Hi, guys." Big white teeth, wide brown eyes, milk-chocolate skin, tango-dancer slick black hair, pinstripes veering in fascinating ways, Detective Maria Esperanza stood over their booth. "I've got something kind of interesting. Mind if I sit down?"

Zimmerman didn't throw himself onto the floor so she could use him as a stile to climb into the booth. But he used his napkin to brush off the seat next to him. Whatever Cullen had been about to say wasn't as interesting as what Maria Esperanza was about to say. "Please."

She sat, her clothing sighing sweetly, and got right to it. "I've been working on this awhile, since I've been helping Suffolk Homicide on the Justice K. Going over the files on Justice's wife's K, I was struck that we never found the cabbie who picked her up. Fliers went out, and turned up *nada*, which doesn't make sense when you think about it, because this was a beautiful woman, a former model, a little notorious because of her husband's murder—her first husband's—remarried to a well-known writer, her disappearance a big story all over the country. So I thought maybe, just maybe, the driver never *saw* the fliers. Maybe he was, just for the sake of argument, a foreigner with green-card troubles, he got picked up by INS the day after he gave a ride to Karen Justice. He had an accident and lost his license. He quit. Whatever.

"A girl at Taxi and Limo owed me a favor, I asked her to pull the names of any drivers who stopped driving, for whatever reason, on or around last September one-seven. It was a very short list, ten or twelve names, most of them foreigners who, just as I'd thought, had green-card problems. One of them was a woman named Julia Strange, who'd driven for Belmar.

"I called Belmar and the dispatcher said they used to call Julia Strange Strange Julia because she was always reading books. He said they also called her Red because she had red hair, and Good-Looking because she was, and Hemingway because all she talked about was moving to Paris to write a novel. She quit last September one-seven and did just that. I asked how he happened to have the date on the tip of his tongue. He said he'd just been discussing it with her, with Julia Strange, asking her when it was she left exactly. I said meaning she's back? He said it didn't work out, she was back, she was standing right there, did I want to talk to her? She's staying at a friend's on Grove Street. I'm on my way over. Want to come?"

30

THE NOVEL JULIA STRANGE WENT to Paris to write was a suspense novel— she called it a *roman policier*—about a New York taxi driver, a good-looking redhead, who goes to Paris to write a suspense novel and gets caught up in a plot hatched by the handsome bastard son of a legendary Congo mercenary and a beautiful Bantu princess to steal the remains of Ayatollah Khomeini and swap them for hostages held by Islamic fundamentalists in Lebanon.

"Sounds commercial," Cullen said. "What do they call it? High-concept."

"I'd like to read it," Zimmerman said. *I'd like to get to know you*, his eyes and face and body said, for he found that he could entertain the notion of a tall pale redhead with a spare name while still remaining true to the concept of small dark girls with big names.

Maria Esperanza saw that he could, and was not amused. She had appreciated Zimmerman's generosity in attributing her failure to mention something to her wish to be brief; she had felt sorry for Zimmerman for taking it on the chin from Chief Ruth for wishing to be brief himself; she had counted Zimmerman a little bit different from other cops for not trying to climb down the front of her suit while still appreciating the fascinating ways in which its pinstripes veered, and she had read the *I'd like to get to know you* in his eyes and had thought she'd like to get to know him too. But now, watching him watching tall pale Julia Strange, she saw the same message, saw that his interest was generic. "Don't forget the Rushdie controversy. A book like that might offend a lot of people."

Julia Strange waved a hand at that—"Rushdie's book was a best-seller for months; I could stand that kind of controversy"—and went on serving them ice tea and Milano cookies on the tiny balcony of her borrowed brownstone parlor-floor apartment. The balcony looked down into the garden of the Greenwich House Music School, out whose windows tumbled a babel of Mozart, Mahler, Mingus, Kern, and Sondheim, coaxed out of pianos, woodwinds, strings, drums, and voices by beginners, adepts, inepts, experts.

The son of a socialite and adept himself at making small talk with his hands full, Zimmerman said, "Sergeant Cullen's son is a musician."

"In fact," Sergeant Cullen said, "he took his first piano lessons at that very school. I used to sit and wait for him in that garden and try and pick out his 'Skip to My Lou' from all the others."

"Does he still play?" Maria Esperanza said.

"Not piano, guitar. His hero used to be Hoagy Carmichael, now he's a Bon Jovi wanna-be."

Zimmerman and Maria Esperanza and Julia Strange laughed more heartily than that deserved. The smallness of the balcony had the effect of making them feel Brobdingnagian, and it took some effort to bring their gestures down.

Cullen brushed cookie crumbs off his fingertips over the balcony railing and blotted his lips with a party napkin imprinted WELCOME HOME, IRA. "Tell us about last September seventeenth, Miss Strange."

And she did, sounding like the opening paragraphs of a *roman policier*: "I usually drove nights, so I could write in the daytime. Graham Greene taught me that, in his autobiography: get a night job and write in the morning; be tired on somebody else's time.

"That night I worked the day shift and some overtime. I was leaving for France on a charter at midnight. I'm a lousy traveler; I always get to airports too early. I wanted to work as late as possible, then go home and change and get there just on time.

"I'd dropped a fare at Grand Central and picked one up for Fifty-seventh and Madison. I kept going uptown and she hailed me a couple of blocks later—north of the GM building, but I don't know the exact street.

"When Officer Esperanza—it is Esperanza, isn't it?"

"Detective," Maria Esperanza said.

"When De*tective* Esperanza called the garage, Larry, the dispatcher, showed me the flier you guys put out. Larry never throws anything away; he's got ten-year-old Lotto tickets. It was the same woman. She had a briefcase and a squash racquet in a, you know, in a bag, a case. I know it was a squash racquet, because I told her I'd never seen anyone carrying a badminton racquet around New York. She laughed. Not unkindly, but she laughed. I used that exchange in my book. Never do anything or say anything in front of a writer that you don't want to see in print. I now know the origin of the name badminton; it's named after Badminton House, the country estate of the dukes of Beaufort, where the game was invented in the nineteenth century."

Zimmerman laughed this time, joke or no joke, to the dismay of Maria Esperanza and of Cullen. Cullen knew Zimmerman to be a royalist, but he didn't think he had to try so hard to appreciate a bit of patrician trivia.

"She gave Eighty-first and Central Park West as her destination," Julia Strange said. "I stayed on Madison, heading for Seventy-ninth. At about Seventy-second, her beeper went off. It was in her pocketbook or her briefcase and at first I thought it was a wristwatch alarm. She saw me looking in the mirror and rolled her eyes in a way that made me like her. She asked me to pull over at a pay

231

phone. There was one at about Seventy-fifth or -sixth, on the, uh, southwest corner.

She left her stuff in the cab and got out and made a call—a local call; she dropped in a quarter. She didn't call a service to find out who beeped her. Some beepers have a display that shows the number that's calling you. If she had one of those—I didn't see that she had it, but she must've—it was a number she knew; she didn't write it down and she didn't take it with her when she made the call." Julia Strange took a look around at that point to see if these professionals noticed how a writer of *romans policiers* had observed that little detail. Zimmerman smiled hugely. Maria Esperanza's nostrils twitched. Cullen said, "Please go on."

A bite of cookie, a sip of tea, a blotting of the lips, an explanation for the napkins: "My boyfriend gave me a surprise welcome-home party. He never has any money; he's a would-be writer too. He got these at a discount paper-supply place. I don't know *who* Ira is."

It was Maria Esperanza's turn to laugh—not about the napkins, but that there was a boyfriend who had bought them. Zimmerman moped.

"I wasn't trying to eavesdrop," Julia Strange said. "But she stood facing me. I could hear every word. It was one of those conversations where it was very simple to fill in the other half:

"She said, 'Hi,' the other person probably said, 'Where are you?'

"She said, 'At a pay phone. I was in a cab,' the other person probably said, 'Going where?'

"She said, 'Home,' the other person probably said, 'Can you meet me at Rusty's?'

"She looked at her watch and said, 'Just for a while.'

"She hung up, she felt to see if her quarter came back, she got back in the cab, she said she'd changed her plans, take her—please—to Seventy-fourth and Third. The fare was around four dollars with the night rate, she gave me a ten, told me to keep it, for my 'trouble.' I put that in my book too—an impeccably dressed woman who fishes for a quarter in a coin return, then gives a cabbie a one-hundred-fifty-percent tip.

"She said, 'Have a nice evening.' I said, 'I will. I'm going to Paris.' She laughed and said, '*Bon voyage.*' She went up to the window of Rusty's and tapped on the glass. The person she was meeting—the guy—was sitting at a table in the window. He smiled and they, you know, touched fingertips on either side of the glass. She went in, I put my off-duty sign on, went to the garage, went home, went to Paris, to write. I couldn't write in Paris, though, so I'm back."

"What did the guy look like, Miss Strange?" Cullen said.

"Like that wrestler, the one with the long blond hair who used to hang around with Cyndi Lauper."

"Neil," Cullen said.

Zimmerman showed Julia Strange the copy of the badly lit, contrasty year-old photograph of Blond Tommy on his last pistol permit. She squinted at it, looked at the flip side, fanned herself with it. "Could be. Definitely. I think so."

"You think it definitely could be," Cullen said.

Julia Strange giggled. She weighed the copy on her fingertips, the ultimate test. "It's the guy. . . . Or the *type* of guy, anyway."

"And she didn't look upset to be there? She looked like she liked the guy?"

"They looked like friends, not lovers. Or maybe it's just that I couldn't love a guy like that."

"Thanks." Cullen got up. "Thanks for the tea. And the music."

Maria Esperanza got up too, and followed after Cullen. Zimmerman moved to the front of his chair, but stayed seated. "I'm interested—you said you couldn't write in Paris. I wrote a paper in college about expatriate American writers in Paris in the twenties, especially Hemingway and Gertrude Stein. My thesis was that being among foreigners took them back to an almost preliterate form of expression. Every day they struggled to make themselves understood in a foreign language and they wrote in English the same way. Their writing is beyond simple, it's almost simplistic. A rose is a rose. . . . We went to the stream and the stream was cold and we put the wine in the cold stream and the wine was cold and we drank the cold wine and it was good. . . . Was it similar for you? Did you feel anything like that? Was that why you couldn't write? I'm just curious. I just thought . . . Well, maybe . . ."

Julia Strange shook her head. "It was more basic. I missed my boyfriend. I missed sex."

"MARIA?"

To see Cullen better, Maria Esperanza sat back in the corner of the back seat of Zimmerman's Saab, inching through the midafternoon jam on Varick Street. (Zimmerman, at the wheel, smoked from the ears over the seating arrangements—though it was far from his custom to let anyone else drive his goddamn car. He displaced his anger by blasting his horn at a white Continental trying to nose into his lane.)

"Yes, Sergeant?"

"Joe. It looks like you're working with us. Do you mind?"

"No, Joe. Not at all."

"We're a little unofficial. As you heard, I'm in Hriniak's doghouse."

"It's not a doghouse full of all kinds of nasty things, is it?"

Cullen smiled. "No. No, it's not. . . . We need to know a couple of things, Maria: Julia Strange said Karen Justice recognized the number on her beeper. It isn't likely she'd recognize the number of a pay phone at Rusty's, it's more likely Blond Tommy called from a residential phone *near* Rusty's. Call Karen Justice's real-estate company, KarWin, get the name of their paging service, see if there's a record of that page. If that doesn't pay off, a messier route is to find the pay phone and run its MUDS. Either way, it'll take a while, so go around to Rusty's, see if anyone knows Blond Tommy, if anyone knows if he hung out anywhere nearby—a friend's, a girlfriend's, his own apartment, whatever.

"If no one knows or isn't saying, Charlie Peck, Manhattan Crime Scene, was in Brooklyn Anti-Crime with Blond Tommy when Tommy was having an affair with Diana Romano. Call Charlie, tell him I'll owe him, ask him if he knows if Tommy has an apartment in Manhattan. Tommy, for the record, lives in Little Silver, New Jersey."

"No kidding? I'm from Asbury," Maria Esperanza said.

Cullen would have loved to pass the traffic jam away talking about Bruce and Madame Marie's and the silly New York virgins. He usually never passed up a chance to talk Springsteen around Zimmerman, the Mike and the Mechanics fan, the man who thought Rod Stewart was Heavy Metal, but he had a feeling in his gut that they were running out of time, though what the deadline was and who was imposing it, he couldn't say. No one else stood to die.

Did they?

31 WHEN ANN WAS A WHOLE LOT YOUN-
ger, with more spring in her step, stars of
great magnitude in her eyes, a fakebook of
toe-tapping songs in her heart, she had a
boyfriend who urged her to read Tolkien from cover to
cover to cover to cover to cover. If the cock is hard, she
reasoned, and complied.

The mismatch of cuteness and portentousness
numbed her, but she liked the part very near the beginning where Dildo or Baggo or whatever his name was was
press-ganged to be the official lockpicker of a treasure-
hunting expedition in spite of his total lack of lockpicking
skills. Whenever Dildo or Baggo would wonder how he
and his companions were ever going to gain access to yet
another apparently impenetrable place, someone would
remind him: "*You're* the burglar."

"*You're* the burglar," Ann whispered to herself now
as she stood in a hallway deep in the labyrinth of the
New York *Bulletin*'s editorial floor, outside the locked
door to Tony Justice's office. Some wag—she didn't
think it had been Justice, but a fan—had put a DON'T
MESS WITH TEXAS bumper sticker up on the pane of
old-fashioned frosted glass, X'd out the last word, and
written in JUSTICE with a felt-tipped pen.

Ann had breezed this far, having told the receptionist by the elevators that she was a press agent—new in
town, in case the receptionist claimed to know every
press agent there was—with a couple of handouts for the
boys back in Drama. That whole-lot-younger Ann had
worked at a newspaper herself, as it happened, and remembered that press agents often sailed through the

various checkpoints unchallenged (while real folks with real stories to tell were turned back and turned out). And she remembered that the press agents with nearly absolute entrée were the ones who provided the Broadway columnists with the jokes the columnists supposedly heard firsthand, the celebrities the columnists supposedly saw with their own eyes, the confetti of gossip that supposedly floated down on the columnists' shoulders as they supposedly strolled the Rialto. (She remembered that the drill had been that the flacks made facedown piles of their handouts on the columnists' desks; when the columnists came to work early in the afternoon, they would turn the piles over and type up the jokes and the gossip, drop the names, in the order in which they had been delivered. The early bird got the lead item.)

"You're the burglar," Ann reminded herself again, in answer to the question she was asking herself: *Now what?*

Credit card. Burglars used credit cards to pick locks. Credit cards or elegant little stainless-steel picks selected from sets of picks carried in handsome leather cases that fit nicely in an inside pocket or in a lady burglar's purse. Ann didn't have a case of picks, but she had plenty of credit cards. Funny how her credit-card companies called her on the phone or wrote saber-rattling letters at the merest suggestion that she had been shopping compulsively or was flirting with her credit limit, but her being a murder suspect didn't seem to bother them a bit. She had gotten a new card in the mail just that morning, a credit line even her mother could love preapproved in recognition, the cover letter said, of her "outstanding credit history." She could, presumably, continue to write that history, shopping by

237

mail or phone, even when *she* was history, behind bars, doing points, in stir, in the joint—that was probably why.

But how exactly *did* you use a credit card to pick a lock? Where exactly did you slip it in? Did it make a difference which way the magnetic strip faced?

"You're the—"

Oh dear, oh shit, oh christ, oh damn, someone was coming. A copy-boyish young man, cute, short, pugnacious, a Sean Penn look-alike. Blue candy-striped shirt with the collar unbuttoned just so, sleeves rolled up just so, dark blue knit tie loosened just so, a pencil behind his ear, horn-rimmed glasses hanging by an earpiece from a corner of his mouth, he was a chorus dancer dreaming of taking over one of the leads. He was on a mail run, but in his fantasy he was returning to his office (no newsroom bullpen desk for him), having impressed the slow-witted brass at the daily editorial meeting with the need to have his piece be at least the off-lead, never mind that he'd been on the front page fifty-seven straight days. The interoffice envelopes under his arm were in his fantasy crucial Central Intelligence Agency files slipped him at a rendezvous in a dark, echoey underground garage by a disenchanted company assassin, a man who had had in the cross hairs of his watchamacallit, world leaders like—

"Hiya." The Sean Penn look-alike took the horn-rims out of his mouth and put them up in his hair. Vain about his myopia, thank God, he wouldn't be able to describe her to the cops.

Ann had always been a hit with copy boys—in those whole-lot-younger newspaper days and now at the magazine, where the copy boys tended to be thirty-year-olds with useless advanced degrees from the London School of Economics, the Sorbonne, NYU Film School. Young or old, they appreciated that she didn't talk down to them, like the bitches who covered fashion, or try to act like one of the boys, like the butches who covered sports. "Hiya."

"Can I help you? Most of the back-of-the-paper people don't come in till one or two."

Inspiration: "I'm with the software people. I'm rounding up the five-point-two. We're replacing it with an upgrade."

The gamble was that the Sean Penn look-alike was computer hyperliterate. His blank face said he was not: Five-point-two, 6.3, 128.9—it was all Pascal to him. Maybe he had a mentor, some crusty chain-smoking old coot who spiked his Styrofoam cups of black coffee with Jim Beam from a bottle in his desk drawer and insisted that the Good Lord hadn't meant for words to be processed on video display terminals, He had meant for them to be formed a tap at a time on good bond paper rolled into battered old Underwoods or Royals or Smiths long before there was a Corona. Ann had had a couple of mentors like that herself, except that hers had been motivated by a desire to sleep with her as much as to impress her with the extent of their traditionalism.

"So if you'll please unlock these offices, I'll collect the disks. The new ones'll be here in a minute. My colleague's on the way up; he had to park the car."

"Uh . . ."

"You can stand and watch. I'm not going to steal anything."

The Sean Penn look-alike laughed, but he wasn't sure.

So now what?

You're *the burglar.*

The burglar in her would never amount to a hill of beans, but the woman in her knew just what to do—unbutton a button—and did it.

And smiled.

And licked her lips.

The Sean Penn look-alike, seeing the button unbuttoned, hearing the hiss of lips being licked, took his horn-rims down from his hair and put them on. *Boing, boing.* "Uh, sure, yeah, okay. I have a key." He unhooked a ring of keys from his belt, but didn't make a move toward the door to Justice's office. "Listen, do you, uh . . . ?"

"What?"

"Well . . ."

Ann put her hand on the clasp of her bag. "Do I have some ID? I sure do."

"It's okay. Really. It's okay, it's okay."

She unsnapped the clasp. "Listen, I understand. You can't be too careful."

He turned his back on her, wishing he'd never suggested she might be untrustworthy. "Let's start with the movie critics."

Ann snapped the clasp shut, and didn't move. "What about this office?"

"*This* office?"

"Doesn't Tony Justice use . . . ? Oh. *That* Tony Justice?"

The Sean Penn look-alike nodded gravely. "I don't think he'll be needing new software."

"No. No, I guess not. But . . . I should still pick up the old disk. Someday someone's going to use this office again, right?"

"Uh, yeah. I guess."

"A star. A columnist, a feature writer, an editorial writer—whatever. A critic."

"You're probably right."

"So I should pick up the old disk, because he or she is going to want the latest software."

He just wasn't sure. That mentor of his, the crotchety old fart. Jason Robards.

Ann said, "Look. On the way out, I'll check with the assistant managing editor, Mister uh ..." She opened her bag all the way this time and pretended to look inside: Trident spearmint gum, Maxithins, Curity telfa sterile pads, a Du Pont nylon comb, a Caswell-Massey hairbrush, a Pilot Precise V7 rolling-ball pen, another one, another one—what did a burglar need with so many pens?—all kinds of coins, scraps of paper, gum wrappers, matchbooks (taken from restaurants and hotel lobbies out of habit from the days when smoking had been the habit and she had always been out of matches), safety pins, paper clips, lint and shit but nothing that looked like an official—

"Quinn?" the Sean Penn look-alike said helpfully, hopefully.

Ann snapped her bag shut again. "I'll check with Mister *Quinn* on the way out and if he thinks that for some reason the five-point-two should stay in this office, well ..."

He laughed, the Sean Penn look-alike, which was what Ann had begged for with her sardonic delivery. He unlocked the door to Tony Justice's office, he stopped aside to let Ann pass. "There's his computer"—he pointed with his horn-rims (which he'd taken off again in the hope she wouldn't think he needed to wear them all the time) at a Toshiba lap-top on a typing table next to the big old wooden desk that wasn't a Purchasing Department acquisition but a true antique—"but where he keeps—kept—his disks, I have no ... idea." He laughed again, the Sean Penn look-alike, for Ann had gone

241

straight to the computer, pressed a button on the side, and out had popped a disk.

"They should be stored in a proper disk filer," Ann said in her best flesh-and-blood modulese, "but most people leave them right in the computer."

Now: How do I distract him so I can get the rest of the disks, the disks I really want?

You're *the burglar.*

"Would you do me a favor . . . Uh, I'm sorry, I don't know your name."

"David."

"David, could you please do me a favor and look out by the elevator and see if my colleague's standing there? He's a big tall white-haired man in a gray suit. I'm afraid he might've gone in the other direction." Ann ran a fingernail against her chest inside the placket of her blouse in case the Sean Penn look-alike needed prompting, but he was gone before she even finished concocting her imaginary sidekick.

She popped out the disk in the B drive of the computer and looked around for the proper file she suspected a classic summerguy, a careful sailor, a thoughtful guide and host and cook like Tony Justice, of having. She found it in the big center drawer of his big old desk, a gray plastic folding file that some disk-maker gave away as a bonus when you bought disks by the score, by the pound. There were eight or ten disks inside. She put everything in her bag. She went out the door and shut it. The Sean Penn look-alike wasn't back yet, he was *really* looking, so Ann went on down the hall the other way and out a fire door and down the stairs to the street.

She wasn't even shaking.

Of course you're not shaking. You're the burglar.

242

32 "JEFF!" RONEE BALDWIN LOOKED helplessly at the roach in her fingertips. "What a *nice* surprise."

"This is my partner, Detective Zimmerman."

"Shit, a*nother* narc?" Ronee sucked on the roach one more time, then dropped it on the rough wooden floor outside the metal door to her loft. She would have trod on it to put it out, but she realized she was barefoot. She smiled when Cullen stepped on the roach. "Thank you, Jeff. Thank you *so* much."

"Tell Detective Zimmerman what you told me," Cullen said. "About when you and Karen started your modeling careers."

"Gee, Jeff, I'd love to talk about the old days, but I have company." Ronee gestured at her black tank top and paint-spattered white jeans as if they were the latest in entertaining-at-home clothes.

Cullen stepped around Ronee into the loft, which had even more mescal bottles than the last time, but no visitors. Ronee stomped after him, bare feet slapping. "Okay, so I'm alone. I *don't* like to talk about the old days. I hate talking about the old days."

Cullen sat on the arm of the sofa that he and Ronee and Og Slate had crammed themselves into. "Tell Detective Zimmerman what you told me."

Ronee made her mouth a bow and put a finger to its corner. Betty Boop. "Which part, Jeff? The changing-room part? You get off on that shit? Lots of guys do. Some of them pay to peep through holes in the dressing-room walls. Some rich, famous guys, guys you wouldn't

243

buh-*leeve*, guys you'd think could get all the trim they—"

She snapped her fingers suddenly, having made a connection. She took Zimmerman by the elbows and held him at arm's length, as if he were a piece from the next season's line. "You *are* cute, Detective Zimmerman. Og Slate *said* you were cute and you *are* cute." She tossed a look at Cullen. "You're cute too, Jeff, don't get me wrong, but you're not my type. Detective Zimmerman's my type—tall, dark, and ever-so-cute. What's your first name, Detective Zimmerman? Or is Detective your first name, Detective Zimmerman?"

Zimmerman got gently out of Ronee's grasp and got her by an elbow. "Have a seat, please."

"Hey, do that again I'll call my lawyer. I'll tell him you mauled me. Police brutality. I'll call Spike Lee. I *know* Spike. Spike came to a *party* here."

Zimmerman found a cordless phone in a mess on a desk and handed it to her.

Ronee tumbled into a big club chair. She draped her legs over an arm and held the phone tight against her crotch, stroking it hand over hand. Her hollow eyes betrayed her awareness that she was the saddest of things—a temptress gone arid.

"Pornography, Ronee," Cullen said.

Ronee laughed her alcohol-and-nicotine laugh. "You guys're assholes, you know that? Every fucking one of you. Tommy Muldoon. You, Jeff. You, Detective Zimmerman. Assholes. Cop assholes."

Cullen was disappointed. He should have surprised her with the name, not let her slip it in first. "How long have you known Tommy?"

Ronee ignored him. "Did you fuck Romano, Jeff? The other night? You wanted to. Did you?"

Zimmerman got a bentwood chair from a dining

table and sat close to Ronee, off to one side. "Have you seen Tommy lately?"

" 'Cause if you didn't fuck her, if you haven't fucked her, then you're the only guy in town." She craned her neck to see Zimmerman. "Unless maybe Detective Zimmerman here hasn't fucked her. Have you fucked Romano, Detective Zimmerman?"

Whatever Ronee was high on, she was coming down off it, coming in for a crash landing. Cullen got up and got a bottle of mescal from a coffee table and gave it to Ronee to postpone the auguring in. "The night Karen disappeared, she met Tommy at Rusty's. What did they talk about?"

Ronee stopped the bottle on the way to her mouth, impressed. Sometimes—once in a great while—you asked the right question, one that rendered answers true or answers false irrelevant. She took a swallow and waited for the surge to make her dumb again. "I don't know what they talked about. How the fuck should *I* know what they talked about?" But she would never be as dumb as she had been; she had surfaced and she couldn't go back under: under was too frightening, too deep. Too lonely. "Maybe they talked about auld lang syne. Maybe they went to Tommy's place and watched one of the old jerk-off flicks."

"Tommy's place," Cullen said, "—where is it, exactly?"

"Across the street. The dump on the corner."

For a moment, Cullen misunderstood, and looked toward the windows, which looked out on the roof of another loft building across Wooster Street.

There was a man on the roof. A man with a hat.

And then there wasn't.

Cullen got up and went to the window. Nothing— just water towers, air-conditioning units, fire escapes, windows, people, taxis, trucks, a Chinese delivering Chinese food on a balloon-tire bike. Where did the Chinese restaurants get all those balloon-tire bikes?

"What?" Zimmerman said.

Cullen came back, shaking his head. "You mean on the corner across from Rusty's, right, Ron?"

Ronee was stroking the bottle now, holding it against her shoulder as if it were a kitten. "It was another cop's. I forget his name. Another asshole. Except he was smart enough to get out; he went to Alaska to work on the pipeline; he left the key with Tommy."

"What's the address?"

"It's the four-story dump. The other dumps're bigger."

"What name's on the bell?"

"It's a dump. There's no bell. You just give the front door a good shove. The apartment's on the third floor, in the back."

Zimmerman picked up the phone, which Ronee had put on the floor next to the sofa. "I'll call Maria. Save her some legwork."

Cullen nodded. "Thanks, Neil."

Ronee craned her neck again. "*Neil?* Your name's *Neil? Neil* Zimmerman?"

Zimmerman took the phone into Ronee's studio. "I like your work," he said as he waited for the call to go through.

Ronee slid her hand into her crotch and wagged her eyebrows at Cullen. "He should see my *work.*"

"I was down in Little Silver last week," Cullen said. "Tommy and I had a chat. Before we did, he made a phone call—to you. While I was waiting, I played with the things in his car. He had a couple of, uh, jerk-off movies in the glove compartment."

"Some people can't get enough of that shit."

"The movies you were in—did Tommy make them?"

"They aren't movies, Jeff. They're *flicks*."

"Did Tommy make them?"

"He was, you know, the producer."

"And you were in some, and Karen, and you and Karen together."

She batted her lashes. "That turn you on, Jeff?"

"What about Diana Romano?"

Ronee laughed. "Ro*mano*? Romano was ten years old when we made those flicks. Romano's a baby, Jeff."

Cullen was relieved. Relieved that Diana Romano had been too young to be in the flicks, or relieved that she hadn't been in the flicks even *though* she had been so young, he couldn't say. "And Karen and Tommy were a couple at the time?"

Ronee gave him a weary look. Like all the very vain, she was offended by interrogation; she felt you should already *know* everything. "It was nineteen-seventy. Peace, love—all that shit. There weren't any couples— except John and Yoko, which is why John and Yoko seemed so fucking weird. Everybody else fucked any- body else."

Zimmerman was back now and sat in the bentwood chair. He'd overheard enough about the movies to know what to call them. "These flicks—was Tommy produc- ing them for some bad guys?"

"Naturally."

"Remember any names?"

"Guido, Vito, and Dumbo."

Zimmerman smiled. "So he was running around with bad guys even in those days?"

"Naturally. Tommy loves bad guys. Why do you think Tommy was a cop? So he could help people? So he could be a public fucking servant? He was a cop because it was a great way to meet bad guys, learn new tricks, do them favors, get favors done."

"Did the bad guys do Tommy the favor of killing his wife?" Cullen said.

Rather than choke on it, Ronee sprayed out her mouthful of mescal. She coughed and hacked and finally laughed and laughed and laughed. She shook her head and shook it and laughed and laughed.

And Cullen understood that there was only one thing that was that funny. "You're Rae Muldoon."

Ronee stopped laughing and shaking and put her head back against the arm of the sofa, spent.

"Baldwin," Cullen said. "Baldwin's where you lived, Baldwin, Long Island."

Ronee wrinkled her nose. "Clever, no?"

"Insurance," Zimmerman said. They were at the point—finally—where the questions were the answers.

Ronee squinted at one of her big abstract paintings—blobs of red, a gash of black—as if wondering how the hell it had gotten on her wall. "What a fucking asshole Tommy was. They don't let go of their fucking money, insurance guys, as long as they smell a rat, and in Tommy's case they got so close and sniffed so hard they could smell a rat's asshole."

"And in the meantime," Cullen said, "as so often happens, you and Tommy split up."

Ronee gave him the finger. "What're you, Jeff, a philosopher?"

"Tommy's affair with Diana Romano—was that the real thing, or was it just to embellish your disappearance?"

Ronee chuckled. "Em*bell*ish? He em*bell*ished her fucking brains out, so don't give me em*bell*ish."

"But she found out about your scam. How?"

"Tommy told her, what'd you think? First he em*bel-*

248

lished her, then he told her. Most guys don't talk in bed—not afterwards. Oh, maybe if they're really sweet they'll say, 'Hey, what's your name?' Most guys, they em*bel*lish you, then they forget you. One minute they need you *so* bad, the next second they don't want to know about you. You should feel what it's like, you guys, you should have the experience of one second having a guy need you *so* bad, the next second wanting you out of his life practically—or until the next time he wants some trim. It's like walking out of a hot hot summer day into an air-conditioned building—except we're not talking just about a change in temperature here, we're talking about contempt. Tommy's different, I'll say that for him. He loves to talk afterwards. He comes too fast, slam bam, like all micks, but he loves to talk afterwards. I used to think it was his orgasms. He had these itty-bitty orgasms, hardly any come. Some guys shoot such a wad, it drips out of you down your leg all day long, Tommy shoots a few little drops. It's like, I don't know, he's got to talk to make up for it, or something. Or the words are instead of the come, or something. I don't know, fuck it."

Cullen looked at Zimmerman, who looked at him. They had asked the right questions and were getting the right answers; they had come here to find out a little and were finding out a whole lot more; they were getting a sense of where this would lead them. And yet: something was wrong, something was too easy. Neither particularly wanted to be the point man for the next part of the way. Cullen pulled rank and nodded to Zimmerman to go first.

Zimmerman went slowly, in the present tense, the tense for writing on water. "A couple of years after her thing with Tommy, Di Romano gets involved with Tony Justice, she tells him about your insurance scam. Justice wants Karen out of the way so he can marry Di, he tells

249

Tommy he'll blow the whistle on him unless Tommy kills Karen."

"What's this *Di* shit, Neil?" Ronee said. "*Are* you fucking her? Are you *both* fucking her?"

"The meeting at Rusty's is a setup. Karen calls Justice to say she's on the way home from work. Justice calls Tommy, who's at his place across from Rusty's, Tommy beeps Karen in a cab, suggests they get together for a drink. Tommy's already been in touch with Karen—for auld lang syne. They've hung out together a little. They probably liked each other, right? I mean, they were kind of wild when they were young, now they're grown up and successful. Karen's first husband was killed, Tommy's wife is missing. They commiserate. Maybe . . ."

"Maybe Tommy tells Karen about Stephen Fox," Cullen said. "Tells her that Tony Justice had Fox killed so he could marry her. Is that what Tommy did, Ron?"

Ronee was *in* the big abstract painting now—mucking through the blobs of red, stepping warily around the gash of black. "What, Jeff? Sorry, I was . . ."

"Did Tommy tell Karen that Justice had Karen's first husband murdered?"

". . . If you say so, Jeff."

"Tommy knew because Justice told him."

". . . If you say so."

"They wanted Karen to think Tommy was trying to help her. They wanted her to let Tommy get close enough to kill her."

". . . If you say so."

"The squash racquet was Tommy's proof that he'd done the job. He brought it to Justice. He probably brought Karen's purse and her briefcase and her clothes too, but Justice destroyed them. He forgot about the squash racquet, though. He put it in a closet and Rickey Henderson found it."

Still in the painting, Ronee mouthed *Rickey Henderson?*

The phone rang.

Zimmerman made a move to answer it, but Ronee scrambled up out of the painting and beat him to it. She took the phone into an alcove where they couldn't hear what she was saying.

Cullen said, "So?"

Zimmerman said, "So we got a lot more than we came for. Which makes me wonder."

Cullen nodded. "She was ready to talk. What spooked her?"

Zimmerman shrugged. "You showed up at her party with Di Romano. Di Romano's a singer. Maybe Ronee figured she sang to you."

Maybe. But Cullen was trying now to catch the drift of Ronee's phone conversation, the way Julia Strange, attempted author of a *roman policier*, had caught the drift of Karen Justice's call from the street-corner pay phone. But while Cullen, *gendarme*, could see Ronee, he could hear only sibilances and changes in pitch. Her shoulders hunched, bent forward from the waist, feet spread wide, her free hand splayed open, palm up, Ronee's posture said *I'm telling you. . . . It's the truth. . . . Honest.*

The caller insisted that Ronee was lying.

Again: *I'm telling you. . . . It's the truth. . . . Honest.*

The caller relented a little, for Ronee straightened up, relaxed her shoulders, let her hand fall, stood hip-shot.

The caller said something that amazed Ronee, for she turned to face Cullen and Zimmerman, as if she were hearing news she wanted to share. "You're kidding. . . . *Really?*"

The caller assured Ronee that he or she was not

251

kidding, and invited her to see with her own eyes, for she came out of the alcove, looking toward the windows, striding toward them, then trotting, then running. "Here? . . . Right now?"

And then what had been so simple became crazy, pointless, inexplicable. What the caller said, what Ronee did, none of it meant anything, none of it mattered. All that mattered was what was to come, which was the end of it all, the finish. That was what was simple, it was the simplest thing of all.

"Neil. *Neil!*"

But Zimmerman was right with the program, he had figured it out too, he was on the ball and halfway across the room when Cullen called to him, halfway to the windows, halfway to the web of floating isolated solitary individual pieces of glass the windows had become, hanging momentarily, hanging forever, still all a unit, still all touching contiguous joined, then slowly, slowly, slowly falling crashing splashing spilling on the rough softwood floor, glittering, shattered, shards, diamonds, slivers, scimitars, slices, pearls, pieces, motes, grains, dust.

And Zimmerman was halfway to Ronee, who was being punched repeatedly in the chest and stomach and thighs by the same mad withering fire that was turning the windows to something like tumbling liquid. She still held the cordless phone in her hand, held it out in front of her. She was—yes, she was staring at the phone, the way poor actors in poor productions do to communicate their dismay, their displeasure, their disgust, at being told off, at being hung up on. We don't do that in real life; in real life we slam the phone down, we turn our backs on it, we punch something, kick something, slash, clench, buffet, stalk, pace, stomp. Ronee stared at the phone she held out in front of her with one hand while with the other

252

hand she made a whirligig in the air to try to keep her balance as the same mad withering fire that was destroying the windows cut her in two; to try to dance the two step-quick step-mambo-da butt-bugaloo-stutterstep-foxtrot-box step-frug-staggerstep-chicken walk-duck walk-cake walk-hustle-samba-dance of life.

"Neil, no. *No!*"

But it was too late, for Zimmerman was already all the way to the tumbling liquid windows, to the dancing-the-dance-of-life Ronee.

Ronee Baldwin.

Ronee Rae.

Baldwin Muldoon.

Ronee Rae Baldwin Muldoon.

Muldoon. Muldoon, Muldoon, Muldoon.

Someone was shouting: *Muldoon, Muldoon, Muldoon.*

It was Zimmerman, Cullen realized. Zimmerman was shouting: "Muldoon, Muldoon, Muldoon." He had his .38 out and was firing. "Muldoon, Muldoon, Muldoon, you son-of-a-bitch Mul*dooooooon.*" Firing out where the window had been at the rooftops on the other side of Wooster Street, shouting toward the rooftops, firing, shouting, although the same mad withering fire that had made tumbling liquid of the windows, that had cut Ronee Rae Baldwin Muldoon in two, was cutting Neil Zimmerman in two too.

"Neil, no, Jesus, no, Neil, no, Neil, get the *fuck* down, Neil."

And just like that, as if following orders, Zimmerman went down, down flat on his face among the shards, the diamonds, the slivers, the scimitars, the slices, the pearls, the pieces, the motes, the grains, the dust. But he wasn't following orders, he was dead. He was dead the way Ronee Rae Baldwin Muldoon was dead, Ronee Rae

253

Baldwin Muldoon dying differently, dying on her knees, on her knees, down onto her knees still holding the phone out in front of her, staring at it, betrayed by it, misled by it, deceived by it.

WE GET THE POINT, RONEE! We really do get the fucking point: your asshole not-exactly-not-precisely-ex-husband, he of the insurance scams and the murders of convenience, of the itty-bitty orgasms and the postcoital logorrhea, of the Resistol hat, the Larry Mahan boots, the something-or-other silver belt, coming to see you, saw instead a couple of cops going up to your place, timed the time they spent talking to you as way too much time, decided no more talking would be about enough talking, called you on his portable cellular phone and invited you to step over to the window to see something he'd brought to surprise you. A car maybe. A Testarossa, a 911 Carrera 4, an MX-5 Miata, a Corvette ZR-1, a Benz 300E. (Cullen didn't know about this shit himself, didn't know that *Road & Track* or *Muffler & Lube* or whatever the fuck had named these cars the top high-end high-performance high-tech high-priced cars of all time or last year or next week or whatever the fuck. He knew about this shit from Neil Zimmerman, down flat on his face among the shards, the diamonds, the slivers, the scimitars, the slices, the pearls, the pieces, the motes, the grains, the dust, and all of a sudden Cullen cared about this shit more than anything else in the world.)

He called you, Ronee Rae, Blond Tommy called you and sold you a bill of fucking goods and you fucking bought it and now you're slowly sinking sideways, rightward, downward, quietly, gently, silently, girllike, like nothing, nothinglike, until you're nothing. No Ronee, no Rae, no Baldwin, no Muldoon.

Poof.

... Quiet. Just quiet. So quiet. So quiet you could

hear a baby crying. A baby somewhere in this building or another building or down on the street, unnerved by the mad withering fire, or maybe altogether unaware of it, centered on the world of which it was the center, the world that was suddenly too hot or too cold, that didn't have a nipple in it, a loving face, a woolly lamb.

A baby crying and a siren. It couldn't be a siren responding to the mad withering fire. It couldn't be. The mad withering fire had just ended, the brimstone smell was still pungent, things—metal things, glass things— were still quivering in resonance with it. Or was it consonance? Whatever it was, the siren wasn't a siren responding to the mad withering fire. It never was, not so soon. Only in the movies, not in life. In life . . .

In life . . .

In life . . .

33 WHILE STASHING HER NEW CREDIT card in the back of a desk drawer where she hoped she would eventually forget it, Ann had come across a couple-of-years-old *New Yorker* cartoon, an Ann McCarthy, four horizontal panels:

In the first, captioned I AM DOING FANTASTIC, a woman and two pigs soared six feet off the floor through the room of a big old house. In the second, I AM DOING REAL GOOD, rays of sunlight poured through dark storm clouds. In the next, I AM DOING SWELL, the woman lay in a bed, covers pulled up to her chin; one of the pigs peeped out from under the bed. In the last, the woman and the pigs sat glumly in chairs in the room through which they had earlier flown, beneath the caption I THOUGHT I WAS DOING FANTASTIC BUT I'M NOT.

Mabel Parker finished looking at the cartoon, which Ann had put up on her refrigerator, and stuck it back on the door with a magnet shaped like a miniature slice of watermelon. "Weird."

"Actually," Ann said, "I am doing fantastic now that I've become a burglar."

"You're *not* a burglar," Mabel said. "You committed several crimes, but not burglary."

Ann leaned over her Toshiba lap-top in the center of her kitchen table. "Look at this list, Mabel. This is a list I've made of the names I've come across in Tony Justice's files so far."

Mabel folded her arms across her chest, grasped her elbows, turned her back. "I told you—no. Looking at those disks makes me an accessory after the fact. No."

"How about if I just tell you some of the names?"

256

"No."

"One, then?"

Mabel covered her ears. After a while, she uncovered them.

"Og Slate," Ann said.

Mabel opened the refrigerator and refilled her glass of spring water. "I didn't hear you."

Ann tipped her chair back and clenched her eyes, trying to imagine herself stretched out in the Adirondack chair at the edge of the bluff looking out over Peconic Bay and up into the sky, the stars dim through a scrim of sea mist, glimpsing shooting stars—silvery elves, quick and clever, like fish in deep black pools. "Tony and I were talking about Rickey Henderson, the cop who was killed at the bus station in the middle of investigating Karen Justice's murder. I said it must be scary when a cop who thinks you might be a killer gets killed. He said he wasn't scared because he hadn't killed anybody. Sit over here, Mabe. Listen."

Mabel sat. When Cullen recommended that Ann retain Mabel, a former prosecutor in the office of Manhattan District Attorney Leah Levitt, in private practice now, specializing in women's rights, experienced at self-defense homicides, he hadn't known that Ann and Mabel had been good friends for a couple of years. They knew each other from a job that Cullen and nearly every other cop in town had caught a piece of, and that Ann and nearly every other reporter in town had written about at one stage or another—the murder of the previous police commissioner, Charles Story. Mabel had been an unwitting player in the drama, a chance witness to the flight of Story's killer from the back entrance of Story's East Side town house, which Mabel had a view of from an apartment on the next street, where she had been having a couple-of-times-a-week affair with an arbitrageur

257

named Norman Levitt, Leah Levitt's husband. Naturally, Mabel had been reluctant to come forward right away with her eyewitness testimony. Naturally, she was very sympathetic with Ann's current distress at having been in the wrong place at the wrong time.

"Tony said he hadn't killed anybody," Ann went on, "but even so, he'd felt Rickey Henderson's contempt for him. He asked if I ever felt contempt for people I write about, people who think I'm writing a puff piece when what I'm writing is a hatchet job. He told me about a piece he was working on, a piece about gay promiscuity—the new gay promiscuity. Leather bars, bathhouses—just when you thought people would never go *near* the water again, they were in over their heads. They have a new clientele—Wall Street types, bankers, lawyers, brokers. Tony seemed to think it went with the territory: a day of unfriendly takeovers, a night of anonymous fucking.

"One of his subjects—one of his *targets*—is married and has a wife who raises money for AIDS research. You can see why a reporter like Justice would like that. Reporters like Justice like stark ironies. The guy has to be Og Slate. He has to be. Michelle Slate is . . . What's the name of the group she's head of?"

"Ann?"

"Women For, Women Against, Women something."

"Ann?"

"What?"

"If you're suggesting Og Slate killed Tony Justice, there's one small problem. I saw Og Slate at a memorial service in the city late Saturday afternoon. For Duane Higgins, the dancer? He left with some people to go to a dinner party."

"So?"

"So Justice was murdered Saturday night on Shelter Island."

"I know that."

"I know you know it, Ann. I just—"

"The Slates have a house in the Hamptons," Ann said. "You told me yourself—it's right near the Levitts'. Is it East Hampton?"

"Maidenform," Mabel said.

Ann laughed. "Maiden*something*, not *form*."

"Maidstone," Mabel said. "Norman called it Maidenform."

"If Og Slate left the city even as late as eleven," Ann said, "and made good time, he could've gotten to Greenport *or* North Haven in time for the last ferry to Shelter Island. Getting to Justice's house, killing him, and getting *off* the island before the ferries shut down—that would've been very difficult. So all that means is he spent the night there—in his car or in Justice's house. It's a *big* house. Gruesome, maybe, but—" She stopped herself and snapped her fingers. "*Nor*man."

Mabel shook her head. "That's over, Ann."

Ann held a thumb and forefinger up to her eye. "A teeny-weeny favor."

"We *never* speak."

"*I'll* call him."

"And ask him what? In between leveraged buyouts, has Og Slate mentioned killing Tony Justice?"

"Ask him about the Frères."

"What's that?"

"I don't know. It's like a club—a Wall Street club. There's a file on it on one of these disks, but it's locked. It's the only locked file on all his disks; eleven disks, and only one locked file."

"How do you lock a computer file?" Mabel measured a tiny piece of air with her thumb and forefinger. "With a little Master Lock?"

Ann turned the Toshiba partway around and tapped at the keyboard. "This key, Text In/Out, lets you create a password for a file. Unless you know the password, you can never again retrieve that file from the disk. See? I've told it I want to save this file, which I've called Names, as a locked file, and it's asking me for a password. We'll make *sesame* the password. S-e-s. See? You can't see the password as you type it. A-m-e. Hit Return, and it asks for the password again. S-e-s-a-m-e. Document to be saved: Names. This light means it's saving the file. Now we'll leave the file—Exit, No, No—and try to retrieve it. Document to be retrieved: Names. See? It asks for the password. S-e-s-a-m-e. Bingo. This light means it's retrieving the file. And there it is. If we've forgotten the password, even we who made it up, there's no way to get the document.

"Justice locked a file called Frères. The only file on eleven disks. I've been sitting here for an hour trying to think of a password. I tried *Frères*; the point of passwords is not to be subtle, the point is to remember them. I tried *password*. I tried *Tony*, I tried *Justice*, I tried *TJ*, I tried *AJ*—A for Anthony. I tried *Anthony*. I tried *sesame*, I tried *open*, I tried *unlock*, I tried *key*—"

"How about *open sesame*?" Mabel said.

"The password can't have more than eight letters."

"*Frères* is French for brothers," Mabel said. "So maybe it's *ouvre*."

Ann shrugged. "Maybe. . . . O-u-v-r-e, right? No S?"

"No S."

". . . Nope."

"How about *ouvrez*—with a Z?"

Ann tried it. "Nope."

"How do you say it in Spanish?" Mabel said.

Ann's Spanish consisted of *Uno gin y tónico. . . . La quenta, por favor*, and *¿Donde está la playa?* "Openo upo."

Mabel smiled politely, but she was thinking hard. ". . . What do you think the Frères is? Or are? Or who?"

"I think it's . . . I think they're . . . Well, I don't know, do I? I guess I think they're . . . homosexuals."

"Homosexuals has more than eight letters. Try *homos*."

"*Ma*bel."

"Come on, Ann, don't be squeamish. You said the object is not to be subtle."

"H-o-m-o-s. . . . Nope."

"Try *gays*."

". . . Nope."

"Try *fags*."

"F-a-g-s. . . . Bingo."

34 AN EAR TO THE DOOR OF THE REAR apartment on the third floor of the four-story dump on the corner across the street from Rusty's, Cullen heard K. T. Oslin singing "This Woman," and knew he'd come to the right place.

He would have found that out in another few seconds anyway when the never-before-experienced yet unmistakable hard smooth maw of a gun barrel kissed his left cheek, kissed it and made it hurt.

"Check your weapons, please, gents, at the door." Blond Tommy took away from Cullen the .38 he had drawn on the way up the stairs. He tucked it in his belt. "Door's open, hoss. Just go inside nice and slow. Then down on the floor with your hands behind your head. Slow, hoss—real, real slow."

If Ann were there, she could do five minutes on the importance of imagining the best possible resolution of this uncomfortable situation, not the worst. She took occasional lessons from a tennis pro whose methods, practiced (he said) by Ivan Lendl, among others, of preventing premature surrender, Ann enthusiastically preached:

"You lose a couple of points in a row, it's very easy to see yourself losing more points, losing games, sets, the match. But it would be just as easy to think the opposite. So rather than let your mind run wild, you have to interrupt the fantasy of losing by concentrating on something insignificant—the spacing of your racquet strings, the positioning of your wristbands; describe, in your mind, a tree next to the court; tie your shoes. Then, when your mind's clear, force on yourself a fantasy of winning—

winning the next few points, the next few games, the set, the match. It seems so . . . California—or maybe it's so India—but it works."

So Cullen tried it: instead of seeing himself going through the door and down on the dirty gold carpet, hands behind his head, and seeing Blond Tommy putting his pistol behind his left ear and pulling the trigger and blood and brains and bone spraying everywhere, he concentrated on the most insignificant thing he could see—the peephole in the door, a tiny metal cylinder was all it was, with a tiny glass lens. *Was* the cylinder metal at all, or was it plastic? And *was* the glass glass, or was *it* plastic?

His mind clear now, he saw himself opening the door and starting through it, then stopping suddenly and driving his right elbow back into Blond Tommy's stomach. He saw himself reaching back with his left hand and then with his right and grasping Blond Tommy's gun hand by the wrist and hauling Blond Tommy over his back and slamming him down on *his* back on the dirty gold carpet. He saw himself kicking Blond Tommy's gun away and kicking him in the groin and stepping, grinding, crushing, hopping on Blond Tommy's face. He saw himself picking up Blond Tommy's gun and putting the barrel in his pulp of a mouth and cocking it, but not pulling the trigger, letting Blond Tommy hurt, letting him sleep in his blood and in the piss and the warm wet shit that his terror had squeezed out of him.

But it was too California, too India, for when it came time to open the apartment door, Blond Tommy kept his pistol to Cullen's cheek and guided him through the door and down to the dirty gold carpet, a lover laying his lady gently on silk sheets. He frisked Cullen's torso and legs, yanked his arms down from behind his head, and just like that had him cuffed. He stood up and stood back to admire his work, a rodeo cowboy astride a hog-tied calf.

If Ann were there, Cullen would ask her to concede that neither she nor Ivan Lendl nor her pro/guru played tennis with .22-caliber pistols to their heads.

"That's the piece that K'd Rickey Henderson, isn't it?" Cullen said. "How the fuck can you go out on a K and buy something with a credit card at the fucking crime scene?"

Blond Tommy whistled flatly along with George Strait, singing on the radio, somewhere in a corner of the room, "Let's Fall to Pieces Together."

"The super let me in, Tom," Cullen said. "I told him if I wasn't down in five minutes to call nine-eleven."

Blond Tommy put the toe of a pointed boot against Cullen's kidney and pressed in mean and steady. "Super? Super lives in the *barrio*, hoss, comes by here once a month to shove the garbage around, calls it maintenance. You came through the front door the way every wino needs to take a leak comes through it; you shoved it. You came entirely without fucking backup, didn't you, Cullen? You're not strapped with an off-duty piece, you don't have ammo for your service piece except what's in the fucking chamber. You want to be a fucking hero, don't you? A fucking dead hero. Was that you in the turbo? Shit, you can't drive worth a lick. You're lucky you made it here alive."

"Yeah, well." The turbo was Zimmerman's, and Zimmerman's ghost had kibitzed from the back seat all the way uptown. Cullen had guessed right that Blond Tommy had come by car, and had spotted the Coupe de Ville—SOUTHPAW—bulling east on Spring Street, horn blaring, half up on the curb, scattering pedestrians.

Cullen had nearly overtaken Blond Tommy on Lafayette, but had fallen for his fake at Astor Place and gone up Fourth Avenue while Blond Tommy spun onto Eighth Street. Taking Twelfth Street to Third Avenue and heading north, Cullen had spotted the Coupe de Ville four blocks ahead, then two, then he hadn't had to close the gap any more, for he had known where Blond Tommy was going. And all through the drive Zimmerman's ghost had groaned from the back seat at Cullen's gear changes, moaned at his braking, shaken his head at his tactics.

Blond Tommy took his toe away. "You *did* come without backup, didn't you, hoss?"

"I've got a call in to Batman. He was out on a job, but I left a message."

Blond Tommy kicked Cullen in the ribs the way he'd forearmed him in the Adam's apple, not as hard as he could, but as hard as he had to.

"No backup, Tommy," Cullen said when he was able. "I want you for myself."

"I'm surprised, hoss. You're such a straight fucking arrow, everything by the regs." Tommy said something else—something about Cullen's being a friend of Hriniak's, probably—but Cullen couldn't make it out, for Tommy had gone off into another room. There was just one other room, wasn't there, besides a bathroom and a small kitchen, probably? Cullen hadn't seen much between the door and the dirty gold carpet.

There was the sputter of urine on water, the toilet flushed, and Blond Tommy came out to where Cullen could see him altogether for the first time. Resistol hat, Larry Mahan boots, something-or-other silver belt, suede sport coat, gingham shirt and chino pants with western pockets. From against the doorpost, where he'd

265

propped it, he picked up a machine pistol. Then he was gone again, out of sight.

When Cullen had thought he had seen a man on the roof, a man with a hat, why the fucking hell hadn't he who was such a straight fucking arrow, everything by the regs, gone with the thought, responded to it, acted on it, *done* something?

Lyle Lovett sang "I Married Her Just Because She Looks Like You."

"Your wife's dead, Tom," Cullen called. "In case you were wondering how the MAC-11 works in the field."

A refrigerator door. An aluminum can pop-top.

A perfect opportunity: Cullen saw himself lurching up onto his knees, then onto his feet, quickstepping to the kitchen door and through it. He saw Blond Tommy with his head back, chugging a Coke or a Pepsi or a Dr Pepper, a Bud or a Miller Lite or a Coors, and he saw himself karate-kicking the can down Blond Tommy's throat. He saw himself somehow slipping the handcuffs off (so California, so India), reaching under the kitchen sink for a can of Drān-O, ripping the bottom off the beer can in Blond Tommy's mouth, and pouring the Drān-O down his throat. He saw himself opening the refrigerator and getting a Coke or a Pepsi or a Dr Pepper, a Bud or a Miller Lite or a Coors for himself, popping the top, pulling over a kitchen chair, and sitting and watching Blond Tommy corrode.

Too California, too India, for Blond Tommy came back into the living room, a whiff of beer around him.

"Can I have something to drink, Tommy?" Cullen said. "Some water."

Tommy snorted. "Water's exactly where you're headed, hoss, soon's the transportation arrangements're worked out."

"Uh-hunh. You going to cut me up, or dump me whole?"

Blond Tommy stepped over Cullen and switched on a big old television set. He sat in a decrepit leather lounger, tilting way back. He hadn't turned the radio off and Cullen got to imagine what the answer to his last question was going to be and to listen to "As My Children's Hospital Turns" and to Dolly Parton singing "You Know That I Love You."

If Ann were there, she would do five minutes on Dolly Parton, on how so many women refused to take her seriously, actually seemed to hold Dolly's body against her, and wouldn't listen to the voice that came out of that body, while men, who made no bones about wanting to hold Dolly's body against *them*, were attentive listeners, appreciated her talent. If Ann were there, she would make them listen to Dolly singing "A Gamble Either Way," the saddest and the wisest song she had ever heard about how hard it is to grow up pretty and sexy.

" 'It's not easy being taken seriously when you're a piece of ass,' " Cullen said. " 'Trust me on that.' "

The leather lounger creaked as Blond Tommy shifted to look back at Cullen. "You losing it, hoss?"

"It's something Ronee said—something sad and wise. Or do you still think of her as Rae?"

The leather lounger creaked as Blond Tommy turned back to the television.

"Or do you *think* of her?"

"Fuck you, Cullen."

Cullen used his shoulders and chin to move on the dirty gold carpet to where he could see Blond Tommy—see his boots and legs and knees. "Ronee had some nice—*I* think of her as Ronee—had some nice things to

267

say about you. She said you were different from most of the men she'd fucked because you talked in bed afterwards. I guess you let her see other guys while she was off the so-called scope, was that it? Or maybe that was a demand she made to make up some for all the screwing around you did.

"Anyway, Ronee said most guys, the most they'll say, is 'Hey, what's your name?' But Tommy's different, Ronee said. He loves to talk afterwards. He comes too fast, slam bam, like all micks, but he loves to talk afterwards. She thinks maybe—she *thought*; she's not thinking anymore—she *thought* maybe it was your itty-bitty orgasms. She said you had itty-bitty orgasms, hardly any come. Some guys shoot such a wad, it dripped out of her down her leg all day long, but you shoot just a few little drops. The talking, she thought that it was like you had to talk to make up for the itty-bitty orgasms, like the words were instead of the come, or something. Is that so, Tom? Is that it?"

On the television, Willard Scott pitched Maxwell House coffee. On the radio, Don Williams sang "Thank God for the Radio." If Ann were there . . .

Cullen turned still more on the dirty gold carpet, so that his face was just inches from the toes of Blond Tommy's boots. "Let me get this straight, Tommy. Tony Justice found out about your and Rae's insurance scam from Diana Romano. He was shopping for someone to kill his wife so he could marry Romano and enjoy the good things that had come to him when he had Stephen Fox killed. He said your secret was safe with him as long as you did him a favor.

"Just killing her would've been sufficient, but you chopped her up to make it look like some psycho did it, not her husband, not someone who'd shared her bed, been intimate with her. Is that it? *Is* that it? *Is* that why you chopped her up, Tommy? Otherwise, I don't get it, it doesn't make any fucking sense."

Cullen was weeping now, real honest-to-God tears of terror and despair. He *had* come there entirely without backup, not strapped with an off-duty piece, no ammo for his service piece except what was in the chamber. He had let Blond Tommy get the drop on him and take him out of the play without any resistance whatsoever. And very soon he was going to wind up in some river, probably in pieces. He had plenty to weep about.

While Cullen wept, Blond Tommy hauled himself up out of the leather lounger and went into the kitchen. He opened the refrigerator and popped the top of another aluminum can. On the television, a woman said, "You've got a lot of nerve, Keith, to say you're my friend." On the radio was the same Maxwell House commercial that had just been on television.

Cullen remembered the walk he had taken along Sinatra Drive in Hoboken: walking to the Hudson and counting the neon drops dripping from the neon coffee cup on the Maxwell House factory; having, after a while, to make himself see them as drops dripping instead of drops leaping upward back into the cup. He remembered the couples making out everywhere and all around him on the windless night, the windless morning, their moans and sighs and shivers and shudders rising up all around in a goddamn symphony of lust.

What's with you and Di Romano? Zimmerman, the late Neil Zimmerman, had said. *You're not addicted to her, are you, Joe? That seems to be what happens.*

And what had Cullen said?

What *had* Cullen said?

Addicted? (Hang on a sec, will you, while I get this

needle out of my vein.) *No, I'm not addicted.* (Turn your back for a sec, will you, while I stash this bottle.)

Blond Tommy came back to the living room and sat in the leather lounger and took a sip of whatever it was he was drinking and put it on the dirty gold carpet next to the lounger and Cullen saw it was a Busch, which went with Blond Tommy's outfit better than a Bud or a Miller Lite or even a Coors, certainly better than a Coke or a Pepsi or a Dr Pepper.

"You want to hear something funny, hoss?" Blond Tommy said. "Only reason you're as right as you are about this is that you're so far wrong. Rate you're going, and in what direction, there'll be a National Hockey League franchise in hell before you put it together." He picked up his Busch and sipped it and kept it in his lap.

On the television, a man said, "I love you, Amanda. I always have." On the radio, Willie Nelson and Merle Haggard sang "Pancho and Lefty." In Cullen's memory, Zimmerman, the late Neil Zimmerman, said, *Something Rickey said once made Lang think Karen Justice's K had something to do with homosexuals. She knew someone who was gay, maybe Justice knew someone who was gay, she got killed because she knew or because he knew or because they both knew.*

The dust and the grime of the dirty gold carpet sticking to his wet lips, his wet cheeks, Cullen said: "Karen's K *was* a contract, but it wasn't put out by Tony, it was put out by someone who wanted to keep Tony quiet. The squash racquet wasn't an oversight, you planted it. You knew Rickey Henderson would find it, or maybe you told him *where* to find it. You expected him to play it, but he didn't. He wasn't ready. He told his roommate about it, but he wasn't ready to play it in the field. But it was in place and that was enough reason for you to K Rickey, so it would look like Justice K'd Karen, then K'd Rickey

270

because he was closing in. Who paid for this, Tommy? And how much? Or was the payment their silence—about Rae? They're the blackmailers, aren't they? Not Justice. So who are they?"

And then it just came out of him. "Is it Slate? Og Slate? Ogden Slate? Is that who it is, Tommy? Was Justice working on a story about prominent gays in the closet? Gays who had AIDS? Was he getting too close to some important people?"

Blond Tommy had put the Busch down on the dirty gold carpet and was sitting forward in the leather lounger, but he wasn't listening to Cullen, he was craning to hear someone on the stairs, someone who, if he had gotten down onto the dirty gold carpet alongside Cullen and looked through the crack under the door, he would have been able to see was standing right outside, an ear to the door, probably, listening to "As My Children's Hospital Turns" and Rosanne Cash now, singing "Runaway Train," listening to the silence where Cullen's voice had been.

Maria Esperanza. Maria Hope. Zimmerman, the late Neil Zimmerman, had called her, to save her some legwork.

"Maria! Back off!"

"Hey, what the fuck." Blond Tommy swung a boot at Cullen's head and grazed his forehead.

The shadow was gone.

But a MAC-11 in the hand is an irresistible plaything to many, and Blond Tommy aimed his at the door and drilled four rows of holes right across the middle at knob level. He rocked a little on his heels from the recoil and the sheer pleasure of it and grinned a cockeyed grin at Cullen. "Take fucking that, fucking Maria. Fuck."

The grin went slack when Blond Tommy realized two things simultaneously—that he had shot the lock off the door and that he had emptied his clip. He threw the MAC-11 down and backed toward the window, tiptoe, moon-walk, drawing his .22 pistol from a shoulder holster under the suede coat.

"Maria, he's taking the fire escape. He's out of—"

Blond Tommy aimed the .22 at Cullen and fired.

35

CULLEN ROLLED AWAY ACROSS THE dirty gold carpet, rolled onto his stomach, rolled again, used the momentum of his roll to twitch himself to his knees, to stagger up, right leg, left leg.

Maria Esperanza, Maria Hope, was in the doorway now, having kicked it open, standing legs apart, arms up, gun hand out and steadied, neck erect, eyes bright.

By the rear window, in the shadows, Blond Tommy swerved his pistol away from a second shot at Cullen and aimed at her.

Her first look had been at Cullen. It was going to be her last, unless . . .

He had never tried it, he had seen it only in the movies, kung fu movies back when it was Bruce Lee the Bon Jovi wanna-be had wanted to be. Had Bruce Lee ever done it with his hands bound behind his back? Probably, but Cullen didn't remember. He remembered that Bruce Lee had at least once done it blindfolded, but blindfolded wasn't as hard as no hands. Or was it?

If Ann were there, she would encourage him to *Visualize, visualize. See yourself succeeding.*

Thank you, Ann.

You're welcome.

"Maria, down!"

And from that warning Cullen formed a yell, a shout, a focus of energy, a lever, a pole with which to lift himself off the ground, kicking out, reaching out, hurling his feet out forward while falling at the same time backward, striving to be more out than down, more forward than back.

And—yes!—succeeding. Yes! catching Tommy's

273

gun hand, his left hand—SOUTHPAW—with the barest toe of his shoe, his trusty Weejun, before he was defeated by gravity, fell more down than out, more back than forward, slammed down hard on the dirty gold carpet, taking all his weight on the shoulder of one cuffed arm.

Cullen didn't succeed, though he had visualized succeeding, in kicking the pistol from Blond Tommy's hand, as in the movies. He did succeed in jostling Blond Tommy's aim just enough that when he fired, the barrel was moving away from Maria Esperanza and the bullet passed by her and ricocheted around the stairway, making a sound like crazy violinists tuning up.

Maria Esperanza, Maria Hope, took one more crossover step onto the dirty gold carpet and swung her braced arms toward Blond Tommy and shot him in the chest. He took two stiff steps backward, slammed into the corner, slid down the wall, knocking, as he slid, the radio from a low table.

On the radio, Steve Earle sang "Goodbye Is All We've Got Left to Say." If Ann were there . . .

Maria Esperanza kicked Blond Tommy's piece into a corner. She put the barrel of her .38 against Blond Tommy's throat and felt for a pulse in his right wrist. She dropped his wrist and slipped her .38 into a hip holster and found the telephone and dialed nine-eleven. She tucked the receiver under her ear and carried the phone to Blond Tommy and while she told the operator where she was and what she wanted she searched for the key to the handcuffs. She found it and hung up the phone and left it next to Blond Tommy and came to Cullen and touched his shoulder gently, firmly—"You okay?" she asked, and he said he thought he was—and rolled him a little and unlocked the cuffs and helped him sit up. She rubbed his wrists for him at first, then let him rub them himself.

274

"Thanks," Cullen said, and Maria Esperanza said, "Hey, don't mention it."

"I need some air."

"Sure."

"I'll be back before the Squad gets here."

"Take your time."

Rubbing his wrists, rolling his neck and his shoulders, feeling free at last, Cullen skipped down the stairs and out onto the street. Third Avenue, clotted with reeking traffic, looked like a mountain stream to him, rainbow trout leaping up out of the dappled current. Seventy-fourth Street looked like the Yellow Brick Road. He restrained himself from shouting and leaping and kicking up his heels and doing cartwheels, but he did do a little two-step as he headed toward the westering sun.

In no time at all, he was all the way to the park, and he skipped across Fifth and vaulted two-handed over the wide stone wall and skittered down the wooded hill.

A holiday had been declared for the most beautiful people in New York, the sleek and the fair had been given the afternoon off and invited to gather at the sailboat pond, to wear their whitest, sheerest clothes, to bring their borzois, their Afghans, their cockatoos, their cherubs. The sun didn't shine but to produce an effect— a halo here, a silhouette there; the breeze didn't blow but to mold a skirt against a pair of stupendous legs, to muss a child's hair, to luff the fine soft shirt of a gorgeous man, to fill the sails of the hundred scale-model boats that sped about the pond, reaching, beating, running in miraculous disorder.

Cullen's children were there, somehow—Tenny and the Bon Jovi wanna-be, Tenny looking all grown-up in a yellow cotton sundress, sandals, wide-brimmed straw hat, the Bon Jovi wanna-be looking human in baggy whites and espadrilles: Heavy Metal meets J. Crew. They were down around a bend of the pond and didn't come closer, just smiled and waved and let him enjoy his solitude.

And Ann was there, coming toward him with purpose and passion, in a white sundress herself, her long strong body dim beneath it, smiling a little, for she knew he was taking her body in, enjoying his taking her body in. She put her arms around his neck and let him lift her and swing her.

"Oh, Joe."

"Hi. Hi, hi, hi."

"Joe, Joe."

He set her down and they kissed, hot, hard tongues delving into each other, hips and thighs surging. They hugged again, tightly, then kissed again, so wet and hot they had to step back or they would not have been able to stop.

"You're all right?" Ann said.

"Yes, but Neil—"

"Neil's all right."

Cullen stared. "No? He can't be."

"He's all right. I heard it on . . . on the radio."

"Thank God for the radio." Cullen put an arm around Ann and as they walked around the pond drew her to him. "I did what your tennis teacher taught you. I saw myself getting out of a jam and I got out of it."

"Oh, Joe."

"Karen Justice *was* killed on contract, but—"

"Don't talk about work, Joe." Ann yanked on his sleeve.

"I'm sorry about Diana Romano. I was—"

"Don't talk about her, Joe."

"I'm sorry."

"Oh, Joe."

Cullen stopped and slipped his arm from around Ann and stood in front of her, taking her shoulders in his hands. "What's wrong?"

"Oh, Joe."

"What's wrong, Ann?"

"Oh, Joe."

"Ann, why do you keep saying that?"

"Oh, Joe."

"Ann?"

"Oh, Joe."

"*Ann.*"

"JOE? . . . JOE? . . . Oh, Joe. Talk to me, Joe!"

The dirty gold carpet stretched away from Cullen like a prairie.

"Joe, talk to me."

Way, way off, almost at the horizon, was what he thought at first was a mountain range, then recognized as Blond Tommy Muldoon, still as death.

"Joe, please, for fucking christ's sake, talk to me."

". . . Ann?"

"It's not Ann, Joe. It's Maria. You want me to get Ann, tell me who she is, where to find her, I'll get her. But first talk to me. Tell me you're okay."

"Maria. Are you all right, Maria?"

"I'm all right. Blond Tommy threw down on me, but I popped him."

"Did I . . . ? No, I know I didn't help you. I thought I did. I mean, I saw myself helping you, but I know I didn't."

"He threw down on you, Joe. He popped you. You couldn't help me. It's not your fault."

"I saw myself helping you, but I know I didn't."

"It's not your fault."

277

"I saw myself—"

"Just hang on, Joe. I can hear the ambulance. Just hang on."

"Neil? Is Neil all right?"

"Oh, Joe, no he's not. He's not all right. He got K'd, Joe. Neil got K'd."

"That was just a dream too, then. I dreamed Ann said Neil was okay, I dreamed I helped you, but I didn't—"

"Joe, maybe you shouldn't talk—"

"I didn't because—"

"Joe, don't talk."

"—because I can't move my legs."

"Oh, Joe."

"Maria, I can't move my legs."

"Shhh, Joe. Shhh."

On the radio, Neil Young sang "Helpless." If Ann were there . . .

"If Ann were here," Cullen said, "she'd do five minutes on how a station that claims to be all-country shouldn't really be playing Neil Young."

"Shhh, Joe. Shhh."

36 ANN JONES AND MABEL PARKER, UR-
ban jungle girls, not afraid (or not looking
it) to be out after midnight on the New
York-Gomorrah border, walked right up
to the Lash, the scene of Noel Cutler's murder and arguably, they supposed, an apt spot for a memorial service—
walked right up as if they belonged, as if they weren't the
only ones there not dressed in leather or denim, as if they
weren't the only women on the block, in the neighborhood, for miles and miles, on the planet.

For a time in the late seventies, Ann had lived on
Christopher Street, in a famous—notorious—apartment building nicknamed Leather Flats. All the building's tenants weren't sadomasochistic fetishists with
cropped hair and military mustaches; they weren't
all trim and hard from hours at the gym, from gallons of caffeine, cartons of cigarettes, pounds of cocaine, drums of amyl nitrite; they didn't all play Patty
Smith full blast day and night—when they weren't
playing Judy Garland; their apartments weren't all
decorated in steel and leather and vinyl, all their ap-
pliances and electronic equipment weren't matte
black; they didn't all buy cock rings at the Pleasure
Chest, Crisco at Gristede's on Bleecker Street, hip-
pocket bandannas, BVD undershirts, and Levl's
501's at Village Army & Navy; they didn't all hang
out at the Ramrod or the Spike and cruise the piers,
giving or getting lips or hips or fist three times a night
on weeknights, six or eight or a dozen times a weekend (unless they went to Cherry Grove for the weekend
and gave or got lips or hips or fist twenty times a
weekend *and* got their bare asses sunburned); they

didn't all drink Miller Lite from cans; they didn't all go home on Mother's Day, Jon Vie cake boxes or Godiva Chocolate shopping bags dangling from their tense fingers. It just seemed that way.

"You scared?" Mabel said as they both became aware they were putting off going inside by pretending they were expecting to see someone among the mourners who kept on arriving, on foot, by taxi, several in stretch limos, many astride Harley hogs. The car and bike headlights turned the exhaust clouds to a glorious silver fog: Brigadoon-by-the-Styx.

"A little," Ann said. But actually, what she felt on seeing all those hairy chests, on smelling the sweat and the piss and the beer every time the Lash's doors swung open, on hearing a florid female vocalist on the jukebox (Bette Midler singing "The Wind Beneath My Wings")— what she felt was nostalgic.

Ann had known at the time she lived in Leather Flats that what was going on around her was weird, outlandish, outsize, immoderate. It was gross and ugly. It was sick. She would never claim she had known that people would actually *get* sick, but she had been sure that they couldn't gorge themselves to that degree day after week after month after year without some indigestion. Still, she had been fascinated by it all. Three hundred partners, some of them claimed to have had. *Five* hundred partners. What would that be like? Wouldn't it be, well, *in*teresting?

Sometimes, hanging out her window on the fifth floor of Leather Flats on a hazy, hot, humid summer evening, watching the faggots come and go, talking of Michael and Angelo, she had imagined that she could hear the semen spurting all over the Village, gushing into mouths and anuses and armpits and crotches and fingers, onto bellies, onto chests, onto loins, into hair and beards, into chammy cloths and silk underwear and jock straps and cotton bandannas and rubber gloves. It made her wet, it made her breathless, it made her want to get out of the house and get her hands on some of the hard cock waving free and brave from Greenwich Avenue to West Street, from Gansevoort to Houston. A *thousand* partners. It made her want to suck and fuck without having to talk a lot, without having to dissemble, without knowing her partners' names, without their knowing her name, without having to go through the rigmarole of *meeting* someone.

Most straight people in those days hadn't had a clue what was going on, and what would they have thought if they had? If the average straight person in the average straight town like, oh, Peoria or Dubuque, one of those cliché litmus towns, knew how many times, how often, with how many different partners, with how many partners at the same time, where, in which postures, wearing what, on top of what, inside what, under what, hanging from what, tied or handcuffed or duct-taped to what, anointed with what, your partner's arm slathered with what *up* to what, with how many watching and doing what while they watched—if they knew all that, would they be revolted, those Peorians, those Dubuquois? Or—come on, admit it—wouldn't they want to, if not enlist, at least check it out, check it out in the hope that maybe heterosexuals could learn to party like that too—without guilt, without jealousy and possessiveness, without a letup?

Wouldn't some of those Peorians, those Dubuquois, be out the door *so* fast, before the information was even fully processed, before the sound of the revelation clobbering them in the forehead had even stopped echo-

echoechoing, heading for the airport, the train depot, the bus station? Wouldn't they hit the road in their cars or even in stolen cars, taking their neighbors' cars, their spouses' cars? Wouldn't they creep out in the darkest predawn while their spouses and their children nestled all snug in their beds, visions of fundamental American values dancing in their heads?

Of course they would. They'd be dying of curiosity. Mabel was dying of curiosity. Ann could feel it. Mabel wanted to know a lot more than just the little she now knew—about all of it, not only the Frères.

WHAT ANN and Mabel knew about the Frères, they knew, of course, from the file on one of Tony Justice's computer disks that had been unlocked by the word *fags*. The file had been created or updated, they couldn't determine which, on the Friday before Tony Justice traveled out to Shelter Island for what turned out to be the last time. This is what it said:

> *Note to Cafferty* ["His managing editor," Ann explained]: *Dear Jim: If you're reading this, I'm dead and someone has figured out the codeword I dreamed up to keep this file from being accessed, as the computer types say, by unauthorized snoops and busybodies.*
>
> *This is NOT repeat NOT a publishable news story and is NOT repeat NOT to be published in full or in part or to be the subject of any news story or stories that might attempt to describe its contents SO LONG AS THE FOLLOWING IN-DIVIDUALS REMAIN ALIVE: my wife, Diana Romano; my stepdaughter, Valerie Fox (the daughter of the late Karen Fox Justice and the late Stephen Fox).*
>
> *In the event that BOTH of the above-named individuals should die, however, then publish the son-of-a-bitch*

*and sit back and enjoy the sights and sounds of the shit
hitting the fan.*

Sorry I didn't get a chance to say a proper good-bye.

Best,
Tony

~ ~ ~

By ANTHONY JUSTICE

Bulletin Special Columnist

I will tell it chronologically, as if that will make it
make sense:

On April 20, 1986, Andrew Steiger, 28, a waiter and
aspiring actor, was killed instantly when he was thrown
from the roof of a six-story tenement on West 49th St. by
his occasional lover, Noel Cutler.

Cutler, 32, another would-be actor who worked as a
counterman in an ice cream parlor, had become enraged
on learning that Steiger had been diagnosed as having
AIDS. He used a typewriter in Steiger's third-floor apartment to forge a note that made the death look like a
suicide.

Unknown to Cutler, there was a witness to the quarrel that ended with Steiger's fatal plummet. Lupe Escalante, a tenant in a West 50th St. building that backs on
Steiger's building, while preparing dinner in her third-
floor kitchen, heard and saw two men arguing in Steiger's apartment. (She would later identify them from
photographs as Steiger and Cutler.)

A short time later, Ms. Escalante saw the men appear
on the roof and saw Cutler lift Steiger in his arms, carry
him to the parapet, and drop him to the courtyard below.
She then saw Cutler return to the apartment, where he

spent twenty or so minutes composing something at a typewriter.

Lupe Escalante's brother, Jorge, had been accused in November, 1985, of killing a former girlfriend. Escalante claimed that at the time of the murder he had been in Camden, N.J., looking for work. He alleged that he was being falsely accused by the dead woman's sister, who he said had several times tried unsuccessfully to seduce him.

Alerted by Lupe Escalante to her brother's predicament, this reporter was able to verify Jorge's alibi and wrote a number of columns that eventually resulted in the charges against him being dropped. As a sort of payment for helping her brother, Lupe contacted this reporter to tell what she had seen on the night of April 20, 1986.

~ ~ ~

I believed Lupe Escalante's eyewitness account, but rather than publish it, I decided to use the information to help me in a personal matter.

In February, 1986, at a party at "21" to celebrate the publication of a new novel by Martin Tractman, I had met Karen Fox, a former fashion model turned real-estate executive, and her husband, Stephen Fox, a prominent theatrical producer. I fell in love with Karen Fox and determined to make her love me.

By July, 1986, I had formulated a plan. I contacted Noel Cutler and told him I knew he had murdered Andrew Steiger. I would keep his secret if he did me the service of killing Stephen Fox and of turning himself in not to the police but to me.

On July 9, in Stephen Fox's office in the Brill Building, Noel Cutler fatally shot Fox with a .32-caliber Beretta automatic pistol. On July 15, Cutler telephoned me

284

at the *Bulletin* and "confessed." I wrote the first of a half-dozen columns recounting Cutler's contention that he had been angered at Fox for refusing to cast him in a leading role in a musical version of the Preston Sturges film *The Lady Eve* that Fox was preparing to produce.

On July 21, proceeding according to arrangements made by me, Cutler surrendered to the police.

On October 14, 1986, Karen Fox and I were married in a civil ceremony at the Municipal Building.

On November 2, Noel Cutler was convicted by a jury of Stephen Fox's murder and sentenced to eight years in prison.

~ ~ ~

I made one additional use of Noel Cutler. I asked him to provide me with the names of prominent men, in business, in the arts, in sports and entertainment, in government, who he might have heard had contracted AIDS. At the time, Rock Hudson was the only illustrious casualty of the disease, but it seemed inevitable that more celebrities and notables would have been infected with it, that some of them would be beginning to die.

Cutler didn't run with celebrities, of course, but he was a kid at the fence that protected them from the mundane world and he would have seen things and heard things. A homosexual is a homosexual, after all, by dint of his having had a homosexual experience with a partner who could very well be expected to brag if *his* homosexual experience was with a famous partner.

Cutler confirmed rumors that I had begun to hear of a return to gay libertinism. After a period of emphasis on safe, smart, monogamous sex, promiscuity was back. Leather bars and bathhouses were opening up anew; gay men were once again cruising streets and alleys in numbers, having abrupt liaisons in vacant warehouses and empty trucks.

Many of the practitioners of this new gay polygamy were men who had been openly gay in the late seventies, and who had gone to ground during the paranoid early eighties. Many were young urban professionals who were still in high school and college—and still in the closet— during the heyday of licentiousness.

Nagged by the feeling that they had missed something, these brokers and doctors and lawyers and lieutenants of industry set out to make up for lost time. Straitlaced, uptight team players at work, and fearful of compromising their standing in the business and professional communities, many of them joined newly founded private clubs that catered to their special tastes while protecting their identities.

The most exclusive of these clubs is Frères (pronounced Frair—the S is silent), from the French word for brothers or comrades. Frères was reportedly conceived by the scion of a prominent manufacturing family, who recruited a second member, who recruited a third, who recruited a fourth, and so on. As in a terrorist cell, the precise identity of each member is known, in theory at least, to only two others—the one who recruits him and the one whom he recruits.

Frères' meetings were held originally in a palatial town house, off Fifth Avenue near the Metropolitan Museum. As the membership grew, it became necessary to find new quarters, and the club acquired an entire floor of a cast-iron skyscraper in the TriBeCa area that had been converted to a luxury residential building.

Oral and anal intercourse, every form of sado-masochism from racks and wheels to testicle vises and nail boards, solitary and group masturbation, coprophilia, and the practice for which, strikingly, there is no euphemism, i.e., fist-fucking (*Note to Desk: You think of a euphemism or put in the necessary dashes, but for God's sake don't take it out. TJ*)—all are practiced during a typical evening at Frères. Almost all encounters take place in private rooms equipped with one-way windows or in the open in one of three small theaters-in-the-round. Some members are merely voyeurs, others like to watch and to be watched. Partners are usually fellow members, but some male prostitutes are permitted into the sanctum with the understanding that none is to be considered the exclusive property of any single member, not even the one who may be paying for his services.

~   ~   ~

The members of Frères will kill to keep their identities a secret. I know this because my wife, Karen, was murdered and horribly dismembered as a warning to me not to publish what I had learned about the secret gay-sex fraternity. Homicide Detective Harold Henderson, assigned to the investigation into Karen's disappearance and murder, was killed because Frères' members feared I would tell him about their organization.

(Why not kill me? Because to kill me would be to run the risk that I would arrange that these revelations be posthumously published.)

Their intimidation was successful. Fearing for the lives of my second wife, Diana Romano, and my stepdaughter, Valerie Fox, I refrained from publishing an account of Frères' activities or the names of its members. I left instructions with the managing editor of this newspaper, however, that freed him to publish this account if both Diana and Valerie should die. In that unfortunate event, I would want some justice done.

Following is a list, alphabetized by me for convenience, of members of Frères as of the date indicated on the directory of the computer diskette on which this file was located:

"Some list," Mabel had said after they had read through it, and Ann had agreed: "Some list."

"I'm surprised to see some of these names," Mabel said, "and then again, I'm not surprised at all."

"I'm not either."

"What does surprise me is ... Well, why write all this down if there was only a very slim chance that it would get published?"

"Journalists can't keep secrets," Ann said. "If you discovered a perfect Caribbean island, you'd maybe tell a couple of friends. Or maybe you wouldn't. A journalist can't get off the island and back to his typewriter fast enough, and writes a story about it. He gets a couple of hundred dollars from some newspaper travel section and gets to write off his plane ticket and hotel bill, and then a year later he's wondering how in hell the place got so overrun with ..."

"What?"

"There he is."

Ann had said she wasn't surprised at many of the names on Justice's list, but watching an ivory stretch limo pull up to the curb in front of the Lash like a liner coming in to its pier, seeing a familiar face get out and look around, just a little bit bewildered by the lights, the coughing bikes, the turbulence, she wasn't prepared for the lurch her stomach gave.

When the familiar face passed close by, Ann said, "Hello, Mark."

37

MARK TALBERT HAD COME STRAIGHT from something that had required a dark blue suit; he hadn't had time to change into his New York-Gomorrah border outfit. He gave a little pinch to the knot of his silk pin-dot necktie (Johnny Carson's tic), knowing full well that it was perfect, that never had a knot of his not been perfect. "Ann."

He said her name just the way she had been expecting he would say it. He wasn't bewildered to see her there on the border, he was ever so curious. He was a newsman, after all—a businessman, okay, yes, but a newsman foremost: printer's ink in his veins, a finger on the pulse of the metropolis, a fever to find the truth—all that. Who? What? Where? When? Why? That was his battle cry. That character defect that Ann had just described to Mabel, that inability to keep a secret, he thought of as a virtue, and demanded it of his staff and cultivated it in himself. (He had devoted a recent issue of his magazine to "Personal Grails: Quests for the Undiscovered, the Little-Known, the Off-the-Beaten Track: a Virgin Beach; a Visionary Landscape; a Mysterious City; a Perfect Restaurant.") To have a dark corner of his life illuminated in a banner headline would be no disgrace. The vanity plate on his BMW said HARDNEWS.

Ann remembered Talbert, just a few days back, standing on the threshold of her office, gripping the doorposts as if a poltergeist were trying to drag him in, then looking like something out of Dickens, someone named Sneep or Grool, and wondering whether he was going to propose that they have an affair, or ask her to

289

understand his giving someone else a choice assignment, or confess that he was an embezzler.

It hadn't occurred to her, it would not have occurred to her in a million years, that Talbert had been bent out of shape because there was a cop there, a Suffolk County detective, a homicide detective, to see Ann about a murder that Talbert had committed.

"We came across your name in a piece that Tony Justice wrote— I'm sorry. Do you two know each other? Mabel Parker, Mark Talbert."

"Mabel." A nod. His eyes—go figure—flicked to her breasts and back. *Boing, boing.*

"Mark."

"We came across your name, Mark, in a piece that Tony Justice wrote before he died. It was what we used to call, back when I was a newspaper reporter"—back when she was a whole lot younger, with more spring in her step, stars of great magnitude in her eyes, a fakebook of toe-tapping songs in her heart—"an HFR. Hold for Release. Hold for the writer's okay—or sometimes the subject's—before publishing it, is what it meant. In this case, the okay would have come in the form of the deaths of two people you haven't gotten around to killing yet, Mark: Diana Romano and . . . Oh."

Ann rocked on her heels for a moment, then shrugged the shrug of the last to know. "I get it. Do you get it, Mabel? Poor Tony. Poor dumb fucking Tony. She's in on it, isn't she, Mark? Diana Romano is in on your end of it. Do you see, Mabe? Mark here killed Karen—well, all right, *had* her killed—to keep Tony from writing about the Frères. But he also had her killed so his pal Romano could have Tony—and all of Karen's stuff—to play with. *Romano*: I should've heard that sooner; you don't call someone *Romano* unless you're tight. Then Mark killed Tony, because Mark's a newsman—and

290

knows how hard it is for a newsman to keep a secret. He also killed him because his pal Ro*mano* was tired of sharing Karen's stuff with Tony, she wanted to play by herself."

Talbert reached for his tie again, but this time crooked a forefinger inside the knot and tugged at his collar to ease it some. A crop of sweat sprouted on his forehead. "Ann, really. This is—"

"Don't patronize me, you motherfucker. You dipshit fuck." Ann pushed at his chest with the fingertips of one hand, liked the sensation, pushed with both hands, using the full palm, then pushed again and again. "You dipshit fuck. You. Set. Me. Up."

Talbert had his hands up to keep his balance, but his eyes were going this way and that in the hope that anyone who noticed would see that he was too chivalrous a man to retaliate physically against a maiden fair. He took a step backward each time Ann shoved at him, and was soon off the curb and backing into West Street, where even at this hour traffic whizzed and rumbled dangerously. He finally planted his heels and grasped her wrists. "You don't have any proof."

Ann jerked her hands free. "You asshole. *I* don't need proof, the *cops* need proof, the cops *have* proof. You made a round trip on the South Ferry between twelve-thirty and one-thirty the night Justice was killed. You drove over from Water Mill and killed him and drove back. Dowdy knows, Dowdy the Suffolk County Homicide detective. Mabel and I showed Dowdy Tony's piece—it's all about Frères, Mark, all about Frères—and Dowdy went out to Shelter Island and showed your picture to the ferry crewmen.

"Your picture didn't tweak any memories—it was dark—but your license plate did. Guess what, Mark. One of the ferrymen *collects* vanity plates. He's a college kid, a smart-ass, he's going to write a book or something, he writes down vanity plates in a little pocket notebook, he wrote down yours. HARDNEWS. You dumb stupid fuck."

Talbert turned away and looked across West Street and out over the Hudson. He saw only the lights of New Jersey and turned back again. "Your boyfriend, Cullen—"

"What about him?" Ann put her hands on her hips and her face close to Talbert's, daring him to shock her.

"He's known for *months* that Justice and Romano had a thing before they were married." Talbert put his hands on *his* hips, which made Ann shiver, there was something so bitchy about it. "He saw them fucking in the church in Sag Harbor after Karen's funeral. Romano saw him watching."

Ann had been in full stride, but now she was stumbling on the flagstone walk outside the church on that blustery day, asking her boyfriend, Cullen, if he'd found the bathroom, her boyfriend, Cullen, saying, "Yup."

"He came around to her studio on the pretense—"

But Ann wouldn't let Talbert get back at her, she tromped all over his words. "So he didn't say anything, so what? So it turned him on, so what? It doesn't make him an accomplice, Mark. You *killed* people, Mark, and *had* them killed. You're a murderer and an executioner. Who does your killing for you, Mark? One of your . . . Oh."

Ann rocked on her heels again, then again shrugged. "That ex-cop. The one *Romano* went around with. Tommy . . . Muldoon. Right, Mark? Am I right?"

All this while, all around them, men of every description, of every size and shape and color, from all walks of life, funneled into the Lash—drawn by what, exactly? The wish to commemorate what about whom?

Or was it just that old adolescent impetus—any excuse for a party? At first the men had given them room, had flowed around them like a stream around rocks, but now, as the appointed hour—the hour for what?—neared, they began to jostle, they began to bump.

Ann stood her ground. "Poor Linda. How do you do this to Linda? Do you ever think about Linda? You don't ever think about Linda, do you? You want to hear something funny, Mark? Before I—before Mabel and I—read Tony's piece, he'd already told me a little about it. Out on the lawn at Shelter Island, looking up at shooting stars—meteorites. He said he was working on a piece about gays—gay bars, gay bathhouses, S&M clubs. Just when you thought people would never go *near* the water again, they were in over their heads. He was especially interested in the Wall Street types—bankers, brokers, lawyers: nothing like a night of anonymous fucking to ease the tensions of a day of unfriendly takeovers. He didn't mention CEO's and publishing barons, but I should've guessed. I should've guessed.

"He said one of the men he was writing about had a wife who's an AIDS fund-raiser. Og Slate, I thought. Og Slate, I said to Mabel, who covered her ears because she's a lawyer and likes to hear only what's admissible and nonlitigable or nonfungible or whatever the fuck. Og Slate, I said anyway. It has to be Og Slate because Michelle Slate is Mommy AIDSbucks. The only human being who does as much to raise money to fight AIDS Is . . . Holy shit, I said to Mabel, Linda Tal— Mark. *Mark!* Oh, christ, Mabel, do something. *Do* something."

Mabel stared. "What? What? Do what, Ann?"

Something like, oh, drag Mark Talbert off her, undrape him from her shoulders, peel him off her and make him stop weighing her down, gasping in her ear, drooling on her, bleeding. Something like, oh, pull the knife out from between his shoulder blades and lay him down on the sidewalk.

Ann had seen it coming and she hadn't. She ought to have been able to stop it from happening and there was nothing she could have done. It was as clear as day and as clear as mud. She replayed it again and again, each time slower and slower, and it still happened so fast that if she blinked she missed it.

Still: she could say this. Out of the crowd of men flowing around them like a stream around rocks had come one who was different. Different because he didn't want to get around them, but to them. Different because he didn't look at them and look away, he looked at them and latched on to them. Looked at Mark Talbert. Latched on to Mark Talbert. Came at Mark Talbert purposefully. No hesitation, no reluctance. An emblem, almost, of a mind made up.

Hispanic, in his early thirties, tall, but slight, black hair slicked back, thin mustache, T-shirt, jeans and jean jacket, motorcycle boots. Wayfarers, just like Ann's. Where *were* her Wayfarers? Shit, she'd left them, she just now realized, in the red rented Lumina. She could see them sitting there on the dash.

Ann had seen the man before. No, not seen him, but heard about him on television and the radio, read about him in newspapers: *male Hispanic, twenty-five to thirty-five, five-eight, one-thirty, straight black hair, mustache, white tank top, jeans and jean jacket, motorcycle boots, possibly riding a racing-type motorcycle, possibly armed with a switchblade*—a switchblade with which he'd killed Noel Cutler.

His mind made up, the Hispanic man came right up to Mark Talbert and thrust a hand out at him, drove it in him, then floated past him, past Ann, past Mabel, floated into the crowd, became part of it, vanished.

Ann saw him again, having slowly lowered Talbert to the sidewalk, Mabel shouting now, screaming *Help! Please! Help us!* She saw the Hispanic man bucking the streaming crowd, swimming upstream, half a block away, then a block, breaking free, swinging a leg over the saddle of a motorcycle, jump-starting it, peeling rubber, doing a wheelie, the front wheel coming up and up and up, the Hispanic man fighting to bring the wheel down, to drive the handlebars down, but losing—the wheel coming up and up and up, the rear wheel under the front wheel now, then ahead of it, the rear fender scraping, a fountain of sparks—and all the while the bike going the wrong way, going south in the northbound lane, cars and trucks and taxis braking, skidding, spinning, crashing, horns shrieking, voices, metal, the Hispanic man's harsh curse as he back-flipped off his flipping bike, the wet gush of his head striking the pavement, then tumbling, flipping, flopping, over and over and over, bent, broken, split, splattered, stopping finally, splayed up against the concrete median, shoulders dislocated, legs turned all the way around, head lolling on broken neck, Wayfarers long gone, mustache—a prop—dangling by the last bit of makeup goo, not a Hispanic man, not a man, Diana Romano.

38

"WHAT DOES IT ... FEEL LIKE?" ANN said.

Cullen said, "All different things. Some of them are actually pleasant—like floating in warm water, like flying. Sometimes I tingle all over, like when your foot falls asleep. Sometimes I hurt—a generic, unspecific hurt."

"And you won't ... They can't ... They don't ... Damn it, Joe, help me."

"It's too soon to know. Sometimes people recover. It just happens."

"Like red hair?"

Cullen smiled. "I don't get it."

"Raymond Chandler," Ann said. "I don't remember the book or the context, but he said sometimes certain things 'just happen, like red hair.' "

"I don't know anybody with red hair, do you?"

"Didn't you tell me Tommy Muldoon was called Blond Tommy because there was another Tommy Muldoon called Redheaded Tommy?"

"Redheaded Tommy wasn't *called* Redheaded Tommy, just Tommy. Blond Tommy was always Blond Tommy. Redheaded Tommy's hair, when I knew him, was gray."

"My cousin Alise has red hair. My Uncle Ed has jet-black hair and my Aunt Janet's a blond gone gray, so I guess Alise's hair just happened."

"Do they live in Lansing?"

"They did. Now Alise lives in Chicago, my aunt and uncle live in Arizona. Flagstaff. My uncle calls it Half-staff; he's the family Jackie Mason. And funny you should mention it, there's a family reunion in Lansing this weekend. My parents' fortieth anniversary."

"You're going?"

"It's just for the weekend."

"I didn't mean that. I just meant . . ."

"What?"

"Nothing. I didn't mean anything. It was my turn to say something, that's all. You said there's a family reunion, it was my turn to say something, so I said, 'You're going?' "

"Don't get angry, Joe."

"I'm not angry."

Ann looked away, looked back, looked away and kept looking away. "I don't know what to do about this."

"About me, you mean."

"About you, about me, about us, about *this*. I'm not especially . . . selfless."

"Who is?"

"My mother is. My Aunt Janet is. Alise is. Mabel. Some people . . . I won't say *thrive*, but some people can *cope* with adversity." Ann made herself look at him. "I have lots of dreams, Joe. None of them . . . Oh, hell."

"None of them has a man in a wheelchair in it?"

" . . . No. I know that's a selfish thing to say, but no."

"*My* dreams," Cullen said, "*all* have me in a wheelchair. My daydreams, my nightdreams. A wheelchair"—he patted the bed's guardrails—"would be progress."

Ann sighed. "*Touché.*"

"It wasn't a thrust, so it wasn't a touch. Ann, I would never ask you to give up your dreams to push around my wheelchair."

She made fists and punched her thighs. "Well, maybe that's the problem. That *is* the problem. You'd never ask. You never ask anything of anybody."

"I don't know what to ask for."

297

"Ask for help."

"Well, there's help and there's help. There's full-time, knock-down-drag-out, spoon-feeding, bedpan-cleaning, sheet-changing, forehead-wiping, dusting, vacuuming, shopping help, and then there's dropping-around-once-a-week-and-bringing-books-and-mag-zines-and-videocassettes-and-having-a-cup-of-tea-and-a-little-chat-and-then-going-on-about-one's-life help."

"What about . . . ? Nothing."

"What about sex?"

"Yes, damn it."

"I don't know. I get erections—nighttime erections—but I don't feel them."

"Oh, hell, Joe." Ann got up from her chair and walked to the window and looked across the airshaft at another window beyond which another woman sat talking to another bed-bound man. How trite.

"What's the latest on Talbert?" Cullen said.

"We're not always going to be able to change the subject," Ann said.

"I know. What's the latest?"

Ann shrugged. "He'll live. Poor Linda. Everybody else died, just about; why couldn't he?"

"Poor Linda, poor Ann?"

"I don't know what you mean."

"Just about everybody else died except Talbert and except me. Poor Linda, poor Ann."

"I didn't mean that. Stop that."

"Connie and the kids were here this morning," Cullen said. "Tracy—the tiny blond nurse—thought James was Axl Rose, which threw him, because it's not Axl Rose he wants to be. Connie and Doug have been talking about adopting Val Fox. There're aunts and uncles and grandparents all over from various marriages, so it's

298

complicated; but Doug's sister's a lawyer who does family law and she seems to think they have a shot."

The woman across the airshaft got up and walked toward the window. If she looked at Ann, Ann was going to have to give her a tentative wave, like some wimpy "Masterpiece Theater" heroine, or a clenched fist. She didn't look, she fussed with the blinds, and Ann was glad. There was sisterhood and there was sisterhood.

Ann turned away from the window and leaned against the sill. "Why do people do the things they do? Why did Diana Romano do the things she did? You were pals with her."

Diana Romano, in her loose black linen boatneck shirt, loose black linen pants, her dry cracked dirty feet in black silk slippers (Bruno Magli?), sat on the fender of a parked car near the corner of Spring and Broadway, waiting for Cullen to catch her a cab. In the damp dawn's early light, she looked like a wraith. She lifted her left arm up alongside her head and with her left hand, palm downward, fingers pointing toward her forehead, grasped her Elvis pompadour and dragged her fingers backward through it to the middle of her skull. This time it was as if she were displaying to him some priceless thing in whose presence he should consider himself very lucky to be.

"There're two kinds of men," Diana Romano had said. "Men who can get a cab and men who can't."

"The Lexington Avenue subway stops at Spring and Lafayette," Cullen had said. "The Eighth Avenue's at Spring and Sixth."

Diana Romano put her head back and roared. "You hate me, don't you?"

"A little."

"Hate, love—you should do them all the way, not a little. You wanted to fuck me a lot, you should hate me a lot for not fucking you." Diana Romano rummaged in her shoulder bag and came up with a business card. She held it out to Cullen. "Call this car service. Use my name. They'll come."

Cullen ignored the card and stepped out into the middle of Broadway and pointed at a cab with its off-duty sign on. If it hadn't stopped, he would have drawn his off-duty gun and shot out its tires. But the driver somehow got the picture that Cullen was just a gofer, that the fare was going to be Diana Romano; off-duty was no longer a place he wanted to be.

Diana Romano hopped down off her perch.

Cullen opened the cab door for her. " 'Night."

She touched his cheek. "No one ever said it would be easy."

"No. No one ever did."

She went up on tiptoe to kiss his lips, but he slid by her and she was suddenly out on a limb and had to grab at the door to keep from falling.

Cullen didn't want to look back at her, but he couldn't help it. One more time, one last time, she grasped her Elvis pompadour and dragged her fingers backward through it to the middle of her skull. And kept on and kept on and kept on until she had hauled the skin from her face and left nothing there but bones and teeth and eyes and a tongue. A tongue that turned into a serpent and flicked and hissed, eyes that ignited into blue flames, teeth that tapered to fangs and dripped bright red blood. With supreme contempt, with a flick of the wrist, she tossed at him the empty sack of flesh that had been her face, and ducked into the cab.

The empty sack turned suddenly sere and the wind plucked it from in front of Cullen's feet and scampered away with it, tossing it playfully, teasingly.

*　　*　　*

"Wow," ANN said. "I say Diana Romano, and you just get sucked into the past, don't you?"

Cullen didn't deny it. "I want to make sure I didn't leave anything behind."

"Anything incriminating?"

"Anything valuable. We weren't pals, no, to answer your question."

"It wasn't a question."

"Whatever."

Ann almost did five minutes on *whatever*, on *whatever*'s being the refuge of scoundrels, on this guy on "Dallas" saying to J. R., "You don't want any killing, do you, Mister Ewing?" and J. R. saying, "Whatever." But she remembered that she had already done it for Cullen in Sag Harbor at Karen Justice's funeral. "So many dead. Neil dead. To accomplish what? To keep what from happening?"

"Neil's mother came by yesterday, with Hriniak, after the funeral. She wants to endow a scholarship, or something, at the Academy. I told her she should endow a fund to give every cop a MAC-11. Hriniak looked like he was going to throw down on me."

"I'm sure she understands." Then Ann flicked her hands, as if waving that statement away. "How could she understand? Who understands? I don't understand. Do you understand? Tell me. Let's hear it: Who done what to whom and why? Start anywhere. Blond Tommy killed his wife because he was afraid she was telling you, you and Neil, that they, she and Tommy, faked her disappearance for the insurance, is that right?"

Cullen nodded. "*And* Tommy was afraid she was telling us he killed Karen Justice."

"All right, why did he kill Karen Justice?"

"Talbert hired him. To warn Tony Justice to back off investigating Frères."

" 'Hired him'? Not blackmailed him?"

Cullen shook his head. "Hired him cheaply, probably. Blond Tommy was as vulnerable to being used to do dirty work as he was to being blackmailed. Talbert was supposed to meet Karen Justice in Boston. He called the night before, supposedly to confirm their date, but really to find out when she was leaving work. Talbert called Tommy, Tommy beeped Karen, Karen met Tommy at Rusty's. Talbert told us all this, in so many words, at the funeral."

Ann held her head very still, as if moving would derail her train of thought, never mind that it was chugging very, very slowly. "*Why* was Tommy vulnerable? Because Diana Romano knew about the insurance scam?"

"She more than knew about it, she planned it. She put Tommy and Rae Muldoon up to it. Her affair with Tommy was just for show, to make people think there was a reason for Rae to disappear. The scam couldn't work: Romano knew that and she didn't care. What she cared about was having Tommy under her influence, so she could use him. Tommy was Romano's gun, her butcher knife, her meat cleaver."

Ann thought some more. "Okay, so killing Karen was a warning to Tony Justice. What was killing Rickey Henderson and who killed him?"

"Tommy killed him, for Talbert, to make it look as though Tony Justice had."

And some more. "And who killed Cutler?"

"Diana Romano," Cullen said, "because he was the loose end that could unravel the whole thing. Talbert was another loose end—that's why she tried to kill him."

302

"And what was she supposed to gain from all this?" Ann said. "This 'whole thing'?"

Diana Romano looked up at Cullen from the table in the corner of the damp and ratty basement off the Bowery. She stopped dabbing up with a fingertip the cocaine that had escaped being snorted up through a silver pipette, she stopped scrubbing her gums, she forbore grasping her Elvis pompadour and dragging her fingers through it. She just sat and listened.

"She wanted to shock," Cullen said. "To disgust, to outrage. She wanted the high, the pleasure, the danger."

Ann rolled her eyes dubiously.

"Hriniak said she has parents, a hometown. Reading, Pennsylvania. You don't expect something like that—someone like her—to come out of Reading, Pennsylvania. Her father's a security guard at an outlet clothing store, her mother's a waitress."

"God."

" 'God,' no wonder she turned out the way she did, or 'God,' who would've guessed she'd turn out the way she did?"

Ann shrugged. "Both. Neither. I don't know. There's nothing very sociologically profound to say about it."

"They're both authority figures," Cullen said.

Ann frowned. "A waitress is an authority figure?"

"You know, no substitutions."

Ann sat back a little. "I don't know why, but I don't think that's funny. I hope you don't think being hurt gives you the right to call people gimps."

"And niggers and kikes and wops and—"

"You know what I'm saying."

"So what're we going to do about it, Ann? About sex? About us?"

Ann hugged herself. "I'm going to Lansing for the weekend. Did I mention that?"

"Your parents' fortieth anniversary. Give them my congratulations."

"You see, the thing is— What're you laughing at?"

"I was thinking, 'If Ann were here, she'd do five minutes on people who say, "The thing is . . ."'"

"Is that how you think of me—as a stand-up comic?"

"Like your Uncle Ed."

"You remember his name. That's a good sign."

"How do you mean?"

"I mean, since you remember his name, maybe I'll tell him about you. Tell him you exist. My Aunt Janet too. And Alise. And my mother and father and my other aunts and uncles and cousins. And my brother."

"Jeff. No—Steph."

"You knew it was Steph. See, the thing is—don't laugh—the thing is, I've been doing with my family what you did, when we first got together, with your kids."

"Keeping me a secret."

"Yes . . . Joe, I'm supposed to be smart. You know— intuitive, perspicacious, all that."

"Savvy."

"Savvy. Exactly. That's the word people use to describe Linda Talbert. But neither of us, Linda nor I, had a clue that Mark Talbert was gay."

"He's more than gay. Gay is a way of living. He's a sociopath, a psychopath. Those're ways of . . . of getting even."

"Have you seen the *Bulletin*?"

"I haven't seen any papers."

"Not directly, but between the lines, they're bashing gays. I'm afraid there'll be more of it."

"Well, you could argue that behavior like the Frères' is inappropriate."

Ann came to the bed. "I guess what I mean is, Tony Justice's death *was* retribution for Stephen Fox's. I wish the *Bulletin* wouldn't forget that. They're treating him like a martyr."

"Martyrs sell papers."

Ann gripped the railing. "Does this thing come down?"

"There's a lock on the right side. I don't know what it looks like, but the nurses—"

"I got it," Ann said. She put a hip up on the bed. "Is this okay?"

"Un hunh."

"Just un hunh?"

"Yes, it's okay. It's fine. It's good. I'm glad."

"I don't know what to do next. I feel like a teenager."

"A teenager, I'm afraid, would know what to do next."

"How is Tenny?"

"She's okay. She doesn't understand any of it either—the motives, the motivations—and I can't explain them very well."

"It was scary, being a suspect."

"I'll bet."

"Everything I said, everything I did, I thought sounded and looked suspicious. I can understand why people confess to things they didn't do: there's so much energy being expended to prove you did do it that you get swept along by it."

Cullen took Ann's hand in his, first by the fingertips, then altogether. "You know, my parents are on their way up here."

"Oh, good. Tampa, is it, where they live?"

"Clearwater. They'll still be here Monday."

"What happens Monday?"

"You get back from Michigan."

"Well. Yeah. Probably. Late Monday."

"Tuesday, then. You'll meet them Tuesday."

"Uh oh."

"As soon as I can, we'll take a trip to meet your parents."

"My father . . . Well, he loves sports."

"I like sports."

"Name a Tiger player. One Tiger player."

" . . . Ty Cobb."

"He'll hate you. You'll have absolutely nothing to talk about. Can you name a Lion?"

"Bobby Layne."

"A Red Wing?"

"Gordie Howe. I know Isiah Thomas."

"He hates Isiah Thomas—that kissing Magic Johnson stuff. He'll hate you."

"I'll talk to your mother."

Ann snorted. "Right. About needlepoint?"

"I can knit. I learned to help me quit smoking. I made a baby blanket for James—white with maroon stripes. It was very collegiate."

"What've you knitted lately?"

"That's the only thing I ever knitted, but I'm sure it's like riding a bicycle."

"Oh, Joe." Ann swung her legs up and lay next to him.

"A wheelchair's kind of like a bicycle. Maybe I can become a wheelchair marathoner. Then I can talk to your father about that."

Ann put a hand under the sheet. "Can you feel this?"

"No."

"Then why're you smiling?"

"It's nice to be close to you. And I was thinking about something you said. It was the night Maslosky beeped me at your house to tell me about Rickey Henderson's K. You said you weren't looking for a four-hundred-pound Samoan oboe player—"

"Who liked Texas lap dancing."

"Who liked Texas lap dancing. You said you were looking for someone who'd take some risks along with you."

"Emotional hang-gliding."

"Emotional hang-gliding."

"You're not going to tell me a wheelchair is like a *hang* glider. Can you feel this?"

"... No."

"You can. Something's happening."

"I can think about it, and remember it, and something happens."

"It *just* happens?"

"Yes."

.